The Sorceress of Karres

Eric Flint
Dave Freer

THE SORCERESS OF KARRES

This is a work of fiction. All the characters and events portrayed in this book are fictional, and any resemblance to real people or incidents is purely coincidental.

A Baen Books Original

Baen Publishing Enterprises
P.O. Box 1403
Riverdale, NY 10471
www.baen.com

ISBN: 978-1-4391-3446-7

Cover art by Stephen Hickman

First paperback printing, June 2011

Distributed by Simon & Schuster
1230 Avenue of the Americas
New York, NY 10020

Pages by Joy Freeman (www.pagesbyjoy.com)
Printed in the United States of America

Johanna Alida Freer 1916–2009

PROLOGUE

Captain Pausert was delighted to have the familiar decks of the *Venture 7333* under his feet again. The Imperial palace and the capital were all very grand and beautiful, if you liked marble and columns. Pausert preferred good, honest, unpretentious hull-metal.

He celebrated their return to space in their own ship with one of his trademark bad take-offs. Goth shook her head. "You'll be the death of us yet, Captain," she said, smiling at him and getting up with her familiar, lithe, catlike grace. "I really need to learn some more ship handling."

She would have to, in fact. With Hulik do Eldel having returned to Uldune with the Sedmons, they had only the old spacer Vezzarn as crew. And, of course, the Leewit. But the Leewit was still only seven years old. She was useful on comms and on the nova guns, but the mathematics of astrogation and the engineering side of the *Venture* were still a bit much for her.

Goth, on the other hand, was soaking it all up like blotting paper. She might only be not quite fourteen Karres years old—the same age now, as Maleen was when he'd first encountered the witches on the Empire world of Porlumma—but she was as reliable as any crewman. On difficult or dangerous sections of their journeys he would split watches with her, rather than with old Vezzarn. She had an iron nerve and a lot of common sense. Not for the first time Captain Pausert wondered what he had done to be so lucky.

But then luck too was a klatha thing. And he'd always been a lucky gambler. He smiled to himself. He wondered if the Leewit, cardsharp extraordinary, had actually figured out that the captain played to lose. Just enough, to keep her happy and bathing without a fight. "We'll put in some teaching time," he said. "It's so good to be back on the *Venture*. Just us, the old team back together again, eh!"

"We need to use the Sheewash drive to get us back to Karres," she said. "A couple of bursts will save us months of traveling, Captain."

"Sure. And I won't try the modification I had in mind," he said cheerfully.

"Clumping well better not," said the Leewit, who had just walked into the control room. "I've decided that I have to learn astrogation math," she announced. That was a reversal of her gleeful announcement of a few days earlier, when she'd told them all that she was going to be a healer and had no need of it.

"Good," said Goth, nodding approvingly. "You never know when the captain might need you."

They set up the focus for the klatha energies of the Sheewash drive—which amounted to nothing more than some twisted wires. The wires formed a three-dimensional pattern and a means of directing the vast amount of klatha force the witches channeled through their secret space-drive. The shape was important, Pausert gathered. But he wondered if it had to be wires. And what happened if you changed the pattern?

He'd experimented with the problem, in fact—but the results of his experiments, so far, had not always been too easy to fix. So for now he'd stick to the tried and tested way. But he supposed that it was in his nature to want to push those limits. That had been why life on Nikkeldepain had been difficult for him. Nikkeldepain worked by the rules. Lots of rules. Rules to be obeyed without question. At least it had until Vala and the lattice ship got there! The show on the lattice ship had been a rare treat. And while it had nothing to do with his eventual decision to part ways with Nikkeldepain, it seemed to be a trigger to the sequence of events that had changed things.

He tore his mind away from thinking about his youth and concentrated on the matter at hand. Soon an orange ball of furious energies danced above the truncated cone of twisted wires and the *Venture 7333* raced along at a pace that the fastest naval chaser could not dream of. Pausert melded well with the two young witches, and the ship hurtled onward through space.

CHAPTER 1

Threbus looked more than a little alarmed at the sudden appearance of the slitty little silver-eyed vatches all around them. "I suppose these are the kind that can't be handled by your mother?" he asked of Goth, his middle daughter. The tone was faintly hopeful. The expression was not.

His daughter shook her head. "I reckon not. Captain, how about you? You're a real wizard with vatches."

Pausert considered the problem. It seemed clear enough that the little fragments of otherwhere, pieces of impossible whirling blackness called vatches, had appeared because of him. Pausert was a vatch-handler, a vatch negotiator, he who had done the impossible, and made friends with the creatures who were normally puppeteers playing with humans for a sort of dreamlike amusement. It would seem that there was such a thing as too much success.

Eventually, he shook his head. "If I tried and failed—even on one, it'd be pretty fatal. I think we're going to have to learn to cooperate with them, Threbus."

"How?"

"Rather as one deals with the Leewit," said Pausert.

Threbus groaned. "One does not deal with my youngest daughter, Pausert. One merely tries to limit the damage and then distract her."

Captain Pausert, who had had plenty of experience of the Leewit, grinned at his great uncle. "Yes. That's it, I think."

Threbus took a deep breath. "Pausert, you have repaid us for what we did to you."

Because of the Karres witches, Captain Pausert had been though more near-death experiences than he cared to think about at any one sitting. He patted his great uncle—and future father-in-law, if Goth had her way—on the shoulder. "I hope so. It was a bit rough at first. But I wouldn't have missed it for all the worlds in the Empire."

"More to the point, the Empire wouldn't have survived without you getting through it," said Threbus.

Pausert nodded. "I understand that now. And I wonder if the vatches are not doing the same thing for Karres."

Threbus looked thoughtful. "You can hardly have spoken to the precog teams, Pausert. It's because of what they're seeing that we're glad you came back here so quickly. They've been giving us worrying and confused views of the future. Not all good, either. I wonder if this is another klatha talent starting to manifest in you?"

"Nope," said Pausert. He'd been through enough of the otherworldly klatha development phases to recognize that feeling. "Just common sense. Karres has faced two terrible dangers. Been all that stood between man and Manaret, and between the Empire and the Nanite plague."

"Could be," said Goth slowly, "that Karres, just by existing, draws trouble."

Captain Pausert felt an eerie prickle at the back of his skull. Some kind of klatha force was at work here.

It was plain that Threbus felt it too. "We can't exactly stop existing. We've always operated, if not in secret, at least not obtrusively. We could hide back in time or something..."

Goth shook her head, her high forehead wrinkled in concentration. "It wouldn't make any difference. Whatever causes this is like Big Windy the vatch. I reckon it's not limited to space or time as we know them. Not even this dimension. Manaret and Moander were pulled from somewhere else. Another dimension, thousands of complicated dimensions away... they *thought* it was by accident. But what if it wasn't?"

"I'd say we're in trouble. Again," said Captain Pausert, shrugging. "We're getting quite good at that."

"Clumping right," said the Leewit, arriving suddenly in their midst. "What are all these stinkin' little vatches doing here? Where is Little-bit? She's okay. I didn't invite all these other ones."

"Perhaps she's here, somewhere. It's a bit confusing," said Pausert.

"Well, go away, you lot," said the Leewit to the vatch-swarm. "Or I'll whistle at you. I don't know if it'll bust you up. You want to find out, huh? Anyway, Pa, I came to tell you Maleen is here at the palace."

Threbus brightened perceptibly. He was a fair man, Pausert knew. He never played favorites among his daughters. But he plainly had a soft spot for Maleen, his oldest child. "If they won't go away," he said, looking at the vatches, "I suppose that we could."

The Leewit looked warily at her father. "Not the Egger Route."

There was a boom as air rushed in to fill the space. The vatches flickered and rippled around where the four Karres witches had been moments before. They'd find them again, of course. They had their flavor.

CHAPTER 2

"I didn't know that it was possible to teleport that sort of mass," said Captain Pausert, impressed.

Goth squeezed her father's hand. "Oh, yes. So long as you've got a hot witch doing it, it works pretty well."

Threbus wiped his brow. "If the range is not particularly great, I can manage large amounts of mass. But I'm pretty well limited to a few hundred yards. A group of us can manage a few miles."

"Still a pretty hot witch," said Goth. "I can only do a couple of pounds."

Threbus smiled. "You've got the range on me though. And you're young yet. When I was your age I had just started to discover a few klatha powers, but they were so slight that I didn't actually believe they were real."

"That must have been just as well on Nikkeldepain,"

8

said Captain Pausert, thinking of his home planet. It was a very conservative and traditional place. Quite stuffy in a lot of ways. Karres witch tricks would not be happily received there.

The thought made him chuckle a little. Most of the people of Nikkeldepain would be horrified by the company he was now keeping. It had not been the easiest place to grow up in, in some ways. Not if one was just a little bit out of the ordinary. Captain Pausert could see now that might easily have been the start of his own klatha manifestations. But it had given him enough trouble at school, and later in the Nikkeldepain space navy.

That, and the infamy of his Great Uncle Threbus, the very man who had just teleported them. It had been difficult growing up in the shadow of the stories about Great Uncle Threbus. Harder because he'd never known quite where to stand on it all. His mother had always stood up for her strange uncle, in spite of what people said. Pausert had had a few bitter fights about it at school. He'd always held out that the stories had to be exaggerated. Now he had to wonder whether it had not been Nikkeldepain that had been the victim, not his eccentric great uncle.

They were joined by Maleen, who was with a young man Pausert didn't know. Pausert hadn't seen much of Maleen since the day that he had left the three witches of Karres back on their home planet after rescuing them from slavery on the Empire world of Porlumma. He'd always been a little suspicious about that. The witches were certainly capable of rescuing themselves from most situations. Maleen was a precognitive Karres witch— which gave him enough ground for extreme suspicion.

Precog was not an exact science. But it was good enough for her to have prepared a tray of drinks for them. Tall green Lepti liquor for Captain Pausert and her father, and a pale frothy brew for her two sisters. When Pausert had last seen her, Maleen had been a pretty blonde teenage girl. It made him sharply aware of the passage of years to see that she was now definitely a young woman.

"Captain," she said proudly, taking the young man's hand possessively, "this is Neldo. My husband."

Pausert extended his hand. "Pleased to meet you." Well, she had said that she would be of marriageable age in two years, Karres time. Pausert was still not too sure just how long a Karres month was. But he, together with Goth and her little sister, the Leewit, had been on quite a number of adventures since then. Come to think of it, he wasn't entirely sure how many months it had all taken.

Neldo shook his hand warmly. "I've heard a lot about you." Then he turned to his father-in-law. "Maleen has got some great news."

"We're going to have a baby!" said Maleen excitedly.

Threbus beamed and hugged both of them. "Would it be too much to expect for a precog to have some idea what sex it's going to be?"

Maleen blushed. "You know we're not supposed to do that kind of thing."

"So you got Kerris, or one of the others, to do it for you," said Goth, grinning.

Maleen and Neldo smiled at each other. "You might be right. We might even know what we've decided to call her."

The Leewit stood in front of them, her arms folded. "There is only one 'the Leewit.'"

Maleen laughed. "We know that. And it still didn't put us off having children. Her name will be Vala."

"Why?" asked Goth.

"We don't know," answered Maleen. "It's not a name that either of us had ever heard before."

Captain Pausert was a little taken aback by the name. It brought back a flood of memories which he had thought were gone for ever. "I knew a Vala once, back on Nikkeldepain."

Goth looked suspiciously at him. "You said that sort of funny. Who was this Vala?"

"Just a girl I knew when I was growing up." Pausert had a bad feeling his ears were starting to grow slightly red.

"I bet she was your sweetheart, Captain." Maleen sniggered. "Hope she was better than that insipid girl, what was her name, Illyla."

"She wasn't a bit like Illyla," said Captain Pausert reminiscently. "Actually, if anything she was more like Goth. Except that she had red hair and was a bit older. She got me into a fair amount of trouble, but I don't remember that I minded too much. Like the lattice ship that came to Nikkeldepain at about that time. She was one of those people that you never really forget. Oh well, it was long ago. It's a beautiful name. I'm glad you chose it."

"Huh!" said Goth, looking at Pausert from under her dark brows. "Anyway, I've never had much time for babies, not until they grow up a bit."

Toll came in. "And then they turn into something like the Leewit," she said, looking at her youngest daughter and smiling.

The Leewit shrugged. "Babies are no fun anyway.

I have decided that I'm going to stay with the captain for the next while. Things happen around him. And he takes pretty good care of us. Makes us wash behind our ears even."

That last was plainly something that she felt was a little unnatural. Pausert had to smile to himself. The Leewit was a handful to deal with, but at least he felt that he was dealing with a child, even if he knew very little about how to do so. With Goth he was less certain. She was growing up. Fast.

According to the Karres precogs this was going to be a very important year for Goth. The year had started with their departure from the governor's palace on Green Galaine, on a life or death mission to escort the Nartheby Sprite Hantis and her grik-dog Pul to the Imperial Palace. Of course no one had seen fit to tell him that the trip was going to be quite as risky as it had turned out to be. It had been a period during which the captain's own klatha skills had grown immeasurably. But although Goth had matured, he could not honestly say that it had been that much of an important year for her development. Except... they still had a couple of months to go. Pausert could not help but be a bit nervous as to what they might bring her.

A little later, when Goth had gone off with her sisters, Pausert broached the subject of his next mission with Toll and Threbus. His relationship with the witches of Karres was an interesting one. At least in theory, Captain Pausert was just an independent trader, with a fast, armed merchant ship. But in practice he was part of the community of Karres. That was more about a willingness to do what was needed, than merely a reference to your citizenship or place of birth. And if Karres needed him, he was willing.

"The Chaladoor," said Threbus, referring to a dangerous and mysterious region of space, the lair of pirates, the Megair Cannibals—and at one time of Manaret and the Nuri globes lurking within the Tark Nembi cluster of dead suns and interstellar dust and debris.

"Oh?" said Captain Pausert warily. He'd survived one crossing of the Chaladoor. Admittedly, he'd been in more danger from those inside his ship—spies and the notorious Agandar—than from forces outside it.

"There is something going on in that area of space. Since Manaret was destroyed, quite a few ships have risked the crossing. And none of them have made it. The Daal of Uldune has also thought to expand his power in that direction. But he has been repulsed."

Pausert raised his eyebrows. He knew the hexaperson that was the cloned and telepathic ruler of the one-time pirate world rather well. Sedmon the Sixth was not a trivial foe. The Empire still trod warily around him and the forces at his command. Whatever the danger was that lurked in the Chaladoor, it was something serious. "You want me to do what, exactly?"

"You will be a kind of bait, to be honest, Pausert," said Threbus. "All we want you to do is encounter the problem, and then run away as fast as you and the Sheewash drive can manage. The Chaladoor is a large, complex region. Karres could hunt for some years without encountering whatever the problem is. Problems tend to avoid whole worlds which are also spacecraft."

He looked at his grand-nephew with a twinkle.

"And we do really mean 'run,' Pausert. You've proved yourself far more than just capable with problems. And you've taken good care of my daughters in the process. But not with something that was big enough to deal with eight of the Daal's cruisers and a battle wagon. They barely had time to say they were under attack on subradio before being destroyed. Whatever it is, it is no easy foe to deal with."

Threbus cleared his throat and continued. "You have a ship which is very nearly the equal of a single cruiser anyway, as far as speed and detection equipment are concerned. We'll have it refitted with some more of the very latest equipment, at our expense. Your armaments are not quite to the same standard, but they are certainly up to holding off an enemy until you can engage the Sheewash drive. Now that you have also mastered the drive, and with Goth and the Leewit to help you in emergencies, we think you should be able to deal with running away. Leave us to do the clean up!"

"You wouldn't take unnecessary risks with the girls anyway," said Toll, smiling. "My daughter has already made her plans for you. And you wouldn't be foolish enough to try to spoil them now, would you?"

Goth's plans were to marry the captain as soon as she was of marriageable age. At first the captain had not taken her terribly seriously—just as Threbus had apparently not taken Toll's similar plan too seriously. And see where it had got Threbus! As time had gone on and Pausert and Goth had shared adventure and danger together, Pausert had come to realize that he was very fond of her too. But he was a normal man, and she wasn't yet properly grown up.

a dope. I like him quite a lot, actually. He's good to have around especially when things go wrong. But I don't see what Goth's all upset about." She sniffed. "And don't tell me that she's not, because she is."

Goth gave her a look that would have sent sensible wildlife running. "It's your baby's fault," she said to Maleen.

"I didn't tell you everything Kerris and the other precogs said about her."

"Don't know if I want to hear," said Goth crossly.

Maleen put a hand on Goth's shoulder and pushed her down into a chair. "Well, you should. Because it is important. I need to talk to Toll and Threbus about it too, but I couldn't with Captain Pausert there."

"Why? What did they say?"

"Pausert's going on a mission to the Chaladoor."

"I know that. We leave . . ."

"Except that you're not going to be with him," said Maleen.

Goth shook her head. "He needs me around. He doesn't have a pattern in his mind to guide him through the klatha stuff. And he . . . experiments. Look what happened with the Egger Route. We ended up back in time. He'll get hurt or killed, for sure, if I am not there."

Goth knew full well that Captain Pausert had actually done all right a couple of times without her. But a girl had to keep an eye on her man. And she was doubly uncertain right now. That episode was well back in his past, but she was not ignorant and naive enough not to know that the captain had given his heart to this Vala. Also, his tone said that she'd meant something very different to him than his former fiancée Illyla.

Illyla, Goth could deal with, just like she'd dealt with Sunnat. This Vala...

Goth hadn't liked his reverent tone. And she didn't like the fact that, in a way, the girl couldn't have been much older than Goth was now, when she got her claws into the captain. Well. He wouldn't have been a captain then. But still.

"You know what precog is like, Goth. No one ever sees the whole picture, but they do see what they see, right? And this is what Kerris said. You—Goth, nobody else—have got to do this or else he's not just going to get killed. It'd be like he never was. It's got something to do with what is going on in the Chaladoor."

Goth took a deep breath. "You tell me all that you know right now, Maleen." This was much more serious than some old girlfriend he'd never got over.

"Well, you know precogs measure might-be's. They predicted Vala's name. We both heard it and loved it—and they said that it was really important that she be called that. And they said that some power from the Chaladoor was going to murder Captain Pausert."

"What!" Goth leapt to her feet. "We could dismind him, like Olimy. Or he could put himself in a cocoon like he put the Leewit and me in."

"And it happened when he was fourteen," said Maleen. "There is a ninety-eight point probability that he died before he ever left Nikkeldepain. Maybe some enemy figured out then it was a good idea to get rid of him before he developed any klatha powers. Before he had Goth and Karres to protect him."

Goth said several words that even shocked the Leewit.

"The captain will wash your mouth out with soap!"

said the youngest witch, primly, as if she herself did not delight in using terms that would make a docker blush. Although she was usually careful to do so in a language that Captain Pausert could not understand. Her klatha gifts ran to the ability to translate and speak any language.

"Not unless you tell him, he won't. And I'll make you swim back to Karres on the Egger Route if you do," said Goth. "You're going to have to look after him in the Chaladoor, little sister. I'm going to have to go and deal with this."

The Leewit nodded, wide-eyed, looking at her sister. It was going to be quite a task. But that was pure Karres. If something needed doing, you did it. Karres people weren't much good at waiting for someone else to take the responsibility. "How are you going to get there?" she asked.

Goth gritted her teeth. "The Egger Route. And there's not going to be anyone else to help me at the other end, either."

That could be nasty. Really nasty. But by the look on Goth's face, that wasn't going to stop her for an instant.

"I think you'd better talk it over with Toll and Threbus first," said Maleen. "And this may not be the perfect time."

Goth took a deep breath. "I am not going to be able to sleep unless...isn't this a paradox? Like, he must have survived or we wouldn't have met him?"

Maleen bit her lip. "You'd think so. But all precog could give us was that somehow they avoided the time paradox."

"Time is too complicated to play around with lightly,"

said the voice of Goth's Toll pattern, issuing from her lips. "Dimensionality comes into it."

They went to find Threbus and Toll. And, not surprisingly, found them in consultation with several of the senior precogs. "You know the prediction that it was important that you spent the next year with my grand-nephew Pausert?" said her father. "We've got a little more clarity on that."

"We're trying to establish the precise dates right now," said Toll. "But you will be leaving on the *Venture* with him, and then we think you're going to have to jump to the past, via the Egger Route."

"I worked that out," said Goth, gruffly. "Been talking to Maleen. But why can't I just go now?"

"Because the flight schedules have been published and we are still trying to establish exactly when you have to go to, Goth. We have established you do—or did—go back to Nikkeldepain. We have only one other insight, Goth. A lattice ship."

The Leewit bounced. "Yay! I want to go too! I want to go too! I love the circus!"

"Well, you can't," said Goth firmly. "I need you to keep an eye on the captain. Anyway, you're the only one beside him that seems to be able to do anything with those little vatches."

Threbus grunted. "We need them to clean out Nanite-infected people. But the follow-up on that has been a bit chaotic. It seems that they only do things because they like Pausert. We don't really have any way of motivating them."

"Little-bit likes me too," said the Leewit cheerfully. "I got used to her."

She seemed firmly convinced the vatch was female, although Goth couldn't for the life of her figure out how you'd determine the gender of a vatch—assuming the distinction between male and female meant anything to them at all.

As if the vatch had known that it—she—was being spoken about, the tiny fleck of blackness with the hint of silver eyes appeared, flickering around the room. **Hello, big ones. I have taken the others to watch a play. They like them nearly as much as I do.**

Goth chuckled. "I guess you've got your motivation."

Threbus nodded thoughtfully. "There are going to be a lot of traveling players visiting the outlying provinces of the Empire in the next while."

"On an Imperial cultural uplift programme," said Toll, smiling. "I'll have some words with Dame Ethy and Sir Richard."

"Should be pretty interesting with that sort of audience! They'd better not let the shows get stale or the little things will liven 'em up," said Goth. "But it could work."

Threbus nodded. "I like it. It gives us something the vatches want. The other issue with the Nanites is that we've had the Imperial scientists working nonstop on the material—dead material so far. They haven't given us anything to use to combat the plague, other than a possible repellant. But they have said that they're absolutely sure that the plague is an artificial creation. The Nanites were engineered. Made. They were programmed to do what they did."

There was a moment of silence. "That's a pretty powerful enemy."

Threbus nodded. "And one that has been around

for a very long time. Working on records from the Sprites of Nartheby, the plague came from somewhere toward the galactic center. We, of course, probably weren't the targets. But it could be that something in there knows that their plague has been defeated."

"So they might be getting the next attack ready."

Threbus rubbed his jaw. "It's also, in a way, why humanity was able to expand off old Yarthe with such ease. We found so many habitable planets with traces of old alien civilizations on them, but no other existent aliens, except for the Sprites on Nartheby. But we have to face the possibility that the Nanite plague might just have been the alien equivalent of a pest-exterminator, cleaning up before the new occupants got there. And the Nanite problem won't just go away. It's with us for the foreseeable future. Even if we track down and destroy every Nanite in the Empire, they could still be hidden away somewhere—inside or outside the Empire, in the smallest colony, and could burst out again. We're going to have to be vigilant. And get people used to having grik-dogs to smell out the Nanite exudates."

"Well, at least I like grik-dogs," said Goth. "And I guess keeping an eye out for Nanites will also mean that we're ready for other problems."

Threbus nodded. "We're going to be stretched pretty thin, though, for the next few years. We'll have to keep Karres people undercover, scattered around. And Karres itself will probably keep a low profile. We will have to find ourselves a new sun to orbit, because the planet will be top of their target list."

"I reckon," said Goth. "And we like the old place."

CHAPTER 3

Pausert was not prepared for Goth to sniff loudly and retreat, when he made a joke about his lousy take-off, instead of teasing him. The captain was almost sure she was in tears. But he couldn't leave the navigation controls just then to follow her and find out what was wrong. When she came back, her face looking recently washed, he started to ask. But she waved the question away.

She remained taciturn for the rest of the day—and all of the next, and the next. By then, Pausert was really starting to worry.

He tried to question the Leewit, to see if she knew anything. But the little witch seemed to be in one of her noncooperative moods.

By then, they were approaching the Chaladoor, and Pausert had something else to worry about.

*   *   *

Neldo stopped vibrating after a while, and started breathing. "Touch-talk," he gasped, just as soon he had enough breath. "The things I do for love. Maleen couldn't come because of the baby. And I've had a team of witches damping the klatha output. We hope that Pausert is unaware of this, but I need to be quick."

Goth put her hands against him, and made contact with Maleen. "What have you got for me?" she demanded.

"Quite a lot. We tracked back the date a lattice ship last landed on Nikkeldepain. And discovered that a girl called Vala, the daughter of Sutherb and Lotl, was a student at the Nikkeldepain Academy for the Sons and Daughters of Gentlemen and Officers, for six months in the same year. Got a picture of her from a yearbook. It's you, all right. But your hair is curled and red. I've sent curling tongs and the dye that mother thought best matched, with Neldo. You'll have to light-shift it a bit longer at first, but long-term it's easier not to have to do light-shift all the time. Oh, and here's a safe set of coordinates for you to go to—an impression of a place on Nikkeldepain. Father supplied that."

The image flooded into her mind. "Suberth and...?"

"Mother and father, you dope," said the Leewit. Complex codes were obvious to her. Mere anagrams were a joke.

"Oh. Yeah."

"The Leewit. You need to know, seeing as Goth isn't going to be here. Someone is spending huge amounts of money on finding the *Venture 7333*. Offering a small fortune for her flight times and schedules.

Whatever is happening in the Chaladoor has fingers in crime in the rest of the Empire. We're digging for whoever has put up the money. But, even by Karres standards, they've been spending it like water. And the odd thing is, they have a description of someone who looks a lot like mother, that they're also looking for."

"What's so odd about that?"

"The person has wavy red hair, and her name is Vala."

Goth put on as many layers as she could. The Egger Route was tough on the body. The captain thought that he had some way to stop the vibration, but she couldn't ask him about it now. Anyway, his klatha skills were very powerful—and a bit scary and off the wall.

The Leewit was oddly silent during the whole process. A little wide-eyed and apprehensive. The Leewit *really* did not like the Egger Route. Actually, Goth didn't like it much herself.

"Well," she said, taking a deep breath and fixing the touch-talk mental coordinates in her mind, "Here goes. Look after the captain for me, Leewit. And don't forget to wash behind your ears."

"I won't," said the Leewit, not arguing for once in her life, her voice a little small.

CHAPTER 4

When Goth recovered from the stresses of the Egger Route, she tried to take in her surroundings. She was sitting on some turquoise mossy stuff, overhung by long fronded purple leaves, that she didn't recognize at all. But just over there was what she was sure was a tumtum tree from her native Karres.

A scrawny, fresh-faced boy was standing just a few feet away, staring at her wide-eyed.

"What is this place?" she asked.

"The Nikkeldepain Xenobiology Botanical Garden. It's part of the Threbus Institute of Xenobiology."

He sounded rather proud as he said that. But within seconds his wide-eyed stare was back. "You were having some kind of a terrible fit," he said. "Shaking and banging yourself around."

With a sudden shock, Goth realized that she recognized his face. She actually knew it very well. She'd just seen a picture of Pausert as a teenager.

"I'm all right now," she said shakily.

He was plainly worried by the whole experience. "I think I could carry you," he said. "I'll get you to a healer."

He possibly could carry her, Goth thought. He was a rather skinny boy, with a rapidly swelling black eye.

"Did I do that to you? Punch you in the eye?" she asked, feeling more than a little guilty.

He grinned. "No. You should see the other guy. He started it. But I'm going to catch it for it." He seemed quite accepting about that. "Look, I need to get you to some kind of medical help. That was really scary."

"Don't worry," said Goth. "It's over. It won't happen again." She thought hastily. "I just got the times wrong. I should have been home already. It's a side effect from the medicine I had to have for Munki fever."

"I've never heard of that. It must be pretty bad," said the young Pausert, plainly impressed. "So who are you, and what are you doing here? I thought I was the only person who ever came here. How did you get in?"

"Uh . . ."

What was she going to say? She hadn't actually expected to meet him. Just to slip around in no-shape invisibility, find out who was trying to kill him, and deal with them. She couldn't exactly say that she was Goth from his future. He might remember and he'd never mentioned it. Surely he would have? She snatched on the first name that came to mind.

"I'm Vala," she said. And then suddenly realized that

Captain Pausert might never have mentioned meeting anyone called Goth, who had apparently been having an epileptic fit when he came across them...but he had definitely known someone called Vala. He'd even said that she'd looked a bit like Goth! Except a little older. The situation made her want to break out into a fit of the Leewit-type giggles.

What else had he said? Oh yes, Vala had had curly red hair. Her hair was hidden inside the padded hood she'd chosen to protect her on this end of the Egger journey.

She just had to remember to do a light-shift, when she took it off—which had better be quite soon. She might have survived the Egger Route, but she was going to boil in this outfit.

"Well, Vala," said the boy, "my name's Pausert."

She noticed that he was rather watchful as he said it. "That's a nice name," she said, smiling at him.

He looked at her rather like a spooked mountain bollem, one of the wild ones. One that could either run away or charge at you. "You don't come from around here, do you?"

That was for sure! she thought. But what she said was: "Nope. And you?"

He nodded. "Worse luck, yes I do. I've lived here for years."

Goth unfastened her bulky hooded over-jacket. And then took off the miffel-fur coat. Pausert stared at her, wide-eyed. "It's not that cold, you know! Actually, it's a pretty warm day for this time of year."

"I'm not used to this place," Goth improvised hastily. "I didn't know what to expect."

"Nikkeldepain only gets snow a little later. And

besides, you never get it in here." He looked a little wary. "Just how did you get in here? Where are you from?"

As Goth had no idea just where she was, that was a question she preferred to avoid answering. And she hadn't exactly expected to have to immediately come up with a good story as to where she came from either. Fortunately, he answered for her. "You're from the lattice ship, aren't you?"

At least she knew something about lattice ships thanks to their time on the *Petey B*. But it was best to be a little cagey. She looked up at the glassed roof, and did her best to make her face into the very picture of innocence. "I really don't think I should say."

He grinned. "Don't worry. *I* wouldn't tell anyone. I want to get out of Nikkeldepain myself. Do they take on apprentices? I'll do anything. Clean out cages. Get custard pies in my face. I don't mind."

Goth resolved to remind him of that one day. But she also had a duty to see that she didn't mess up her own history and timeline. The captain had stayed on Nikkeldepain until his trading mission with the *Venture 7333* when he had rescued her, Maleen and the Leewit from slavery on Porlumma. "No," she lied valiantly. "And don't try and stow away, either. Promise you, it's not worth it. They'll just catch you. Kids try it at every stop."

He looked terribly disappointed. It had obviously been on his mind.

"Don't worry," she said. "You'll get out of here soon enough, I reckon."

He shrugged. "I don't really see how. Ma hasn't got the money to send me to the space naval academy.

I guess I could sign on as a crewman one day. But not a lot of ships come to Nikkeldepain these days. It's a pretty dead-end place, I suppose."

He studied her for a moment, a bit squinty-eyed and looking much more curious than Goth was comfortable with. "Don't you remember how you got here?" he asked.

"Uh. No, it's rather vague. One of the other side effects of the medication I've had to take." Out of the miffel-fur coat, she then pulled off the thick sweater beneath.

"Oh," said Pausert. "I just wondered how you'd got in. It's supposed to be securely locked, to prevent any chance of cross-contamination, see."

She had to wonder just how the captain-to-be had got himself in here, then? He was always so strictly law-abiding. She had to admit that it was something that she admired about him. The Pausert that she knew would not have voluntarily broken any law. He was scrupulously honest.

"So how did you get in, then?" she countered.

He scowled. "I've got a key. My great uncle built this place. In spite of all the other trouble he caused, nobody's ever asked for the key back. I've got a sort of right to be here. I come in here to hide out," he admitted. "I had a fight, and now some of them are looking for me. They plan to give me a beating."

Goth felt her fists ball. "Just let them try!" she said fiercely. "They've got two of us to take on."

It occurred to her then that the great uncle he was referring to was probably her father, Threbus. Well, he was supposed to have caused a fair amount of trouble here, before moving to Karres.

Pausert grinned at her, looking terribly young and vulnerable. "I wouldn't do that. They don't like strangers around here. Nikkeldepain is pretty conservative. I'm surprised that they even let that lattice ship land."

"Huh," said Goth, wishing that she knew just which lattice ship it was. But most of the traveling circus ships had dealt with hostile local governments before. She hoped that this lot took the officials of Nikkeldepain for every penny they could!

As usual, the journey down the Egger Route had left her ravenous. "So where do we get something to eat?" she asked. "And if anyone out there tries to pick a fight with us, we'll sort them out," she added militantly.

"It's been a while," said Pausert. "They've probably moved on and gone to look somewhere else by now. But I'm afraid I don't have any money right now."

Looking at his clothes, Goth could see that penury probably did not apply to just right this moment only. He was a little too large for what he was wearing, and his clothes looked elderly and threadbare. There was a patch on the one elbow of his shirt and a fresh-looking tear on the opposite shoulder.

He must have noticed her looking, because he grimaced and touch the tear. "Ma is not going to be very pleased with me. She keeps telling me to stay out of fights. It's just not that easy."

"I know," said Goth. "Look, I've got some money. Let's go and get something to eat before I start on these plants. Is there any place I can stash this coat and stuff?" The part about having some money was not strictly true. She actually did have a few Imperial maels, but they would not have been printed yet.

That could be a little tricky if someone looked too closely. But Goth figured that she could do something about it. The captain's honesty had had some effect on the way that she saw the universe, but as far as she could work out, there were a lot of people on Nikkeldepain who owed him. She could 'port some repayment. He was always very careful to pay exactly what he owed. Goth was not naïve enough to believe that others always treated him as fairly. He'd taught her to behave just as honorably as he did. And she would, for herself. But she might just right the balance as far as he was concerned. Just as soon as she had managed to get something to eat.

"I can show you where to go," he said. "But I can't let you pay for me. We don't need charity," he said stiffly.

Looking at him in his old, patched clothes, Goth reckoned that he probably did. He also looked like he could use a few more meals. But she was experienced enough with people from other places besides Karres to recognize the last phrase as a direct quote. Suddenly she was very glad that she'd taken the Egger Route back to Captain Pausert's childhood. She had needed him a good few times during their adventures. And it looked like he really needed her now. Besides, he was rather cute. She could see that she was going to be a very busy young Karres witch for the next while, besides fulfilling her mission to prevent Captain Pausert's untimely demise.

And then she had to stifle a chuckle that he probably would have taken the wrong way. To think that she'd been jealous of Vala!

He saw her smile anyway, and smiled back. That

did odd things to her. Whoever gave him that black eye was going to suffer!

"And this kit?" was all she said, though.

"Oh. There are lockers under the plant-beds. Most of them are empty. Here. This one will do."

He pulled it open, reading from the label. "You just have to remember which plant. This one's *Mularina tremblence* from Coolum's World. Big maroon leaves. Easy to find."

He seemed totally uncurious as to why she would have a full-length miffel-fur coat. He simply helped her to push it in, along with the bulky sweater, and closed the locker.

They went down a corridor between the huge beds of vegetation from various alien worlds. Squat little robot tenders trundled around constantly. A taller, stilted robot was trimming a tree with heavy basketball-sized fruits.

"It's all automated. That's why the place is still running, I guess," said Pausert, when she asked if there were any human gardeners. "The robotics must have cost a fortune, my mother says. It's a pity uncle Threbus didn't leave us the fortune instead."

"There's some pretty valuable stuff here," said Goth, looking at the tillipwood tree and the berry-hung bushes that she was sure came from Margoli.

Pausert shrugged. "I suppose so. But it all goes into the laboratories. My mother works in one of them. There's not much new stuff coming in, but there's years of work still, mother says."

They had arrived at a small doorway. Pausert produced an elderly looking key, and unlocked it.

Several boys came bundling in through the doorway.

"I told you we just had to wait for him!" shouted one of them.

They were all quite a bit bigger than the scrawny Pausert. Goth wasted no time. She head-butted the first one in the stomach, kicked the next one. Pausert was already fighting, but they had plainly not expected him to have any help. She 'ported a small object inside the shirt of the boy Pausert was wrestling with. It was a fleshy and very thorny leaf from a nearby cactus. He yowled most satisfactorily.

"Quick!" she shouted, pulling at Pausert's sleeve, seeing there were at least another four of the gang still pushing their way in through the door. "There are too many of them. We'd better run."

So they did, dodging the little maintenance robots, sprinting along the corridors between the raised beds, as the boys chased them. Goth spotted the tree she had been looking for, with its spreading branches and large basketball sized spiky fruits. "Up there," she panted. Toll had taught all her children: if you're in trouble, go up until you're above it. It was always easier to deal with it from up there. And if she had recognized the tree correctly, dealing with it could be a lot of fun.

They climbed into the growing-bed and then up into the tree. Doing this had set off some kind of alarm—but that didn't seem to worry the seven boys. They were into the growing-bed and starting to climb the tree too, when Goth 'ported one of the fruits down on their leader. It was near the limits of the weight she could manage, but the effect was well worth the effort. The Leewit would have just loved it. The fruit exploded in a shower of thick glutinous mauve juice full of tiny seeds. The boy fell out of the tree, knocking the boy behind him down too.

By this time the two of them were out near the end of the branch in the foliage, and among the fruit. The young Pausert was no dope when it came to getting the idea. He picked and flung one of the Tyrian fruits at the crowd helping their leader to his feet. It hit the tree trunk and showered them all in its jellylike juice. The boys scattered like a picnic that has just discovered a zark-scorpion on top of the potato salad. Goth and Pausert sent a few more of the fruit hurtling down at them, sending them running for cover.

Pausert yelled in delight, beaming from ear to ear. Goth thought that it was no wonder he and the Leewit got on so well. They must have been very alike, once.

"Well, I'm sorry I have got you into such trouble," he said, apologetically. "But it was worth it."

"Why are we going to be in trouble?" asked Goth.

"The alarm. Someone will come to see what the problem is. They'll be able to run away, probably. We are not supposed to be in here."

"Uh huh." Goth looked around for a way out. "Suppose we climbed down the tree a bit and out onto that branch there, and out along it. Might be able to get down and to the door first."

Pausert shrugged. "Maybe, but we shouldn't be here. It would only be right to stay and take our punishment."

He hadn't changed that much, thought Goth. "You are allowed to be here," she said. "I mean, you have a key. They don't. And I'll bet they would say it was all your fault they are here."

"Likely. Rapport and his friends are always pretty good at saying it was all my fault," he admitted, with a rueful grin.

Goth smiled nastily. "So follow me along the branch."

Goth hoped that he would not wonder too much about the fact that Tyrian fruit kept flying down at the little gang hiding behind a nearby stone-palmetto, even after they'd left. And that the gang could run, but they weren't getting out, because she had the key safely ported into her pocket.

They shimmied down the branch and dropped into the pipelike thicket of bright yellow-stemmed plants. With an awkward slither Goth descended into their midst. They creaked but did not break. She celebrated by 'porting another couple of Tyrian fruit down on the boys who had been persecuting Pausert. It was a very good and almost indelible dye, as she remembered. Quite expensive too.

Pausert followed her lead. Only he must have weighed a little more than she did, and the yellow stems gave way. He landed, with a lot more of a crash, on top of her. Hastily she ported a couple more fruit down at the gang just in case they had heard the commotion. But by the sounds of it there was another kind of commotion coming.

"You lot! Just what do you think you are doing here?" yelled an angry-sounding adult voice. "Stop! Come back here! You can't get away! We'll catch you!"

Goth took advantage of the fact that Pausert was winded and a little stunned to hide both of them with a light-shift, as the purple-spattered group of boys ran for the small door they had come in through, hotly pursued by a couple of uniformed men. She listened in satisfaction as someone yelled, "It's locked!" They sounded suitably horrified.

Soon they came running past again. "Time for us to go, I guess, Captain."

"Captain?"

"Uh. I mean, Pausert. You just reminded me of someone that I call captain."

"You don't think that we should go and turn ourselves in to security?"

He really hadn't changed! "No," said Goth. "Then I'd be in a lot of trouble too."

That worked. "I'll get you out," he said.

"Good. Because I'm still hungry. Come on, let's go. Just keep calm and keep walking. Pretend we belong here. I'll be right behind you."

With any luck he wouldn't realize that what was walking behind him looked very like one of the little maintenance robots. Actually, hopefully he wouldn't realize that he looked like a security officer. She hoped she'd got it right. She hadn't managed to get a very good look at them. She snickered. She had done exactly what he suggested: turned him into Security. And herself as a maintenance robot—that was appropriate too.

They walked on. A security officer ran past in a cross corridor, and one of the purple boys ran down towards them, saw them and fled. "They didn't realize who we were," crowed Pausert.

"Shut up and keep walking," hissed Goth.

They got to the little door. "It's shut! The key is gone."

"No farther than my pocket," said Goth. "Now let's get out of here before they come back."

So they did, carefully locking the door behind them. "Maybe we should leave it open. Give the others a chance," said Pausert.

"Just like they were giving you one," said Goth. "Come on. I am ravening. It'll serve them right."

"Rapport's father will get them off anyway," said Pausert. "He's a big cheese with the council."

"Smelly, is he?" said Goth.

That reduced the youthful Pausert to laughter. "Vala! You're amazing."

"Yeah," said Goth. "And hungry, too. Come on. Let's go and eat."

CHAPTER 5

So they walked together into downtown Nikkeldepain City. You could see, right then and there, that
Nikkeldepain was big on order. Probably law too,
Goth reflected, but certainly order. The streets were
straight, neat, and very uniform. All the shop-signs were
the same size, precisely. People all wore clothes that
were the same style and cut, within a certain range.
Goth used a little light-shift to subtly alter her own
appearance. Captain Pausert had never been too good
on dress and noticing. She just had to remember what
Sunnat had worn—and he had barely noticed. Hulik
too, although to be fair, the Imperial agent hadn't
really been after the captain, like that Sunnat had.

They stopped at a pastry cook. "He's probably going
to ask to see the money," said Pausert.

"Then I'll show it to him," said Goth. The problem
with 'porting things was first the energy it used, and
second that it really helped if she knew exactly what
she was teleporting. When she'd teleported Wansing's
jewels around she'd been able to see them. That was
easy. She'd watched the Syrians load the cargo she'd
teleported from their holds. Things she couldn't see
in closed drawers was a bit like guess-work. You had
to visualize them quite carefully.

Sure enough, the pastry-cook took one look at
Pausert and demanded to see the money first. "I
know you. You'll be like that Threbus," said the
shopkeeper.

"And what was wrong with Threbus?" demanded
Goth, taking offense.

"And who are you, missy? Never seen you before,"
said the sharp-eyed proprietor. "Anyway, unless you
have money to spend, out. Or maybe just out anyway.
You lower the tone of the place, just by being here."

"I have money to spend," said Goth, letting hunger help her to hold her temper. It wasn't holding
it very tight.

"Let's see it."

So Goth focused her mind on his cash box. Then it
was merely a case of taking something the right size
from it. 'Porting it into her pocket. She pulled it out.

The shopkeeper's eyes bulged. "How..."

Goth looked at her hand, and then hastily returned
what she had 'ported to the drawer. But it was a bit
late for that. It was time for turning and running.

They ducked into a side street.

"What was that picture?" asked Pausert. He hadn't
seen it too well, apparently, to Goth's relief.

"I really don't know," she said. "But I would avoid going back there for a while."

She had the locality of the cash-box now. And her second attempt did feel a bit more like cash. She knew that Pausert would look on it as theft, so she did a quick check to see what she had. A twenty-mael note. Well, she had one of those. If the pastry cook didn't spend it in a hurry, he would be all right. Anyway, it would serve the shopkeeper right for keeping that sort of picture under his money.

"I can't really afford to buy pastries anyway," admitted Pausert. "There is a sausage seller down the next street that's not too bad. He used to have a stall near the school. Just don't think about the sausages too much."

It was good advice, Goth reflected, as she ate a few minutes later. Still, if it didn't kill her, it'd probably do for food, or at least something to fill the hole where her stomach used to be. And Pausert was obviously good at following his own advice, as he ate three of them.

He had been a bit difficult at first. "No. I couldn't. Really. I am not hungry," he said.

"Huh," said Goth. "I owe you for helping me when I had that . . . fit. And I won't eat alone, and I'm starving and you wouldn't want me to starve, would you?"

The sausages smelt reasonably good. She could see that he was tempted. "Look. I'll hire you to show me around Nikkeldepain City. Payment will be some of those sausages. If I had to get a proper guide they'd skin me for a lot more. You get to eat, and I get a guide. How is that for a deal?"

He nodded. "Okay. If you're sure."

"Sure as can be," said Goth. "Now, what'll you have?"

They washed the sausages down with some lime-green juice that Pausert liked, and Goth thought was rather like the sausages—best avoided. Now that her hunger was eased, Goth began to think about why she was here. It was really neat meeting the captain as a boy her own age, but there had to be some terrible danger threatening him.

She began fishing for details as they walked. He was determined to give her a full sausage's worth of a guided tour. Nikkeldepain City didn't have a lot of sights, but he was going to show her all of them. On foot, and not by the monorail that seemed to be the normal mode of transport here.

She got the feeling that he was also fairly lonely. Well, judging by the gang of boys back at the botanical institute, he didn't have a lot of friends. She began to tease out bits of his life, school and family from his conversation. She was surprised to find herself learning a fair bit about her own father in the process. Threbus had also come from here, years before. And he had left quite a mark. His niece, Pausert's mother, was a widow. She'd come back to Nikkeldepain after Pausert's father had been killed in a military action somewhere on the borders of the Empire.

He was not from Nikkeldepain, and the locals didn't like that much. "I'm an outsider," admitted Pausert. "And Great Uncle Threbus managed to make himself infamous here. Ma says when she was growing up it was a bit different. I mean his practical jokes were still talked about, but after the Flidean expeditions on the *Venture* he made quite a lot of money. And where there is lots of money Nikkeldepain will turn a blind eye."

"I bet," said Goth. But, as interested as she was in finding out what had happened—she was pretty sure that a lot of Threbus' "practical jokes" were the start of his klatha skills manifesting themselves—Pausert was curious about life on the lattice ship, or just life off-world in general. It became very clear that long before he had rescued Goth and her sisters on Porlumma and gotten himself into trouble with the authorities on Nikkeldepain for associating with the prohibited planet of Karres and its notorious witches, he'd been getting ready to leave, anyway. Their intervention had forced him to flee to the life of a vagabond of space, but he seemed more than happy with it. Thus Goth was willing to feed that desire, although she had to be careful not to mention Karres. After all, Captain Pausert had, in perfect truth, said that he had never heard of it.

It took her a little while to realize that they were being followed. And whoever was doing the organizing was good at it. If Nikkeldepain's memorials and prominent sights had been a little more popular with visitors, she would not have noticed. But it was improbable that the same man with tan shoes and blue trousers would be visiting the corn exchange, the statue of Nikkerliss, and the old fortification, at exactly the same time as them.

Goth could not really see any reason for ever visiting any of them at all. It was obvious Pausert couldn't either, but he was doing his best to earn his meal. They'd seen nearly everything except the Central Museum of Historical Nikkeldepain—which not only charged entry, but her guide said had nothing but moldy old rubbish that they took school groups to see. Goth wouldn't have minded taking the monorail to several of the spots, but Pausert plainly never considered taking it. He walked with a long-legged easy stride, and kept forgetting to walk at her pace and then guiltily slowing down. Goth had always considered herself a good bollem hunter, happy to walk and track, but Pausert had plainly got himself very fit legging it about the streets of Nikkeldepain.

At the next sight, a grain mill, the follower had changed. Now it was a woman with a cone hairdo. But now that Goth was aware of them, the information she'd absorbed talking to Hulik do Eldel, who had been a top Imperial agent, made them easy to spot.

It occurred to her that if they were being tailed— and she assumed it was Pausert they were tailing, not her—they were probably using a spy ray to listen in to their conversation too. That made her blush slightly, and also made her angry. There were going to be some painful lessons learned around here.

"I have a challenge for you, Pausert," she said cheerfully, just short of a street corner. "You close your eyes and I'll lead you. I'll take you somewhere. Then you tell me which of Nikkeldepain's sights it is!"

"Sure," he said, and obediently closed his eyes. She took him by the elbow, and they stepped around the corner and into no-shape. She just hoped no one noticed them disappear. But they'd probably just not believe their own eyes. She turned him around and set off the way they'd come.

To nearly get run down by a hurrying woman with a cone hairdo, speaking into a wrist communicator. Goth hurriedly led Pausert away in the other direction. They got to a particularly ugly building with a nice bench and she said, "open them."

"The old power station," he said, grinning. "It's harder to walk with your eyes shut than I thought!"

And easier to lose a tail, thought Goth. And then she got a horrid surprise. The man with the tan shoes was idling along the pavement, reading what appeared to be a guide book. And, yes. Over there. That had to be the woman with the cone hairdo.

They weren't tracking him by sight.

There was no way they could have found them so quickly, if they were. She felt terribly alone and vulnerable. The little witches of Karres traveled around the galaxy perfectly cheerfully, exploring and learning. But they never went alone. She wasn't quite alone this time, either. She was in the company of one of the most powerful klatha operatives that Karres had ever encountered. A real Wizard of Karres. The only trouble was that Pausert wouldn't develop into one for quite a few years. Right now he was just a poor boy from Nikkeldepain with a black eye. A rather nice poor boy, but nothing more.

She gave him her best smile. "I have to get back. But you have been a great guide."

He bowed and blushed. "A pleasure. So, um, are you going to be around?"

Very definitely! thought Goth, *and for a lot longer than you realize.* But all she said was "Maybe. You take care, huh."

"I can't walk you back to the lattice ship?"

"Nope. I'd get into trouble. See you. Maybe." And she got up and walked off. She could see his reflection in the plate glass of the nearby shop window. He really looked quite tragic.

But cone-hairdo was watching her. So she walked

on, and into the shop. It was a fairly busy lady's dress shop. Goth went into a fitting room and emerged in no-shape, bending light around her, moments later. She found cone-hairdo reporting on her wrist communicator. She had an oddly flat voice.

"Yes, he's alone at last, Franco. We should be able to make the snatch soon."

Goth could only hear one side of the conversation. "Well, it's not our fault," said the woman. "That bunch of kids were following him around like glue. And you said we were to avoid witnesses. Then he acquired a girl with red hair. You've got the stills pictures of her that Mirkon took. And a name from the spy ray. Track her down in planetary records. They're obsessed with records in this place."

In the meantime Pausert, now bored, had gotten up and begun to saunter his way down the street, whistling. Goth was surprised. He still whistled the same tune, years later.

"He's moving off. Got to follow him," said the woman. "Mirkon has just gone to collect the van. Keep him on the trackerscope. Out."

Goth followed quietly behind her, her mind seething. Someone was putting a lot of effort into this, but why? And something about Pausert's circumstances stank. She knew, from casual comments over meals and in conversation, that her father had left behind a small commercial empire on Nikkeldepain, the results of several lucrative discoveries, when his last expedition had stumbled on Karres. She also knew that he had been declared legally dead there—which was a source of some amusement to the family. He'd gone to some lengths to protect Karres and to provide the

Nikkeldepain authorities with this conclusion, even sending back an empty ship—the *Venture 7333*—and a log that pointed at disaster in a different quarter of space.

Pausert's mother was his only heir on Nikkeldepain. He'd thought well of her, and said that it wasn't surprising that the captain had come out so well. So where was the money?

CHAPTER 6

The incident happened in a little side street, and it was done so slickly that, even forewarned, Goth was nearly taken by surprise.

A grubby little white air-truck slid past young Pausert and slowed to a crawl. The back door opened and a man beckoned to Pausert, who smiled and walked forward to speak to him. It was tan shoes, the follower from earlier—"Mirkon," presumably. And cone-hairdo was closing in, fast, from behind, a transdermic syringe in her hand.

Goth had to take action herself, just as fast. This was no time for finesse. She was between the woman and Pausert. She 'ported the syringe into Mirkon's hand—the wrong way around. He instinctively squeezed the sudden apparition that smacked into his palm.

48

Goth didn't wait to see what effect it had. She was too busy head-butting Cone Hairdo in the stomach. And as the fast-striding woman staggered back, she kicked her. It wasn't exactly great fighting, Goth knew, but her victim didn't know what had hit her. Cone Hairdo tripped over the curb and landed hard on her back. The cone-shaped hairdo turned out to be a wig, which went flying.

Pausert had heard her explosion of departing breath after the head butt, and turned to see her inelegant crash-landing on the sidewalk. Being Pausert, he turned to help her up. He retrieved her wig, unaware that the man he'd been about to speak to had keeled over sideways in the back of the air-truck.

"Are you all right, ma'am?" he asked politely, handing her back her wig.

Goth decided that as the driver too must be an accomplice, it was time to get rid of him and the vehicle. The throttle was controlled by a small foot-pedal, just like most of the air cars in the Empire. The driver couldn't see her because he was looking backwards, his hand on the door handle. Peering past him, Goth happily saw that it was the kind of pedal that had a spring to keep the cable taut and off the floor. A cheap model! She knew from experience that the throttle stuck full if the spring broke, so she 'ported the spring elsewhere.

The air-truck, its door now half open, suddenly roared to full throttle and accelerated down the narrow side street, swaying wildly with the brakes squealing as the driver-accomplice tried to control it. He should have paid more attention to his steering, as he hit a lamp-post, ramped the curb and crashed into the corner.

Goth hadn't intended his departure to be quite that spectacular. Luckily, no bystanders were hurt. The driver leapt out and ran away.

The woman had obviously realized that this was no time to be present, either. She snatched her wig and ran away from the open-mouthed Pausert.

Of course, at this point, the local flat-feet turned up. "And what is going on here?" demanded the policeman of the one person he could see on the scene: young Pausert.

"I really don't know," said Pausert. "The lady fell over. I was helping her up. Then...Where has she gone?"

The woman and her wig had disappeared.

More policemen arrived, one on a hover cycle, siren howling. He had the sense to check the air-truck, find the unconscious man in the back, and call for an ambulance. In the meanwhile one of the policemen was staring inquisitorially at Pausert. "You're related to that Captain Threbus, aren't you?"

Pausert, incurably truthful and with a strong familial resemblance, nodded. "He was my great uncle."

"Hmm. Well, you'd better come along with us then," said the officer sourly.

"But I had nothing to do with it!" protested Pausert. "The driver ran away."

"We'll check on that."

So Goth had to follow as the young Pausert was led off towards the police station, and the unconscious Mirkon was driven away in an ambulance. It would seem that her father had had quite a reputation here on Nikkeldepain. On the positive side, if the enemy had been trying to capture or harm him out of sight of any witnesses—Pausert was surrounded by witnesses now.

A horrible thought occurred to her. What if they too were villains? She walked a little closer. No-shape—bending light around herself—was not something she had to consciously exert her mind to do. But it took energy. She was already tired and hungry again.

And then came the next problem. Someone had plainly called for a patrol-car. Goth realized that there was no way that she could fit into it, along with the three bulky policemen who seemed to believe that they'd gotten their man. She had to do something quickly. She had no idea where the local police station was and she had no intention of letting Pausert out her sight. She settled for the advantages of no-shape to reach in and remove the starter-bar from the vehicle's ignition, and dropped it down the grate of a nearby drain. It landed with quite an audible plop, but fortunately the policemen were too busy telling their comrade to radio for a tow for the crashed air-truck.

"You can do it when we're back at the station," said the driver irritably. "I don't know why you couldn't have walked anyway. I was just on my break."

"You're always just on your break," said one of the other officers, pushing his way in. "Come on, Hasbol. Get the kid inside, and let's get down to the station."

So they did. The door was closed. Goth waited and watched the searching and commotion. The door was opened again, and Pausert and the officers got out again. "So how do you think I got here?" yelled the driver irritably. "One of you must have taken it. Or him. You'd better search the kid."

They emptied out Pausert's pockets, which had all

the useful things a fourteen year old boy might have in them—string, some odd bits of scrap metal, a bottle cap, a broken penknife, but no starter-bar. They patted him down but still did not find the missing starter-bar.

"We may as well walk back to the station," said one of the men eventually. "And you'd better call in, Bryton. There's something very fishy about all of this."

So they marched off together, escorting Pausert— who was struggling to hide a grin at their misfortunes. The captain that Goth knew would have been better at keeping a straight face. Goth was able to walk along behind them, having taken the step of light-shifting to the shape of one of the local constabulary. It was less effort than staying in no-shape indefinitely.

It was a mere two blocks away and round one corner, so, other than to protect the way their uniforms bulged over their belts, there'd really been no reason to call a patrol car out. Still, from what she could gather, Nikkeldepain City did not have much crime to entertain them. They were grumbling about the extra duties that the presence of the showboat lattice ship had put onto their poor overworked selves, and, so far, they'd been unable to arrest anyone for their troubles.

"That circus master—Petey. He'll be behind all this. Mark my words. I don't trust him."

Goth's heart leapt. *Himbo Petey? Here?* Then the lattice ship must be the *Petey, Byrum and Keep*, the Greatest Show in the Galaxy. Her friends here to help! And then she realized...

They weren't yet her friends.

It was still comforting to think of them being here. Of course over the years, lattice ships did visit nearly every inhabited planet. Quite a coincidence—but one of the things that the people of Karres had learned about klatha force is that there really were no coincidences. Just patterns, some of them too enormous ever to see.

Pausert was stoical throughout all of this. Goth, who knew him well, could see that the boy was quite nervous despite his stolid expression. He just wasn't letting the police see it. Well, that was hardly surprising. She just wished that she could tell him that she was here, and that she'd see that he was all right.

A few minutes later, she discovered that she was not alone in her task of shepherding the young Pausert. His mother was quite a fearsome one-woman army herself.

"He happened to be in the same street as a car crash and you arrest him? He can't even drive yet! Anyway, where would he have got this vehicle from? Tell me that! Are you accusing my son of theft?"

"Uh. We're still following up on that," admitted the desk-policeman. "The vehicle was hired from Porklotta vehicle hire. But we've been unable to trace the ID of the person who signed for it."

"And who presumably was an adult, produced a driver's license, and paid a deposit," snapped Pausert's mother. "Even if my boy had the money, no one could take him for an adult. And where in Patham's name would he get a license that matched his ret-ID? They would have checked that, you know, or you should know, if you weren't a bumbling idiot."

"Who are you calling a bumbling idiot, ma'am?" demanded the bumbling idiot, drawing himself up.

Her eyes narrowed. "I'll leave you to think about that one. It might take you a week or two. In the meanwhile I am taking my boy home. You have no reason to keep him here. I gather that there was somebody else in the truck, and that they have been taken to the hospital. Why don't you go and check on their ID? They can probably tell you what happened."

"Uh . . . As to that, the patient seems to have absconded," admitted the desk sergeant.

"Oh. And I suppose that was somehow caused by my son, although you had him here."

"Well, there is also the matter of the starter-bar from the patrol vehicle."

She raised her eyebrows. "And just what is Pausert supposed to have done with that? From what you told me on the telephone you found him at the scene of the accident. I presume that the patrol vehicle managed to arrive after that. Or did it cause the accident?"

"Of course the vehicle arrived after the accident, ma'am. But we believe he managed to make the starter-bar go missing."

"But how did he do that? Turn himself invisible and walk around the vehicle and snatch it out? Put it in his pocket? Toss it down a drain?" she said sarcastically. "This is all about my uncle, isn't it? Well, Pausert isn't Threbus. He's just a very ordinary little boy. I wish you would leave him alone. Now. He's coming home with me."

And, a few minutes later, after a little bit more verbal bludgeoning, Pausert's mother proved correct. Goth was very relieved, and decided to use their bathroom before following her. It was a little childish to express her relief by blocking the basins in the officers' bathroom and removing the washer that allowed the faucet to seal. She left quietly in no-shape.

There was a startled exclamation, and Goth looked

back to see an officer staring at the row of wet footprints that she was leaving behind her. Sometimes
behaving like the Leewit just wasn't worth it.

Goth ran for it. Fortunately, the officer seemed
more stunned than quick on the uptake, and she was
out of the door before he had time to do more than
make incoherent noises and point.

Outside she ran to a nearby piece of public parkland.
The grass didn't show wet footprints, and in no-shape
she was happy enough to ignore the sign that said
that she should keep off it. Two of Nikkeldepain's
constabulary did follow the rapidly drying footprints.

"Must have taken their shoes off, whoever it was,"
said one, scratching his head, looking at the sign and
then peering at the pavement. It appeared that if one
lived on Nikkeldepain, one took rules very seriously.

"Wonder where the water came from?" said the
other.

Goth discovered the second problem with behaving
like the Leewit. She had to stuff her own sleeve in
her mouth to stop from betraying herself. After a few
moments, the answer plainly dawned on the two and
they turned to run back to the station. It was then that
she realized the third problem. She had lost sight of
young Pausert and his mother. She was in a strange
city, on a strange world, with absolutely no idea how
to even start looking for him. She'd have to find him
before those others got to him. And then she'd have
to deal with them.

Right now, however, wet feet or not, she desperately needed to eat and rest. But could she afford
to do either or should she rather immediately try to
find Pausert?

She decided, after a few moments' consideration, that while he was in the custody of his mother, he was probably reasonably safe. Whoever was trying to kidnap him without witnesses would probably not risk it while his mother was with him. Goth slipped into a public restroom and undid the no-shape. That at least saved her some energy. She went off in search of food and ideas of where she could find Pausert.

She got help with both from the sausage seller. "Aren't you the kid," he said, in friendly tone, "who was here with the boy from the botanical place? The Threbus Institute?"

He seemed no more than idly curious. "Yes," admitted Goth, "but he's gone home now."

"I used to have a stand near there. Saw the kid most days back then. Nice polite boy, not like some of the rich riff-raff at the academy. I hadn't seen him for a while."

"Oh," said Goth artlessly. "And where did your stand used to be?"

"Pilking Street. Over toward the old power station."

Goth set out, armed with a street name, a direction, and the energy from digesting some greasy sausage. The lights were coming on across Nikkeldepain City. It was a rather flat and uninspiring place. In the distance beyond her destination she could see the trails of multicolored fairy lights flickering seductively from the lattice ship. That called to her, but her duty now was to find and protect Pausert.

So she studiously avoided thinking about the lattice ship, about the journey they'd had across the Empire with the *Petey B*. It was like not thinking of pink fanderbags.

She was so busy not thinking about it that she nearly walked into the woman whom she'd last seen wearing a cone-shaped blonde wig. She had curly auburn hair now, but it was the same woman. She also plainly recognized Goth.

"Hello, little girl," she said, clutching Goth's arm. "You look thirsty. Can I get you something to drink?"

Goth shook the hand off. She hated being called "little girl" at the best of times. Her look made the woman start back. "No," she said coldly.

And then it occurred to her that she might be able to extract some information from her. Best to play it cautiously, for now. "I am not thirsty. Thank you."

"It's very late for you to be out. It's not really safe for a young girl to be out the street after dark."

Huh. Not with you around, thought Goth. But, in general, she thought Nikkeldepain was probably one of the safest worlds she'd ever been on. It was the kind of place where even the thought of crime was just too complicated.

"I'm fine. I live near here," she said crossly. "And they're expecting me. Goodbye." She walked off, around the corner, and then used light-shift to make herself look like an elderly man she'd seen earlier.

A few seconds later the woman appeared, talking into her wrist communicator. She looked up when she saw the light-shifted Goth. "Hello, gramps," she said curtly. "Have you seen a young girl come this way. Brown eyes. Sharpish chin?"

Goth didn't want to try imitating an old man's voice as well as his appearance. The more klatha powers of imitation you used, the harder it was to do each of them properly—and the energy requirement was exponential, not simply additive. So she just pointed toward a side street and continued shuffling on her way.

The woman did a rapid U-turn and was back around the corner in a few seconds. Goth followed in no-shape. Now, maybe, she could get close enough to listen in on the woman's communicator conversation.

"—snooping around here," said the woman. Goth listened but could not hear the reply. "The reason you can't find her on the police records system could just be that she's working with them, Mirkon."

Her informant replied.

"That leaves the lattice ship," said the woman, "although why the circus people would have an interest in the target is beyond me. I admit it's good cover, though. Look, I think tonight is off. There's only one window and unless you've got the Rubilon three to dope them—"

Mirkon plainly interrupted. "Don't make your problems mine!" said the woman crossly, getting into a parked air car.

Goth waited for her to drive off, but the woman stayed there, continuing her conversation. Only now Goth could hear neither side of it. Goth pondered her next step. It would be fairly easy to deal with this woman. But that was just the surface of the plot. It seemed that they planned no further action that evening, and she couldn't follow Pausert everywhere in no-shape forever. She was already pushing her energy reserves too far.

In fact, Goth found herself nearly swaying with exhaustion. Traveling back here by the Egger Route, not to mention everything else she'd done since arriving on Nikkeldepain, sure took it out of you. She needed a safe place to lie up for the night. In the morning, she'd find out just why they were after the captain, and just who they were. She had a feeling that could be vital information. But now, she had to rest. And burgling Pausert's home seemed just too hard.

The *Petey B* was close enough. She knew where to find a quiet spot in the props store for a bit of sleep, and there were always cushions and some fabric for a bed there. The "props" had been a veritable treasure house, as well as the perfect hideout for her and the Leewit, when they'd traveled with the lattice-ship circus. So she walked towards its lights, trying not to think just about how tired her feet were.

The ship was secured and guarded, of course. The *Petey B* did not want stowaways or petty thieves. Well... it would take stowaways, sometimes. But Himbo Petey was a man with a conscience and Goth didn't plan to test it. She knew how the security system worked, and she still had enough energy left to use no-shape in a pinch.

As it turned out, she made it to the old hulk that was the second props store with no problems or incidents. Despite the fact that she was a decade and a few years early, the setting was so familiar, so comforting, that she might have indulged in a happy snuffle or so when she reached its sanctuary.

It was dark and warm and comfortable in the bed she'd made for herself. It easy to sleep here.

Too easy.

When she awoke it wasn't dark anymore. And the crimson-faced man staring down at her was not pleased to see her.

"Manicholo!"

The thermosensitive crystals tattooed into the man's dermis shifted color slightly, in a wave of cooler purple across the red visage. The reaching hand stopped. "What did you call me?"

Goth, still only half awake, struggled for an answer. "Uh. Manicholo. Isn't that your name?"

The plump sideshow entertainer scratched his head. "Weird," he said. "I've been considering it but I'll swear I haven't told a soul, yet. Look, kid. I'll have to see you off the premises. The local authorities would love something to bust us for, and although I understand your wanting to get off this dump, I don't want Himbo ornamenting their jail for juvie-kidnap. This isn't the Empire and they have laws about kids here. Personally, I'd like to get off Nikkeldepain altogether, but the marks are still cranking through the turnstiles."

Goth nodded. "It's okay. I understand. I'm not from here, but I met the local flatfeet yesterday. They aren't the sharpest scribers in the box. I just needed a place to sleep, that's all. Don't worry, I'll go quietly."

Manicholo-to-be looked at her thoughtfully. "How did you find the store? How did you get in?"

You showed it to me somewhere in the future. I should have guessed it was a favorite spot of yours. But that was not an answer that she could give. "Luck, I suppose."

"Exceptional luck," said the chameleon-man dryly.

"Um. I've been on a lattice ship before," admitted Goth. "So I knew what it was that I was looking for, and how to sneak in. Promise I will go now and not bring back any trouble for Himbo Petey. He's a decent old dope."

Manicholo had a disconcerting habit of noticing just

what you didn't want him to. "He's not that old. And just how did you get past the perimeter?"

Himbo *wouldn't* be that old yet. Goth found herself very curious. How big was his moustache? And . . . "Is Dame Ethy with the Show?"

Her captor shook his head. "That does it. You're coming with me to talk to Himbo Petey, young lady."

Goth ported a glass lamp-stand five feet above a display of Medoirian armor and let it fall, then slipped away into no-shape as Manicholo turned to see what had happened.

"Wha—where . . . ?" Manicholo wasted precious seconds looking for her instead of closing the outer lock to the hulk that served as the second props store. By then Goth was outside. It was already quite bright out. The Greatest Show in the Galaxy was busy with its familiar morning chores, mucking out, cleaning up, preparing for the return of the crowds.

Pausert was probably already at school. She hadn't meant to sleep that long. Klatha. It took it out of you! She needed breakfast and to get back to her task—and not necessarily in that order either.

But on a whim, she followed Manicholo as he hurried along to the main part of the lattice, where the circus offices were. It wouldn't take her much out of her way—well, not more than it took to skirt the fanderbags' tail ends carefully. No-shape bent light around her, not more solid things.

Sure enough, Manicholo had stopped by to see a younger Himbo Petey. He was working on the mustachios, but he had a few years to go. They looked faintly ridiculous on his younger face, and Goth had to stifle a giggle.

"—intruder of some sort. A young girl. She seemed to know a great deal about the circus."

Himbo twirled his mustachios. "They do, you know. They find out as much as they can. So where did you find her, and how did she get away? We've got to be careful here, Fenn. The local authorities are ready to jump on us for anything."

Manicholo nodded. "I know. She was in the Props store. No. 2. Distracted me and ran, I think. Means she's probably hiding out somewhere."

Himbo sighed irritably. "We'll do a search. And contact that local councilor fellow, Onswud, and ask if they have any missing persons. Give me a description so that we can say we saw her. That way if it goes pear-shaped, we're on record as having tried and having reported the incident to them. I'll have a word with security. And you'd better make sure that she's not still in that rat-warren of a store, and see that it is locked."

Goth slipped off before he did all of that. She was right in her earlier judgment—Nikkeldepain City was already at work. She could just hope that young Pausert was safely in his school as she made her way along the street to his home.

"Why aren't you in class?" asked a sharp-eyed fellow in gray coveralls. He radiated *self-important minor government official* without having to say so.

"Great Patham! Look at that!" said Goth, pointing. He looked and she did a subtle light-shift on herself, making herself look a little more like her mother.

"What?" The minor official turned back. "What are you pointing at?"

"You should have looked faster," said Goth, shifting her voice too. "It's gone now. Some kind of animal."

The official peered again. "What color? I'm here to catch strays," he said proudly. "Sorry, I thought you were a lot younger."

He went on his way, followed by hard thoughts from Goth. The man's petty officiousness had required her to use a fair amount of her klatha energy for no good reason. The last night's sleep had restored some of that energy, true, and a good meal would restore still more. Still, she'd have to be careful.

Goth noticed that a vehicle sitting in the leafy street close to Pausert's home had an occupant, who was staring at her. She could only hope that they hadn't seen the subtle shift in age. She recognized the fellow as the man from the back of the air-truck yesterday.

Pausert had been rather disappointed when Vala had had to go. She'd been, well, quite unlike any other girl he'd ever met. The affair with the air-truck and police were just the way things happened in his life. But Vala wasn't. He indulged in a little daydreaming about her.

His mother sighed and tugged his ear. "I suppose that was a no."

"Huh? What, sorry . . . I . . . ah, was just thinking about something."

"Never mind. It's been quite a day," she said tiredly. "We had an incident at the institute today. That horrible Rapport boy and some of his friends broke in and were vandalizing the gardens. You should have seen the mess that they got themselves into. I'm glad you have better taste in friends."

Pausert wanted to say he just didn't have any friends, but that would have upset her, so he held his tongue and thought about Vala and the fight. And the sausages. He seemed to be hungry all of the time at the moment. It wasn't easy, growing up and being saddled with Great Uncle Threbus's debts. It didn't seem fair.

"So how was school?"

That was not a question Pausert really wanted to answer. So he tried a well-known diversion tactic. "The lawyers haven't got back to you yet about Great Uncle's will?"

She rubbed her eyes. "No. I'll have to go in and see them again tomorrow."

She'd been trying, determinedly, for the last three years. She was nothing if not stubborn, his mother. But lawyers were a money pit. "So what happened about Rapport and his gang?" Pausert asked.

"Oh, security was all for throwing the book at them. But he howled for his daddy and eventually they were let off with a caution and a very large bill for damages."

Pausert took a deep breath. That wouldn't make life easy. But then, life wasn't easy. The sheer joy of seeing his enemy splattered in Tyrian fruit juice was worth it. And although his mother had seen the tear and the black eye, apparently she'd decided not to say anything. Maybe she thought the police had done it. How could he tell her the truth, without giving away Vala's part in all of this? Anyway, there was no harm done, was there?

The next day when he saw Rapport and a few of his little friends, he realized that it wasn't that simple. The Tyrian fruit dye didn't come off easily. It didn't even scrub off that easily, judging from the red, raw skin. And it was apparent that the experience had some of the boys looking for new company—probably warned off by their parents—but the three who were the core of Rapport's crew were hoping for a rematch. He'd take on any one of them. He'd take any two of them. But four…

They let him know that they'd be waiting, after school. And this time he wasn't going to get away.

He couldn't walk any slower. And he couldn't find any more reason to delay. He took a deep breath and walked out through the gates of the Nikkeldepain Academy for the Sons and Daughters of Gentlemen and Officers. That was why they always had had it in for him. Because he really didn't belong here. He was a scholarship boy. And worse than that, they said that he hadn't got the scholarship fairly. That it had just been given to him because his great uncle had endowed the school with it. They could hardly have given it to someone who really deserved it, when Pausert had applied, could they? Huh. He'd won it fair and square. But it wasn't something that he could tell people who had already made up their minds.

"You took your time getting here," said Vala, leaning on the gatepost. "I explained to a couple of purple-splattered boys that were hanging around that they needed to get along home to mummy."

Pausert gaped. "You did what?" he finally got out.

Goth was quite proud of herself. Not only had she dealt with one of the watchers, but she'd had breakfast, and had also had her morning ablutions. She'd decided that the captain was pretty much family, and, if she'd asked him, that he'd have had no problems with her climbing in through a second-floor bathroom window and making use of the facilities. While she was at it she had a snoop around the family home. She felt a bit guilty about that, but, well, the captain really wouldn't mind. The younger Pausert might, but she wasn't planning to tell him until he was much older.

The home was clean, just like the captain always kept the *Venture*. The signs of scraping by on a limited income showed. There wasn't much in the way of food or spare clothing. But there were a lot of signs of travels to exotic places. Bangras from Gilars World hung on the wall. There were other items she didn't recognize. The walls were studded with pictures of various strange animals and plants. There were a number of excellent space-shots. And a photograph of an Imperial officer in pride of place, in the small lounge.

There was a report card from a school, too, which Goth found rather fascinating. She'd never been to a formal school of that sort. Karres did not teach its children like that. She studied his grades proprietorially. He was good at Math. Nikkeldepain Academy—she noted the name, and worked out just how she could use her 'porting skills to get the key for the back door to the house if she needed it again, before setting off to the school.

The boys had been easy to spot hanging about just outside the school's gates. The purple-blotched red faces did make them rather obvious, even if their behavior hadn't done so.

Obviously, they were waiting for Pausert. And he was going to make things worse by waiting until everyone else had dispersed. So Goth took steps herself. She'd learned a thing or two about Nikkeldepain from the captain and his attitudes. It was a pretty masculine society, rather like the Empire and very unlike Karres. She smiled nastily to herself. Toll always said that it was worth quietly fitting into a society—after all, Karres people were just passing through. Threbus said there were times for that, and times for establishing some respect. She'd do both.

"Hello, boys," she said, smiling at them. "Remember me?"

By the looks of it, they did. "You're the tough guys here. Are all these people going to be impressed when I tell them how I helped to improve your looks? I can improve them some more if you like. And I will do both, if you're still around when I've finished counting to three."

They were plainly torn between teaching her a lesson—huh! like that was going to happen!—and being seen fighting with a girl. One girl, at that, and the real threat of having that girl telling the locals just how they'd acquired purple blotches. Rapport's nerve broke first. "You can't protect him forever," he said, sniffing and turning away.

Watch me, thought Goth. *But he'll be able to deal with worms like you himself, any day.* But she kept this to herself and waited. Pausert emerged, wary and fists balled, a few minutes later.

It did not take Goth very long to penetrate Pausert's armor. He was naturally gregarious, and liked to talk. And, well, she knew him. The most difficult thing was not to give that away. But, sitting on the rails of one of Nikkeldepain's many iron bridges, swinging their legs over the water, in compete contravention of the sign telling them not to, she heard the story of most of his life to date.

The surprising thing was just how little of it she had learned in all the time that they had spent together on the *Venture*. He'd obviously made the decision to put all of this behind him. And it wasn't really surprising.

"—and so he's still MIA. Mother says they think he deserted. She says that's impossible."

His father lost after a minor skirmish on an otherwise routine patrol. His one-man scout ship was never found. He was assumed to have fled the scene and dumped the ship somewhere.

The Imperial navy stopped paying his salary.

And then things got worse.

They'd come back to Nikkeldepain.

"Mother had an offer of a job at the Botany Institute." Pausert kicked the rails. "She's a xenobotanist and a plant pathologist. They really need her, but there are not a lot of other people who do, here on Nikkeldepain. Like, they don't need me either."

"Nonsense," said Goth. "But why did you even come back to Nikkeldepain? There are xenobotany places inside the Empire. There's one in the capital, and one on Green Galaine. There must be lots of them."

Pausert shrugged. "Probably. But Mom had inherited the house. Seeing as my father is looked on almost like a traitor or something in the Empire military, I suppose she wanted to get out of there. And she had a house and job offer here. Only when we got here, that's when things got really complicated. See, the law around here says that your heirs also inherit your debts. And it seems like Great Uncle disappeared owing a few people some money. Not a lot by his standards maybe. Nothing much against the estate. But a lot of money for us."

"I don't really understand these things," said Goth. "But don't they just sell off his property, and pay people?" She was vaguely horrified that her Captain Pausert should have ended up in clothes that were plainly a little too small for him, because his mother was paying off Threbus's debts.

"The law here is a bit odd about that, Mom says," said Pausert. "They are not allowed to take more than the estate is worth from the heir, but they don't have to wait until the whole thing is wrapped up. And it can't be wrapped up, because the Nikkeldepain Office of Records refuses to declare Great Uncle dead."

Goth knew a moment of righteous indignation. Of course her father wasn't dead! That was followed by the pragmatic realization that for Karres's sake he had set things up to look like he was.

"So, um, what is happening?" asked Goth.

Pausert kicked the bridge railing angrily. "Nothing. We spend more of the money we haven't got on lawyers who don't do anything. I go to school, Mother goes to work. And things just go on the same way. Sorry. Enough. I shouldn't have even told you about it. It's our problem. So what are you doing here?"

Goth hadn't thought much about that part of her story yet. "I'm going to be going to your school," she announced. It was a sudden decision—and a tall story—but better than anything else she could think of right now.

It did at least serve to distract him. "You are?" He smiled, and the smile chased the gloomy expression off his face. "It's a good school. But you better not tell anyone that you know me. I'm not too popular."

"Huh. Too late," said Goth, grinning. "So, tell me about it." He did. And talking of school successfully steered the subject away from Goth's own back history. She really would have to think about that. She was also going to have to do something about the mess that the local law had made of Captain Pausert's life as a young man. There was no doubt that it was an appalling mess. And yet, somehow it must have all come right in time for him to go to the Space-Naval Academy. Goth was willing to bet that she had had something to do with it. She just wished she knew what it had been. That would have saved her having to work out what it would be! Time travel was needlessly confusing.

CHAPTER 7

Here in the Chaladoor, Captain Pausert was finding out
the hard way just how intrinsic Goth had become to
the running of the ship. Yes, there was still old Vezzarn.
The spacer was an experienced hand, and these days
the captain felt that he could trust him. But he lacked
Goth's incisive decision-making. The experiences they'd
been through had made Goth aware of what the dangers
actually were, and when it was wise to wake the captain.
Vezzarn . . . the experiences seemed to have made him
timid instead! "There are too many strange things I
really don't understand, Captain," he said. "I reckon
that it's best to leave that sort of deciding to you. Or
to the little Wisdoms," he said, referring to the Karres
witches by their Uldune honorific. "Only, well, better
if it's Missy Dani, uh, Goth."

That was all too true. The Leewit had grown a great deal since her sister had left her here on the *Venture*. But she still was some years younger. And, unlike Goth, the Leewit did not wake easily, or in a good temper! The end result was that the captain was getting very little sleep, and what he was getting was being interrupted all too often. Besides that, he just missed having Goth to talk to. They'd been companions now for some time. To his shock Pausert realized that it was heading on for a good year or two since the incident on Porlumma—hard to say exactly!

He tried to quiz the Leewit on just where Goth had got to. But on that subject he might as well have tried to ask the bulkheads questions. The Leewit could stonewall with the very best. And she could fend off too much questioning with a threat of a few of her shattering whistles. That was enough to stop him asking.

Besides, he had a lot on his plate. The trip had had far more encounters than he expected, and something, he found, was bothering him. It felt as if they were being watched. Maybe even manipulated. He was tired, off-balance, stressed, and missing his familiar helper. But that did not stop the captain noticing that there was a certain pattern to the incidents. He talked about it with both the Leewit and Vezzarn, in one of the relatively rare times when all three of them were awake at the same time. One couldn't just leave the ship running on automatic in the Chaladoor, as they might have in the empty areas of Imperial space, relying on the detectors and alarms—which meant watches.

"I'm beginning to feel as if something is trying to herd us," he said tiredly. "We've just had to change course again. Not only is this adding quite a lot to our trip time, but it is beginning to worry me. It's almost as if these attacks are being orchestrated. But even subradio doesn't work reliably here in the Chaladoor—not without repeaters. That means the best anyone trying to track us could do, would be shorter range. And that implies a lot of coordination and a lot of ships. Unless, of course, they have some kind of leech or tracker on us. And we made sure of that not being the case, after last time!"

"Or else we've some pretty fast enemies," said the Leewit. "Maybe we should not run next time. Shoot them up and ask questions later." The Leewit loved her work on the nova guns, even if they were erratic, old and rather dangerous—even after the very best of the Daal's armorers had serviced and refurbished them.

It was a tempting idea, Captain Pausert had to admit.

Vezzarn shuddered. "In the Chaladoor it always feels like it is out to get you, Captain. But even the Agandar would have struggled to organize something like this. I think this must be more witchy stuff, Captain. I reckon we better cut and run."

"It would take us just as much time by now to go back as it would to go on," Pausert pointed out. "But I don't like playing their game for them. We might try a little extra speed."

Vezzarn coughed. "Uh, I'm feeling really tired, Captain. I think I'll go and take a sleep now." Vezzarn strongly resisted seeing "witchy stuff" in action. He really did not like to be around when they worked the Sheewash drive. It was quite an eerie thing to watch, Pausert had to admit. The more he thought about it, the more he decided it wasn't a "drive" at all. The *Venture* did not gain momentum in the process. It just traversed vast amounts of space. He wanted to understand how, but not right now. Right now, he needed to get away from the harassment and get some rest.

Soon, in the control room of the *Venture*, a cone of strangely twisted wires had a ball of orange energy dancing above it, as the captain and the Leewit worked the klatha pattern that produced the Sheewash drive. They did not keep it up for very long. Captain Pausert found that he did not mesh nearly as well with the Leewit on her own as he had with Goth and her sister. Besides, right now they had nothing to run from, except a feeling that the captain had that they ought to follow a course of their own choosing, rather than being steered down one. Using the Sheewash drive took it out of him. Captain Pausert was not particularly experienced at using it. And the Leewit was still quite young for doing so. They really couldn't afford to push it too hard or far. For all they knew, they might be needing it soon in earnest.

"You'd better go and rest, brat," said the captain afterwards, as the Leewit wolfed down a double batch of pancakes and Wintenberry jelly.

The Leewit nodded. "Need to bathe first," she said.

The captain smiled to himself. She was growing up. Imagine her suggesting washing herself! Times changed. But what he said was: "See you wash behind your ears." It was by now a traditional thing for him to say. He wasn't prepared for the Leewit to hug him. "Miss Goth," she said thickly, before hastily walking away towards her stateroom.

He went back to his chair in front of the control panels and viewscreens. Watching.

He didn't have long to watch before trouble came looking for them.

CHAPTER 8

Goth had always been around while the captain was organizing things, but until now she hadn't realized just how useful the experience would be. At least she had some idea of the actual mechanisms of renting a house, which was not a custom on Karres. She decided that it would be easier than trying to find a safe spot in the circus lattice ship—which would be leaving anyway, pretty soon.

On the other hand, she also began to appreciate Karres's habit of simply ignoring bureaucracy when you could. The Karres people never made waves deliberately among societies of the Empire and the other worlds they visited. Their work was far too important to waste time causing trouble for mere entertainment. But fussy, meticulous bureaucracies that seem to like paperwork for its own sake were a real temptation, Goth had to admit.

Before you could rent a house on Nikkeldepain you had to provide a whole lot of paperwork, most of which would be easy for a criminal to fake, but was guaranteed to cause maximum inconvenience for an honest citizen. And, unfortunately, documents posed a problem for her. Goth could very easily appear to be an adult. Light-shifts could provide the appearance of most things—but every use of klatha drained some energy that could only be restored by sleep and food. If she pushed herself too much in any one day, she ran the risk of being exposed or having something else go wrong. Multiple klatha tasks were especially draining, such as documents which had to feel right in someone's hand as well as look right.

And it appeared that she would need an amazing number of documents in order to rent a house legally. Bank statements, previous utility payments—the list went on and on. It was truly amazing—and that was before the estate agent discovered that the smartly dressed woman in front of her was a foreigner, from off-world. Oh, they were very keen on off-world investment here on Nikkeldepain. They never lost the chance to tell foreigners so. But that didn't mean doing something ridiculous like making life easier for them!

The experience started to give her a real idea of the minefield that Pausert's mother had to cope with. She smiled politely at the estate agent. "I think I will just stay in the hotel that you recommended in the port area."

The woman allowed herself a relieved smile. "You wouldn't believe the paperwork it will save me."

Goth was tempted to make a very sarcastic comment. Or several comments. But she just nodded, and took her leave.

She had to face up to the fact that this was all going to be more complicated than merely coping with the Egger Route had been. She still hadn't worked out why someone was trying to kidnap Pausert. She knew that she would be here for six months. That was considerably longer than any jaunt that she'd ever undertaken as a young Karres witch to the various planets in the neighborhood of Karres. Karres approved of their youngsters going out and learning about how life was away from home. But, generally speaking, they went in twos or threes. There was nothing much that two or three Karres witches couldn't deal with! But, as the second-in-age sister, Goth had left quite a lot of the organization to Maleen.

Now, she found that she had to deal with issues like money. It was easy enough to 'port it, of course. However, living with Captain Pausert had left her feeling guilty about doing that. Anyway, to live for six months she was going to need quite a lot of money. It wasn't like she didn't have it. The *Venture*'s account was nicely into the black. Goth had found a lot of satisfaction in managing the captain's money for him. He probably hadn't even realized she was doing it. But there was one small problem to spending any of that money: it was all safely in the Daal's bank some years into the future.

She was so busy thinking about all of this, and how to deal with it, that she did not notice a nondescript vehicle shadowing her. In fact, the first thing that she knew about it, was that somebody had pressed something over her mouth and she felt the sudden brief sting of a transdermic injection.

She awoke somewhat later, feeling groggy and sick, and lying tied up on a narrow bed in a dim room. Two people were talking in the next room. They were plainly quite upset with each other. Goth recognized the toneless voice of one of them. It was the woman with the cone hairdo, which had turned out to be a wig.

"—should have come to a while ago," said the male voice. "She was smaller than we guessed."

"You're hired to know that kind of thing, Franco," said the woman.

"Listen, we found her for you. And I still think you're taking a chance. She's been seen with two of the agents of the police force."

"Yes," said the woman. "When Mirkon got himself arrested by the local dogcatcher."

"He may not really have been a dogcatcher."

"Which is why he was shown in the newscasts as one for his heroic capture. To cover his secret agent tracks," she said. "Anyway, we've got Mirkon back in the ship. They assume that he's escaped off-world. That just leaves us a bit shorthanded for this. Let's go and see if the girl is awake yet."

The lights came on. Goth immediately closed her eyes and slumped in the bed. The woman poked her in the ribs. "Wake up, sleepyhead. We need you awake to call that little boyfriend of yours."

Goth groaned, and kept her eyes shut. She needed time to think about this. Huh! Boyfriend, was it? He was going to marry her, he just didn't know it yet. Even though she had told him so. In the meanwhile she really needed to think, and also to drink some water. And somebody was going to learn a lesson about catching and drugging a Karres witch. She had every intention of making it a very memorable lesson, but now that her mind was beginning to clear a bit, this might be the perfect opportunity to find out why they wanted Pausert.

The woman slapped her face. "Wake up! Come on, girly, wake up. We've got some work for you."

Goth decided that it was time to stop pretending to be unconscious when the man emptied a glass of water onto her face. She spluttered and immediately regretted doing so. That was a waste of water that she really needed right now.

"Ah, sleeping beauty has decided to join us after all," said the woman, now wearing a curly coppery head of hair. "Now listen to me very carefully, little girl. Do exactly what I tell you and you're not going to get hurt. Don't even think of trying anything clever. Do you understand me?"

Goth wondered just how stupid they thought she was. They were making no attempt to hide their faces. She'd bet that either they did not plan to leave her alive, or they were going to get off-world very quickly. The man had a Nikkeldepain accent, so it seemed unlikely that he was going anywhere. Goth was sure that kidnapping, in a society like this, was not going to be looked on as a minor crime. The local authorities on Nikkeldepain got very serious about such offenses as walking on the grass and spitting on the sidewalk. But all she did was nod.

"Good. Now Franco here is going to give you a caller unit. You're going to tell that Pausert boy to bring us the Illtraming map."

"The what?" asked Goth, doing her best to memorize the word.

"The Illtraming map," she repeated.

"What's that?"

The weasel-faced Franco fiddled with the handle of his blaster, which was protruding from a hip pocket. "You don't need to know. He's just got to bring it to us and we'll let you go."

"Well, what does it look like? I need to tell him what to look for. Does he know where to find it?" She tried to sound frightened rather than angry.

"He'd better. Seeing as we couldn't," said the man.

"Shut up, Franco. It's in among his great uncle's things. A sheet of metal about as high as a door. It must be hidden somewhere in the house."

"What is it for? I mean where is it a map to?"

The woman's eyes narrowed. "You ask too many questions. Franco, bring her that caller."

"You promise you won't hurt him?"

The woman snorted. "We just want the map. We'll arrange a pick-up point. He won't even need to see us and you'll be as free as a bird."

She was busy talking and so did not notice that a piece of paper that had been lying on the table under a brass paperweight a few moments before was now in close proximity to the gas flame of the heater. She did notice, however, when it set fire to her wig. The fake hair was apparently made of something quite flammable. That struck Goth as being very poor design, but she wasn't about to complain.

The woman's companion was unable to assist her. As he'd bent over to pick up the caller, the brass paperweight had dropped on him from the ceiling, where Goth had 'ported it. The paperweight fell a lot harder than the piece of rope that she had chosen to teleport out of the entirety of her bindings.

As the woman danced up and down on her wig, Goth slipped away into the security of no-shape. Fortunately, the blaster in Franco's hip pocket was a small one apparently designed for concealment, not the much heavier variety that were normally used by law enforcement or military personnel. So it was—just barely—within the limits of Goth's teleporting ability.

After 'porting the blaster from Franco's hip pocket, Goth quietly flicked the light switch off and stepped back into the corner to see what happened. The handle of Franco's weapon felt very comforting in her hand.

The light came on again.

"Where in Patham's seven Hells has she got to?" groaned Franco, who had staggered up to turn the light on.

The now wigless woman, whose hands had suddenly filled themselves with a pair of Blythe pistols, nearly shot him. "After her! She can't get far, the outside door is locked!"

Goth had always been good at teleporting, and by now her klatha skills in that area were as good as those of any Karres witch. Part of those skills was the ability to visualize—by what amounted to a sort of mental "feel"—the inner workings of any reasonably small object. She didn't quite know *exactly* how Blythe guns worked, although she understood the basic principles of the weapons. But it seemed only logical to her that removing *that* particular part from both guns would make them inoperable. She was pretty sure they were the power units without which the guns were just awkwardly shaped bludgeons.

The pair of hoodlums rushed through the door together. Goth followed at her leisure. The two frantically looked around the next room, and then charged off down the hallway. Goth sat down on top of the desk and had a good look at the books and papers there. Oddly, two of the books were xenoarchaeology tomes.

There were several other useful bits of paper for Nikkeldepain's paper-obsessed bureaucracy. Goth doubted the authenticity of any of them but folded them up and put them into her pocket anyway. The two kidnappers returned, considerably more warily now. Franco had plainly discovered his missing blaster, and was now armed with one of the Blythe guns. They searched cautiously in the cupboard, and under the desk, and behind the door. And then went back into the room where she'd been held captive. "She's got to be here somewhere!" said Franco, his voice fearful. "We can't afford to let her get away! They'll put me away for fifty years for kidnapping."

"Stop whining!" said the now wig-less woman. "We caught her once. We'll catch her again."

"It's you who don't understand, Marshi. I should have guessed when we couldn't find any record of her in the Nikkeldepain database. She's some kind of special agent! That Threbus had something to do with them. There are lots of stories..."

"She's a kid. We took her easily." Marshi peered behind the door again.

"She's no kid and she's got my blaster," said Franco nervously. "I think we'd better cut and run. I'll take the rest of the money you promised me right now.

You go your way and I'll go mine. Wha... what are you doing?"

What she was doing was pressing her Blythe gun against the base of his skull. "Drop it," she said.

He did. "Look, I've got friends."

"Not many," she said sardonically. "So long, Franco." She pulled the trigger.

However, instead of his skull exploding in a shower of bone and Blythe needles, nothing happened. She tried again. Franco was not the quickest thug on the uptake, but two attempts were enough for him to get the idea. He dropped, snatched his fallen weapon and tried to shoot her.

The expression on his face, when nothing happened, was so comical that Goth had to push her sleeve into her mouth to stop from laughing. The two of them, both wild-eyed, stood there squeezing the triggers of their useless weapons at each other.

Franco was the first to realize that nothing was going to happen, no matter how hard he squeezed the trigger. He flung the weapon at Marshi and ran off down the hall. Meanwhile, Marshi had staggered back and opened up her Blythe gun, and was staring incredulously at the empty space that Goth thought was the charge-socket.

Seconds later, she too was heading down the passage. Goth followed. Outside, she recognized the area. They were in a side street barely a block from Pausert's home.

The woman rushed up to a red people-carrier with an enclosed back. She fumbled out an electronic key and scrambled into it. Coming just behind her, Goth popped the hatch and climbed into the back as Marshi pulled away. Then Marshi skidded to a halt, jumped out, and peered cautiously into the open back. She slammed it closed, and soon they were off again.

Goth wondered where they were going. Sitting in the back-hatch, she had time to examine the various packing crates sharing the space with her. It would appear that her would-be kidnapper was in some way involved in mining. The crates claimed to hold heavy-duty rock drills, but Goth had no way of making sure that they actually held what they claimed.

They came to a halt at a customs barrier at the Nikkeldepain City port. The official who peered into the back insisted on opening one of the crates, after examining the papers. Goth had time to get herself out of the way, although she had to move slowly and carefully. No-shape was not the same thing as no-sound—and for whatever odd reason, Goth had always found no-sound to be a lot more difficult than no-shape. She found it almost impossible to do both at the same time except for mimicking voices, which came easily to her. Apparently there was a difference between "no-sound" and "no-voice." Klatha could be tricky that way.

The crate did indeed contain large heavy-duty mining rock drills.

"For which ship is this cargo destined?"

"The *Kapurnia*. Registered in Lepper."

"You don't look much like a Syrian," said the official. "Passport."

This was duly presented and examined. "What happened to your hair?"

"Accident," said the woman, in her curiously flat voice.

"Well, I hope it grows back," he said, in a tone that exuded indifference. In the same tone he added: "Thank you for visiting Nikkeldepain."

"I'm not leaving yet. Just delivering this cargo."

So! thought Goth. The game was still afoot. She pieced together what she knew so far. They were looking for some large metal map, which was hidden among her father's things in Pausert's house. They'd plainly broken in and searched for it, before deciding on kidnap and force. They had books on xenoarcheology and they had rock-drills. And they were quite prepared to kill people.

Goth did not know quite what to expect of the Syrian-registered *Kapurnia*. She didn't, however, expect what she was driven to, which was not a grubby battered freighter or a miner-ship. It was a gleaming, state-of-the-art space-yacht. A rich man's toy.

Goth slipped into the front of the vehicle—and realized that the doors were electronically locked. It took her precious seconds to open a window, and to jump out of it and run to the ramp. The lock was just closing.

Goth stuck her foot in—and then pulled it out hastily. The lock wouldn't seal with her foot there, true. But it would also crush her foot first. She watched in impotent fury as the door closed. She was a skilled klatha operative, for her age. She expected to get a lot better. She could teleport and bend light. She could power a spacecraft to travel faster than any conventional set of tubes. She could even swim through space-time by the Egger Route, albeit with great discomfort.

She still couldn't do much—anything, really—to hull-metal. She resisted the temptation to thump on the door. Instead she walked back down the ramp, leaned on the car and studied the ship. It was sleek and lean, with a bulbous but opaqued viewpod. Grudgingly, Goth had to admit that she wouldn't mind owning it, even if it was not a patch on the *Venture* for real work.

Well, sooner or later they would come and fetch the rock-drills. In the meantime, Goth could attend to the sort of pressing personal needs that somehow never got included in adventure stories.

She walked across to the spaceport control buildings. There, thankfully, she found a bathroom and put it to quick use. As an extra bonus, there was a water-cooler just outside the bathroom which supplied the drink of water she'd been longing for also.

That done, she found her way into an office, not occupied at the moment, with computer access to ship registry listings. She looked up the *Kapurnia*. The owner was apparently somebody named Mebeckey, of Arc's World in the Republic of Sirius. She had a good view from here. Nobody had yet come out of the *Kapurnia*. Goth decided to make use of her access to the data-net, and searched for information on Mebeckey.

She didn't really expect to find anything. But, there he was. Rich. Famous. And, if you read the sub-text, ruthless in getting the prizes he sought in the world of xenoarchaeology. He'd made some extraordinary and valuable finds, by all accounts. But it was still obvious that he was not very highly regarded in academic circles, by what was not said. There was one story about some very valuable pieces fetching up in a private collector's hoard, valuable pieces associated with a dig that Mebeckey had conducted.

It was all beginning to fit together now. Somehow

her father had brought back a map of some sort that this Mebeckey wanted. Goth couldn't help wondering just what it was a map of, and why they hadn't been able to find it when they'd burgled the house. There weren't that many possible hiding places for something that size. How did they know what they were looking for? And surely this was all a bit much for a map? Pausert's mother was poor. She'd probably happily have sold it to them. But they might not have wanted to let on that there was something of value in Threbus's bric-a-brac.

Besides, it wasn't Pausert's mother's to sell yet, strictly speaking. She might very well have gotten stiff about it. That was the sort of honesty—stubborn to the point of crankiness—that the captain would have displayed.

Goth knew that she was really going to have to sort out the mess. She scowled at the sleek space yacht. And teach this fellow and his lackeys a painful lesson!

She went back to the *Kapurnia*'s registry record and added to the custom notes: *Possible smuggler. Search and check identities of all passengers before allowing take-off clearance.* If something went wrong, that should give her a little extra time. And she might also get some of the gang punished for planning to kidnap Pausert. They might sing about their friends. You never knew.

She walked back down, pausing only to do a little teleporting on a sandwich vending machine in the lobby, and went back to watch the ship. It was like hunting wild black bollems. Sometimes you could track them and stalk them. Sometimes you just had to wait.

CHAPTER 9

Three ships, needlelike and of some alien design, came hurtling out of cover from where they must have hung, hidden from instrument detection, close to the radiation of a giant blue-white star. Pausert hit the laterals, sending the *Venture* into a steep curve away. What sort of shielding must they have on those ships? He would never dare to take the *Venture* that close to a B-class supergiant.

And yet it seemed they were content with just that—a chase and seeing the *Venture* off. That was not, he would have thought, what hunter-ships in the Chaladoor should be prepared to do. This was a place of aggression and predation, not defense.

The captain began setting the course to take them back toward their original route—and within an hour the ships were back. Either they were much faster than the *Venture* or there were a lot of them.

The Leewit had woken up again and was looking over his shoulder. "They look the same as the ones from two watches ago, Captain. Do you think someone is taking over the Chaladoor?"

"Let's try hailing them. If they don't want to fight, they're welcome to it. We're just passing through. We don't need trouble."

The Leewit nodded, looking just a little disappointed. She loved those nova guns. But not having her sisters around was forcing her into a different role, making her just a little less of a wild-child, showing that she could act with sense and maturity when she had to. Pausert thought Toll and Threbus might appreciate the change.

She'd seated herself and was working the communicator, scanning likely calling frequencies, sending out standard Empire hailing pulses. If she got a reply of any sort her linguistic klatha skill would allow her to translate it.

The communicator howled like a banshee. The pitch was sharp and eerie enough to make Captain Pausert's hair stand on end. The Leewit snapped it off, mid-caterwaul.

"What was that? What did they say?"

"Nothing," said the Leewit, her voice unusually quiet. She got up and came and leaned against his shoulder, a totally uncharacteristic thing for her to do.

Pausert put his arm around the littlest witch.

"It was just ... hate. And almost a kind of hunger. And fury."

"We'll deal with the ships if they try anything."

"It wasn't the ships sending it. It came from that star."

"What?"

The Leewit shrugged. "They hate us. And they're trying to do something to us. That's all I got. But it's not the ships. They didn't answer."

As she said that, the lead ship fired on them. A torpedo of some sort, according to the detector board. The captain glanced at the readouts. The torpedo was not going to intersect their course, unless it changed vector. But the mere act of firing it showed intent.

The Leewit saw that too. "They mean business, Captain."

He nodded, hands moving over the controls, increasing thrust and pushing the ship onto a slightly different trajectory. "Get Vezzarn up."

"I'm here, Skipper," said the grizzled old spacer.

"Unlock the nova gun turrets. Vezzarn, stern turret. The Leewit, take the other. See if you can deal with that torpedo."

It would not be an easy target. But the Leewit's ability with those guns verged on the uncanny.

And once again, she proved it so. The torpedo exploded into a vortex of amber incandescence, far enough away to be harmless, although close enough to set the *Venture*'s radiation detectors squawking.

"Nasty stuff," said the Leewit. "The lead ship is coming into range, I reckon, Captain."

As she said that, the mysterious ship fired two more space-torpedoes. That seemed to be its chief armament.

"Let them have it," said Pausert. "They asked for it. We'll run, if need be, after that."

The captain readied the wires for the Sheewash

drive. He was sure he could do that on his own, if need be, even if he never had before.

The Leewit took out the torpedoes, and then launched a volley of purple nova gun fire across space.

She did not miss. But for all the effect that she had on the attacking ship, she might as well have.

"Give them some more," said Pausert tersely.

It was almost as if the nova bolts were just going through the ship. Pausert checked his instruments. There was something very wrong here. The visual and radiation detectors were giving readings—but the mass-detector wasn't. The attacking ships were pushing out power, and they could be seen . . . but they were as insubstantial as snow-flakes, mass-wise. He commented on it, as the Leewit continued to fire.

"It's Chaladoor Phantoms, Captain," quavered Vezzarn's voice over the intercom.

"What are they?" asked Pausert.

"Stuff of legends of the spaceways of long ago, Captain. But you can't escape them, apparently. And you can't kill them, either. You can drive a ship right through them, and it has no effect. But they sure can kill you."

"Huh! Those torpedoes sure got hit," said the Leewit. "Anyway, how did any legend start if no one gets away, Vezzarn?"

"Well, *we're* going to get away," said Captain Pausert. "Seal those guns and let's do some special running."

CHAPTER 10

Goth found the waiting tedious. She whiled away the time by climbing back into the car and checking out the contents of the glove compartment. Those would have given the customs official more pause than the rock-drills had.

For starters, there was a pair of gloves. Quite a normal thing for a glove compartment—except these had artificial fingerprints embossed onto them. Then there was a transdermal syringe and a set of ampules, one of which was empty. Goth was willing to bet that that was what she had been dosed with.

She pocketed the syringe and ampules, and then carefully damaged the embossed fingerprints on the gloves. That took a further five minutes. Then she sat and thought about their adventures on the *Venture* and about *Petey, Byrum and Keep*, the lattice ship. Sat and thought about the Nanite plague. Just sat.

Eventually, she got bored and searched around the car for more entertainment. She found a book under the seat on xenoarchaeology. Specifically, the book was about the Melchin culture, the ruins from which had been found on several worlds on the fringes of the Chaladoor relatively near to Uldune. It was not the most interesting thing that she had ever read, but it was what she had, and it was better than just sitting. The pictures of the Melchin spacecraft—alien, spiky-looking sleek things—were some of the more fascinating parts of it.

Eventually she started to get hungry and thirsty again. By the looks of the light, it was getting on for late afternoon. Was she going to have to spend the night here? She couldn't keep up a light-shift indefinitely.

Hunger and impatience finally got the better of her. She left the book. Confiscating the syringe was one thing, taking someone's book another entirely.

There was an airbus service into Nikkeldepain City. After someone nearly sat on her, Goth realized another one of the less obvious disadvantages of being able to hide in no-shape.

She was beginning to think that the reason that the precogs had seen her traveling back in time to Pausert's youth might be a bit more complex than just to save Captain Pausert, as she'd originally assumed. Marshi had been callously unconcerned about killing her criminal associate. Yet they were steering clear of obvious clashes with the law. It could be that if they could have found this map that they were looking for, they would just have quietly gone away. Goth wondered briefly if she should find it and give it to them. But the thought was dismissed: even if they were mere treasure hunters, if anyone had a claim to the map or whatever treasure they could find using it, it was Pausert, or her father, or, for that matter, herself.

She'd deal with them in her own way, once she'd dealt with issues like supper and where she was going to sleep tonight. After some thought, she took herself back to the apartment where her kidnappers had held her. The door was still open, with a key inside the lock. There were also a pair of good solid old-fashioned bolts. Goth had no faith that someone like Franco—or his friends, if he had any—could not pick a lock, if he decided to return. But bolts were a tougher proposition. She knew that much from old Vezzarn. He'd been, under some protest, quietly teaching her his lock-picking skills. The poor old fellow was nervous of what the captain might do to him if he ever found out!

When you weren't being held captive there, or dodging searchers, it was actually quite a pleasant apartment. The most serious fault Goth could find with it was that there was very little food in the cupboards or the fridge. A meal of crisps, some cookies and water was not at all satisfactory.

Mostly, though, she was very tired. Using klatha so constantly would do that to you, even klatha that you were especially good at. Goth found that she had a good view of Pausert's home from the third room, which also had two unmade beds in it. She was tempted for a moment—she was *really* tired, now—but Goth decided that while she didn't mind sleeping in a props store, sharing Franco's bugs was a different matter. She found a spare blanket, still in its store wrapping, and a sofa, and slept the sleep of the very tired. The sleep of the just would have to wait until she caught up with the perps.

The next morning she locked up the place. She'd have to get fresh bedding and some food. She was already considering it her apartment, she thought with some amusement. Well, maybe the criminals had done the bureaucratic work for her. She'd just have to check it out.

The question was: what to do next? Did she go and lay siege to the *Kapurnia*? In the end, she decided to go and have a look through her father's things in Pausert's house. That probably wasn't the right decision, she knew. But she was very curious about this map. En route she stopped at a money dispenser and, using her teleporting ability, swapped the maels she had for ones that were currently dated. Since it was an even swap, she figured it didn't count as stealing. After that she bought herself some breakfast, which consisted of a curious bunlike pastry with seeds and cheese in a neat little cardboard box.

She let herself in to Pausert's home, and began to look in the obvious places—and then decided that was probably a complete waste of time. Franco and his friends would have done that, anyway, and done it better than she could.

She could always pump Pausert for clues, but instinct said that would be a mistake. She felt that quite strongly, and one of the side effects of being a klatha-operative was that sometimes those feelings were in themselves klatha side effects. Perhaps what she needed to do was to tap into those feelings.

She wandered around the house looking at the

souvenirs of fifty worlds. They were interesting but she felt no draw towards any of them. She wandered into the kitchen, and then the bathroom, feeling like a bit of an invader. From there she peered into the bedrooms, feeling even more uncomfortable. She walked back downstairs.

Her attention was suddenly caught by a piece of patterned cloth on which the communicator rested, on some kind of wall bracket. She touched the cloth, which was plainly some kind of handwoven material, pretty enough in a primitive sort of way. The cloth didn't feel special, just reminiscent of a hot place of tall fronded trees—but it was covering a small metal box that stood on the shelf. The cord of the communicator would be too short otherwise.

Goth touched it, then pulled her hand back abruptly. The metal was oddly cold and felt repulsive, almost slimy. Carefully, Goth pulled the cloth aside and peered at the box.

It looked disappointingly like a box, although there was some patterning etched into the metal. Goth carefully took it off the shelf, balancing the communicator against the wall. She didn't really like touching the thing. It reminded her, in a way, of the synergizer from the Lyrd-Hyrier ship, except that it felt old.

She felt a flood of strange, unpleasant images coming into her mind, and put the box down hastily on a small table. It still just looked like a box. She could see a thin line where the lid fitted onto the lower section. There were neat little hinges at the back. There was no sign of a lock or any way to open it.

Braving touching the box again, she shook it. There was a faint sound, too dull to be a rattle—as if whatever was inside was heavy and fairly soft. She put it down again. The box did odd things to her head. Images. Strange images. Enormous trees spanning whole continents, and little animals dying.

Goth couldn't be sure quite what was in the box, but she was willing to bet that this was the "map" they were looking for. It would seem that they were wrong about the size. Or perhaps this was a sheet of metal that could be folded. The question was: what was she going to do with it now that she had found it?

She was quite reluctant to even touch the box again. On the other hand, she was now very sure that she shouldn't let it fall into the hands of Mebeckey and his cohorts. If she left the box here they might come back and find it. But she couldn't just take it, since that would be rather obvious. Looking at the wall and the faint line where someone had obviously dusted often, the box had been lying on that shelf for many years. The box, however, was almost the same size and shape as the box her breakfast had come in. That was now in the previously empty trash can attached to a post just down the road.

Goth went and fetched it, and put it under the cloth. It was much the same height, and nearly as wide. Unless they looked closely, no one would never know that a substitution had been made.

She couldn't cope with actually touching the box for more than a few seconds. But with a little experimentation, she discovered that a bit of cloth—anything— between her and it, and she felt fine. She settled for taking two squares of kitchen towel and wrapping it in that and putting it in a carrier bag. It wasn't a very large box. She'd have to get something else to put it in once she got back to what she had decided would be "her" apartment.

Perhaps it was having been taken by surprise once before that made Goth more wary. This time she actually spotted her assailants before they got to her, although they were well hidden. She didn't have time for any fancy maneuvers. She just ducked under the reaching hands and ran.

There were three of them: the woman Marshi, a tall balding man with a few grizzled whiskers and an aquiline nose, and, although wearing a hooded top and sunglasses, the fellow from the van who Goth had had arrested. They ran after her.

As she dived over a fence, Goth cursed her ill luck. They must have been watching Pausert's home.

Then she realized that she had a more immediate problem. The garden she had jumped into had a squat but vicious looking dren-hound, still blinking itself awake from where it had slept in the morning sun. The beast was looking at her incredulously, as if to say "you dared jump into *my* garden?"

Goth knew that the one thing she dared not do was to run—and even no-shape wouldn't help. The dog could certainly smell her, and she really hadn't completely mastered no-scent yet. Not well enough to fool a dren-hound, for sure.

Her pursuers appeared. One of them, the woman, had a small clype gun in hand. Goth ducked behind the dren-hound's kennel. A clype needle screamed off the roof. That distracted the dren-hound. He noticed strangers leaning over his gate. The toothy animal plainly wasn't too bright. It barked and rushed at them.

The laughter of the tall bewhiskered man and his companion stopped abruptly as the dren-hound jumped up at the gate, which was swinging open under their weight. Goth ran, jumping the fence into the next yard, ignoring the noises behind her. Someone yelled at her, but Goth just kept right on running until she got behind a small greenhouse. There she took refuge in no-shape. That still left a locked gate and an angry householder between her and getting away. But a little patience and she was able to go on her way, as the irate woman told the local policeman all about the disturbance.

"Some people chasing a young girl. About fourteen years old, I'd guess she was. They ran off when I came out. Lucky for them my neighbor's dren-hound is a soppy old thing. Doesn't bite."

Goth slipped away, grinning. It was a pity the dren-hound wasn't a biter. She'd take the long way back to the apartment and to make absolutely sure she wasn't being seen, go in no-shape.

Within a hundred yards it became obvious that no-shape wasn't going to be enough. The three in the red people-carrier were very slowly cruising towards her. The hooded fellow was driving. The man with the grizzled whiskers was reading out coordinates from a wrist communicator.

They must have a tracking spy lock on her. Just as they had followed Pausert, they could follow her, even if they could not see her. Then, belatedly, it occurred to her—they had probably been using a spy ray to watch Pausert's home. And what had she done? Walked in and shown them where to find the map! And now they knew what they were looking for, and knew how to find her, too. Being in no-shape wouldn't protect her from projectiles or blaster-fire, or even just being grabbed.

A short way down the road was a stop for the monorail system. Goth could see a monorail car arriving, and took off for it at a sprint. She vaulted the automatic ticket gate and then hastened to find a place to change via light-shift into someone unobtrusive. No-shape on crowded public transport really didn't work.

A frumpish old lady appeared on the platform—she looked rather like the woman who had called the police earlier. Goth needed models to get the light-shift right and she figured this one would do fine. She started to run, and then slowed to a hasty shuffle when she realized that frumpish old ladies usually didn't run as if an enraged bull-bollem was after them.

She boarded the monorail car. It was fairly full, but Nikkeldepain folk were generous about letting an old lady past, or even offering her a seat. She politely declined the offers and made her way to the back door, which was intended as an exit. In typically orderly Nikkeldepain fashion all the cars had a forward entry door and a rear exit. And people were of course scrupulous about using them as intended.

Nikkeldepain had some good points, if you liked everything done just so. Goth had often wondered what made the captain, and indeed, to a lesser extent, her father, behave as they did. The answer was obviously growing up on Nikkeldepain. Whatever else she achieved back in time, Goth realized that she was learning a lot about what motivated Captain Pausert. That was probably a good thing, she supposed, given that she was going to marry him.

The car jolted, and, just before it took off, three

panting red-faced passengers forced their way into the crowded monorail car. They were looking around, and looking puzzled.

Grizzled-whiskers was talking into his wrist communicator. There were various shields available that could scramble the satellite-tracking. Goth wished she'd thought of getting herself one. She could 'port the communicator elsewhere. But that would be quickly replaced, and Goth didn't want to advertise her klatha powers further than she had to.

Her pursuers began making their way down the car towards her as the car sped on toward its next stop. The Nikkeldepain citizenry were much less polite to the three now pushing their way through the crowd. They weren't old or infirm, and they were lacking in manners, as far as the locals were concerned.

The car slowed and stopped at the next station. Goth stood up and got off along with five or six others, as the pursuit pushed their way through. The automatic door mechanism wasn't a complicated one, and Goth had had a few minutes to study it. She 'ported the person detector away, and joined the group walking off, as behind them the three struggled with the door. The car began to move again. The door was closed and the car's safety system said that it could.

When they were out of sight, Goth turned back and waited for the next monorail car. Given the way the system worked, they'd be getting off at next station to come back at the same time that she got on at this one—unless they were sharp-witted enough to wait for her, or to split up, of course. She'd deal with that if they were.

The car rolled and swung on, on a rail to somewhere.

Goth had no idea where it was going, or what she would do when she got there. She was also not at all sure about the strange box in the carrier-bag. Was it their "map"? And, if so, where was it a map to?

The monorail car slowed to a halt again. Goth looked warily up from her reverie and saw a familiar, heart-warming sight. The lattice ship, its gaudy synthasilk covering bright in the morning sun, decked out with bunting and flags. She nodded to herself. Spy lock or no spy lock, let them try following her around the lattice ship. Here on Nikkeldepain she was the one who didn't know where she was going. And security on the lattice ship was fairly tight for areas that were off-limits to the paying public.

She set off with the crowd who were obviously heading for the morning show. No-shape wasn't really an option right now, so she settled for buying a stalls ticket and a box of CarniPops. There was no food value in them, but if she couldn't enjoy some artificial flavorants for old-times' sake, then what could she enjoy? She went with the flow, past the side-stalls and on into the main stages. They were doing the Scottish play again, she noticed. Out of pure nostalgia, Goth went in.

And discovered that live theater still had the same mesmerizing magic for her. Seeing Dame Euthelassia playing the third witch was different, though. Distracting. She almost didn't see her three pursuers sneaking in. She actually might not have seen them if it had not been for the "hush" and "sit down" from others in the audience.

Huh. *When shall we three meet again?* She was meeting those three all too soon!

She slipped under her seat, down into the scaffolding

that held the bleachers up, then swung down to the lattice tier. Once there, she moved along one of the beams toward the animal enclosures.

The carrier bag on her arm was a nuisance for this sort of work. It was heavy and awkward. And just there was the props store. There was junk in there from a hundred productions.

Goth dropped onto the beam, next to it. The door was locked. No matter. She knew the lock-keypad sequence backwards.

It took just a few seconds to bury the map-box in her old lair and get out of there, locking the door behind her. And there the three were, after her. She stepped behind a stanchion and assumed no-shape again. There was a choice of three directions in which to run from here—so instead Goth went up. That was always her first instinct.

Once she was a comfortable three body-lengths above the beam, at a convenient cross-rail, she stopped and listened.

"Where has the little witch got to this time!" snarled Marshi. "I'm going to kill her when I catch her. See what I mean, Mirkon. She just disappears."

"We need answers out of her. The readouts say that she's right here," said grizzled whiskers.

"Could be up or down, boss," said Mirkon.

"True. It's got an altitude reading." Goth didn't stick around. She climbed and railed along, and then dropped down to the fanderbag section. Fanderbags were loveable and huge. Especially huge. And Ketering, their keeper, even slept in there with his big children. He never left them alone.

He was with the gentle behemoths now, washing

and scrubbing them. Goth balanced her way to the top of their sleeping-house. The fanderbags twitched their big noses at her, plainly smelling her. But this was scrubbing time, a treat not to be missed.

Onto the scene burst her two of her three pursuers.

"Oi. What are you doing here? This is off-limits to the public," said Ketering.

"We're from the Nikkeldepain police," said Mebeckey, flashing a card. "Looking for a dangerous fugitive. We believe that you have her hidden in that structure. Now, just bring her out for us and we'll say no more about aiding and abetting criminals. We don't want any trouble, do we?"

"You think someone is in my fanderbag house?" said Ketering. "They have babies in there. No one is in there. But here, Nellie. Take him and show him the babies. Show babies. Go, girl."

The startled Mebeckey was whisked off his feet by the long prehensile tusks and transported over to the fanderbag house. "See?" said Ketering. "Babies. No criminals. Now get out of here, see. They don't like their babies being disturbed. Gowan!"

Goth kept still, watching. Any sign of weapons and there was going to be some serious 'porting—and shooting back. She liked the fanderbags and Ketering.

Mebeckey was plainly not used to being manhandled by a three-ton animal—gently manhandled, but it had still demonstrated just how light the fanderbag found him. Mebeckey carried himself with that arrogant assurance of those accustomed to getting their own way. Right now that assurance was badly rattled. "Er . . ."

The closer fanderbag snorted at him, leaning forward. Goth had seen Ketering's prompting hand, and she'd fed and petted the big animals often enough to know that they were utterly harmless. Mebeckey and the woman didn't know that. Where was the third man, though? "Thank for your cooperation," said Mebeckey meekly and retreated back the way he had come.

"You can come out now," said Ketering, a few moments later. "The fanderbags know that you're there."

Goth slipped down the side of the house and back into visibility.

"Thanks," she said. "They're not cops." Instinctively she was petting and caressing the sensitive, curious noses that snuffled at her, just as he'd showed her how to do, years ahead of now.

He raised his eyebrows. "You know fanderbags." His tone, a little sharp earlier, was now much gentler.

"Adore them. And I'm not leaving before I see the babies. Then I'll be gone. No trouble for you or Himbo, I promise."

A smile spread across his face. "They like you too. Come and have a look."

The two baby behemoths were miniature quarter-ton versions of their parents. Goth thought that it was just as well the Leewit wasn't here. There really wasn't room for a baby fanderbag on the *Venture*!

Ketering watched her pet them. He sucked his teeth. "Look, kid, you know young Himbo, it seems. You hide on the ship now, and they find you, and we could be in all kinds of trouble. You want to get here about an hour before we lift. I'll give you a pass."

She hugged him, even if he smelled of fanderbag. "Can't," she said gruffly. "Got stuff to do here. But you tell Himbo those are not cops. One of them is a wanted escaped felon."

He bit his lip. "By the way the fandies are sniffing, they haven't gone far. You're in some kind of deep water, kid. Do you need help?" He patted a prehensile tusk. "I've got some big friends."

"Who wouldn't hurt a fly," she said, smiling. "I'll be fine. Just tell Himbo he's got some bad guys—three of them, backstage where they shouldn't be. I'll lead them off now. Head for the sideshows. A few roustabouts around there would help."

"You know lattice ships?" he asked.

She nodded. "Yeah. And I know what I'm doing. Take care of those little ones."

She was reluctant to leave, Goth discovered. She had never thought that she'd appreciate a champion. That was not the kind of thing Karres witches found necessary too often. Mind you, they'd let Pausert be one. It had seemed right. But the lattice ship would leave Nikkeldepain soon, and she still had the better part of six months to spend here.

She clambered up the beam like a monkey, and was not that surprised to see the third member of the chase-pack waiting up there in the high shadows. And he'd seen her, too. Well, he was probably their cat burglar. She should have realized that they'd have hired one for the break-ins. She'd just have to hope that she could climb quicker, and that he wasn't going to start shooting.

The light up in the beams and rafters of the lattice ship was not that good. It made moving fast risky. Goth just hoped it made shooting riskier. He was climbing about as fast as she was. She was tempted to 'port a small bird perched on a nearby rafter into the folds of her pursuer's coveralls, to distract and delay him.

But she knew she didn't have much klatha energy left and figured she'd be smarter to save it for later.

She swung down to the aisle behind the sideshow stalls where she and the Leewit had had their act. It was quicker to run than it was to climb, so, no surprise, Mebeckey and Marshi were very close. She dropped into the gap next to Timblay the folding man's stall—he was bad-tempered at the best of times—and slipped out of the narrow passage that led to his boxes and paraphernalia as quickly as possible. Within seconds, she was back onto the main aisle.

They'd seen her drop into the gap and ran there. So did several other people, some of them of considerable size and bulk. Goth had to dodge sideways to avoid being flattened.

"What are you doing here?" demanded one of the large men who had now cornered the two perps in the narrow passage.

Once more, Mebeckey attempted to use his false identification. "Special Investigations, Nikkeldepain Police. We believe you're harboring a fugitive," he said, flashing the card.

"Yeah? Let's see that card again."

"You're obstructing police investigation. We're in hot pursuit—"

"Let's see the card again, mister," said the big roustabout, his arms folded.

"I will warn you just once more. You're obstructing the course of justice!" Mebeckey reached into his jacket. It was going to be a gun that came out this time, Goth suspected, and readied herself to act.

A shriek, a crash and the tearing of synthasilk turned heads. It was the third member of the group, who'd apparently tried to climb faster than he could really handle. He fell right through a sideshow awning, which probably saved his life. But landing in the same environment as Merisco and his dancing jungle-cats nearly lost it for him again. He did, however, cause enough of a distraction for Mebeckey and Marshi to flee.

Goth stood quietly in the shadows and watched as the cat burglar was very ungently evicted from the premises of the circus. The images of Mebeckey and Marshi had also been captured, even if they hadn't. They had been chased. The ticket office was informed, and given pictures of the three. Goth wished that they'd caught them and turned them over to the local police, but that wasn't the circus way, unless the crime involved was something like murder or kidnapping. It wasn't worth getting bogged down with local law enforcement.

Goth couldn't be too sure they wouldn't be back. She couldn't spend too long in the circus, either. The security systems were on full alert now, and there were some fairly sophisticated gadgets and some very-far-from-stupid people here. They were plainly still looking for her, or anything odd. She figured it would be best to get out while the getting was good. The map could wait for a day or two until she could collect it.

So Goth left, quietly, into an open field on the far side of the lattice ship. Walking along toward the monorail, she spotted the red people-carrier bumping its way towards her. She was getting powerfully tired of them by now! At least the vehicle had the advantage of being very recognizable.

Reluctantly, she decided she had no choice but to use some more klatha. The limit on her 'porting was a few pounds and had slowly increased with age. There

were a few rocks of the right size in the field. She
'ported one into the motor of the red vehicle. She had
the satisfaction of seeing it come to an abrupt halt,
and the three climb out and open the hood. They'd
not fix that in a hurry!

For good measure she also 'ported Mebeckey's
wallet—she'd seen it twice and that was enough—into
her hand. That would cut, temporarily, his access to
cash for things like replacement vehicles, although the
others would probably have at least monorail fares.
A pity, but she couldn't see any easy way of dealing
with that. So she left them trying to fix the vehicle
and boarded the monorail car.

She soon realized that she had underestimated
Mebeckey and his cohorts. The woman, still panting,
boarded the monorail just before it left the station. She
looked around and sat down, making no attempt to get
closer to Goth. But she had her wrist-communicator.
Goth wondered why the desperate need to keep her
in sight. They could track her anyway.

Then it occurred to her. The map-box! They were
worried she might stash it or pass it on to someone.
Ha. A light-shift image of a carrier bag was not a hard
task, even as klatha-depleted as she was.

So, just as the monorail was about to leave the next
station, she jumped up, raced to a door, and appeared
to throw a carrier bag onto the dock, then made as
if she was going to follow the bag onto the dock.

That last little subterfuge probably wasn't necessary,
though. Marshi wasn't even looking her way anymore.
The woman was frantically pushing back the closing
door in her part of the car. She managed to leap onto
the dock just as the monorail took off again.

Goth kept the image of the carrier bag intact until the very moment when Marshi, with a triumphant little yell, bent over to snatch it up. The look on the woman's face when the bag just vanished was priceless.

The monorail was much too far away by now for Marshi to continue her pursuit. Goth leaned back in her seat and considered her situation. First and foremost, it was by now obvious that she had to lose the spy lock and put these three out of commission for a long time. That was easier said than done, of course. It was at times like this that she would have appreciated getting back onto the *Venture* and getting as far as the ship could take her—and Pausert—away from here. Or even, as awful as it was, the Egger Route. But there were things that had to be sorted out here. And she knew that she would be here for another six months.

The monorail took her back to the center of Nikkeldepain City, with the car getting fuller and fuller. Goth was grateful now for the tour that Pausert had given her. The Central Museum of Historical Nikkeldepain seemed like a place that would upset the locals sufficiently.

CHAPTER 11

Vezzarn shook his head. "They're not using normal space-drives to chase us, Captain."

Pausert looked at the instruments. "They're not normal spacecraft, Vezzarn. I've been searching the records and I've yet to find any known ship that looks like them in the galactic ship-registry. I was hoping for some kind of clue on how to deal with them. I haven't found anything quite like them."

That was disturbing in itself. The registry went all the way back to fabled Yarth, and had almost every ship ever to pass through human space recorded in it. Names changed. But basic ship configurations stayed the same. These ones were just not there.

Hello, big dream thing, said the tinkling vatch-voice in his head. **This is a strange place, this.**

Little silver-eyes was back. As if his life wasn't complicated enough already. Still, he'd wondered quite where the vatchlets had got to. "Been busy?" he asked conversationally. "I haven't seen you for a while."

While? Oh yes. The linear time thing. I don't really understand that, big dream thing. Why are you here? This is a very funny place in space-time. Full of cracks. And things.

"What sort of things, Little-bit?" he asked.

Half not here-things, half other things and half dreamthings.

"That's a half too many," said Pausert.

Not here it isn't.

On that mysterious statement, the little whirling bit of blackness vanished. Seconds later the intercom chirped. "Little-bit's back, Captain."

The Leewit actually sounded very pleased. It occurred to Pausert that the littlest witch might have been a bit lonely without a partner in mischief or even a sister as a companion. Well, the *Venture* had survived vatch-visitations before. Maybe he could get Little-bit to lure a big one down on them, then he could get his vatch-handler hooks into it, and get it to take them away from a bit of space that was "full of cracks. And things."

Pausert knew vatches well enough to know that if the silver-eyed vatch hadn't told him more than "things," then his vocabulary didn't have the words to comprehend what it was talking about. It was a young one, and as far as he could establish, still learning. Anyway, as far as vatches were concerned, this was an odd, illusionary dream-universe anyway. Their universe was bigger and more complicated. Pausert was glad he merely had to cope with his own universe. He just wished he knew exactly how to do so.

He went back to his instruments, to study the records of their encounters with the Phantom ships. There had to be a clue somewhere. A way out of this situation.

There was. Just how they could use it was another matter. The Phantom ships had become something which had mass for a brief instant, as they'd fired those torpedoes, the instruments showed. So: if he could anticipate the launch of the torpedoes, there was a fraction of a second in which they could be hit. And the Phantom ships kept well clear of the gravity wells of stars and planets. In extremis the *Venture* could land on one and wait them out. Of course that assumed that any planet in the Chaladoor was itself a safe refuge. It was probable that—in these parts—they weren't.

Pausert began to strategize. He wished, for the many-th time, that Goth would come back from this mysterious mission of hers. He was beginning to toy with the possibilities of the Egger Route. But he couldn't do that on his own, let alone take the ship down the mysterious spaces between continua. And of course the Leewit would resist the very idea. She hated the Egger Route, and probably couldn't manage it, not taking the ship along as well.

The Egger Route was traumatic, but Pausert was sure it didn't have to be. There had to be a pattern change in using the klatha force that would make it better. After last time, however, he was reluctant to experiment while there were others around. His talents were still quite unpredictable.

On the other hand, he was usually a lucky gambler. So he took a gamble on a new course. Something—it felt like a prickle at the back of his scalp—made him go to the hold and take out the map-boxes from the ship's old exploring days. She'd probably never been near the Chaladoor. But Pausert set the new recognizer-unit they'd bought in the Imperial Capital to work on the stack of maps, comparing them to the stars visible outside. The *Venture* had been in space a long time—several hundred years—and you never knew.

The machine found a map of the area of space just to the celestial north. But it wasn't from that long ago, a mere thirty years back. That was odd. The captain didn't know that the *Venture* had been in this part of space. But Threbus had used her for a number of his earlier expeditions.

Pausert set the *Venture* on a vector to intersect that previously surveyed track. The Chaladoor was not a safe, constant piece of space. Everyone knew that. Things moved. The bulk of it was uncharted, and even charts were not too reliable. But it was also a lot safer to follow some sort of previously charted course. That was what they had been doing earlier before being forced astray.

CHAPTER 12

The Central Museum of Historical Nikkeldepain housed a collection of artifacts from the first settlers. The room Goth chose had their Charter of Rights, signed by the first councilors, on display. And, for good measure, the Mayoral Chain of Nikkeldepain City too, a relic of old Yarthe itself, if the label was to be believed. It looked like a trumpery bit of stuff to Goth. She'd seen more real-looking fakes in Wansing the Jeweler's shop. But it had an impressive high-security glass case.

Goth slipped into no-shape and waited until the troop of bored schoolchildren was escorted out of that particular display room. Sure enough, she didn't have long to wait. Mebeckey and his two confederates appeared. They'd apparently been watching the entrance. That particular display room had only one way in or out.

"She's not here, Mirkon," said Marshi. "Must have slipped out with the kids. That teacher looked a bit odd." She moved toward the exit, drawing out a blaster.

Given what she'd seen of Marshi's murderous temperament, Goth was afraid the woman would attack the children and their teacher. So she allowed herself to become briefly visible, huddling behind the display case of the charter.

"There she is!" Mebeckey snapped. "Don't let her get away! We need that map."

All of them had drawn weapons, now, even here in the museum. The one that could cause problems was a tangle-gun—which fired a spreading stream of thin, glutinous fibers. Goth supposed that she could get out of it, but a Goth-shaped tangle would give them a target.

Goth used one of the light-shift tricks she'd learned from the little vatch. It could create multiple images of itself, and she did the same. Suddenly there were four of her, one in each of the far corners of the big room.

Marshi immediately took a shot at one. Fortunately it was an illusory one, but Goth decided right then and there that Marshi was the first candidate for a shot from the transdermal syringe she'd taken from the glove compartment of Marshi's vehicle. In no-shape she came up behind her and injected her broad behind. Then she darted away as the woman turned.

As he was armed with the tangler, Goth dealt with the cat burglar Mirkon next, then with Mebeckey himself. It was all ludicrously easy.

And then Goth realized it hadn't been. Mirkon had fallen over, Mebeckey had sat down, head lolling, but was still trying to raise his weapon. Marshi hadn't done either. It seemed the transdermal injection had had no effect on her. She was in the act of thumbing her blaster to rapid fire mode, searching the room for a target. From the expression on her face, Goth was pretty sure the woman had decided just to sweep the whole room with fire and never mind whatever damage might result.

Marshi's heavy, powerful blaster was beyond Goth's weight limit for outright teleportation. She didn't have time to fiddle with some internal mechanism, either. But her 'porting ability was great enough to allow her to force the weapon out of Marshi's grip and make it to fall on the floor. Then, with an effort, she was able to send it skidding across the smooth surface to come to rest again the pedestal holding up one of the exhibits.

Marshi went racing after the blaster. Goth snatched up the tangler that Mirkon had dropped. She fired just as Marshi was bending over to retrieve the gun. The woman's own momentum sent her into a tangled sprawl. She was out of the action and would be for some time.

Not surprisingly, however, by then the ruckus had drawn one of the museum guards. He stopped, his mouth agape, and drew his own gun—which was a tangler, of course. Museums frowned on weapons being discharged on their premises that could destroy the exhibits, even in the hands of their own guards.

Marshi was still struggling in the tangle-net, which drew the guard's attention. Cautiously, he moved toward her. Goth saw her chance. She still had one ampule left in the transdermal syringe. She dosed him just as he finished saying "All right, whoever you are, put up your hands!"

That made her feel a little better about the business. The guard was a completely innocent party, of course. But Goth figured anyone dumb enough to order someone in a tangler-net to raise their arms was barely conscious anyway.

After he collapsed, Goth 'ported the charter in with Marshi. Then, as the alarms began ringing and security doors crashed closed, dropped the mayoral chain around the slumped Mebeckey's neck. For good measure, Goth tangle-webbed both him and Mirkon. And then put the weapon in the unconscious guard's hand, swapping it for his own. She wasn't positive, but she thought criminal investigators could determine which specific tangler had fired which particular net. It wasn't likely anyone would bother with such a detail, but why take the chance?

That left the one obvious drawback in her grand plan—she was stuck in the room with the three of them, with a tangler in her hand. But she was pretty sure she still had enough klatha energy left to stay out of sight in no-shape.

She didn't have to wait very long. The heavy steel security doors were cranked open and the guards scrambled under them before they were halfway up. At which point there was enough confusion to tempt Goth into staying.

"Great Patham. The Charter is gone!"

"They've murdered the guard!"

"But that's young Ziller with the tangler in his hand."

"I think he's still alive, too."

"Do you think he was in with them?"

"Get the cops to set up roadblocks! Somebody might . . . well. Might have escaped. Who knows?"

Goth decided to intervene. Light-shifting in a back corner, she became yet another museum guard. That was a little tricky, because she had to combine a real tangler with the illusory guard holding it. But such complexity was more a matter of skill than available energy. She didn't have much energy left, but she had a lot of skill.

She walked forward to the captive Mebeckey and pointed: "He's wearing the chain."

They all crowded in, exclaiming. Goth stood back. So she was the only one who saw Marshi—who must have been painstakingly sawing at her tangle-web—make a break for it. Goth saw her stagger to her feet, and start sidling toward the now open door.

"She's getting away!" yelled Goth. Marshi was able to move, but not quickly. She was leapt upon by several museum guards and wrestled to the floor.

"What's happening?" demanded a panting guard captain who arrived at this point.

"Young Ziller caught them in the act," Goth said immediately. "Have the entrances been sealed? They might have accomplices."

She was quite proud of that story. The people of Nikkeldepain would believe what they wanted to believe. Better a hero museum guard than more mysterious happenings.

The guard captain looked startled. "Run. I'll radio the office."

So Goth ran. The Leewit would simply have come back, but Goth decided that it would be a good time to leave, even if it would have been fun to stay and watch. She'd have to follow the rest of the story in the newscasts. She even stopped to pass on the message about closing the main entrances. Of course, she made sure she got outside before they did that. Then she went off in search of a hyperelectronics dealer. She had Mebeckey's wallet, and it seemed fair to spend some of his cash on a spy-ray shield, just in case there was someone still at large to follow her. It was quite a fat wallet. She'd sit and investigate it when she'd spent a little more of the money on sugared pastries and a long cool bitter-sweet caram juice. Nikkeldepain had some things worth discovering.

Later, full of pastries and almost awash with caram-juice, she made her way to join the curious crowd peering at the windows of a holo-vid store. Nikkeldepain had seldom had such excitement, it seemed. A brave young museum guard had foiled the heist of the century, although when he modestly said that he could remember almost nothing of doing so. Goth had to grin. The three criminals included a known felon who had escaped custody barely days before, and two suspicious off-worlders.

So far, so good. Unfortunately, the talking heads of the media, always in search of material to keep their prattle going, now began voicing dark suspicions about the presence of the lattice-ship carnival and the undesirable people who came with such entertainments.

Goth rolled her eyes. Ha! Still, she'd bet Himbo Petey had started the roustabouts working as soon as he heard the first suspicion uttered. She'd better go and recover that strange box. She went to the nearest monorail station and headed for the lattice ship, eavesdropping with quiet amusement to the lurid stories of museum derring-do.

But Himbo Petey, it turned out, had moved even faster than she'd thought he would. When she got to the monorail's final station, she realized that there was something missing from her view. The lattice ship, with its bright silks and bunting, was gone. There was nothing but a big skytrail of rocket exhaust.

Himbo must have started breaking the circus down almost as soon as she'd left it. The mysterious map-box was still in its second props store, and had headed off to trundle between the stars, heaven knew where next, with the Greatest Show in the Galaxy.

Goth took a deep breath. She didn't really know what to do about it. She'd have to think. She shook her head irritably. She really missed the captain, partly because he was turning into a clever planner, and partly...just because. And because chasing after the lattice ship in the *Venture* would have been relatively easy.

Right now she needed to sort out so many things. School. Pausert's inheritance. Those other kids. And if she could definitely stay in her kidnappers' old lair. The map-box on the *Petey B* would just have to look after itself. After all, there was centuries of junk in that props-room. No one ever threw things out and no one knew she'd left it there.

She retraced her steps and caught up on the latest excitement about the Museum heist on the wall-holovid at the monorail coffee-shop. It appeared the authorities had identified one of the off-world desperados as none other than the famous Sirian archeologist Mebeckey. The police had surrounded his spaceship at the Nikkeldepain spaceport and could be seen trying to force entry to it. Revolt ships had been scrambled and circled overhead. Goth scowled. She should have thought of the ship and gone there straight away to search it for herself. In among Mebeckey's possessions in the wallet was a key-card door-coder. It could easily be for the ship.

Goth took the monorail to the spaceport terminus and the crowded airbus from there. She might as well go and look. Everyone else on Nikkeldepain seemed to be.

The spaceport was probably busier and more crowded than it had been at any time in the last fifty years. The police had cordoned off the onlookers, and had started deploying a heavy duty ion-cannon to blast open the lock of the *Kapurnia*.

Goth decided that it was not the right time to try the key-card, and it probably never would be again.

It soon became apparent that, despite her rich-man's-plaything appearances, the *Kapurnia* had a military grade lock. The ion-cannon had to be recharged and fired at the lock again. And then again. On the fourth try it did finally give way. The military went in first: a small contingent of Nikkeldepain's Space Marines. The little Republic might be stuffy and a bit backward in some respects, but that was not something Goth was prepared to say about those Space Marines. They were, in her opinion, as good as anything that the Empire or Daal of Uldune could field. She began to understand where the captain had learned some of the skills that made him such an asset to Karres.

No wonder the Empire had held back from gobbling up this little Republic. They were pretty good at making allies with those worlds that were going to cost more to take and hold than they were worth.

A planet against an Empire had always seemed bad odds to Goth. But Captain Pausert had explained that any attack on a well-defended position would be difficult and expensive. In the case of Nikkeldepain, Goth could believe it.

If there was going to be any resistance on board, Goth felt sorry for them. A few minutes later a Nikkeldepain Space Marine popped his head out of the blasted airlock. "All clear," he said to the commander of the police and customs officers waiting outside in the shelter of their armored vehicles. "We've taken a couple of crewmen and the cook into custody. The ship should be safe to search now, sir."

"No trouble?" asked the commander.

"None, sir. But the delay with the lock did give them time to shred some of what look like star-route maps."

"Well, that won't help them to claim to be innocent, will it?" said the commander. "Thank you, Lieutenant. If you can just bring the prisoners out, we'll start our search." Goth had used no-shape to cross the cordon, and then had joined the ranks of customs men waiting behind the armored cars. She joined them in marching into the *Kapurnia*, too.

It was, in many ways, internally, very much of a rich man's racing space yacht. The engines were outsize and the tubes would have done for a space navy patrol cruiser of five times the size. But that, of course, was not necessarily abnormal for that kind of ship. Rich men liked expensive excess power.

The heavy weapons turret hidden behind slide-back bulkheads was enough to get the customs men very excited. Mebeckey went from merely being a robber of museums to being a space pirate, or worse.

Goth was less sure. It was the kind of armament that you might want to have if you were on an archaeological expedition somewhere outside of the writ of the Empire and other safe, civilized worlds. The contents of the hold were more convincing evidence of a hardened criminal to the Nikkeldepain police and customs than it was to her. After all, an archaeologist might actually need to have rock drills and explosives, although she thought that they were supposed to do the excavation with trowels and great care. But maybe you had to get to the place to do that careful digging? Still, it, and the selection of personal weaponry, excited the locals a great deal. Goth found the large library more interesting, and more revealing too. It was indeed principally made up of archaeological books. But there were several on botany that just didn't fit in with the rest.

Goth felt she'd had enough trouble with botany. These books looked old. They even felt really old. Perhaps Yarthe relics. Well, science had taken a back seat during the wars of expansion. They'd been pretty advanced back when humans lived on one world. Looking at the dense text and strange archaic words, Goth was glad she wouldn't have to read those.

Of course the customs men were seizing all the paper and computer records. Goth didn't get much of a look in there. But somehow she doubted that the crew would have destroyed star-maps and left much else that was incriminating intact. Forensics on Nikkeldepain were not likely to be up to much, she was sure. Goth left the *Kapurnia* carrying a box of papers to the customs air-truck, feeling that she might have dealt the threat to Pausert a blow. But she'd come no closer to discovering why the threat existed in the first place. It niggled at her. There was something she had to do about it, but she just wasn't sure what.

The rest of Goth's day was taken up with the dull practicalities of an ordinary life. They were more time-consuming than she'd realized. She spent time checking out the apartment's rental, and was happy to discover that the criminals had cheerfully forged all the documentation the bureaucracy of Nikkeldepain required to keep itself busy with purposeless paperwork. She was quite grateful to Mebeckey and his criminal cohorts for shortcutting all the supposedly preventative paperwork.

Now, for as long as she continued to pay the rent, she had a place to live. It was rather fun going shopping to make it into a home. To furnish it with the paraphernalia of parents who apparently lived there with her and paid the rent, by means of those convenient envelopes she could drop through the letter slot on the rental agency's door. Nikkeldepain's authorities would not take kindly to her living on her own.

By evening she had a new robo-butler, well stocked with food and fresh bedclothes that had not been occupied by a louse like the thugs who had kidnapped her. She had doubts about how often Franco had bathed and just what kind of lice or bedbugs had shared the bed with him. She'd tossed out the burned wig, tidied the place out, and made it quite homey. She'd even put some effort into faking signs of a mother and father being there. She had to laugh thinking of what the authorities' reaction would be if they found out that it was the infamous Threbus she was faking.

Goth was very proud of her new apartment. She

even entertained thoughts of going across to Pausert's long, narrow home and bringing him here to see her new place, but she put that aside. She wondered how his day at the school had been, with the gang of boys. If they'd stayed frightened off? Pausert was a match for any one of them, she thought stoutly. Only they didn't hunt in ones. And that Rapport struck her as sneaky.

CHAPTER 13

Deep in the Chaladoor the *Venture*'s engines thrummed on steadily, pushing the ship forward into the unknown. Pausert's choice of a new course proved that his gambling instincts were still sound. They hadn't had any further harassment from the Phantom ships, or any other problems, for nearly a week now. For the Chaladoor, it was worryingly peaceful.

The only problem was that it had increased the length and the duration of the journey through the Chaladoor. The original route had been the shortest possible. The incidents with the Phantom ships had forced them to curve away from the Galactic plane, toward where the stars lay farther apart, as well as farther from the Empire. The captain's new course took them back into a region where the stars cluster densely—but the Empire was still farther away out along the spiral arm.

It was seat-of-your-pants navigation along the *Venture*'s old course, as the stars and beacons giving star map coordinates were now very distant. Undoubtedly, other ships had ventured this far, but none had come back with their records to add to the Galactic survey. Of course, not everyone wanted their records added: pirates, rogue-traders risking all trading with unknown worlds, buying rare goods that would have to be smuggled back into the Empire past the quarantine cordon. You could not hide the fact that you'd landed, and the decontamination and confiscation of the cargo meant it was worth keeping quiet about it. The Imperial survey service didn't pay terribly generously for those records—it would certainly not cover the costs. Well, a childhood on Nikkeldepain had taught him that bureaucracy was seldom sensible.

It was fairly likely that the people of Karres had better maps available to them—they'd ventured farther afield, taking their whole world with them. Pausert regretted now that he had not asked Threbus before they left. It would have enabled him to get a little more sleep. There were a good few asteroid clusters and comets out in the deep dark that were as much of a danger as any Phantom ship could be. At these speeds anything bigger than interstellar dust was to be avoided. The Leewit and Vezzarn weren't quite up to it. And after a week, neither was the captain. Instinct and the buzzing of the alarms told him to fire the lower port thrusters, but he just didn't react quite fast enough. The *Venture* rang like a bell. And a sleepy Leewit and Vezzarn staggered to the bridge as the captain struggled with the controls.

"One of the tubes is out of alignment. I just didn't dodge quite fast enough and a big, fast-moving rock-chunk brushed past our stern," he said. "I'll have to set her down and see if we can do some kind of repair job. That is, if we can find somewhere safe to set her down."

But he did succeed in doing that. The *Venture* 7333's own records showed she'd safely set down on a planet in a nearby star-system. Off route, a little, but at least safe. The encounter with the Phantom ship, close in, was an unwelcome surprise. But the captain managed to outthink it and head downward into the gravity well. It was a tricky landing, but by cutting the thrust to the malfunctioning tube and its direct opposite number, Pausert set down. Fortunately, it was a smallish planet that they set down on, with fairly low gravity. The captain was good at his landings. It was his take-offs that usually left the passengers a little shaken.

"Well. I guess we'd better check the atmosphere—and I think the Leewit better keep watch on the world outside with the forward nova gun turret, eh? We don't want someone to take us by surprise. I hope that the damage can be fixed."

The air-check showed that the atmosphere outside was breathable, if a little cold and full of helium, so, warily, Pausert went out with Vezzarn on a scouting trip. The landscape was a jagged and torn one—it looked as if the place had been a volcanic area once. There was no sign of life on the blackened, scarred terrain. Fortunately the tube was in a better state than the planet. It was merely one of the brackets that had sheared—a welding job and some recalibration and it should be usable, even if not at full thrust. It was the kind of task the captain would have preferred to hand over to a shipyard, if there had been one within light-years. Still, they'd got off lightly.

He and Vezzarn set to work. They had to uncouple the fuel lines and then attempt—using ingenuity, brute force and a hydraulic lift from the cargo bay—to get the huge tube correctly lined up, before the captain could weld. Even under the small, red sun it was hot, hard work, for which they could have done with a dock-crane instead of a makeshift ladder. Still, the captain was proud of his welds. He was just giving them a final inspection when the Leewit spoke in his earpiece. "Something coming towards the ship, Captain. It looks like a man."

"Patham's seven hells. What would a man be doing out here? We need to get the fuel-lines coupled up, the Leewit, and we can be out of here. Alignment will just have to wait. Fire a warning shot," said Pausert, clipping in the first of the fuel lines.

The Leewit loosed a single discharge from the nova guns. "He's still coming, Captain. Waving a white cloth now. I've got him on the 'scope. He's skinny and his clothes are ragged. Could be a castaway."

"Could be a trap too," grunted Pausert, forcing the next fuel line into place. "Keep watching him. And scan further out too. He could be a decoy. We're nearly ready. We'll deal with him if he can convince us he's a real castaway."

"Hello, the ship. I am unarmed. Please, can I approach?"

There was desperation in that call. A slight quaver in the voice. Pausert sighed. "Just stay put until we've finished," he shouted down. "Then we'll talk. Move before that and my gunners will shoot to kill."

"You won't just leave me here again?" called the stranger plaintively. "I'd rather be shot then. Anyway, I am near the end of my supplies. I'll die of starvation."

Pausert pushed the coupling seal onto the next line. Swore quietly to himself again. It was all very suspicious. Here in the Chaladoor everything was suspect. And just what brought them to this castaway? Chance? More klatha manipulation—or possibly his luck?

"Just wait," he said again. "We'll give you a chance to talk."

"I can pay, handsomely," said the stranger. "I'm worth a lot alive, safe back on Arc's World."

Syrian. They were a pretty stuck-up bunch. But the Republic of Sirius was nowhere near the Chaladoor. It was right across the spiral arm, near Nikkeldepain. What was the fellow doing here?

Captain Pausert clicked the last hose in place and climbed down the rickety ladder Vezzarn was supporting. "Reckon we should just scamper," said the old spacer. "They wouldn't have left him here for no reason. Maybe he had space plague or something."

"We'll keep a distance—but he must have recovered if he did. Cover me. The Leewit?"

"Yes," she said tersely.

"I'll keep out of the line of fire," said Pausert. "But set the charge as low as possible. I don't want to be collateral damage. I'll keep the microphone open so you can hear everything."

"Yes, Captain. Be careful, please."

That from the Leewit? She must be feeling the same oddness about this as he did. "Do my best."

He walked towards the man sitting on the lava-plain. The closer he got, the more the fellow looked like a starved scarecrow. That didn't stop the captain keeping his blaster in hand. "Who are you, and what are you doing here?" he asked.

"Dr. Mebeckey. I am a xenoarcheologist. Oh, thank Patham someone has come. You can't believe how good it is to hear another human voice, to see another human face. I've lost track of time. Please. Please, you have to get me out of here."

"Just what are you doing here, Dr. Mebeckey?" Where had he heard that name before? It rang vague alarm bells.

"I led an expedition here. A xenoarcheological expedition."

Pausert looked at the volcanic landscape. "Here?"

"Yes. It was the war damage that led us to pinpoint it. The crustal melting. That and the transmissions."

"Transmissions?" asked Pausert warily.

The ragged xenoarcheologist shrugged. "They stopped when we broke into the bunker. They must have been a distress signal, I suppose. I could have used one. We weren't the first ship to set down here to investigate them."

"So what happened to your ship?"

Mebeckey tugged his ragged beard. "They deserted me. We fell out about what to do with what we found here. In the end it came down to a fight. I barricaded myself into the room we'd set up as a store, with an M20 Blaster. Then . . . they just left me there." A tear trickled down his cheek. "What year is it now?"

Pausert told him.

The gaunt man shook his head. "I've been here more

than twelve years. Please. Please take me away with you. Even if you are pirates. I'll do anything. Pay anything."

"Pirates? No, we're just a fast, armed freighter. We just set down to do some repairs..."

"Ask him what they found, Captain," said the Leewit. So Pausert did.

The man shuddered. "An alien. And I think it was somehow alive after all these millennia. Will you take me with you, please?"

Pausert nodded. "Can't really leave you here."

The marooned xenoarcheologist fell to his knees. "Thank you. You won't regret it, I promise, sir."

Pausert already suspected that he was wrong about that. But there was no way he could leave the poor man here.

A few minutes later they raised ship, with a new passenger. The repairs left something to be desired with the ship-handling, as the calibration was not very good. Still, at eighty-percent thrust the vibration was not too bad. At full thrust it was enough to start your teeth rattling.

Mind you, that might have shut the xenoarcheologist up. He couldn't stop talking. Pausert thought that it might be that he had a lot of isolation to recover from. The Leewit said darkly that that might be the real reason that his crew abandoned him there. He was also going to eat them out of house and home. His expedition had landed with two years worth of supplies for nine people... he'd had to eke it out since. Now he was all for catching up. If he used up all the Wintenberry jelly—the Leewit's favorite flapjack topping—he'd catch one of her whistles, let alone catch up, the captain reflected with a smile, looking at the maroon's plate.

CHAPTER 14

"Your daughter Vala has a very impressive scholastic record, Lotl," said the Chief Administrator of the Nikkeldepain Academy for the Sons and Daughters of Gentlemen and Officers. His tone was doubtful.

Goth, light-shifted to appear like her mother Toll, tried not to look affronted at the tone. She'd put a great deal of effort into faking those results. It had meant a late night visit to this very office, and a painstaking and confusing dig through the papers in the filing system. And she wasn't claiming any abilities she didn't have. True, her math was skewed toward astrogation, and she was a little wary about the essay-writing, but . . .

"What is the problem, then?" she asked.

"It's the subject choices she wishes to register for here." He must have read the militant look in Goth's eye. "I see she's done them before! It's just that she'll be the only girl in several of those classes. And some of the teachers have complained that she'll be a distraction to the boys."

"Oh." That idea was so alien to Goth that she literally had no idea what to say.

"So . . . if you could prevail on her to do Housecraft instead of Advanced Mathematics . . . ?"

"I really don't think so," said Goth. She hadn't known before that frost could actually form on words.

The administrator tried one more time. Nikkeldepain's parents must be a browbeaten lot. "It's not going to be pleasant for her, you know."

Goth raised her eyebrows "Really?"

"Well, she'll have to keep up or we'll transfer her out," said the administrator irritably. "Now, about tuition and fees . . ."

By the time she walked out of the office, Goth knew two things. First, she needed to make sure that her math was as good or, preferably, better than the class, and second, she was going to need quite a lot of money soon. The stock of cash from Mebeckey's wallet was running out.

Goth started to cast her mind around, looking for ways of making sufficient money to fund an education that was beginning to look more like a war zone. The obvious and simple answer was to loot the law-abiding citizens of stuffy Nikkeldepain. But she knew that the captain would not approve, no matter how deserving some of the local citizenry were of being looted. So she'd have to turn to money that actually belonged to her. Well, money that belonged to her father. She was going to have to take steps.

Yes, it would mean that Pausert's mother got a little less. But at the rate she was going, she'd be glad to get anything at all. And the captain was going to need that money to get some pilot training and a bit more food and some new clothes.

But that would take a little time. Walking past the windows of the expensive furriers on the high Street, Goth had seen the prices of the miffel-fur coats displayed there. Of course, to a citizen of Karres, a miffel-fur coat was hardly worth owning. Tozzami and gold-tipped lelaundel were much finer quality. The miffel coat that Goth was wearing when she came down the Egger Route had been chosen for practicality, and Goth had been quite cheerful about the idea that it might get scratched or damaged. It had a rather fine gold-tipped lelaundel collar.

She would have to go and fetch it from the botanical institute. She could find somewhere to sell it, but she hardly knew where to start. The logical place seemed to be with young Pausert.

But when she found him it appeared that it would not be quite so simple. "You're coming to join our class!" said Pausert. "It's almost causing a riot. Half the boys said they shouldn't let a girl join the math class." He was grinning from ear to ear. "Rapport was really quiet, though. His face is still purple."

"They'll get used to it," said Goth. "Or I will make them used to it. Huh. Look, I need to go and collect that coat of mine."

His face fell. "That could be difficult. They've upped security a lot since then."

"Oh."

He nodded. "My mother told me. I think she

suspects I may have had something to do with last time. It was a sort of warning, I guess. She took the key."

Her face betrayed her. He smiled. "We'll just have to take a chance, I guess. Get in somehow, although I just can't think how."

"Tell me about it. Maybe we can work something out."

He did. It wasn't very high tech. New patrols, and some infrared sensors. Still, she had fairly limited resources. She could bend light. She could even go in no-shape. But they'd still show up on infrared. She hadn't figured out heat yet. Of course, to bust up the machinery by teleporting bits out of it or into it was doable. But that didn't seem fair. The institute was her father's legacy too, in a way, and Pausert's mother's job. Goth didn't want him caught there.

In extremis she turned to every young Karres witch's first resort: go up. "What about the roof?" she asked.

"The roof?" Pausert looked puzzled. "It is quite high. I don't think you can get onto it."

But after they'd been to look at it, Goth realized that he just didn't think of heights the way she did. "I need that coat back," she said firmly. "I can go up that pipe. Then there are those skylights. I'll get me some rope."

"But that's burglary," said Pausert, shocked. "I don't think we can do that."

"It's my coat. I'm not stealing anything. And your great uncle left the key. Therefore he must have meant that you could go inside." Goth was already rather fancying the idea. She'd always liked the excitement of the hunt, and this was similar.

Pausert was less morally certain than he had been as an older man. "Are you sure? I mean, it seems wrong."

"There's a *don't walk on the grass* sign. There's no *don't climb onto the roof* sign."

"That's because nobody would," he said grinning. "Anyway, I am not sure I can climb a rope."

"I can. You're not coming with me. You could get into trouble."

"Ha, and you? Anyway, I am not letting you do it alone," he said determinedly.

In some ways, he was already just like he grew up to be. Knowing the captain's obstinacy about these sort of things, Goth didn't even try. She let him show her where to buy rope. She was pretty sure the local police would take a dim view of it all if they were caught. She took extra care, therefore. She made sure to leave him outside, and the person who bought that rope looked nothing at all like the young woman who had just been enrolled at the local academy.

They found a tree with a convenient branch. Rope climbing lessons followed. And very shortly after those had not succeeded, rope knotting. That did make it easier. By now, Pausert was entirely carried away by the excitement of it all, and Goth was feeling guilty. She tried to call it off, planning to come back quietly that night. But Pausert read her too well. "You're not going without me," he said.

So they walked around to the back of the building. Goth was now really quite nervous. She would have done this in no-shape or light-shifted to look like something that belonged here, but she couldn't do that in his company. The "close your eyes" trick would never work twice.

She found herself appealing to the Toll teaching pattern in her head. And yes, there was an answer.

Not quite as good as no-shape or a light-shift, but it would make them a lot harder to notice, without being obvious to young Pausert. He could go on imagining they were just incredibly lucky. She'd bent light around herself and others before. Made refractory illusions of light-shifts. She could also bend light around the air. It was tricky. Air was not cooperative about staying in the same place. The molecules moved unpredictably. But an illusion could be created in it.

Goth tried to trace the klatha patterns in her head, but it was like herding smoke. The best she could do, unpracticed, was to create a greenish haze around them. And that made her sweat.

"Guess we just hope no one is looking out of the window," said Pausert, his voice sounding a little uneasy.

"Nothing to stop us walking here. You said the gardens are open to the public. Try to look like you're having fun."

"Oh, but I am. Really. I haven't made a lot of friends here."

"You don't fit here too well," said Goth. "Don't worry, eventually you'll find a place and people that you do fit in with perfectly."

"You sound like you know," said Pausert, half-smiling.

"Do, I guess. I've been a lot of places." She did not add that quite a lot of them had been with him.

By this time they had reached the down-pipe, in among some bushes. Here, at the back of the institute, the gardens sloped away to open land beyond the city edge, and scattered small-holdings and farms. There was nothing that close at hand that they were likely to be seen, unless it was by someone wandering in the slightly unkempt gardens.

"You first," she said, pointing at the pipe. That way she could hide him in a light-shift while he climbed. He stood just a little straighter at what he plainly perceived as a responsibility, and set off up the pipe. Goth hid him in a light-shift, merely patterning his back to look like the wall and pipe. By the way he huffed and puffed, she thought critically, he was not as fit as he could be. About time she got to work on that! She wondered if there was some local equivalent of the mountain bollem she could talk him into hunting with her. There was nothing like that for getting you in shape.

When he was up, she followed him, climbing the pipe as easily as a staircase. Soon they were both on the roof tiles, moving to the rows of skylights. The institute roof was taller than any of the other buildings in the area, and so not overlooked. It was gently sloping and not difficult to move on, just a little hot. Goth was glad it was winter. Pausert was sparkling with the sheer adventure. It was Goth's turn to be wary now. She was learning a great deal by being responsible for him, for a change.

They peered down through the first skylight. The plants looked quite different from above and Goth couldn't be sure just where her patch of maroon leafed markers were. But Pausert had a good sense of direction—or just knew the place very well—and had them move on. At the third skylight he tried, he found what he was looking for. "Okay, now if we tie the rope to that bar..."

"If we just sit still and watch for the patrols," said Goth firmly.

"Well, all right. It's just that I have math homework to do. You will tomorrow, too."

Goth had not previously encountered "homework."

It didn't sound like she was going to enjoy it, though. They watched. After about twenty minutes they had the patrol schedule sorted out. It seemed that orders had come down for more patrolling, and maybe even IR beams, but the security patrol had had many peaceful years of drinking tea and occasional saunters through the beds of plants from a hundred worlds, and weren't about to let a bunch of kids change that.

They tied the rope securely, after a short but fierce debate about who could tie the better knots, and dropped down into the dense foliage of a makemake tree. At least, that was what Goth thought Pausert said. It seemed a strange thing to call anything. After another heated debate both of them went down. Goth did put her foot down a little this time and went first in spite of his protests. She soon wished that she hadn't. Makemake was obviously "make you itch," but after her first brush with the leaves she carefully avoided them. She could think of no way of telling Pausert about it, so he just had to find out for himself.

Once down onto a narrow little walkway, they stood and scratched their arms and legs, until, avoiding any more leaves, they made their way to the edge of the bed and down into the corridor between the botanical beds. It had all seemed quite easy so far, but a few yards from the locker below the planting of maroon-leafed *Mularina tremblence* from Coolum's World, they must have walked through one of the infrared beams. Goth had forgotten them.

A siren sounded. "Back to the rope, quickly," said Goth. They ran back and crawled under the stinging foliage. Goth did a light-shift on the rope, just where it was visible above the tree.

"It came from here. From this sector," said the lead guard.

"Probably a bird or something," said the second security guard. "They keep getting in."

"Someone could be hiding in the bed. It's one of the ones with a sampling walkway."

"Don't be crazy. That's a makemake tree. No one would go near it. You itch for days."

Goth knew all about that. It was hard staying still and not scratching. She still didn't have her coat.

"I think we'll just have to keep watch here for a bit. Radio in and have them activate the beams again. That way we'll know if whatever it is decides to go anywhere."

After a while Goth decided to risk a peep. And a quiet scratch. The two guards were sitting on the edges of the plant beds, right next to the locker that held her coat. It was probably too big to 'port, but she tried anyway, out of sheer frustration—and was rewarded by her miffel-fur coat. Her teleporting abilities must be getting better with practice and age. And so they need not have come down here, and had the encounter with the makemake tree. Now, would patience serve? The itching was something fierce.

"I'll have to get back," whispered Pausert. "I have math to do. I need to have it done before Ma gets home."

"Give it another minute or two," whispered Goth.

"You got your coat. Great!"

"Yes, it would be nicer if I wasn't itching like mad," said Goth, scratching.

"I just knew the name of the tree," he said, defensively. "Didn't know what it did. Or at least I didn't remember."

"Well, at least I'll have a coat to protect me, climbing up." Goth concentrated on thinking about the air just a bit farther down the corridor. Making the image of something in the air, not just a refraction, was going to be tricky. But making the air opaque . . .

"That looks like smoke," said the guard.

"It does. Better go and look."

The alarms went off again. Goth realized they'd forgotten to radio in, in their haste and surprise.

"They've got enough problems," said Goth. "Let's go."

"Vala, you're amazing," said Pausert quietly. "How did you do that?"

"Do what?" asked Goth innocently. "Now climb."

So they did. Goth had to leave the rope visible—but from below Pausert looked like a piece of roof. An itchy piece of roof. She followed. Even if the security men had not been busy explaining what they'd seen and done, they could not have seen her. Once they were on the roof they hauled the rope up and then closed the skylight. Except for the rash on her hands and Pausert's legs, they'd come away without a scratch, and with her coat. They dropped back down the drainpipe and into the bushes and headed out of the park.

"We will stop at the drugstore and get something for the itch," said Goth, firmly. And Pausert didn't even argue with her.

The pink goo helped for the itch. It wasn't beautiful. A sort of payback for the purple they'd covered Rapport and friends with, Goth decided. She'd talked Pausert into letting her join him in this math homework at his spartan house—so that she could see what level of work she would be expected to do. The answer was a combination of very frustrating and quite simple. She was used to harder problems—but not at all used to having to show how she derived her answers.

"What's the point?" she demanded crossly. "If it's right, it's right."

"But if it's not right, they can't give you any marks for the part you had got right."

"If it's not right, your ship is a crater."

"There are other uses for math besides astrogation," said Pausert, defending for the sake of it.

"Oh. Like what?"

"Like biology, for starters," said another voice. It was Pausert's mother. "But getting it wrong there can actually be just as bad."

Pausert leapt guiltily to his feet. "I didn't hear you come in, mother. Vala's joining my math class and—"

"Glad to see you have brought her home. I think she's right, though. My uncle was apparently forever in trouble for not showing his work. He always said he could tell which answers were right. Nearly drove his teachers mad. He never learned the method as prescribed."

It had never occurred to Goth that other people might not know when their math calculations were right. "He sounds like a good man," she said gruffly.

Pausert's mother laughed. "Depends on who you ask. Growing up, I thought he was pretty wonderful."

It was all Goth could do not to agree with her. She stuck to nodding.

"So. A girl doing advanced math—and who believes the only purpose of it is astrogation. I wonder if the Nikkeldepain Academy for the Sons and Daughters of

Gentlemen and Officers has any idea of what is going to hit it. They'll give you a rough time, my dear."

"Huh. I'll give it right back."

"You could. But it is probably not how you'll win the fight, Vala."

"I'll be there too," said Pausert, staunch and solid as ever.

"I am sure you will, Son," said Pausert's mother, proudly. "But seeing as I did it, long ago, without any supporters, maybe you should go and get us some fresh bread, and leave me to chat with Vala about it."

When Pausert had gone, Pausert's mother smiled. "First, let me get you something better than that Darmin lotion for the makemake stings. So it was you two, was it?"

Goth blushed to the roots of her hair. "We didn't do any harm. I was just fetching something of mine I had left behind last time." She took a deep breath. "You ought to do something about those boys. They're making his life a misery."

Pausert's mother smiled sadly. "I know. But it's actually quite difficult not to do something that would make it worse. Nikkeldepain's not a bad little place. But they don't like incomers here. I wanted to give you some advice on how to deal with it best. Being a tomboy and trying to punch your way through all of it is just too difficult. Ask me. I found out the hard way. Of course I was a little younger than you, and it took me a while to learn to be a social chameleon. I didn't like the idea at all. And I was delighted that that Rapport boy got what was coming to him, by the way. But I can't tell Pausert that."

CHAPTER 15

"Captain, he's been sneaking around the ship. Trying his hand at lock-tickling," said Vezzarn, disdainfully. "Even Missy Goth is better than he is."

Pausert raised his eyebrows. "What? Have you been teaching Goth your tricks?"

"She asked me to," said the old spacer. "And you know, Captain, their little Wisdoms are hard to refuse."

"I suppose this means that you are teaching the Leewit too," said Pausert dangerously. "Now look here, Vezzarn, I gave you another chance..."

"I explained how you'd feel about it, Captain. They said they wouldn't steal anything. They just thought... in their line of work, well, it might be useful," said Vezzarn, looking as if he might turn and run at any moment.

On the ship, of course there was nowhere to run to, and that probably was all that was holding him back. Captain Pausert got himself under control with a deliberate effort of will. When he'd first met the three witches of Karres, they'd seemed to have no more morals than a jungle-cat. He'd thought that had improved a bit, but he felt responsible for them. He knew, now, that that was why Toll and Threbus were happy enough having him ride herd on them. The girls didn't seem to have much respect for property, but they didn't lie. Not to him, or, as far as he'd been able to establish, to anyone else. The work of Karres could indeed lead to lock-picking being an important life skill.

"Well, you'd better teach me too, then," he said, trying to keep his tone even. "I can't have them knowing things that I don't. Anyway, what do you mean? Mebeckey the castaway has been picking locks. How do you know? Been using spiderwebs?"

Vezzarn shrugged. "I'm good at it, Captain. He's not. He leaves little clues for someone like me. Scratches on the surface of the lock. Locks with the tumblers half-turned. That kind of thing. Amateurish. But you need to watch him, Captain. He tried the armament's cupboard last night."

"But didn't succeed, I assume."

"He got in all right, but I think he was disappointed. He didn't find anything," said Vezzarn. "I thought something was going on, so I moved the blasters to my cabin. I've got a lock-up there that would fool anyone but two or three of Uldune's best."

"And fool me, or even the Leewit, if I need them," said Pausert. "Did that occur to you, Vezzarn?"

"I reckon her little Wisdom would just bust it with

one of her whistles," said Vezzarn, grinning. "I set her too hard a lock, to give her a bit of a lesson, and she did that. Gave me a bit of a lesson instead."

"So what are we going to do about him, Vezzarn?" asked Pausert, getting to his feet. "Locking him into his cabin, without a guard, seems futile. We don't have the manpower to guard him. I presume he can pick the stateroom door locks easily enough?"

Vezzarn nodded. "Yes, Captain. They're not a big challenge, you know."

"I think, when we get though to Uldune," said the captain with a scowl, "that I must get this ship fitted with a brig. I could use it for you, and the Leewit, not to mention any other people we might pick up in the middle of nowhere, or take as paying passengers. I wish Hulik do Eldel was here."

"She'd be all for just shooting him now," said Vezzarn. "She was pretty harsh, was Hulik."

"Considering who she's ended up with, she'll have to be," said Pausert, rubbing his jaw wearily. "Look, I am not prepared to just shoot him out of hand. He seemed a genuine enough castaway, though I'd like to know what he was doing there. He's not explained that very well. And this does rather throw doubt onto his story of being a rich archeologist. Why would a rich archeologist be a proficient lock-tickler?"

"He's not. Not proficient, I mean," said Vezzarn. "But it is all very suspicious, Captain. I think we need to be more careful, at least. Maybe we need to ask him what his game is? Or drop him on another world?"

Pausert knew that was probably the right thing to do, that or Hulik's response. But he also knew he could not actually bring himself to do either. "Let's talk to the Leewit," he said. "Then we'll go and ask him a few pointed questions and decide just what steps to take next. If he turns nasty, the Leewit can always whistle at him. Serve him right."

The Leewit was about due to get up for her watch, so the captain made a mug of coffee and took it to her stateroom. She was not asleep, though. Actually, she and the little vatch were playing something that could be called tag—if the captain could figure quite how you touched an immaterial being, and how it touched you. The game seemed to involve a fair amount of acrobatics and giggling.

They also seemed to think that he and the cup of coffee would be a good addition to the game. It took him some time, and spilled coffee, to persuade them that this was not the case. But as he was persistent and quite used to dealing with the Leewit, he did succeed, and explained what Vezzarn had told him and what he planned to do about it.

"Don't like him much," said the Leewit. "He's a bit slimy. What do you think, Little-bit?"

The silvery-eyed peck of whirling nothingness seemed to briefly pause. **Doesn't taste nice**, it projected.

Pausert wondered quite what that meant. He also wondered if he, Vezzarn and Leewit had a "flavor" too. It could explain what drew vatches to certain people.

"I don't think he has any weapons. But we neglected to search him when he came onboard," admitted the captain. "We should have done that, but it is too late now. So I want you to stay back just at the door— maybe even around the corner. You can give him one of your whistles if he gives me any trouble."

"Coo. I *hope* he does," said the Leewit, militantly.

She was destined to be a healer, one day. But she was still very fond of breaking things and causing chaos. Actually, that was one of the oddest things about having Goth away. The Leewit was being much more Goth-like—at least, when she remembered. The mask did slip every now and again.

The captain hoped Mebeckey did cooperate. The Leewit's whistles were quite devastating, even if you were not their target. The captain collected a blaster from Vezzarn, and quickly field-stripped it, reassembled it, and made very sure the charges were intact and full. The Leewit's eyes got quite wide at this.

They went along to knock at Mebeckey's door. He took a long time about answering it—to the point where the captain was considering shooting out the lock with his blaster—but Mebeckey did open it, eventually, looking a little guilty, the captain decided.

"You've got some explaining to do, sir," said Pausert grimly, still with the blaster in his hand. "I want some straight answers or I am going to have to choose between shooting you or putting you off my ship."

"But I haven't done anything!" protested Mebeckey. "My hands are clean. You can trust me. Really. I'm just an archeologist, worth much more to you alive than dead."

"But you were trying to pick the locks on the armaments locker," said Pausert roughly. "Now come out of there. You can come down to the bridge and do some explaining. Vezzarn, while I keep him under my gun, search him."

"I haven't got any weapons, truly," said Mebeckey, wide-eyed and frightened now. "And I can explain. Truly."

"You're going to," said Pausert. "All of it."

"I will. I promise."

Vezzarn patted him down professionally, all the time keeping out of the captain's line of fire. "He's clean, Captain," he announced after a very thorough search—down to the soles of the man's borrowed boots.

Pausert holstered his weapon. "All right. Come down to the bridge and explain yourself. I want to get back to the controls. It's not the safest place in known space out here."

"I would much rather you were at the controls, Captain. I want to get out of the Chaladoor. More than anything. I wish I'd never come here."

"Explain exactly what did bring you here, to a burned out husk of a world in one of the most dangerous regions of space."

"Greed. I suppose," said the scarecrow of a man sadly. "I told you I was a very wealthy man. Well, that is true, or it was when I went to Garandool—the world you rescued me from. I don't know if it is anymore. I doubt if Bocaj or the others will have been able to loot all of my assets, but with that fiendish thing at his side, I do not know."

"I did understand the part about greed. The rest may make sense to you, Mebeckey. Begin at the beginning. Include an explanation of how come you pick locks. Rather ineptly, it would seem."

Mebeckey sighed. "It began a long time back, before I was wealthy. I was archeology graduate from a small community college in the Empire. It was not a particularly wise choice, when it came to making a living. The best job I could find was as an underpaid assistant to a very wealthy and rather unpleasant dilettante. He . . . well, he had a habit of locking things up. He locked everything. One day I caught someone breaking and entering. A little rat of a petty thief who used to pick locks. I threatened to hand him over to the police unless he taught me. I thought I might be able to, well, relieve my employer of some of the money he didn't pay me. I found that what he was locking up was not cash, but some of the little bits of loot he'd helped himself to from sites. Illegal items in themselves, but very much in demand with collectors. They were not particularly wonderful locks, and with my new assistant thief, I collected a generous share of his collection and shipped it to myself and fled to the Republic of Sirius. It was enough to set me up as a dealer called Becker, and also as a man of private wealth called Mebeckey who had an interest in xenoarchaeology. Thereafter, I would do exactly as my erstwhile employer had done. Loot and sell through my dealer persona. I never forgot how to pick locks, and over the years the skill has been quite useful."

"Still doesn't explain what you were doing in the Chaladoor," said the Leewit.

"A sequence of things. A piece of loot that came to Becker the antiquities dealer. Something that a pirate had looted off another ship, which in turn had come off a hulk they found drifting in space. Star pictures cut into the surface of two strange-shaped goblets which arrived several years apart. A book which turned out to be the log of the *Derehn Oph,* the ship of an expedition that had ventured into the Chaladoor not long after man left old Yarthe and expanded across the galaxy. The log mentioned the finding of the world the goblets had been taken from.

"It must have been part of a much larger set, perhaps commemorating a galactic empire of some alien lifeform. Some of the star patterns were quite distinctive, and the log spoke of other things found on Garandool—a vast half-melted fortress, cities buried in lava ash in the mountains, signs of huge war. And from the most obvious landing plain, a radio signal. An alien radio signal, still operational. Buried under a basalt flow. It's not something that had ever been found before. Alien machinery is worth more than relics. Artifacts that still worked... That would be worth more than just a fortune. And those goblets—they were a lead to the planets of this alien empire. The captain wrote in his log that he took these particular goblets as they showed the star system that Garandool was part of, and the next one over. There were about twenty more, he wrote.

"It was simply too tempting. I set about mounting an expedition out here, following the route in the old ship's log, with heavy drilling equipment and explosives to deal with the basalts. We had to work very secretively, and I fitted out my ship, the *Kapurnia*, with some heavy armament and some very powerful new drives. I thought back then that the stories of the Chaladoor were mostly superstition." He shuddered. "By the time we got to Garandool, I knew that wasn't true. But we got there, and there was the radio-beacon, sending out a repeat signal."

He took a deep breath. "There were also signs that someone had tried to dig there. That someone had unleashed nova guns at the rock from close range."

"How could you tell?" asked Pausert. "I mean, the range, the weapon..."

"It's an important aspect of xenoarcheology. The damage left on alien structures—quite a lot during the time of the Nartheby Sprite empire, some on the other alien relics we've found—help us to date them. Naturally, faking the damage is part of the trade. So radiation signatures to modern human weapons are well documented. And the scatter gives the range."

"Oh, so had they taken your treasures and gone?" asked the Leewit.

"Hardly. We did a space-survey just to make sure that they weren't still around. The world had a number of suspicious refined metal sites, above the rock melt. But careful examination showed them to be wrecks. Disintegrating wrecks. Old. Alien ships. That alone was valuable material. But deep radar showed structures still under the basalt, so we started excavations, going deeper than anyone had previously with space-guns and shovels. It took us a few months—in the meanwhile we had some members of the expedition checking out the wrecks. They were all of a similar design—Melchin or Illtraming—if the Nartheby Sprite records were to be believed. The Melchin were a legendary culture, even to Nartheby Sprites. The Illtraming had rebelled against them, so their ship design is similar. Anyway... they'd plainly been attacking this world with all the force they could muster. They'd literally melted the surface and sterilized the world. My crew collected quite a lot of material from the wrecks, even though they'd plainly been picked over before—they found enough to pay for the expedition twice over, and I was tempted to cut and run right then. But what had they been trying so hard to destroy? Greed kept me, and my people, working away with drills and geological lasers.

"We'd cut a storage bay—and with the sort of people I worked with, you understand I'd put a grade-four safe door on it, and I kept most of the food and artifacts in there. Pieces of alien ship. Bits of half-decayed equipment we had no idea of the original purpose of... a fortune of sorts. In the meantime we kept right on excavating. Then we hit the tunnel— the walls had been made of osmite—heat resistant, vastly expensive material. The stuff was harder than battle-armor. We couldn't cut through it. It took us a month to find the entrance. But we did. And it was still intact, under the melted rock."

Pausert had to admit that he was enthralled. It had even dispelled his tiredness for a while. "And what did you find there?"

"The reason why someone tried so hard to destroy their enemy. And, thanks to us, they'd failed. Oh, and of course wealth untold. For an alien value of wealth."

CHAPTER 16

One of the nicest things about Pausert as a younger man, Goth decided, was that he looked to her for leadership. Not that she wanted him to all the time, but she could see how their roles would change as they grew older. Now, he was very trusting of her. If she'd said to almost any other person, "I need to sell this miffel-fur coat," they would have wanted to know why, and formed opinions about her because of that. Pausert had just smiled and said that there really was only one place to sell that kind of thing, and that he'd show her the way straight after school. Now she just had to survive school.

The new uniform prickled and scratched, especially on her makemake-stung parts. The boys and the girls stared. And talked. Taking Pausert's mother's advice, she did not punch them for doing so. She just smiled politely. She did, during the recess on the large quadrangle, 'port a frog from the biology dissections in among a gossiping bunch of them who had been studiously ignoring her. It was foolish of them to assume that she couldn't hear them or it didn't matter if she did. She was able to sit, demurely, hands together on her lap, through the screaming and subsequent fight with the boys they thought responsible.

She went to math class and carefully made two mistakes, just enough to be good but not as good as some of the boys. There'd be time to move soon. Once again Pausert's mother's survival course on "how to be a social chameleon at school" made that rite of passage possible. Only Pausert seemed in the slightest suspicious—possibly because she'd done one of those problems with him yesterday. Or possibly because he knew his mother. The teacher put her to sit beside him, plainly intended as a punishment, a social solecism. It was the sort of punishment she was happy to endure. He didn't seem too put out by it either.

They left the class with a sea of homework . . . and smiles on their faces. Goth was aware of the reaction from the other children. The looks. It was a steep learning curve, this. She'd followed the captain, and observed Hulik do Eldel and Sunnat with the captain. She'd of course seen other Karres teens, and the interactions between them. But in a society of klatha-users, with adult teaching patterns resident in their heads, interactions were more restrained and yet more advanced and mature. This was different. She was indeed learning a great deal on her "very important year." She hadn't anticipated learning it from

ordinary school children, but from deadly dangers and
the defense of Karres and all it held dear.

That would have been easier, really.

Later, with the miffel-fur coat, Goth and Pausert set
out for the narrow streets of a poorer part of town.
This was plainly one of the first areas settled here
on prosperous little Nikkeldepain—back when there
had been neither prosperity nor much in the way of
building materials. Grik-dogs had bigger kennels. It
was the kind of area that spacers avoided, unless they
were looking to sell something they shouldn't have or,
equally, to buy something stolen or illegal. Goth had
to wonder just how come a boy like Pausert knew
his way down here.

She asked. He shrugged. "We have had to sell a
few things. Some of Great Uncle's souvenirs. We're
not supposed to do that until the will is finalized,
even though all of it has been left to my mother, and
they're things he left sitting in Ma's house for her.
So we had to sell it down here. And, well, this is
Nikkeldepain. You won't get kidnapped or anything."

Goth wondered if she should tell him how wrong
he was, but decided it wisest to keep that part of the
story to herself for the next few years. They arrived
at an unremarkable doorway—unremarkable except
that it had a small surveillance camera hidden in the
archway. Goth, well trained by both Hulik and Vezzarn, professional spies, spotted it at once. Seeing as
Pausert was knocking and absorbed in this task, Goth
did a little light-shift on both of them. One never
knew just who was watching.

The door, obviously controlled by some kind of
remote locking device, creaked open. They went inside,

up a flight of stairs into what, unless Goth was very much mistaken, was a room that would make the local flatfeet almost ecstatic to find—if they were not fooled by the appearance of a small secondhand junk-store.

They might be pleased to find the proprietor too. Franco was a lot less pleased to find Goth staring at him. His mouth fell open, and the second or two's shock gave Goth the opportunity to reach over his desk and slam his fingers in the drawer.

Franco clutched his hand and stared at her in naked terror. "How...did you find me?"

"Followed my nose," said Goth. "You should bathe more often."

"She made me do it," protested Franco weakly. He wasn't, sadly, referring to the bathing.

Goth nodded. She'd already got her own back on him, her Toll-pattern said. He could be useful. But she needed him scared. "I think you know who I am," she said in a steely voice. "So don't make me angry. Or you'll suffer the consequences."

"Uh. Wouldn't dream of it," said Franco, wringing his fingers. But Goth noticed his eyes flicker towards the far door.

Escape? Or backup? "Unlike you, I really have got friends," she said as Pausert looked on in puzzlement. "A friend who knows exactly where I am, and who I am with." Goth neglected to mention that he was also standing next to her, but under the circumstances, not even the captain could have felt that was dishonest.

"Uh..." He suddenly must have realized that Goth must have at least heard Marshi deciding to kill him. "What can I do for you?"

Pausert provided him with a wobbly smile, trying

to smooth over whatever the hidden undercurrent was. "We've brought in this coat to sell."

Goth could literally see Franco's mind jumping to the wrong conclusions, as he looked at a previous seller. He thought Pausert was selling it, not her. That she was accompanying him, not the other way around. "From your mother," he said, attempting a false smile too.

"That's for him to know. Not you," said Goth sternly. "It's not hot property. That's all you have to know."

"As if I would touch stolen property..." He withered under Goth's gaze. "It's not new..."

"It's in good condition and it has a collar of gold-tipped lelaundel. The collar alone is worth as much as the coat. I put that at about four thousand maels."

"You must be jo—uh, yes. A very fine coat. But not new."

"New would be twice that. Or more."

The fence swallowed. "It's a lot of money."

Goth just stared coldly at him.

He sighed. "Four thousand it is, then. And, uh, no...no comebacks?"

Goth smiled her nastiest smile. "Not about the coat. Give him the money, Franco."

So the fence did. Pausert, of course, tried to pass it to her. "Hang on to it," said Goth. "I might need a free hand or something. I'll be seeing you, Franco. Don't go anywhere."

The fence's imagination was obviously a vivid one. He started to sweat. "Look..."

"Later," said Goth. "I have to go now. You behave yourself."

"Uh..."

"Open the door, please."

And they were out in the dingy street, walking away.

"Quite soon," said Goth quietly, "we're going to run. 'Kay?"

Pausert nodded. "What was that all about?"

"I'll explain sometime."

"He gave you a really good price," said Pausert, plainly surprised.

"He'll do that for you in the future too. His conscience just started working."

Goth didn't mention that she was Franco's new conscience. And that she'd be going back later. She just said: "Let's do some running." So they did. Whether it was necessary or not, Goth actually enjoyed the exercise.

By the way he was panting, she was going to have to see Pausert got more of it. He was walking fit, but he needed more running. And he needed to get more to eat. She began to vaguely understand how her mother felt!

Once they got back towards the better part of Nikkeldepain City, Goth called a halt. Panting, they stopped. Pausert fished out the bundle of money and handed it to her. Goth immediately toyed with the idea of giving half of it back to him. Regretfully she had to shelve that idea. First, getting him to take it would be an enormous effort. Second, he'd probably give it to his mother. And that would make a whole new layer of explanations that Goth did not want to deal with. She'd have to do it more indirectly. "I need a drink and something to eat. And before you say anything, it's my treat—you've earned it. Commission. That's business, see. You took me to a place

that I would never have found on my own and got
me a fair price for the coat."

"I am worried about that," said Pausert. "He's
not usually very generous, you know, but at least he
pays. Some others didn't. Took us a while to find out
about him."

Goth resolved to quietly find out about those who
had plainly taken Pausert's mother to the cleaners.
She wasn't into general retribution, but this ... this was
family. "That was a good price, more than Thr—my
father paid for it new, but this is a different planet,
I guess. Now, let's get some food."

Pausert looked around. Looked up at the building
they were standing in front of. His face twisted with
fury. "Not here. Unless you want to eat paper and
excuses." That was not an expression Goth had seen on
his face before. Also, she could feel the rising klatha
energy that he certainly didn't know he was putting
out. She noted the name of the building, something
called the Nikkeldepain Central Records office. She'd
better get him out of the area, before he, or it, caught
fire. "Let's run a bit more," she said.

"Yeah. I've got the energy for it now," he said tersely.

So they did. A little farther on they came to a small
deli, out of sight of the building. Goth had it figured
now. The records office that refused to declare her
father dead. A little spurt of laughter nearly made
her choke on her pastry. They didn't know how right
they were.

Later, back in the apartment, preparing supper
and with her homework behind her, Goth got back
to thinking about just how she would straighten up

Pausert's money problems. And quite what to do about Franco. Once she'd eaten, she decided, she'd go back there. In no-shape.

It was twilight and the narrow streets of old Nikkeldepain were beginning to come to life. Goth was glad to be invisible. Compared to some of the places she'd been it was very mild. But she'd been to them with the captain or with her sisters. She waited until a "customer" knocked at Franco's door, and slipped in through the door behind him.

The fence had added a bodyguard to his room furnishings. He was also nervously holding a blaster just out of sight, below the edge of his desk. Goth 'ported away the charges out of both it and the blaster of the low-browed heavy he had watching over him. Then she had a quiet snoop around. The interior of this room merely held what any small dealer in secondhand goods might possibly have in their possession. Goth waited. She'd had to wait a while for the "customer."

Business for a fence on Nikkeldepain was not brisk, it seemed. The small packet of jewelry of dubious provenance was dealt with, then the bodyguard saw the man out. Goth waited. The bodyguard came back, and the still nervous Franco took the packet through into the next room. It was a storeroom, to all appearances. But Franco carefully locked the heavy door behind him, pushed his handkerchief into the keyhole and moved to the fireplace. The mantel-shelf held a clock. The fence adjusted the time and a piece of wall slid away. Inside was yet another door, which the fence unlocked to give access to his stash-hole. He put the packet into it, and locked it again.

Goth considered her options. The hidden safe was

easy enough for her to access. Yet she'd bet that the fence would get really nasty about defending it. No point in that. She wanted answers, not his loot. So she let him leave again, locking her in there. Then she investigated the locked room. It had a bathroom, which was in the sort of state she should have expected from Franco. But that had once had a window, and that window had been welded shut with a steel plate and some bars.

Goth quietly 'ported bits of the weld elsewhere. It fell away with a clang that Goth just had to hope wouldn't be noticed. It did let some welcome fresh air into the place. Then she sat down on one of the secondhand chairs Franco claimed to deal in, and took a school set-work out of her pocket and did some studying while she waited.

Franco did eventually return. Goth was actually quite relieved. Why didn't they choose books that anyone might wish to read for set-works? He went through his process of locking himself in and poking his dirty handkerchief into the keyhole before Goth interrupted him.

"A decent spy ray could work out what you're up to anyway."

He started like a frightened bollem and nearly knocked himself out trying to run through the sturdy closed and locked door, and then fumbled for his weapon.

"I wouldn't do that," said Goth. "I'd hate to have to shoot you, even if you were planning to shoot me." Goth held his blaster—the one he'd lost back in the apartment—pointed steadily at him.

"That ... that was her. It was her idea, I swear."

Goth shrugged. "You were part of it."

"She'd have killed me otherwise. She tried."

"I'm not really interested in your excuses. Or even in you," said Goth. "I just want some answers. If you cooperate I'll let you live. And unlike you, I have nothing to lose by doing so."

"You're not really a young girl . . . are you?"

"What do you think?" asked Goth, her tone chillier than the methane glaciers of Metrone III.

"I mean . . . you can't be. How did you get in here?"

"That's for me to know. I'm here to ask the questions, not you. Now start by telling me all that you know about Marshi and Mebeckey."

"But . . . you've just sentenced them to forty years in the Kaba mines."

Ah. He was rather mistaken as to who Goth was. Well, she wasn't going to change that. "The locals did that for us, yes. But I haven't—yet—told them about you. So: you tell me all you know and I'll leave it that way."

Franco nodded eagerly, and started to spill his guts.

"I get things, some things that are just too hot, or too distinctive to sell here. I got a contact from my days on the freight run . . . I send stuff to this dealer on Arc's World. In the Republic of Sirius, see. He also ships into the Empire worlds. Different laws and not a lot of talk between their police and ours. I sell things he can't get rid of because their cops have a treaty with the Imperials. It's mostly small stuff. He'll take gems and he pays top mael for antiquities. Not many of them come my way. But I got some bits from the kid's mother. He was happy to take stuff like that off my hands. And then there was this odd-shaped goblet."

Franco chewed his lip. "About three weeks after I sent it through with my usual courier, I got a long-distance subradio call. They needed me to track that seller. They said the information was worth a lot of money to me. I knew who it was, of course. It wasn't a secret. So I told them I could find the seller for a fee, see. Money for old rope. Next thing Mebeckey and his ship came here. And Mebeckey wasn't shy about parting with a cool ten thousand maels for that information. I thought I was onto a good thing. I don't make that much of a living at this," he sniveled. "Not a lot of hot stuff here."

"Concentrate on going on living," said Goth.

"Well, see, I knew where the woman works. I just had to ask a few questions and it turns out she's the niece of that Threbus—the explorer-captain who caused a lot of uproar here. They had me follow up the ships he'd used for his voyages. So then they wanted to get hold of the logs. I got scared. Said they could do the digging themselves... That Mebeckey told me I'd be digging my own grave. And he came up with more money. Gave me some rough dates—about twenty Imperial years back. Turned out he was using an old pirate chaser—a ship called the *Venture 7333*, back then. So then they wanted to break into to the ship registry, and try to get hold the ship's logs that way. But turns out the boat's been mothballed and was sitting in that old crook Onswud's shipyards, and Patham alone knows what had happened to her log."

"And then?"

"They pretended that they wanted to buy her. Onswud was all over them. They had their 'engineers' check out the ship—which was just me and Mebeckey and two of his crew. They searched the ship from stem to stern, but they never found what they were looking for. They wouldn't tell me what it was back then either. But when they couldn't find anything there, they dropped out of the deal. Onswud was spitting, offering them a cut-price deal. The old shark hadn't had a lease on the ship since Threbus last used it. But they sloped off and started on checking out Threbus's niece, seeing as that was where the goblet-thing came from. I don't see how any human ever drank out of it... Anyway, they tell me to find them a cat burglar. So I got Mirkon for them. He isn't the best, but he was available for a bit of rough stuff—and I wanted him involved. He owes me. And I thought maybe, seeing as they're looking this hard, it must be really valuable, see. Only now Mirkon's doing ten to twenty in Kaba, so I guess I am not going to get that money," he said disgustedly. "Anyway, up to then, they'd been being very cautious. Ruthless, but cautious. And then this woman arrives. Marshi. Seems like it was Marshi, not Mebeckey, that was in charge. And once she got here... well, she stopped at nothing."

"Not at first. She was cautious at first."

He nodded. "Scary woman. Even before she tried to kill me. Almost not human. There is a sort of desperation to her, like I've seen with drug addicts who can't get their drug." He shrugged. "I wouldn't cross her. She didn't really care about anything else. She just wanted that map."

"My organization has a history of dealing with desperate and dangerous people," Goth reassured him.

He looked warily at her. "How did you get in here?"

He'd earned some sort of misleading comfort—which

would help to protect her too, Goth decided. "Your bathroom window."

He actually looked faintly relieved. "So... What are you going to do to me?" he asked warily, his little weasely eyes looking for a way out.

"Tie you up and leave. You have told me what I wanted to know. Or rather confirmed it. We'll deal with the rest of them. But just one word of warning. You take one step out of line with Pausert or his mother, and..." She drew a finger across her throat. "He has some very powerful relations." That was the best word she could come up with on the spur of the moment.

Franco took "relations" as meaning something entirely different to the grand-nephew of Captain Threbus. "Oh. I didn't know," he said, sweating anew. There were some powerful crime families in the Empire. The Shinn-Borozo were almost a law unto themselves.

"Now you do. Leave him alone. We'll be watching. Now turn around and put your hands behind your back."

He did. Goth tied his hands with some rope from his own stock. She did a good job of it and gagged him with a piece of cloth before tying his feet. She then went through his pockets. By the way his eyes bulged, he assumed he was going to be robbed, but all she did was to remove his blaster and the key. She unlocked the door. "You should be able to wiggle your way over and kick it," she said. "At the moment you are worth more to us alive than dead. Better hope neither I nor my friends have to come to see you again, because that may mean that that has changed."

She stepped into the noisome bathroom and assumed no-shape. Franco was already frantically wriggling his way across the floor to the door.

It took a little while to get clear of the building—she had to wait until the bodyguard left to go and fetch someone to repair the bathroom window—and then she still had to walk home. But she felt that it had been an evening well spent. And she had got part of the way through the set-work book! Tomorrow she would be the good little schoolgirl Vala again. But for tonight, she was back to being Goth of Karres. All that was missing was the captain.

Then . . . she'd have to brave the Nikkeldepain central records office. She had a feeling that dealing with that creep Franco might be easier. She was getting some idea of Nikkeldepain's obsessive bureaucracy by now.

CHAPTER 17

"What do you mean by 'alien values of wealth'?" asked the Leewit. The Leewit had a healthy interest in treasure and finance. Goth was good at it too, the captain recalled, rather nostalgically. He remembered her delight at figuring out the *Venture*'s cargo values for the Daal's officials, and working out cargo and passenger rates—and searching for the Agandar's loot.

Mebeckey shrugged. "Things which were valuable to an alien species. That had collector's value, but were of no use to humans. Much of it we didn't understand. But it was plainly a mixture between a fortress and a palace. There were no jewels. If there were ornaments, they were things that looked like lumps of coal. There were many bones. Everything was very uniform, very ordered. There were thousands of patterned long planting-beds of dusty earth, all the same. There was alien machinery. Weapons not designed for human limbs. There were freighter loads of stuff that did have a value. Rare metals. The treasure of dozens of worlds that they'd conquered—some of it they had plainly understood as little as we understood them."

His expression got a little dreamy. "For a little while I had made the greatest find of xenoarcheological treasure anyone ever has, and I was rich beyond my imagining. But we kept going deeper. Looking for the source of the radio signal. We should have loaded the *Kapurnia* and got out. But greed kept us going deeper."

"And what did you find down there?" asked Pausert, warily.

"We found a stasis box of some kind. I cleared the area. Wanted to send the Waldo-robot down."

He sighed. "My associates were perhaps less scrupulous than they should have been. One of my assistants sneaked back. Or hid herself and remained behind. She opened it as soon as we were out of sight."

He sighed again. "We heard her scream. And we ran back. But by then it was too late."

"Why?"

"She'd opened the stasis box."

"And..."

"It had been full of the dust—and she was covered in it."

"Dust," said the Leewit. She'd plainly, by the tone of voice, been expecting treasure.

"Everything becomes dust eventually, child. I expect their stasis box hadn't worked," said the captain, faintly relieved.

Mebeckey shook his head. "It had worked perfectly. It had preserved viably what it was meant to preserve. We just didn't recognize it for what it was."

"So what was it?"

"Seeds of a kind," said Mebeckey, his voice quavering slightly. "Or spores, perhaps. Everything was so different that we should have guessed that the aliens were not an animal life-form. We are animals that eat plants and other animals.... These were plants that used animals to grow in, and to disperse their spores. I say 'plants' but really they were all one plant. One vast telepathically linked plant, with various lifestages, with only one vegetative goal: to cover all, to harvest, to bring back to the mother-plant, to breed, to create more seedlings in the motiles, to spread, to cover all, to harvest, to bring back to the mother-plant, to breed, to create more seedlings in the motiles to cover all, to harvest, to bring back to the mother-plant, to create more seedlings."

His voice had become a monotone, his eyes glazed, and he was was plainly caught in the hypnotic repetitive chanting. The captain interrupted. "We get the point. But how do you know all this?"

"And what were the bones from, if it was a plant?" demanded the Leewit.

He looked calmly at them. "Because I too became part of the mother-plant. The haploid stage takes over animal life. Marshi got most of the spores, but the rest of us must have breathed in a few. She was the dominant plant. It grew in us, spreading hyphae through us, taking over our nervous systems and then our bodies. That's what it does, until it is ready to sporify. Then it begins to grow rapidly, devouring the host, using the animal for nutrients and producing millions of spores, haploid spores, that then mix and make new mother-plants—which are all part of the great mother-plant."

"What?" Pausert had his blaster out, pointed at Mebeckey. "Are you telling me you're full of some alien parasite?"

The man shook his head. "Not anymore. I was. It controlled me. But at least one of my crew may still be. My assistant Marshi, the woman who got most of it. Except she was not part of my crew anymore. She'd just become part of the plant."

"You mean this plant is out there, spreading?"

"No," said Mebeckey. "Well, they must have some spores with them. But they need Melchin to finish the life-cycle. The species they coevolved with, that they used as reproductive hosts. They can live in other animals, but not finish the breeding cycle. They left me there, left me to seek for the Illtraming. I don't know if they survived."

"I get the feeling that there are big gaps in this story," said Pausert. "And I don't like it. Who or what is the Illtraming?"

"The mother-plant used its motiles—Melchin that had been infected with the haploid stage—to colonize other places, then continents, then planets. Only, somewhere...the Melchin hosts were infected by some disease before sporification. It killed the mother-plant haploids in the hosts. It did not kill the Melchin hosts. They survived. And bred. They are the Illtraming. The Melchin who are no longer ruled by the mother-plant. They are the mother-plant's most deadly enemies, with a fear and hatred of the mother-plant as deep as the

universe. And also the mother-plant's only hope of
survival. The bones we found . . . the bones are all that
is left of the hosts, the Melchin. The haploid mother-
plant can manage with a female human host. But to
produce viable spores they need a male Melchin. And
then more Melchin to breed for hosts. My crew—or
what used to be my crew—left me so they could go
and search for Illtraming."

"Why didn't they just take you too?" asked Vezzarn.

"I tried to get to them." He held up his scarred
hands. "But I had locked myself in when I started
getting the shakes. I was scared they'd think I was
infected with some alien disease and kill me. I was
scared that they had been infected. I still thought it
was a disease. It took a while to become one with
the plant, and its control of the nervous system took
a while too. And then it takes control. It can't properly read your mind or know what you know. You
are just part of the plant. And the plant didn't know
how to open the lock. I could have picked it, but
the mother-plant couldn't control enough dexterity or
access my memories sufficiently. It tried, but I think I
only had one spore, and I think the more plants the
more complete the control. Anyway, I was trapped.
Then maybe the plant needed something more than
my body could supply. It was adapted to parasitize
Melchin, not humans—although it could use other
animals, just not to breed. The plant mind faded and
I was myself again. Alone. Alone!"

"In the meantime those are some blips on our
screen, Captain," said Vezzarn, pointing. "It looks like
the Phantom ships are back."

Mebeckey looked at the screen too, at the fast

approaching needle shapes. "Melchin. Or maybe even Illtraming."

"What?"

"Xenoarcheologists have found Melchin-mother-plant ruins and the wreck of a ship. And there are Nartheby Sprite illustrations. That's what their ships look like."

CHAPTER 18

Goth found herself negotiating several morasses. First, there was the morass of high school politics. Yes, she could physically and mentally dominate almost any individual there. But as a group, as a system...well, it was like wading through thigh-deep, sticky mud.

The same could be said of her attempts to make head or tail of the bureaucracy that had enmeshed her father's estate. The locals seemed to delight in paperwork for paperwork's sake. It took her a full week of early morning prowling to find the right file. She found that in between keeping house for herself and seeing to the demands of schoolwork, she had a limited amount of time that could be spared to peruse the files through the jungle of the Nikkelde-pain Central Records Office. Gaining entrance to that had been easy enough. She'd let them lock her in in no-shape one evening, and had then arranged to be able to get back in via the fire-escape door whenever she wanted to. The next difficulty had been that she did not want to switch on lights and call attention to herself—and a paper chase in a huge dark building was impossible. So she'd had to settle for the early mornings, before the office opened, and before she had to go to school. There was a strong temptation to simply set fire to the entire place, except she suspected that would just make for more complications.

Eventually she tracked the file down. It was a very thick folder. Marked "confidential." She decided that she could trust herself.

She soon discovered, as she dug through it, that the paper-chase society gathered everything, even though it now had computerized records. It had copies of the logs of various expeditionary voyages. It was surprising how far afield he had roamed—even, from what she could work out, into the Chaladoor—before escaping Worm Weather there. There were reports of various "misdemeanors." To Goth they were obvious klatha flares. There were tax returns. Medical details. And a final report on the last voyage. Which went nowhere near the Iverdahl System. Or the Talsoe Twins. An addendum appended to that log did however give Goth pause. It bore the crest of the Imperial Security Service, and took the form of a query about one Captain Threbus. And it related to two things: the prohibited planet of Karres—it appeared Threbus had been seen in the company of a suspected Karres witch, in the Regency of Hailie—where there was no record of his ever having been. The second query in the letter related to the missing Lieutenant-Commander Kaen, a distinguished young officer in the Imperial Space Navy married to Pausert's mother. It appeared that he had vanished at much the same time as Captain Threbus. The log data put Threbus's last entry to within a few light-weeks of where Kaen was last known to have been.

Goth slapped her head in irritation. The log was a forgery, put together, as she happened to know, to lead away from Karres. To lead as far away as possible. The fact that it placed the *Venture* on the rather troubled and unstable border that Lieutenant-Commander Kaen had been assigned to was pure happenstance. At least, she assumed so. With Karres and klatha, sometimes coincidence wasn't. But no wonder they were suspicious about declaring Threbus dead. Karres was going to have to do something about the ISS, now that it could. And in the meantime, she'd clear out these inconvenient records.

Or would she? Given the fact that Pausert's mother— and the various lawyers she'd hired—had caused this file to be dug up rather often, and that Threbus was well-known and remembered, it could just make things worse. She needed to be a bit more subtle.

Like coping with high school's hidden mudholes, she might get further by not just blundering in. Next big step was going to have to be the Imperial embassy. They could certainly provide confirmation that Threbus wasn't alive. She just wished that she had the Daal of Uldune's skilled forgers to do it for her, instead of having to try to do it herself. In the meantime there were short-term measures. She'd looked up the Threbus Institute's records while she was at it. She wondered if it had ever occurred to Pausert's mother that she was, in a technical sense, employing herself. Threbus still was the majority owner of the unit. It didn't make a fortune, but it could afford to give her a raise.

She'd ghosted around in no-shape often enough following the captain with that Sunnat and kept an eye on him. So figuring out who the director of the Threbus Institute was and how their system worked was relatively easy. She helped herself to a staff evaluation form and a recommendation form as a model and soon had a neatly printed instruction awaiting signature in his in-tray. Doing light-shifts on entire documents was difficult, required a lot of concentration. But a name and percentage, those were easy.

Pausert was finding this term at school far more pleasant than any other had ever been. For a start, Rapport and his cronies had backed off. Yes, Pausert was sure they were just waiting for a time and place of their choosing. But before this it had been anytime, anyplace. This state of affairs was a distinct improvement. And for a second thing, his luck seemed to have changed since the lattice ship arrived. First off, Vala had joined the class. She hadn't done anything hugely obvious. Just smiled at him. But it had resulted in a subtle shift of the power-politics in the class. She was a pretty girl...and the other guys had noticed. He walked a bit taller just thinking about that. He wondered if he should tell them that they often did homework together. But she hadn't, so he didn't. She was smarter than she let on. Smarter than he was, and he was smarter at math than the rest of the boys.

Second, mother had got a pay increase! The first

in all the years she been there. It wasn't a lot, but it was something extra. And Pausert had the feeling it wasn't just the money. It was the gesture. "They didn't even tell me about it. I had to go and query my payslip. But the increase is there on my file with the director's signature on it! I thought he was such an old skinflint."

Pausert still thought so. But it did make the world seem just a little less crushing.

She should have actually have used logic and worked it out properly earlier, thought Goth, angry with herself now, as she dodged back out onto the street, away from the alarms. It was obvious that the Imperial embassy would have complex alarm systems. No-shape was not going to be enough.

She went back in daylight, two days later during her half-term holiday, light-shifted into a grumpy Nikkeldepain housewife but carefully not carrying weaponry or anything to worry their security systems. The visa section of the embassy had, inevitably, long queues. And, of course, a bathroom. Goth was horrified to find that it also had a hidden monitoring camera. Probably spy rays too. Had they no sense of privacy? she thought crossly, before admitting to herself that, realistically, she'd been about to use that privacy to fool them. So she had to evolve another plan.

Goth visited the embassy again in the ambassador's air car. It developed sudden severe vision problems just outside the embassy gate. A problem that could relate to a light-shift of the air, if anyone understood that. The driver set it down in haste. He got out of his door—and Goth, having studied door mechanisms carefully a little earlier, 'ported a piece of it into her pocket. The driver's door would not close.

That was enough to cause the ambassador's security detail to hustle him out of the car quickly and into the embassy. So quickly that they didn't even worry about closing the door behind them. That wasn't quite what Goth had planned, but she slipped in through the open door and sat down, and 'ported the piece of the driver's door mechanism back into place. The driver, left with a door that suddenly worked perfectly on his eighth try, scratched his head, wiped the windscreen, and then walked around the car, closed the ambassador's door, walked back, got in, and drove to the motor-gate, and in through the compound to the garages. He got out, carefully locked the ambassadorial vehicle, put the lockbar in his pocket, walked to the security card reader, and went up into the embassy.

Goth waited a few moments, and then ported the lockbar and his security card back to her. She returned them to him a few minutes later as she made her way to the ISS office. It was an excellent place to see how the security worked around here and how to organize a suitable proof of Threbus's death from the very people who had caused the problems in the first place. Besides, she got to watch how several neat spy-devices worked. She'd heard about some of them from Hulik, but it was interesting to see them firsthand. That might be useful too, one day.

Next step, now that she knew how to avoid detection, was to find out when and where the diplomatic bag came in. The bag itself was a ratty old green thing with the Imperial crest almost worn off. Goth picked it up and dropped it again. Shook herself, nearly losing no-shape. It had been around, that bag. Been in places a lot more alarming than Nikkeldepain. Something involving klatha force was going on, and she wasn't quite sure what it was yet.

Nikkeldepain was far enough out of the way to only get two Imperial deliveries a week, and to have a very bored clerk go through them and assign them. It was interesting to see, subradio or no, that requests for information were still passed through to the Nikkeldepain Central Records Office in writing. Identity was the subject of two of those. The clerk sent them back to the ISS office. And the ISS sent a junior duty officer to Goth's favorite building—The Central Records Office. Goth followed, grateful that the ISS woman had decided to walk.

Goth relieved the ISS of some stationery. She could have inserted the letter into the diplomatic bag, but it seemed a much harder way of doing it than merely becoming an ISS officer. She'd seen Hulik in full uniform. Even practiced it.

She waited a week, and then timed her visit for just after the officer had been to check on the identity of someone who claimed to come from Nikkeldepain. A few minutes later, Goth went in instead. In appearance she was the duty officer. She even wore the same perfume, figuring that she'd mastered no-scent enough for something that simple and blatant. She carried an official request to match the DNA record and dental record of a corpse, which had been carrying the documents that identified him as one Captain Threbus, of the Republic of Nikkeldepain.

The clerk greeted her perfunctorily. "Back again?"

Goth nodded. "Yeah. This one got to me via the ambassador's office instead of via the sorting clerk."

"What is it? Another smuggler or pirate claiming citizenship?"

Goth handed over the request. "Body that was found in a military area. A couple of soldiers stumbled on the remains during an exercise. It was an old corpse, but we got DNA off the bones. The documents found with it say it's one of your citizens. A Captain Threbus. Do you mind checking for me?"

The clerk nodded. "Sure. I'll have it for you next week."

"The ambassador asked if you could expedite it." Goth was very proud of that word. "He was going to call someone."

The clerk sighed. "Let me ask my supervisor."

So he did. And a little while later the clerk brought the news that the DNA match was perfect with the record.

It should be. That was where it had come from.

Goth thanked them politely and left.

The next task was considerably harder. The starting point consisted of finding out just how Pausert's mother was pursuing the matter of Threbus's will. And that was nearly impossible. Over the months Goth had come to know Pausert's mother Lina relatively well—as well as any young teenager gets to know the mother of one of her friends. But Lina was very good at separating the private from the social. She didn't talk about it, and was very skilled at not saying anything but getting others to talk. Goth had to watch her tongue. And still was no further along with finding out details. Eventually, she resorted to pretending her parents needed to consult a lawyer, and, as foreigners, didn't know who to start with.

Lina gave her a long list of whom to avoid, including her current expensive and ineffectual practitioner.

Goth went off to investigate him.

It didn't take long to discover that he had a lot in common with Franco. For a start, he had a secret wall safe. And for a second, he was a slimeball. Goth 'ported all the documents out of the secret safe and spent a good many hours working out what he was up to. Some of it was beyond her. But some plainly involved trust-funds and money. None of it appeared to concern Threbus, which at least removed that complication.

CHAPTER 19

In the Chaladoor the two blips had become four, and then six. Captain Pausert was doing his best with evasive maneuvers, but the numbers were stacking up against them. In the meanwhile, Captain Pausert was learning more about the value of history. He wasn't sure that he wanted to right now, but Mebeckey was telling him anyway.

Decades had passed while Worm Weather spread out of the Chaladoor, possibly from some place in the Galactic East. But, for an historian like Mebeckey, whose studies had spanned eons, history was dates and records—and how they fitted together. From what was known of the Great Eastern Wars when whole planets had died in the gargantuan battles between the men spreading out of old Yarthe, the date of the coming of Worm Weather, of the Nuri globes and the voice of Monster Moander who crouched on the surface of tunneled Manaret were the stuff of those records. So was the Chaladoor of yesteryear, and so was the danger before the coming of Manaret, that great dimension-crossing ship of conquest filled with the Lyrd-Hyrier lords.

It had always been a dangerous piece of space. Few reports existed of why this was so, but those few reports did record the presence of the Phantom ships. Mebeckey hadn't had any access to reports of what they looked like. But he could tell the captain this: the last report of the Phantom Ships had actually been recorded just before the first reported encounter with Worm Weather.

The Chaladoor had actually, briefly, gotten safer to cross with the onset of Worm Weather—with the arrival of the great ship that was Manaret.

"Looks like one set of problems chased the other out," said Pausert. "Now that Manaret is gone and the Nuris have all faded away . . . the old menace is back."

"So it would seem," said Mebeckey.

"You don't know something useful, do you? Like how ships got away from them in the past?"

The archaeologist shook his head. "Other than very rarely, no. But the Phantoms certainly didn't occur in the whole of the Chaladoor region. Most reports of survivors—there were quite a lot, really—came from the Galactic South—the area around Uldune."

That was useful, Captain Pausert supposed, but only to give him some idea where to run to. And, of course, if your destination wasn't Uldune. "If we can't run, we'll have to fight."

"How do we fight them?" asked the Leewit, sparkling. "Shoot their front end off, shoot their rear end off, and ram 'em in the middle?" She quoted her favorite phrase of the captain's vocabulary.

Pausert nodded, and tousled her hair. "Exactly what I would do if they were solid enough to do it to. But they're not, so *you* will have to do some clever shooting. It's a question of timing!"

The Leewit nodded thoughtfully. "Got to guess what they're doing. Those missiles of theirs are nasty."

"They may have other unpleasant surprises too. Remember, they took on the Daal's battlewagons and won. I'm not really sure what keeps them off us."

The Leewit looked thoughtful. "Could be Littlebit. She makes us a bit different, eh? She says there is definitely something vatchlike about those ships. I think she means the way they have no mass, but can still do things like launch torpedoes and move between stars. If she can feel something there, maybe they can feel her here, looking after us."

Pausert thought it was odd to think of the little vatch as a "she," but since the Leewit seemed determined about the matter, he saw no reason not to accommodate her.

"Is she still around?" he asked. "I thought she'd gone elsewhere again. And she hasn't pestered me for more pieces of vatch-stuff."

"Doesn't need to. She's growing, and she's got to stop eating."

"Kind of the opposite of us."

"S'pose so," said the Leewit, who was going through "constantly hungry" at the moment, and putting on inches in height, too. "Anyway, what are you going to do? We can outrun those torpedoes, but if we turn toward them or get boxed in, we'd be in trouble."

"Yes. I was hoping to use..." He looked at Mebeckey. "Our booster drive to get us out. Maneuver us into a position where we can fire on them and then run. But the firing is the trick. We'll need to anticipate. To fire the nova guns just as they launch."

"Pity neither of us do premote," said the Leewit.

"You just fire on my command," said the captain. "Both you and Vezzarn. Mebeckey, you get yourself strapped in. In your cabin. You're supercargo at this stage. Get."

Vezzarn plainly also got the hint. He really did not like witchy stuff. "Going to ready the guns, Captain."

"Do that. The Leewit and I need to talk."

He scarpered. Mebeckey blundered away too. "Don't see how we can do it, Captain," said the Leewit. "I can't operate the guns and do the Sheewash drive with you."

"That's why I am going to have to do the Sheewash on my own. You are much better with the nova guns than old Vezzarn is."

The Leewit looked doubtful. "But can you, Captain?"

"I guess I'll have to. A few more of these ships and they can achieve an englobement. Then we're toast. And I reckon we're going to have them pop up on the screens any time now."

The Leewit looked serious and worried. "They kept up with us when we used the Sheewash drive, Captain. And without Goth, we can't keep it going for too long." She bit her lip. "The Egger Route, Captain. If things get really bad, will you use it?"

Pausert blinked. The Leewit suggesting her pet

hate? "Not without you. I am responsible for you, you know."

The Leewit scowled. "Got it imprinted in us kids, with the Toll pattern. Get badly hurt and I prob'ly can't stop it happening. But you're different, see. And I worry about you, too. Because I'm *also* responsible. Goth told me so." It was plain just then that she felt that responsibility very heavily. But she was Karres. They took responsibility when there was the need.

Pausert had learned, over the years of dealing with the three Karres witches, that when they were this serious, they weren't just children to be humored or jollied. He nodded back. "I'll do it. I think I can. But I have a ship, a crew and a passenger to worry about."

"If it's that bad, you won't have," said the Leewit.

He nodded. "Sure. Well, let's go and shoot their front end off, shoot their rear end off, and ram 'em in the middle, then. Because I really don't want to use the Egger Route."

"Me neither!" said the Leewit. "Sing out when you want us to fire the guns."

Soon the captain was alone in the control room, assembling a blunt cone of pieces of wire from a drawer. The wires, the captain suspected, were no more than a focal point for the klatha pattern. He built it in his mind. The strange swirl of orange energy began to build too . . . in his mind, and then, before it burned him up, he transferred it to where the tip of the cone would be. The *Venture* leapt like a startled bollem and then screamed off toward the upper left quadrant of the approaching Phantom ships. The captain heard the Leewit shriek with glee. He realized the *Venture* was accelerating—but in a jitterbug corkscrew fashion. Belatedly, it occurred to him that one of the more experienced witches—and even the Leewit was more experienced than he—must have controlled directional vector before engaging the drive. But he had no idea how to do that.

The ship was tumbling wildly about, closer to the Phantom ships. "Fire!" he yelled. One set of nova guns responded immediately, and the second set, the aft ones, seconds later. The captain was just glad he wasn't trying to line up cross hairs while the ship was doing a drunken dance. Blue sheet-lightning leapt across space and intersected one of the spiky Phantom ships...to no effect. But then the ship must have tried to launch a torpedo.

The Leewit yowled in triumph like some wild thing out of the jungle. "Got 'im!"

The captain was too busy trying to concentrate on the twisted pattern of klatha energy to look. They went through the containment barrier the inadequate number of Phantom ships had been trying to mount and—without meaning to—cut a high-speed broadside across another. Instinct prompted the captain to yell "fire" again. The truncated cone of wires collapsed as they spiraled out again. The captain gave all the tubes full thrust—the repaired bracket and roughly calibrated tube made the old *Venture* vibrate and wobble—but compared to his ill-controlled Sheewash it was steady and easy. Vezzarn stumbled into the control room a few minutes later. "The little Wisdom got two hits on two different ships. The first one was a real disabling shot, I reckon."

"They're still behind us, but they've pulled back. Barely in detector range."

The Leewit bounced into the control room. Punched

his upper arm and beamed at him. "You are one hot witch pilot, Captain. They couldn't have had the least idea where to fire."

There were times for accepting praise—no matter how misdirected—gracefully. Making the crew feel that the captain was in control and good at it.

This was not one of those times. "They didn't know what we were going to do... because I didn't either. I didn't have any directional control at all."

The Leewit dissolved into helpless giggles. "I'll show you next time. You did pretty clumping good anyway."

"Yes, Captain," said Vezzarn, a sly grin creeping onto his face. "Now they think we're completely mad and they're keeping their distance because they don't want to catch it."

Pausert rubbed his eyes tiredly. "They could be right, at that. Now can you get me something to eat? Because I sure am starving."

"Coming right up," said the Leewit. "I could use a second breakfast myself."

"Actually, that'll be your third, child," said Pausert, chuckling.

"Pooh. Who's counting?" said the Leewit cheerfully. "You want some cone-seed coffee with that?"

"Sure. It'd be good."

Pausert examined the screens while the Leewit went to enforce her will on the robo-butler. They'd managed to lose one of the pursuing craft. But unless he was very much mistaken, they were going to be joined by two more ships.

He was not mistaken.

They'd be properly boxed soon. And then not even the Sheewash drive would get them away.

CHAPTER 20

The lawyer that Pausert's mother had been seeing was greasily polite. He held her chair for her, and smiled in a way that made Goth feel faintly uneasy.

She was not used to the way men treated her, light-shifted to appear to be Hulik do Eldel. It was a little bit creepy, really.

"What can I do for you, Ms. Dolkan? A matter of a will..."

Goth produced a very authentic-looking ID card and showed it to him, obscuring the name, but showing a photograph of Hulik. The card was the real thing, and the agent at the embassy was going to be very worried if Goth didn't 'port it back. The picture was a mere light-shift.

"Imperial Security Service," he read. "We are not

part of the Empire, Ms. Dolkan." He spoke cautiously, but without any of the fear that might have crept into the voice of a citizen of the Empire.

"I am actually aware of that," she said. "I'm clearing up some unfinished business of ours. Your cooperation would be appreciated."

"Ah. Well. I'd be happy to help, where I can, for a fee."

Goth smiled falsely back at him. "I have an appropriate fee for you in this envelope. Now, I believe you have a client, Lina, the niece of one Captain Threbus."

"Yes, I do."

"She is trying to get her uncle's will settled."

The lawyer pulled a face. "Look, to be frank with you, ma'am, if Captain Threbus's niece hadn't been so insistent, I wouldn't be pursuing this matter. I can't really discuss a client's affairs with you." He rubbed his fingers together suggestively, an expression of greed on his face.

Goth spilled the copies of the contents of his secret safe onto the table. "Look at those. I think you'll find you can discuss anything I want to talk about."

The lawyer looked at the papers and stuck his finger in his collar as if it had suddenly decided to choke him. "Where did you get those papers?" he said in a frightened whisper.

"They're copies. We have more. Now I suggest that you assist me properly. I need to know just what the problem is regarding that inheritance."

"These . . . ?" he pointed to the copies.

"Will be destroyed just as soon as that matter is dealt with," said Goth smoothly. She was proud of herself, even if she suspected that the captain would call it blackmail.

The lawyer tugged at his goatee. "I have investigated the matter. Really. I've got connections inside the Central Records Office. The file is security locked. The evidence says that he's probably dead. He's certainly never returned, and it is over the legal time to declare a missing person dead. But they suspect some foul play. Collusion." He raised an eyebrow. Looked at the light-shift of Hulik do Eldel. "It's true, then?"

"It's true that he died in our service. It's also true that we don't want the heir to know about that area of his work. There is, however, a certain prominent person in the Empire who was extremely upset to find that the matter had been left hanging. I suggest that you actually go through with the steps to have the will finalized. There has been some fresh input from our side. Talk to your contacts inside the Central Records Office."

"It'll take a few months to get onto the court roll."

"Months?"

He nodded. "It's not a process you can speed up. And it's quite expensive."

Goth picked up the papers she'd spilled onto the desk, and put them back in the envelope.

"Um. I am sure this time I'll be doing this *pro bono*."

Goth wasn't too sure what that meant, but she was pretty sure an Imperial agent would. So she smiled in the way that she'd seen Hulik do while dealing with something nasty. "I hope I won't be seeing you again, sir. It's a hope you should share."

"Could . . . couldn't you leave those with me?" asked the lawyer.

"No," said Goth. "And it wouldn't help you if I did. There are further copies sitting in the embassy. I think it's time you changed your ways. Goodbye."

"Uh, can I see you out? Look, it was just a temporary loan."

"I am sure it is. And the inheritance and the will should therefore be sorted out very soon, won't they? I have an escort waiting to drive me. Stay here." Goth slipped the appearance of a gray cloak around her, much as Sunnat had once done. She walked out, into the corridor, which was conveniently empty, and disappeared.

He stuck his head out of the office like a snapping wilfer a few moments later, peering up and down the passage, and using language that would have made even the Leewit blush.

Goth followed him back into his office and was nearly hit by the slamming door. Moments later he was on the communicator. "We're in trouble deep, Voks."

Goth could only hear one side of the conversation. But Imperial Security Service was mentioned, rather a lot, along with some very bad words. Goth didn't mind the fact that some Nikkeldepain politico would be campaigning hard to get the Imperial embassy—a nest of spies—under close surveillance. Her work there was done. She waited while the nervous lawyer paced and then called his contact in the Central Records Office, and asked him to pull a copy of Captain Threbus's file. Goth waited, irritated at wasting her afternoon.

The lawyer decided that the sort of day he was having called for strong drink and took a bottle out of the cupboard. Goth 'ported the glass to her apartment before his fumbling hand reached it. He blinked. "Sure I had a glass here." He went out to the secretary's office, and returned a little later with a coffee mug—having sent his assistant home for the day. It must, belatedly, have occurred to him that he'd been shouting at his friend Voks. Goth waited until he had returned to his office before calling him on his own secretary's phone.

"I forgot to mention," she said, when he picked up the call, "That we're watching you and your friend Councilor Voks. Listening to your calls too. You should wash your mouth out with soap."

She put the communicator down and listened with some glee to the faint sound of a coffee mug smashing in the next room. It was time to go.

So she did.

The hearing did not attract much attention. Pausert's mother. A few of the estate's creditors. The lawyer. The judge. Goth had expected it to be an open and shut affair. It turned out to be more complex than she'd imagined. But, on the other hand, it appeared that the right way, here on Nikkeldepain, to get the legal profession to earn their keep was to have them very afraid.

"I appreciate, Mr. Shand, that the latest information in the file held by the Central Records Office does point to the unfortunate death of Captain Threbus on Thambar's world. Nonetheless, owing to previous suspicions, and the fact that no body has been produced—we can't rely on these Imperials, you know—that I cannot reach a decision and order that Captain Threbus be declared dead."

Goth, reclining bonelessly on a seat near the back, relaxed in no-shape, uncoiled and nearly forgot to maintain her invisibility. After all the work she'd done! There was a judge in severe trouble...

The lawyer coughed. "Your Honor."

"Yes, Mr. Shand."

"Your Honor, there is the matter of the debts against the estate."

"The law is quite clear on that, Mr. Shand. Creditors will not suffer, and the rights of property must be respected. Heirs are held responsible for first settling those."

"Yes, Your Honor. Except in this case, the heir cannot fulfil the sum of the obligation completely until probate is granted. Hitherto they had agreed to terms in the expectation of an early settlement. But given that an order will not be given, they will have to sue the state and appeal to a higher court."

"Then they must do that, Mr. Shand."

The lawyer coughed. "You would be a substantiative part of such a case, Your Honor. And, as you know, the law is clear: a member of the bench who is a substantiative part of case may not serve whilst the process is ongoing." He paused. "I will be acting for several of them. I assure you that we will pursue it with as much haste as the court allows. Of course there is one other possibility which could avoid this inconvenience for the creditors."

The judge scowled at him. "I notice you are choosing your words very carefully to avoid anything that could be construed as a threat. You avoided, for example, stating the fact that such cases can take years, or that such suspension is without pay. What are you suggesting?"

"Your Honor, I wouldn't dream of threatening any member of the judiciary. I was merely wanting to remind you of a possible way out of this dilemma. The case of *Madelwud versus Board of Estates*."

"Jog my memory, Mr. Shand."

"Madelwud could not be established as dead, Your Honor. He simply vanished one day. He had substantial properties and was heavily insured—but was also considerably in debt. His widow and principal heir was, *de facto*, bankrupt and penniless. The creditors could institute civil proceedings against her, but not reasonably expect to recover anything at all. They petitioned the court to order the granting of a provisional certificate of death, with full liability to the heirs, should Madelwud be found to be alive. The insurer pleaded for some form of surety. They were granted leave to merely pay Mrs. Madelwud the interest accrued, and the properties were sold off to provide payment for creditors."

"A good solution. Yes, *Madelwud versus Board of Estates*. Very well. I rule that a provisional death certificate should be issued, allowing sufficient property of Captain Threbus to be sold to pay off any creditors. If there is any income derived from the rest, it may be divided among the heirs, although properties themselves may not be sold."

Shand smiled, and Goth saw that Lina was smiling and crying with relief. Goth felt quite choked up herself. It wasn't what she had hoped for, but she hoped it would do.

She had Pausert bouncing into her apartment to tell her that it was good enough for them a little later. "Vala! Come! We're going for cake!"

"What's the celebration, Pausert?" asked Goth, grinning at his pleasure.

"Oh, my great uncle. He's semi-dead. And that means we don't have to pay any more of his debts. We didn't even have to pay the lawyer. He was very apologetic about it, Mum said. She insisted on paying him anyway."

Goth, whose own exchequer was running a little low, resolved to relieve him of that fee. A little later, Lina, for once prepared to talk about their personal affairs, filled in the gaps. Pausert had gone to fetch more tall glasses of caram, so it was just the two of them. "The Threbus Institute can't be sold, as it has various shareholders and wasn't a sole possession of my uncle's. But he owned several other businesses and some land. Even after the debts have been settled, I'll get a dividend. Not a fortune, but we don't need that. Pausert can go to the Space Naval Academy. I have a job until then."

"And then?"

"I'll be going back to the southwestern border zone of the Empire. The Duchy of Galm. To see if I can find some trace of what happened to Pausert's father." A flicker of sadness crossed her face. "We couldn't stay there, you know. Moreteen was a garrison town. Not a place needing a specialist like me. But I'll have a small income from the estate, and just myself to look after."

"He'll miss you," said Goth.

She shook her head. "He'll be too busy with a young lady of his own dreams to even notice. And what are your plans?"

That was a bit too close to the bone for comfort. Goth felt herself color. "My family are leaving at the end of the year. I...uh, they have done what they set out to do here."

"I'm sorry. You've done a lot for my boy."

"I won't forget him," said Goth gruffly.

Pausert's mother smiled, but sadly. "Sometimes it just doesn't work out."

CHAPTER 21

The precogs had said Goth would stay here for six months. At the time that had seemed like a very long time to her. Now, as the end neared, it seemed very short.

And what difference would it make? She could stay a year. Three years. Long enough to see him into the Nikkeldepain Space Naval academy—before leaving him to become affianced to the insipid Illyla. Deep in her heart, Goth knew that there was no point in staying on, as much as she wanted to.

What had started off as something a young girl had said, without fully understanding its meaning, had become a lot more tangible as time passed. She'd said that she was going to marry Pausert when she was of marriageable age. She'd even toyed with age shifts. Over the last couple of years or so, as they battled the Agandar, and then Moander and Manaret, and then the Nanite menace, she'd gone from simply liking the captain to assuming he was hers. Still, the age difference had remained a barrier, making the whole thing seem rather abstract.

But now . . . having encountered Pausert when he was her own age, she'd found she had a real crush on the young man he'd once been. She'd come back in time and space to save the captain. Now she really did not want to leave.

And she knew she'd have to. Vala was part of his childhood memories. If she'd stuck around . . .

Yes, logic said she had to go. But just a few more days?

Then came the news that changed it all.

A jailbreak.

Nikkeldepain remained a poor place for crime on any major scale, partly because of the culture of the colony, and partly because it had a very useful moon. Kaba was the ideal place for removing people from Nikkeldepain society and serving as a reminder of what could happen to those who broke the law here.

A grim mining penitentiary that no one had ever escaped from . . . until now. The breakout had been stunning in its unexpectedness and more stunning in its violence. The guards had been captured, tortured into cooperation, and then murdered along with the crew of the ore-freighter.

The escapees had landed at the spaceport and hijacked a small passenger vessel. They'd used the passengers as hostages and fled—and left more dead bodies in their wake. The somber announcer admitted that as they had fled into the beyond and been lost track of, there was little possibility of recapture.

The escapees were none other than the desperados captured by the brave Ziller during their raid on the Central Museum of Historical Nikkeldepain.

Goth decided that it was time she checked up on her old "friend" Franco.

She went light-shifted as a young woman of questionable virtue, with a bundle. Goth had been watching—with slightly more mature eyes—the people of Nikkeldepain. She looked like the sort of person that one could expect in this quarter, who might be accosted. But not with a bundle that looked like a baby.

When she knocked on Franco's door, the bundle had somehow become something else. Possibly stolen. And she'd changed her expression to one of furtiveness.

No one answered.

She knocked again.

And again.

Someone from inside said, "Go away."

Goth had learned—in order to do good light-shifts—to be very precise about remembering details.

That voice she remembered well. It was enough to make her nearly forget her current light-shift.

They hadn't fled the system. They were right here! Mebeckey had just spoken to her.

Goth turned and left.

It took her a while to gather her thoughts, but her first action was to check on the well-being of Pausert. She found him in the act of being spoken to on the street outside his home by a woman in a small runaround. Some instinct made her slip into no-shape to listen in.

He was looking at a photo-cube of her. "Vala?" Goth knew young Pausert well by now. In some ways he hadn't changed very much on growing up to become the captain, either. She could now detect the hesitation and slight change in tone when he ventured on those very rare lies. "I haven't seen her for a while, since the end of term. I believe she was going off-world with her parents."

"She has parents?" said the woman. Goth was almost certain it was Marshi. She had a peculiarly flat voice.

Pausert nodded. "I haven't seen much of them. They run an import/export company."

"Do you know its name?"

Pausert shook his head. "Nope. Don't think she ever said."

Goth waited, tense. If the woman gave any sign of wishing to harm Pausert...

"Thank you," she said mechanically, turning away.

"Sorry I couldn't help," said Pausert with equal insincerity.

The woman drove off.

Goth bit her lip, trying to decide what to do.

Pausert plainly had no such doubts. He was heading straight for her apartment. Goth ghosted along, making sure that he wasn't being followed by anyone else.

He knocked, and when he got no reply, turned away, his forehead knotted in a worried-puppy frown. Goth decided that she couldn't deal with his distress. She slipped in between two tall ornamental rechi trees and called him as he walked past.

"Vala?"

"Keep walking. Just wanted to tell you I'm fine. Keep to the story of my having left."

He hesitated briefly. And then determinedly kept walking. "I'll help."

"You already did. Really. I'll see you later."

He kicked a rechi cone, dribbled it around, like a bored teen. "What's up?"

"Stuff my parents do."

"I always wondered about that. But your mother seems nice. She's sort of like you. But always busy."

Goth wasn't surprised at his assessment. But all she said was: "I'll see you later."

He nodded and kicked the cone up the street. "Later."

Goth followed him. There was no guarantee there was no spy ray tracking him. There plainly wasn't one tracking her, or they would have found her.

She followed him home. Then, at a brisk walk, she set off for the old quarter of Nikkeldepain. Time for preemptive action.

It didn't take her long to get to Franco's den. If she had to 'port pieces of the door away...

But it wasn't necessary. The door was just ajar, swinging gently. Goth went inside, up the stairs.

The room bore mute testimony to the fight that must have happened. Franco's bodyguard had had his head severed neatly. It lay on a smoldering, tipped rack of used clothes, the eyes still wide and staring.

It took her a little while longer to find Franco. He was in the long unused bath in the bathroom. Unconscious, bleeding badly, and dying. They'd plainly tortured him, and he was lying in a pool of his own blood. She went back to the front room and used his communicator to call the emergency number. She gave the address and told them they needed the police and an ambulance flier.

Then she went back into the bathroom. The window was now bricked up, she noticed. That hadn't helped him. Franco opened his eyes, screwed them up, trying to focus.

"Emergency services are on their way," said Goth, keeping her voice and feelings firmly under control.

"I told them to lay off. I told them you had 'nections," Franco slurred. "She don't care. Not interested in you...thought I mus' have box, 'cause I said you'd been to see me. Illtraming..."

His eyes shut again, and his head lolled.

Goth wondered if the ambulance would be in time. And she wondered if the escaped prisoners had headed for Pausert. She decided that making sure of that was more important than any assistance she might give to Franco, or whatever more she might learn from him.

She'd pick up some stuff and camp out in Pausert's loft.

When she got back to her apartment and saw the door swinging, she realized that it was not Pausert that was their target.

She went in. And realized that she'd been a little too quick. There was still someone inside, and they'd heard her.

Hastily, she light-shifted into the form of an elderly woman. "I've called the police," she said sternly.

Marshi stepped out from the door she'd ducked behind. "Where is the girl, old woman?" she demanded, waving a blaster.

"They...they left," quavered Goth. "A few days ago. Same day as that jailbreak." At the same time Goth was trying something new. She'd split light-shifted images of herself before, leaving herself invisible between them. That was a trick she'd learned from the little vatch. Now she left a light-shifted image of herself standing in place, while she stepped aside in no-shape.

Just in time! Marshi shot the image. No warning, no compunction. Goth projected it crumpling as soon as she realized what was happening.

She'd been caught by surprise, so there was a noticeable lag between the image being shot and starting to fall. And there was the additional awkwardness that the effect of the blaster on the wall behind the image made it obvious to anyone observing carefully that there'd been nothing in the way.

Fortunately, however, Marshi had looked away the moment she fired the gun. That casual indifference to the effect of her own murderous action underscored Marshi's ruthlessness. But it was a ruthlessness so complete that it was also careless. Goth decided the woman wasn't really even sane.

"We need to get out of here," said Marshi. "She may actually have called the police."

Mirkon came into them room. "Where now? That Pausert kid? His mother?"

Marshi shook her head. "No point. They plainly scampered when they heard about us. I suppose we could check flight manifests, but I think false papers would be easy enough for this kind of operator."

"Or an unlisted flight. They happen, you know, if you've got the money."

"I think that's what we need to do ourselves. Get off-world, and use Mebeckey's money to find this woman. We've got a picture, we have finger and retina prints, we have DNA. We'll set up a search across every populated world if need be. Find her and we find the Illtraming."

"You make it sound important. More than money."

"More than life," said Marshi in her flat voice. "Now move."

They stepped over the light-shifted corpse, paying it no more attention than a carpet. Goth could only be glad that they hadn't stepped on it, which they were certainly callous enough to have done. An illusion of solidity would not have survived that.

When they'd gone, she went into her apartment to decide what to do next. They'd torn the place apart. Even the pillows had been slit.

Goth's first reaction was fury. This was her place and her stuff!

Once that passed, though, she was almost amused at the pointlessness of the wreckage. Not even with fingerprints, retina prints, pictures and DNA were they going to find Vala. Karres was not going to be a place they'd search!

They hadn't found her on Porlumma or Uldune, or Green Galaine. Or the Imperial capital. But somewhere, ten years in the future, the trail had come to life again. They were searching for Vala, still, and their precious box. But that was tramping around the Galaxy, with the *Petey, Byrum and Keep*. They wouldn't still be looking for her if they'd found it.

Nikkeldepain was now too hot for them. The attack on Franco and the killing of his bodyguard, coming right on top of the jailbreak, would have the Nikkeldepain police in an uproar for some time to come. But it wasn't likely they could get off the planet immediately, and in the meantime they'd surely be watching for Vala here. They'd be back.

Goth took a deep breath. It was time to go, as in her heart of hearts she'd known it was. But first she had to say good-bye to Pausert. And find some thick padding to wear on the Egger Route.

His first reaction was: "Whatever's going on, we'll deal with it." Goth came closer to understanding what Threbus had meant when he said that the community of Karres was a state of mind, not a state. Without meaning to, she hugged him. He looked a bit startled. He'd probably never been hugged by anyone apart from his mother before.

But he hugged her back. "No need to get upset," he said, trying his fourteen-year-old best to sound mature and like a real man.

"I'm not," said Goth, her voice a little gruff and choked. "It's dealt with. And you did the best thing ever, telling them I'd left. But it's good to know you'd stand by me."

He looked faintly surprised. "But you always stand by me."

Goth nodded. That was easier than talking around the lump in her throat. They stood there, awkwardly, looking at each other. "You remember me, see," Goth eventually said, wishing she had something more that she dared say. But he had hardly remembered her.

"Like anyone could ever forget you. Ever," he said, trying to smile. "You're really leaving, aren't you?"

Goth nodded again, knowing that talking wasn't going to happen. Not without her saying a great deal more than she should. Some of it about the insipid Illyla.

Then she could bear it no more. She wrapped her arms around him and kissed him. Hard. Then walked away without a glance backward. She knew if she looked back, she'd be lost.

For once the Egger Route was a welcome thing.

CHAPTER 22

Pausert watched the screens, trying to figure out the best possible next move.

The Phantom ships were definitely heading towards an englobement formation and seemed to be able to use their here/not-here nature to counter the speed advantage of the Sheewash drive. He was going to have to try something. The fact that they'd actually succeeded in hitting the Phantoms seemed to have made them even more determined to catch and destroy the *Venture*.

And then there was a distant droning sound. Pausert heaved a vast sigh of relief. That would be the Karres witches, thrumming down the Egger Route to the rescue. The bait had drawn the Phantom ships, which had, in turn, called Karres to his aid. The staccato humming came ever closer, the heavy sound filling his head, covering vast distances at incredible speed. Pausert went to fetch as many blankets as the *Venture* had in her store.

Perhaps they could tell him just where Goth had got to. She was supposed—by their own precogs—to spend at least a year in his company. She'd certainly not been in it for the last few weeks.

And then it stopped . . . and there in the middle of the floor was Goth. Goth bundled up in a turban, a hooded jacket and about four layers of clothing. Eyes unfocused, she turned over onto her knees. Pausert, knowing what was coming, hastily wrapped her up. Plainly the Leewit had been roused from sleep by the klatha sounds and came and helped him with rolling Goth up like a mummy. Mebeckey came in while they were busy, and exclaimed in puzzlement, "What's up?"

"Later," said the captain. Goth began to twitch. And jerk. And vibrate like a tuning fork. It took all the captain's strength to hold her still. By the sounds of it she was grinding her teeth and making small angry jungle cat noises. Well, at least she didn't screech like the Leewit did!

The shuddering slowed and the captain began unwinding. "Hurry up." said Goth. "Hot in here. I'm wearing too many layers of clothes."

They de-cocooned her, and a smiling Goth sat up. She hugged the captain and the Leewit together. "Kept the ship in one piece without me, I see."

She peeled off the hooded jacket. Then pulled off a towel-turban in a scatter of ringlets of wavy red hair.

Pausert looked at her, with his mouth open.

"What's up, Captain?" asked Goth quizzically. "You're looking at me like I suddenly grew another head."

He took a deep breath. "You did. Or at least another head of hair, Goth. Or should I say...Vala?"

"Wondered just how I was going to explain that to you."

"You might have told me."

"I only found out myself just before I left."

"I meant back then. I tried very hard to make contact with you again, but I couldn't find any trace of you or your parents. I was hoping you might write to me or something."

"I suppose I could have made a plan. But then you might not have got involved with that wet fish Illyla," said Goth, tartly. "I need to eat."

She looked at Mebeckey, standing nervously in the doorway. "Hello. Who is he?" she asked.

"A xenoarcheologist that got marooned out here," said the Leewit. "We rescued him from some wreck of a planet. Says his name is Mebeckey."

Goth stopped and put her hands on her hips. "Can't be. He's got the wrong face shape, even without the few face-hairs. And he's quite a lot shorter."

"What?" said Pausert warily.

Goth cocked her head on one side and jerked a thumb at the castaway. "Mebeckey. I don't know who this old guy is, but he's not Mebeckey the archeologist. Mebeckey the archaeologist was the fellow who tried to kill you back on Nikkeldepain. He was part of the crowd that kidnapped me, too. Although Franco says they were all under Marshi's control."

"Marshi?" said the castaway archeologist incredulously. "Is the monster woman still alive?"

"I reckon it's probable," said Goth. "What color was her hair?"

"Blond."

"Not the same woman, then. This one is as bald as an onion." Goth took a mug of cone-seed coffee from the Leewit, who had plainly been programming the robo-butler in preparation while the captain had been hauling blankets. "Got to have food too, Leewit. I don't think too much of the food back on Nikkelde-pain, Captain."

Pausert grinned. "You used to drink enough of that caram juice, though. Great Patham. Some of those incidents make sense now. Klatha tricks! I haven't thought about them for years!" He shook his head. "I can't say how glad I am to see you, Goth. I had quite a crush on you back then."

Goth was having enough problems with her own feelings right at the moment. She was delighted to see the captain again, and delighted to see Pausert also—and trying to merge the two people into one. It wasn't easy. She wished that the Leewit and this arbitrary stranger—who wasn't Mebeckey, whoever he thought he was pretending to be—would just go away and leave them to talk privately for a bit. "You did, huh?"

"It's very strange. You're Vala... But I'll swear you've shrunk. Yet for Goth you've grown."

"Grown, I reckon," said Goth, swallowing a mouthful of seed-cake. "Both of us. You were pretty short back then. Now, what's the problem, Captain?"

"We're being followed by some vessels. Phantom ships. They're trying for an englobement," said the Leewit. "I shot up two of them and the captain..." She glanced at Mebeckey. "He did some real hot-shot flying. But they've caught up with us again. Weird ships."

"Yeah? Well, I reckon you'd better have everyone strap in. Because we're going to do some more." said Goth. "Including you, mister whatever-your-name-really-is. Scram."

But the new supercargo did not move. "This person you call 'Mebeckey.' Was he a tall man with a hooked nose and white, spiky hair? A little goatee beard?"

"Pretty much, yes. Except no hair to speak of. The beard's a few wisps. Like you."

The man sighed. "That's my former first mate, Bocaj. He must have taken on my identity. How did you meet him? And how did you get here?"

"Enough questions," said Pausert. "Get to your stateroom and strap in. The Leewit, wake Vezzarn. We'll see if we can break out of this before they take action. Man those guns. Fire on my command!"

"Yes, sir!" said the Leewit happily. "Get on with it, Mebeckey," she said, pushing him down the passage. "There'll be time to answer questions later."

The captain smiled at Goth, almost shyly. "Not having you around here for a while has made me appreciate just how badly I need you."

"It worked both ways, Captain," said Goth. She was feeling a little shy herself. Not often that happened, huh!

They went to the chairs on the bridge and strapped in. "Didn't the Leewit take care of stuff?"

"She's been better than good. To the extent that I was quite worried about her," said the captain. "Even bathing by herself. Helping with everything. Working hard on the astrogation math. But ... I missed you, that was all. And even with the Sheewash drive we haven't been able to shake these ships. They're . . . well, at least most of the time they have no apparent mass. You can shoot them and it has no effect."

"But the Leewit got two?" asked Goth, smiling inwardly at his missing her.

Pausert nodded. "Just as they launch their missiles they become objects of mass. She had to time her firing right. They've kept at greater range since then. But they're following in greater numbers. And it seems like they're going try a classic englobement. Those torpedoes of theirs are slow, but the warheads are pretty bad news. And if they're all around us, we will get a radiation soaking that the hull-metal can't keep out, even if the Leewit shoots them well before impact. We may have to try the Egger Route with the whole ship . . ."

Goth shuddered. "It's a bit soon after the last time for me. Not good for the body, you know. Maybe if we worked the Sheewash together—all three of us?"

"Maybe if you explained how I'm supposed to do vectors in the Sheewash. I was all over the place on my own. Whizzing and bouncing about like a piece of popping corn in a closed pot. I must have wasted light-minutes of power."

Oddly, under the circumstances, Goth felt gleeful all of a sudden. All her unease at being back with the captain after six months with his younger self had vanished. They were a team. She just understood him better, now.

"Forward nova gun turret manned and ready for action," said the Leewit over the intercom.

Pausert clicked the bridge manual firing relays

off. "You have fire control, forward turret," he said formally. "Stern turret?"

"Stern turret ready too, Captain," said Vezzarn over the other channel. "Let's go get them. Only I hope we aren't going to fly so wild this time, Captain. It was all I could do not to lose my lunch, let alone keep shooting."

"We'll try a steep dive toward that star cluster there. The colorful one on the starboard bow. We're going to try to skim the gravity well of that white dwarf on—"

"Captain," interrupted Goth. "Do you recognize that star cluster?"

There was something familiar about it, about the reddish-brown dust haze of space debris and dust that hung about it, in the blackness of space. "I should," said Pausert. "I know I should. What is it, Goth?"

"I reckon it's the Megair cluster, Captain. From the other side."

Pausert looked again and nodded. "You're right. That's what . . . ? About four ship days from Uldune controlled space at normal cruising speed, I figure. I didn't realize we were this close to being on the far side of the Chaladoor."

"It's also a pretty bad neighborhood, Captain."

"We don't have a lot of choices, Goth."

"Guess not." She started assembling the wires as the Phantom ships edged closer. "I've seen those ships somewhere before. Weird shape they've got."

"Mebeckey said they were Melchin. Or maybe even Illtraming."

Goth paused in her laying out of the lattice of black wires. "Illtraming! That's what Marshi and her crew of thugs were looking for. The Illtraming map. And she said finding the Illtraming was more important than life."

Pausert tugged his chin. "There has to be a tie-in somewhere."

"They're closing on us, Captain," said the Leewit. "Nearly in firing range. And two more bandits coming in from twelve o'clock."

"Time to Sheewash," said Goth firmly. She reached out and took his hand. The wires rose and twined like snakes, forming a truncated cone. A ball of incandescent orange fire sparked into existence above it, roiling with wild energies. The *Venture* leapt like a stag and the starscape blurred. Distantly, the captain was aware of the nova guns with their shivering blue fire sheet-lightning. There was a burst of retina-searing amber incandescence to the portside. Chatter from the radiation meters.

"Got that torpedo a bit late, Captain," said Vezzarn apologetically.

"Keep firing!" yelled the Leewit.

The ridged, spiky hull of the Phantom alien ship was very close in the viewscreens, with them driving a straight line towards it, alive with the electromagnetic dance of the nova gun lightnings. Goth seemed to twitch them over at the last moment, sending them diving in an escape curve toward the Megair cluster, where the stars loomed out of the debris.

Debris at this speed would be hard to dodge. But then they were among them, jinking . . . and the Sheewash pattern wires collapsed. "Can't do it too long, Captain. Tired after the Egger Route," said Goth.

She looked exhausted. Pausert still could not get over the fact that he'd never realized that Goth had looked like Vala. One just didn't see what one didn't expect to see.

Abstractly, he understood what had happened. When he'd first met Goth, she'd been only ten years old. Very intelligent, precocious—sometimes even disturbingly so—but also clearly still a child.

Vala and the Goth of today, on the other hand...

Uncomfortably, Pausert finally accepted something he'd been almost studiously ignoring for months now. More than three years had passed since he met Goth, and she was well into puberty by now. Her figure was still girlishly lean, but there was no longer any way she could possibly be mistaken, even at a distance, for a boy.

Neither could Vala—and, for the Pausert of the time, a fourteen-year-old boy who was himself undergoing puberty, that had made for a very different emotional introduction. Years had passed, and the memory of what Vala had actually looked like had gotten fuzzy. Between that, and the red hair, and most of all meeting the two girls on either side of puberty, he could understand why he'd never spotted the identity. As Goth had changed, in the years she'd been with him, he hadn't seen her growing resemblance to Vala. She'd just been Goth...growing up.

And grown up a lot more than he'd realized! The kiss that Vala had given him as she left was something he'd never forgotten. Now, it came with a real jolt to realize that for Goth—today's Goth—that kiss had happened just yesterday.

He wondered for a moment if their looks had had anything to do with that fateful decision so long ago now, back on Porlumma, when he'd rescued the witches of Karres. Being fair to himself, though, probably not.

He didn't like to see anyone abused. Anyway, he'd already rescued Maleen and the Leewit before he'd even set eyes on Goth.

Not long after he'd met Goth, she'd announced her intention to marry him once she reached marriageable age—which was sixteen for the people of Karres. Pausert hadn't taken the whole thing seriously, of course. At the time, the difference between ten years of age and sixteen had seemed enormous. But it came with another jolt to realize that more than half that time had already elapsed.

And Goth still seemed as determined as ever.

As for Pausert... He really hadn't ever been able to forget that kiss.

He wasn't ready to deal with this. It was almost with relief that he forced his mind aside to deal with the perilous situation of the moment.

"Not too safe here anyway," he said, untwining his fingers from hers and taking control of the ship. The Sheewash drive was plainly not a "drive" so much as some kind of sequence of tiny jumps through space-time, because it left the *Venture* far ahead of the pack of Phantom ships, but also with no extra velocity. The captain pushed his throttles forward, causing the *Venture* to increasingly shake and sway because of the roughly aligned repaired tube.

"She doesn't feel so good, Captain," said Goth. "You think we got hit back there?"

"No, we had a run-in with a space rock earlier. Broke a tube-bracket. We did a repair job on the cinder-block world we found Mebeckey on. The alignment's not perfect, I'm afraid. I just hope it's a good enough weld."

Goth cracked an enormous yawn. "Sorry. It's been a very long, full day for me. Back on Nikkeldepain and here."

"Sleep a bit. I'll call if I need you," said the captain, keeping a wary eye on a cloud of shattered rocks that was showing on one of the screens. The dust in the system made guiding the ship even more difficult, hanging in drifting curtains obscuring both the view and the instrument detection. On the positive side, the same factors should make it a good place to hide and evade pursuit—which was probably why the Megair Cannibals used this system themselves.

Then Pausert looked at the rear-screens and realized how wrong he was. He had to dodge space debris—but Phantom ships appeared to go straight through them. And whereas the *Venture* had been dealing with twelve in the englobement, there were more of them now. Far more.

At the same time, he noticed that they did appear to avoid the really, really big rocks—anything with enough mass to have a gravity field worth mentioning. He got that gambler's feeling, the prickle on the back of his neck, that he'd come to realize was a klatha sense too. This was valuable information for Karres. The intangible Phantoms didn't take to gravity. That was why they'd avoided worlds. Some kind of gravity tractor would make a weapon against them.

Goth gave a quiet little snuffly snore from the control chair next to him. "The Leewit," he said quietly into the intercom. "Can you bring Goth a blanket? I think you can stand down from the guns. I've got to keep a look-out for obstacles."

"Sure thing, Captain. I got a couple more. You got

to anticipate them," said the Leewit gleefully. "I'm glad to have Goth back. It was hard being told I had to be responsible for you on my own."

Which, Pausert was ready to bet, was exactly what Goth had told her to be. That explained the un-Leewit-like behavior. He smiled to himself. It was a question of perspective, he supposed. He'd had the delusion that he was the one being responsible for them. Oh well, it worked both ways. He concentrated instead on the crowded region of space ahead. A couple of light-hours away was a reasonable sized world with a slew of moons and a series of rings. If the Phantoms didn't like gravity, that would be a good place to hide up and rest. He really didn't want to push the *Venture* too far on that slightly misaligned tube. The vibration would probably shake loose something else, let alone break his weld.

"They're coming up fast, Captain." said the Leewit quietly, leaning over his chair while Goth slept in the one next to him.

"I know. And I'm going to have to cut the throttle a bit. Look at the telltales. Tube seven, the one we repaired the stanchions for, is overheating. Must be the effects of the vibration. I'll have to throttle down soon or she'll blow. And to keep us running in a balanced fashion, I'll need to cut the throttle on tube three by the same amount."

"Could correct a bit with the laterals," said the Leewit, showing that she'd absorbed a great deal in the time that her sister had been away.

"Yep." The captain's hands moved over the controls, adjusting throttles. "Means we can still keep the other

seven at full thrust for a bit, but dodging rocks...
well, it's a recipe for disaster."

The Leewit grinned. "Disasters are what we deal
with best on the *Venture*. We going to Sheewash
again?"

Pausert shook his head. "If we can get into the
gravity well of that fourth planet from that greenish
star before they get close enough, we can rest up a
bit. With all three of us doing it, we can try. Dodging
debris while doing the Sheewash is even harder. But
we're just four light-days from the edge of Uldune's
space sphere of influence. I'll be pretty glad to see it."

"Yeah. Turn this lot of spooks into a Sedmon of the
Six Lives problem," said the Leewit. "They just keep
right on coming, Captain. I hit the one ship pretty
hard. It's almost as if they don't care."

"They're keeping a greater distance, though. So
something must have got them a bit wiser."

"Uh huh. But give me targets that I just have to
aim for and hit. Not things where it doesn't matter
most of the time."

Pausert smiled to himself. The Leewit was very glad
to have her older sister back, to hand over responsibility
again. But listening to her, Pausert wondered if she
realized that it had been a one-way street that she'd
walked down. She could never go back to being quite
the little hooligan that she'd been before, no matter
how much she still *looked* the complete blonde urchin.

They reached the upper edge of the gravitational
tug of the mass of the greenish-white world below,
and Pausert was happy to discover that his gambler's
instinct had been right. The Phantom ships that had

been steadily gaining on them began to drop back as they got closer to the planet.

It must be a gloomy place, Pausert thought. It had a good eighty-five percent cloud-cover. The clouds, of course, reflected the light of the local sun, giving their white tops a greenish tinge.

Goth stirred in her chair, possibly the change in note from the *Venture's* tubes getting through to her. "Boy, I could murder some breakfast," she said, stretching. "What's up, Captain? Where are those . . . Melchin . . . Illtraming ships? That is weird, you know. The guys I was protecting you from back on Nikkeldepain—did you ever guess you nearly got kidnapped? They ended up taking me as bait for you. They'd been to search the old *Venture 7333*. She's been this way before."

Pausert nodded. "I found star maps. That's how we ended up stopping on the world we picked Mebeckey up at. They indicated that the ship had made a safe landing there. Right now we're hanging just inside the stratosphere of one of the worlds in this cluster. The Phantoms don't like gravity. We can rest and recuperate a little before we need to use the Sheewash drive to get out of here again."

"Had. Yeah. I reckon that place you stopped at . . . that must be where Threbus picked up the Illtraming map they were so busy looking for. It was inside your home. With the other bric-a-brac Threbus left behind there."

"Lucky we didn't sell it. We were pretty hard up when you arrived on Nikkeldepain."

Goth smiled. "And all because Threbus chose to fake his death and disappearance from the same part of space where your father also happened to go missing.

A coincidence, but it made life pretty tough for you. I must say I'm sorry on my father's behalf. I'd like to have told you then. But I couldn't, of course."

"I bet whoever tried to kidnap you regretted it," said Pausert. "I only wish I'd known. Back then I would have thought it was enormous fun."

"They were a tough bunch of crooks," said Goth. "And they're still out there if the information I've got is correct."

An alarm sounded from the detectors.

Pausert looked at his screens. "We're under attack!" he yelped, hitting the throttles.

Goth strapped herself in again. "The Leewit, strap in! I thought you said the Phantoms wouldn't come this close to a gravity well, Captain."

"This is not the Phantoms," said Pausert, putting the ship into a steep dive. "The attack's coming from below!"

The Leewit had stood down from her guns. The captain flicked control of them to Goth, moving the firing relays to her board. Below, rising rapidly out of the greenish clouds, were two atmospheric craft. There was something vaguely insectlike to the design.

"Fire at will," said the captain, banking sharply. "I'm sorry, Goth. I think we just came for a lovely rest in the Megair Cannibals' back yard."

Red balls of fire leapt toward them.

Goth and Vezzarn answered fire, and the captain flung the *Venture* toward the clouds, looking to use the gravity to add to the ship's thrust.

More atmospheric craft came boiling their way out of the clouds like a seethe of roaches.

"Going to have to go Sheewa—"

Something hit the *Venture* with a terrible bang, and the old pirate-chaser spun out of control, hurtling downwards, no thrust coming out of her stern tubes at all. Pausert fought for control as they plunged down through the cloud. He tried, desperately, for reignition in the tubes. Nothing. He hit the laterals, and was rewarded by a burst of power from them. The winds tore and buffeted at the ship as the captain tried vainly to slow her descent. But he just didn't have enough power.

Inside the control room there was a storm of debris blowing about, and a white mist of icy air. Hull integrity must have been lost. A good thing they were losing altitude—a bad thing that they were losing it so fast.

"Vezzarn here, Captain," said the old spacer over the intercom. "I've managed to get to the engine room, Captain. The main interfacer unit has blown, sir!"

"Get strapped in, Vezzarn. This is going to be a rough landing." Pausert began hastily rerouting control through to the test firing circuits. Testing wasn't run through the main interface system. It was also not meant to be run in more than ten-second bursts. He was going to have to set the *Venture* down, manually firing her tubes in ten-second sequential bursts. If he could slow down their descent enough, he could set the *Venture* down on her laterals.

That was going to take all his skill as a pilot to do it.

It didn't help that someone was shooting at them at the same time.

CHAPTER 23

The ground was coming up entirely too fast. Goth saw how, face impassive, intent with concentration, Captain Pausert fired the main tubes in a sequential burst sending the *Venture* corkscrewing but slowing. Their plunge to the gray-green vegetation slowed. The *Venture* swung over onto her side, and the captain fired the laterals on full thrust.

With a rush of cracking and hissing, the *Venture* 7333 settled onto the trees, and then lurched and fell. The captain fired the laterals again and the *Venture* came to a final rest on the surface with little more than a dull thump.

"We're down," said Pausert with relief. They were certainly neck deep in trouble, but at least they were down. That in itself was a huge weight off his shoulders.

"Neat flying, Captain," said Goth. Other congratulations came in over the intercom, from the Leewit, Vezzarn, and in a shaky voice from Mebeckey.

Pausert unclipped from his webbing. "Touch and go, at times. I better go and see if we've got spare parts for the drive sequencer, or if I can rig some kind of manual override. And we need to find out where the hull integrity is breached. We're not leaving here, Sheewash or no, without fixing that. With luck, it is something we can weld a patch onto."

Goth got up and followed him. "The locals might not be too pleased to see us. After that reception, they seem more likely to go after us with a space-gun than offer us the use of their shipyards."

He nodded. "We'll just have to deal with them as they arrive. Do you think we can do anything with a light-shift? The little I saw of the local landscape, it didn't seem like the most populated of places."

"Looked like a cross between a forest and a swamp. With the worst parts of both," said Goth. "I'll check it out."

"They can probably find us with an instrument search," said Pausert. "The hull-metal must be pretty hot. And then there is radiation off our tubes. But let's not make it easy for them."

"They sure didn't seem too friendly."

"No," said Pausert. "I think we may have jumped out of the deep-space frying-pan and into the planetary fire. I think—looking at the design of those ships—this world might be not just the back yard, but the base of our old enemies, the Megair Cannibals."

Goth whistled. "Just the perfect place to crash-land, huh? Okay, you see if you can get anywhere with

the sequencer. I'll stay here. Check out the screens
to see what sort of light-shift I need to do, and I'll
test the atmosphere. We're still alive breathing it, but
who knows whether we'll be able to go on doing that
indefinitely."

"Good thinking. Keep the Leewit on the nova guns—
she's uncannily good—and get Vezzarn and Mebeckey
looking for breaches in hull integrity." He squeezed
her shoulder. "I can't tell you how good it is to have
you back, even if we're straight into a deeper mess."

Goth found herself smiling, despite the disaster.
"We're alive, Captain. And we have three witches
of Karres. What's a mere Cannibal's planet to that?"

Pausert made his way down to the engine-room,
trying not to get too upset by the mess that the conflict
had made of the *Venture.* It could be repaired if they
got out of here. *Not if. When*, he said determinedly
to himself.

Big dream thing, said the littlest vatch, **life
around you is fun. More exciting even than the
dreamplays.**

"Hello. I didn't know you were still with us," said
Pausert with a sort of calm resignation. After all, a bit
of little-vatch mischief was fairly harmless compared
to the situation they were in. It could make things
worse, of course. But it might also help. There was
nothing to be gained by getting upset with it.

**Been here and gone. I talk to the Leewit.
Learning quite a lot about you, big dream thing.**

Via the Leewit, that could be a mixed blessing,
thought Pausert. But all he asked was: "There are no
big vatches around, are there?" One of those could

take them out of here easily enough, once Pausert got klatha hooks into it.

There came a tinkle of vatchy laughter. **Big ones near you? I don't think so! They know your mind's taste by now. Not going to come close. Different for us little ones.**

"Pity. Oh well, I'll have to try and fix the engines and the hull then. Fight our way out, if we have to."

This seemed to amuse the vatchlet. **Never dull around you, big dream thing**, it said, and vanished.

Pausert was left alone to squeeze into the crawlspace behind the electronics banks of the main sequencer. The air stank of burning back here. The captain sighed. He let klatha-energy guide his hands towards which modules to pull. Three of them were almost totally fried and hard to get out of their sockets. Even with the little long-necked atomic lamp, the captain found he couldn't see well enough to read the module numbers in there. Besides, he'd have to get them from the stores—if they had them at all. You couldn't carry everything, and sequencers—the link between the spacedrive and the tubes—didn't often go wrong. The captain was worried. It was a long way to the nearest human spaceport and spare-parts shop.

With two of the three they were lucky. They were standard T-071 units, processors the ship used in half a dozen places. The third...

Pausert stifled a curse. The third was a multiplier link, and he knew already that they didn't have one. The things were virtually indestructible bits of solid-state hardware. This one was probably as old as the ship itself. It would have survived almost anything except a solid—and obviously white hot—fragment of Megair shell. That must have been what caused the hole in the hull-metal. He was standing there, biting his lip, trying to think if he'd ever read how you could do without a multiplier link. It was such a little thing, barely the size of a book—and without it, the ship was helpless.

Vezzarn coughed. "Found the hole, Skipper. Punched straight through the outer hull, into the hold, into the sequencer housing. Dunno what it hit in there or if it kept going."

"It stopped here." Pausert showed him.

"That's the multiplier link, eh?"

"Yes. That's what it is. And no, we don't have a spare. And, no, I don't think it is fixable. The ship is stuck here, unless they find us."

"The Cannibals or the Wisdoms?"

"Now there is the question! I don't know."

But Pausert's mind was already working on the idea of taking the *Venture* down the Egger Route, away from here—no matter how the other two felt about the Egger Route.

The intercom squawked into life. "Captain. We got visitors."

"Get patching, Vezzarn. If we can patch it quick enough, we can get the ship out of here." Pausert made haste back to the control room. Goth had the external screens on. The view outside was a bubbling swamp with the mud plainly at half viewscreen level. The *Venture* lay next to some tall lobate trees of a peculiarly virulent shade of maroon—but that could just be the light. Between the cloud—which here was more like a swirling mist—and the faint light of the green sun, this was not a very attractive piece of real estate. Goth pointed to the upper screens. "Some kind of flier, Captain. I've light-shifted us, but they're keeping station."

It was. With its two clumsy whirling rotors and spikes that could only be some kind of weaponry, it was making a slow circle, cutting swathes through the mist. "Want me to bring it down, Captain?" said the Leewit.

"Um. Just before we do too much..." said Goth. "The mud on the screens is rising. Or, to put it another way, the *Venture* is sinking. Fast."

As Pausert looked out of the viewscreen, a lanky gray-skinned being stepped into sight and then slipped behind one of the lobular trees. The creature held what was plainly some sort of weapon. It looked like it fired the cruelly barbed harpoon that protruded from the barrel. Worse still, it had been talking into a communicator.

Moments later, a flat sledlike craft slipped into view, with half a dozen of the gray creatures on board. They took cover, except for the one gray man who took careful aim with some sort of heavy weapon on the sled.

"I guess there's not much point to light-shifted images of the ship as jungle foliage, then." said Goth disgustedly. "They must have the tubes' radiation pinpointed."

"More ships coming," said the Leewit. "Big 'uns."

That was an understatement. There were nine of them, discharging a truly impressive number of armed gray men. And now a large armored hover-carrier was sliding above the trees, guns pointed at the *Venture*.

"We're getting something on external sound, Captain. Nearly loud enough to make the hull-plates vibrate."

"What are they saying, the Leewit?" asked Pausert.

The littlest witch answered over the intercom, seconds later. "They say we're for coming out. Or they're for boiling the mud and precooking us, before they're for cutting open the hull, and for coming in and eating us. Shall I fry a few of them first?"

The captain sighed. "No. I don't think we could hold off long enough to take the ship down the Egger Route. What if we do a quick Sheewash hop out of here? We can't get too far—not off-world—because we have a hole in the hull and no real use of the main drive. But it could buy us time."

Goth nodded. "Let's do it," she said, reaching into the drawer for the wires.

The carrier above loosed off a bolt of red energy, sizzling the mud. The Leewit replied with a nova gun burst as the *Venture* leapt clear of the glutinous steaming muck in a burst of speed that left the charges of the Megair exploding far behind them. A brief second of Sheewash, and the captain used the laterals again to set her down in what looked like a glade, several hundred miles away.

"Scary stuff, Captain!" said Goth. "The drive's not really for use so close to solid objects. We hit the ground or even these soft trees while moving at this speed and it's going to turn us into jelly."

"Still, we must have shaken them off. If we can just get a patch on the hull, we can out of here. We're going to be in subradio range of Uldune pretty quick using nothing but the Sheewash. I'd rather not try to take the *Venture* down the Egger Route again."

"Too clumping right!" said the Leewit. "You aren't safe doing that. But I could probably do it with Goth."

"Uh, Skipper," said Vezzarn over the intercom. "There's mud coming in the hole, and I can't stop it. I can't put a patch onto the hull unless we get out of this stuff and we manage to get the surface really, really clean. It'd be best put on from the outside, I reckon."

Pausert looked out at the viewscreens. They were settling even faster into what he had taken for a meadow. And there was a Megair atmospheric chase craft bearing down on them already. It wasn't one of those they'd fled earlier, but a larger vessel.

"I don't think we're going to get the chance. We're going to have to abandon ship, I'm afraid."

"More ships coming, Captain," warned the Leewit. "They must have a real hot-shot planetary defense system."

"I guess eating travelers does tend to make people want to come to your planet and exterminate you," said Pausert wryly. "Now the question is, can we take the Egger Route out with the ship holed?"

Goth shook her head. "The hole is not the issue, Captain. It's—"

"Great Patham!" said the Leewit. "They have some kind of gravity tractor on us. They're lifting the *Venture*!"

The ship pulled free of the clinging mud with a resounding plop.

"And now?"

Pausert took a deep breath. "Now we play it by ear. Let's get ready to go Sheewash—it could be interesting with that tractor on us."

"Would be possible but exhausting, Captain," said Goth. "Couple of Karres operatives got caught by a Megair ship. They don't eat their catch at once. So they had time to teach those Cannibals a lesson or three. We could stall for time ourselves, maybe, long enough to fix the *Venture.*"

"Are they human, Goth?"

"Hard to say, Captain. If we have it right, they're humans as humans would have been if things had been a whole lot different."

Pausert took a deep breath. "Okay. Then we play things by ear. If they start to try to cook us, we'll take them for a Sheewash ride."

The *Venture* hit against the large floater with a clang. The ship began moving off.

"Hopefully they're taking us somewhere dry," said Pausert, as they moved through swirling cloud and rain.

"I think that'd have to be off-world," said Goth.

"Looks like it. In the meanwhile, let's see if we can get some kind of patch on that hole, even if it's not a perfect seal. If need be, we can all put on pressure suits and then look for a moon to go and repair it."

"I'll go, Captain. You stay here and watch 'em."

For a moment Pausert nearly demurred. But then he realized that if he couldn't trust Goth, he couldn't trust anyone. And she'd grown noticeably, too. For him, she'd only been gone a few weeks. But for her, he'd gathered, something like six months had passed. She'd always been quick to take on responsibility, but this was a new Goth moving out of childhood and becoming his equal. He rather liked it, actually. As Vala, she'd been the one leading him, he reflected, thinking back.

A little later, as the big Megair floater continued to fly with them, now escorted by several atmospheric craft, Goth came on the intercom. "Next time, let's not set down in the mud," she said. "It's patched, Captain. It's not space tight, but it's the best we can do. We'll lose pressure. But it shouldn't be any worse than the door-seal damage from the pirate-Imperials fight. We could manage a day or so, for sure. Going to take longer than that to get the mud out of here. It's sprayed all over."

"Now all we need is the chance to get away."

"After our last little hop, I reckon they'll be quite cautious about that."

"I could stick my head out the airlock and whistle at them a little," said the Leewit. Her whistles had shattering effects on solids—and people. "I reckon I could bust that grav-tractor up good. They have resonance crystals in them."

"Wait until they're not expecting trouble," said Goth.

"I'm just a sweet little girl," said the Leewit cherubically.

"Yeah, but they like them sweet, young and tender. They make better eating."

A few minutes later, the Megair floater began settling toward a rocky plateau. It was rain-swept and gray-green lit, but for Megair 4 it was probably prime real estate. Nikkeldepain wasn't as beautiful as Karres, but it was a long step up on this place. You could see, by the instruments, if not through the rain, that a large number of other craft were converging on the landing ground. It was already quite crowded, and off on one edge was a testimony to the Megair Cannibals' normal piracy—a junkyard of wrecked Empire ships. On the opposite edge, the Megair spaceport was dominated by a squat hill, which was studded with pill-boxes.

"They've got at least fifteen different types of space-guns there," said the Leewit professionally, examining the protruding muzzles—most of which were pointed at the *Venture*. "I recognize some of them."

Goth peered with narrowed eyes. "Yeah. This is the Cannibal nest, all right. Furnished with their loot."

"It's a good spot for a lair," said the captain thoughtfully. "This cluster could be defended quite easily. They'd know where all the rocks are and could put weaponry on the moons. And they could be on any one of twenty planets orbiting five stars. The only way we could get here was with an escort of those Phantom ships. And by all accounts I've heard, the Cannibals keep their piracy down to attacks on occasional ships. Not like the Agandar."

"Yes," said Mebeckey, who had come out of his stateroom and was peering nervously around. "But they've been at it for a lot longer, Captain. And with the Agandar, there was at least a chance of ransom. The Megair pirates eat their catch. Is there nothing we can do?"

"We'll certainly try to do something," said Pausert.

"If you'd eaten less of my Wintenberry jelly," said the Leewit, "you'd still be skinny and unappetizing."

Mebeckey tugged his hair. "How can you be so calm? Don't you understand? They're *Cannibals*."

"I have the captain and Goth here. We've been in worse messes," said the Leewit stoutly.

"Actually," said Pausert, "we might learn a thing or two from those incidents. In the meantime, I suggest you get some rain-gear and warm clothing. It's both cold and wet out there. Goth—a word in your ear. You too, the Leewit. Off you go, Mebeckey. I know I gave you one of those allweather cloaks I had left over."

When the xenoarcheologist had gone, Pausert closed the door. "I still don't trust him as far as I can throw him. He has a bad habit of sneaking about. I think we want to keep the Karres stuff under our hats. He's already seen a bit too much, with you arriving. Goth, if you and the Leewit go no-shape..."

"Won't work, Captain. We need to talk to them, and the Leewit is the only one who can do that for you."

The smaller, blonde witch nodded. "But you go no-shape, Goth. We'll tell that old snoop you've gone again."

Pausert nodded. "A secret ace in the hole. That's good. And don't forget old Vezzarn. He's a good lock-tickler. Now get yourselves some warm gear." The captain pointed at the readout on the control panel. "It really is cold and miserable out there."

"And they're trying to talk to us again, Captain," said Goth. "On the communicator screen." Goth abruptly wasn't there. "I'll get you both something warm and waterproof," said a voice from midair.

The face staring out of the screen was lean, gray-skinned, red-eyed and feral-looking. When it spoke, its teeth showed. They were distinctly filed into points. The speech came across to the captain as a series of guttural croaks, an odd set of clicks and a sibilant whistle. But Pausert was not surprised when the Leewit answered in the same fashion.

"They say we're for coming out and behaving ourselves. Guns are locked on to us. If they have to come and fetch us, we're for eating alive. If we behave and answer their questions, they'll let us die first. I said we weren't for eating."

The speaker appeared to be having trouble swallowing that one. It took it a good few moments before it spoke.

"It says all life is food. What shall I tell it?"

"Say we'll give it indigestion," said Pausert. "Tell it it would be very wise to help us fix the damage it did to our ship and let us go."

There was a longer pause. Then another burst of croaks and clicks. "It wants to know how we know the holy language. And it says we're for coming out now because they will start opening the ship up with lasers if we don't. What do we do, Captain?"

Pausert took a deep breath. "Go out, I reckon. If they open up with those space-cannon, they can cut the old *Venture*'s hull open like paper."

"And then?"

"I wish I knew. But we'll work it out. We have to," said Pausert with a confidence he did not feel. He could protect them all with the klatha force cocoon that he'd learned to make, except he'd also have to remain at liberty to free them later. But it was plain the Megair Cannibals wanted them alive, at least at the moment. They wanted to ask them questions. Well, Pausert had a few himself. And he still had a few tricks up his sleeve. His gambler's instinct said that going out of the *Venture* was dangerous, but less dangerous than staying here would be. "Tell them we're coming. Tell them the ship is booby trapped, and to leave it alone. And then let's go."

So they collected the very nervous Mebeckey, and the less nervous Vezzarn. "What about the other young lady?" asked Mebeckey.

"Gone back where she came from," said Pausert.

"Ah." Mebeckey looked relieved only for a minute. "They'll find her. We should have fought."

"You leave the decisions to me," said Pausert,

aware that something invisible had taken his hand. He gave it a brief squeeze. And he relled the baby vatch too. Well, it would probably enjoy them being eaten. After all, it described people by taste. He had a feeling that that didn't mean quite the same thing to vatches, though.

They opened the airlock and lowered the gangway. Megair 4 was, if anything, more bleak and miserable in reality than it was on the viewscreens. That was quite an achievement, Pausert thought. The gray-skinned Cannibal squad that came across to the *Venture* at a dogtrot seemed unperturbed by it. Other than small leather loincloths and belts plainly intended for the weaponry that dangled from them, the Cannibals wore nothing but a layer of wetness. They didn't even seem to notice being wet, let alone the chill breeze. The bulbous things in their hands were plainly guns of some sort, Pausert decided.

The lead gray-face spoke in their odd code of croaks.

"What did he say? Come this way, we have a nice fire and hot drinks, while we fix your ship?" said Pausert, with an attempt at a smile.

"He said 'Meat, walk or be butchered,' " said the Leewit.

"Nice people, the Megair Cannibals," said Pausert sardonically.

"Yeah. Can I whistle at him? Just a little? I've got one you can't actually hear. Does some neat stuff."

"Save it for whoever sent him."

The Leewit wrapped her hand in his other one. He had a Karres witch on both sides now. "You have some pretty good ideas sometimes, Captain," she said.

Escorted by the gray squad of Megair Cannibals,

they walked across towards the pill-box-studded hill.
As they got closer, the squad leader gave a whistle
of his own. A complicated one. It might have been
less destructive than the Leewit's, but it did make two
massive doors set into the front of the hill slide open.
They walked forward into the dim green-lit passage.
"Cheerful looking place, isn't it, Captain?" said Vezzarn,
his sharp little eyes darting about, taking in details.

The walls were a polished stone, smooth, but with
regular panels of intricate carvings to shoulder height.
Above that, the constructors seemed to have run out
of patience and just roughly hewed it. "I'm surprised
they don't try to market it as a vacation destination,"
said Pausert as they came to a halt in front of yet
another massive door. The leader of the squad whistled
again with a slightly different series of notes.

That door opened. Inside, on couches that looked
as if they might be carved from stone, lounged several
of the gray-skinned ones—only these all wore collars
of leather, ornamented with hanging bits of bone,
spreading out onto their chests.

The escorts licked their sharp teeth and bowed
their heads respectfully.

The croak and whistle ensued.

"He says the meat has been brought for the masters of devouring," whispered the Leewit. "He says
the little one is for his share."

"If he tries, you can do as much whistling as you
please," said the captain quietly.

One of those who lounged about looked rather like
the one who had spoken to them earlier. He grunted
something that was plainly a curt dismissal.

The squad leader paused briefly and snarled. And

then hastily turned away, backed off to the doorway, and waited.

The high Megair Cannibals stared at them, red-eyed and unblinking. Then one of them spoke imperiously.

"What's he say?" asked the captain.

"He says they have waited to capture one of our kind for a long time. We're for answering questions. He wants to know: Why are we keeping them from their prey?"

"What?"

The Megair Cannibal leader let loose with another collection of grunts and whistles and a small shriek.

"He says they're for examining our ship and finding out how we cannot be shot. He says he's for driving us out of the Megair cluster. He says we're for talking, spilling all our secrets. He says they're for destroying us."

Pausert rubbed his forehead. "Great Patham! Has he ever got the wrong end of the stick. They must think we're the one of the Phantoms. Tell him that, please."

The Leewit let loose with her own collection of grunts, whistles and shrieks. And got a reply that Pausert guessed the content of by the tone, even before the Leewit translated.

"He's not for believing us," said the Leewit. "He says put us in the fattening pens. They're for examining the ship and finding our secret. And for dining on one of us tonight. Alive."

CHAPTER 24

Goth found no-shape in the rain was actually one of the most difficult things she had ever had to do. Light was easy enough to bend around her. But the constant, moving raindrops meant that there appeared to be a Goth-shaped piece of rain doing the wrong thing. She had to light-shift raindrops onto it. It was tiring and took a lot of concentration.

Going inside the Megair fortress was at least a relief from that. Of course no-shape had its usual problems there too. People didn't know you were there, and the entire burden of avoiding collisions fell on you. Not to mention the fact that nothingness should not leave wet footprints. Fortunately, those mingled nicely with the rest of the wet footprints. She seriously considered the possibility of becoming, via light-shift, one of the guards. But it was the Leewit who could understand them and speak their language, not her.

Besides, this place was making her feel really, really weird. As if she was having some kind of hallucination. She worked out what it was, after a time. It was touching the walls. Peculiar . . . hope. Abject terror. Small furry animals with too many limbs . . .

Goth shook herself. She didn't have time for this right now. She held the captain's hand and walked into the chamber full of Megair muck-a-mucks, lounging about and staring.

She let go of the captain's hand and moved about, exploring the room. Always learn as much about your opponent as possible, Threbus said.

There was a limited amount to be learned here, other than the fact that the ceiling was quite low. She noticed that the guards had to stoop slightly. This was plainly just a meeting room. All she could say, feeling the surface of the couches, was that the Megair Cannibals didn't go in for creature comforts much. They were exactly what they looked like. Stone. Carefully indented, polished and carved stone, but still as hard as rock. The only other things the room contained of interest were vast screens up on one wall. They appeared to show the map of Megair 4 and tiny moving lights—presumably atmospheric craft—moving across its face.

She listened to the Leewit's translation of the croaks and whistles, and the last comment.

She was lucky not to be cut when the vast screens shattered and fell into fragments. Looking at the Leewit's face, Goth was sure that it had been one of her newest whistles, and that she was quite pleased with it.

The Megair Cannibals weren't. There was a lot of

noise, shouting, croaking and yelling—but the end result was two things. One was that Goth got knocked tail over teakettle by a running Megair Cannibal guard. The other was that the prisoners were hustled out of there.

It took Goth a few moments to get to her feet and try to set off after them, only to discover the heavy doors of the Megair bunker had shut.

They plainly thought they were under attack, realized Goth. Well, they were. Just not in the way they thought.

She had a long and fairly boring wait before she could set off to look for the others. That was when things got really complicated, as she realized that she had absolutely no idea where they'd been taken. She was alone inside the Megair mound with the locals running about as if they were a colony of ants stirred up by a big stick. To make matter worse, she couldn't understand a word—or a croak or a click or a whistle—that they were saying. And no-shape meant keeping out of their way. Eventually she got tired of it. She found a quiet corner and light-shifted to look like one of the lordly ones who had questioned them, complete with the thoracic collar of wire and finger-bones. She found the other Megair Cannibals avoided her. That helped in some respects. It just didn't get her any closer to finding the others. She went deeper. Found some strange places—a vast indoor arena—she wouldn't have thought that the Megair Cannibals were in the least interested in the performing arts, as Dame Ethy would have put it—and other rooms with loot that she recognized—a fire control center, plainly using looted computer elements that must have come from ships plying Empire space. A communications center. Other areas were more mysterious. And the lower

she went down the ramps, the more Megair Cannibals there were with the same collars. After a while
it occurred to her why. In most places, deeper was
where the dungeons were. Here, deeper was where
it was safer and warmer—for the more important
people. Here, the prisoners would not be deeper...
they'd be shallower... or even outside.

And that was where she eventually found them.

Outside, in the rain.

They had been provided with a roof and walls.
Well, one wall.

And an ample supply of vegetables. Lots of starches
to fatten them up.

Captain Pausert, too, had expected to be taken down
to a cell, somewhere in the bowels of the mound. He
had not expected to be marched back outside.

They were taken to an enclosure on the edge of
the swamp.

As prison camps went, it was not particularly bad.
There were no watchtowers or huge fences. There
was a wall, with an overhanging roof on the inside,
but it wasn't particularly impressive.

They were pushed in through the gate. The enclosure was quite large, but they didn't have it entirely to
themselves. There was certainly room for a thousand
people inside. At the moment, though, it held just
three men. They looked at Pausert and his companions with the lifeless eyes of those whom hope had
deserted, although they were still alive. They didn't
bother to get up or even say anything as they lounged
against the wall underneath a makeshift awning that
kept off the rain.

Other than the three, there were stacks of vegetable matter in troughs next to the wall. Spigots protruded above that.

The gate clanged shut behind them.

"I suppose we might as well get out of the rain," said Pausert. A cold trickle was making its way down his neck. So they moved under the awning. The three old prisoners stared at the newcomers. They still hadn't said anything.

"What's wrong with you?" demanded the Leewit. "Don't you known how to talk?"

"What's there to talk about?" replied one of the men, shrugging. He was short and squat and covered with spectacular tattoos. The other two were rather alike—tall men with deep-sunken eyes. They were skinny to the point of being emaciated.

The Leewit planted hands on her hips and scowled. "Well, you might say: 'Hello, where are you from and when are we leaving?'"

The tattooed man shook his head gloomily. "You only leave here to get eaten, kid. And you don't want to get to know people too well. Then you get to thinking about it too much."

"Huh!" said the Leewit. "You are a bunch of losers. We're getting out of here and going home, see."

"This is Megair, kid. There's no way out and there's nothing you can do about it."

"I know that accent," said Vezzarn. "You're from Na'kalauf, aren't you?"

The tattooed man showed the first sign of emotion. Sadness. "Yes. I'd rather not think about it."

"We'll get you back there," said Pausert, taken aback. Na'kalauf wrestlers were famous. The small planet did not have much in the way of resources, but its men hired out as bodyguards and bouncers across the Empire. They were famed for their courage, their skill at unarmed combat—and their swirling tattoos. Those were part advertisement, and part warning.

"We're breaking out of here soon." He thought of the threat. "Before this evening."

The prisoner shrugged. "Good luck. The back wall is easiest."

"What's wrong with you?" demanded Pausert, exasperated by the man's behavior. "And what's your name, anyway?"

"The name's Ta'zara. And there's nothing wrong with me except being here," said the tattooed man. "If you climb that pole, you can get onto the roof and over into the swamps easy enough."

The pole in question was not much of a challenge to the Leewit or Pausert. The wall beyond was not very high either. Pausert could certainly reach the top of it.

Pausert tugged his chin. "Just what is wrong with you? And your silent friends?"

One of the two tall men said. "There were twenty of us, once. And when we were brought here, there were some others from other ships. Some went over the wall. You can go too."

Their tone said they wouldn't be going along.

Pausert sighed and sat down. "Look. I know this may seem unbelievable to you, but we are going to get out of here. I'm willing to take you with us. But the more you can tell us about this situation, the more likely that becomes. The Megair Cannibals made some mistakes thinking they could take us captive. They got panicked and they haven't searched us for weapons."

"You don't understand," said the tattooed man. "They never do. They don't mind you breaking out. They want you to run. They want you to try to fight. If one of them gets killed, they don't care. He was obviously a weakling—and they eat him too."

"The only thing you can do is stay thin, and not give them what they want," said the other skinny man. He cackled suddenly. "Starvation'll kill you eventually, and Patham have mercy on us for what must seem like suicide. But if you die skinny, you deny them what they need."

He looked like he was a fair way along toward his goal.

"Well," said the captain. "You might as well eat, get your strength up, because we are getting out of here."

"No one gets off Megair except inside the Cannibals' bellies," said the tattooed man. "Sorry. There is no way out."

"If I have to take one of their ships instead of my own, we're going to prove you wrong," said Pausert.

"It's no good," said one of the tall thin ones. The two were as alike as two peas in a pod. Pausert wondered if they were brothers.

"Their ships don't work the same as ours," the man continued. "That's been tried. We can't fly them. Besides—escape from under those space guns? Ha. We're here to be food."

"I'm here to give indigestion to the first one of them that tries," said the Leewit. "Why do they want to eat people, anyway?"

The other tall skinny man cackled again. "They have to. The plants of Megair 4 can't provide all the micronutrients they require. They need meat, and there's not much in the way of animal life in these miserable swamps except small animals and slugs and bugs."

"Yeah?" said the Leewit. "We have news for them. We're not dinner."

Pausert had to agree with her about that. As soon as Goth got here, it would be time to go. With or without these captives—but he couldn't really leave them to be eaten. The question was, where was Goth? He was starting to get worried.

Goth, having now applied logic, had finally arrived at the surface, and was making her way to the walled compound. Only, whereas below surface the collar of bones and wire had caused the other Cannibals to avoid her, here it was attracting unwanted attention. Obviously she was in the wrong place at the wrong time—or the wrong place, unescorted. The problem was that changing her appearance was a bit more difficult. She needed someplace where she was not observed, and the gray-skins seemed to be all over the place.

Several of them had started towards her, and had then sheered off, as if their courage deserted them. Goth wished that she had a slightly better idea of what was going on! Still, the low-walled compound on the edge of the spacefield was about the only place she hadn't been yet. Her sister and the captain had to be there.

She had barely a hundred yards to go when a big gray-skinned Megair Cannibal lurched out of the rain at her. He was going to attack her! But she'd walked all over the inside of their mound and they'd just gotten out of her way. What was wrong now?

Whatever it was, she had to deal with it. She decided to do a light-shift split, the trick she'd learned from the vatchlet. There were suddenly four of the nasty looking Cannibals with a collar of bones at their throats—none of which was actually her.

The attacker paused mid-stride and almost fell over. Then he retreated, whimpering. Goth noticed that as well as the teeth being filed, the nails on the Megair Cannibal's hands had been cut into points. He hadn't been about to attack her with his weapons, but with his hands and teeth!

It started to rain even harder, really sousing down in thick sheets. The sooner they got off this horrible world, the better, Goth decided, as the four images walked toward the stockade. So far, all she could say about the place was that the Megair Cannibals deserved it. They were a problem that Karres needed to turn its attention to. Moander, the Nuri globes, and Manaret had preoccupied her world's attention for some time now. But those threats had been dealt with, and it was Megair's turn soon, if not maybe right next.

She wondered just how the Cannibals had dealt with the Phantom ships and how they'd survived the Nuri globes. They weren't that far from the dead suns of the Tark Nembi cluster here. She knew that their ships had prowled the edges of the Empire for a long time, even outside the Chaladoor.

Nearly at the gates now, Goth was wondering how she'd get in. Then she spotted some more dim figures approaching through the rain. Figuring that no one could see her disappear in this rain, Goth slipped away into no-shape.

The party of Megair Cannibals approached. It was

one of their high ones, by the collar—and what Goth had plainly been missing, which was an escort of lesser gray-faces. If the rain was bothering them, they were certainly not letting on. A lone gate-guard, whom Goth had not even seen in his gate-house, hissed a challenge at them.

A quick, nasty fight ensued. The gate guard was overwhelmed and the collared one left his followers outside. As Goth slipped in behind him, she realized that they were tearing the corpse apart.

"It's one of their lords," said the tattooed Ta'zara in a hushed whisper. "They never come out here,"

"How do you know?" said Pausert, keeping calm. Could this be Goth? Where was she?

"The collar. They hang a finger-bone from each kill on it. The more bones, the more rank."

"Rank all right. They smell," said the Leewit, smiling suddenly. The littlest witch had been putting a brave face on it all, but Pausert could tell that this place made her uneasy. That was hardly surprising, really. She'd also plainly found the dispirited prisoners depressing.

A moment later, the captain felt ghostly fingers squeeze his. Goth! His relief was of such an order that he smiled at the oncoming Megair Cannibal lord.

The Cannibal lord seemed to find that cause for wariness. He stopped short of them and spoke. He did not speak in croaks and whistles, but in heavily accented Imperial Universum. "We find no special things on ship. Ship do not go."

"That's what we told you," said Pausert.

"Ship not same as enemy." He made the statement as if calling for an explanation of that.

"I could have told you that too. We tried to tell you, in fact."

"The enemy still is there. We find nothing—three huntership try to leave. If you get here, we can go. We can go to hunt. We need meat."

"We are busy dealing with them. We are going to get rid of them." Pausert certainly wasn't telling the Cannibal anything useful. The one advantage to having the Phantom ships patrolling the Chaladoor was keeping creatures like these from raiding ships in the civilized parts outside it.

A thought crossed the captain's mind. They had loot, generations worth of loot, probably including various electronics. Maybe even a multiplier link. The Megair Cannibals were no soft target. But compared to the Nuri globes or the Phantom ships, easy to deal with. The Daal of Uldune could probably do it, let alone the mighty Empire. The cluster would be hard to capture and a bad place to fight, but it could be effectively blockaded.

On the other hand, the Phantom ships could not be blockaded or easily fought.

"We need a part to fix our ship," he said, "and we'll get away and have our people deal with them. We just came to establish what the problem was."

"The enemy cannot be escaped," stated the Cannibal.

"We got here, didn't we?" said Pausert reasonably. "Let us go. What do you lose if we don't succeed?"

The gray-faced Cannibal lord stood wrinkling his nose, obviously searching for words. Eventually he resorted to grunts, croaks and whistles of his own strange language.

The Leewit translated. "He says he's for losing

nothing. But the high lord Gwarrr gave the orders about you. He'd have to be for being eaten, first." The Leewit paused, frowned. "If I'm understanding it right, Captain, these guys are not very good at ever admitting they're wrong. If a leader gets challenged, well, the challenger has to beat him. And the loser gets eaten."

"Literally dog-eat-dog politics!" said Pausert. He smiled thinly. "I wish I could get some of the councilors from Nikkeldepain to visit here for a bit. Ask him what he wants to do. I think it'll be clearer in his own language."

The Leewit did, and then translated the reply. "He says nothing is for the doing, then. The Phantom ships have got them trapped. Maybe they will find a way to defend against the Phantom ships, just like they did against the Nuris. If not, they're for eating each other on this terrible planet they've been trapped on."

Pausert was surprised to find himself agreeing with the Cannibal about anything. And surprised to hear one of them describe their home as a terrible planet.

The Leewit was plainly taken aback herself. She asked something, and the gray-faced man with red eyes and sharpened teeth replied. At length.

"What was that?" asked Pausert.

"I asked him why they live here, if it's so miserable. He said when heaven broke—that's sort of what he said, I think—their fleet was trapped here. At first, they thought this place was like home, just colder. But the prey was slow and stupid and they hunted them all out. What's left isn't worth hunting. So now they have to hunt off-world, but they cannot get off because of the enemy."

"I have to ask," he said, thinking that once they got out of here they'd have to deal with these... From close up, if you ignored the color of their skins and the red eyes and the sharpened teeth and nails and the receding chins, they looked almost human. "Why do you hunt and eat people? Why don't you just farm? Or if you have to hunt, hunt animals?"

The Megair Cannibal drew himself back, obviously offended. He rattled off some words that the Leewit translated as: "Hunting is high honor. Cannot look for prey that is lesser."

That was a rather different way of looking at it, the captain had to acknowledge. It still didn't clear things up too well, as far as what to do with them in the long term, or even how to get out of here in the short term. There was always the Egger Route, but not for the dear old *Venture*.

Pausert faced the Cannibal lord, with the one question that was still on his mind. "So why did you come and see us, then?"

The red eyed being stared back at him. "To know." And it turned and walked away, back to the gate.

CHAPTER 25

"They're just plain weird," said Goth, when he'd gone. "Let's go and sit on the far side over there, away from these people. I need to tell you all the things I've seen. And then we need to break out of here."

"I can't tell you how good it is to have you with us again, Goth," said the captain quietly, as they walked around the edge of the compound, keeping under the eave. "I worry. I know. I don't need to—you're a hot witch. But I do anyway."

"Just to keep in practice," said Goth, with a chuckle. "You know how much trouble you caused me with that whistle, Leewit? I got to explore that whole anthill before I could find you. They're not nice, these Cannibals, but they're not stupid either. That's quite a fort."

"I really don't like this place," said the Leewit. "It's like the whole place is sick, sort of."

Pausert felt the vague prickle of klatha force. The Leewit was a healer—or would be when she'd grown up. Most of the time, she was a little girl and something of a hooligan. He squeezed her hand. "I think we need to get out. I think we need to go and do some scavenging in among those derelicts in the junkyard, fix the *Venture,* load these captives up and get out of here, double quick time. Only thing is, how are we going to leave? Egger Route? We can't leave these captives to get eaten, but I am reluctant..."

"We can deal with their communications and even their detection system," said Goth cheerfully. "I can break them up pretty well without the Leewit—or I can take her in there and let her whistle at them."

"Let me whistle down the communication system!" said the Leewit gleefully. "That'll bust up more than just the command post. It'll bust everything that's listening in too. Remember? Like we did with Moander!"

Pausert couldn't help but smile at the thought. "I like it. I like it a lot."

"Good. Then I think we should go before they start adding the *Venture* to the scrap pile, after they've pulled everything out of her."

"I hadn't thought about that," said Pausert, taken aback. "Well. Up the pole and into the swamp, eh. We can't leave Vezzarn, but what about the others?"

"We'll come and fetch them. Mebeckey hasn't said a word since they took us captive. It's a bit worrying. He usually talks all the time, and now he's shut up."

"Could be fear, I suppose. This place is enough to give me the willies. But what do we do with him?"

"Leave him," said the Leewit and Goth simultaneously. Obviously something about the fellow prickled both of them too.

Vezzarn had come sauntering over. "What now, Your Wisdoms?" he asked. "I assume Missy Goth is around somewhere. 'Cause I see you smiling, Captain. That Mebeckey is trying to find out how they decide who gets eaten first."

"We're about to make a break," said Goth, still invisible. "I assume they're watching this place somehow, and they'll follow us. Except we're going back to the *Venture* before they loot bits of her. The captain thinks we might be able to get a replacement multiplier link out of one of the wrecks."

"I reckon they must have some kind of spy-ray tracker on the people in this place," said Vezzarn. "In my old line of business I had to fool those a few times. I brought a scrambler from the ship. It's in my boot heel, with the lock-picks and my UW."

"Okay. Are we going to tell them?" The Leewit jerked her thumb at the other prisoners.

The captain nodded. "I'll tell them we'll be back for them. It's only right."

The three prisoners that had been there when they came looked resigned. The tattooed man bit his lip and took a deep breath. "They like you to do that. Expect you to do that. I'm waiting my chance. Leave the kid with me. Or kill her quickly."

It was the first real sign of emotion Pausert had seen from him. "We'll be fine. Really. Just be ready when we come back, because I plan to blast out of this planet as if my tail was on fire."

"Almost," said the one tall thin man, "you make me believe in Patham again. Or in more than his mercy."

Pausert grinned. "The locals are about to start believing in his seventh hell. The really nasty one." He turned to the archeologist. "Mebeckey. We'll be back..."

"Guards! Guar—"

Vezzarn rapped him smartly over the head. "Mister nice guy. Sorry, Captain. I should have been quicker."

Ta'zara shrugged. "Doesn't matter. You can shout all you like in here. They never come."

"Well, then we'd better go anyway."

The tattooed man from Na'kalauf sighed. "I have never known any of them to come and talk to prisoners. But... anyway, it won't help you, but good luck."

Pausert warmed to the man. He must have been through hell, waiting to be eaten. "We do have a few tricks up our sleeves," he said. "Have faith."

"It hurts too much to do that," said Ta'zara.

They left via the pole. It had very obviously been put there for just that purpose. Only, unlike the many who must have tried it before them, the four of them did not drop over the wall into the swamp for the hunters.

Instead, they switched on the scrambler and sat against the wall. Goth did a light-shift of them to appear like a part of the wall. "I've gone to temperature and scent, too, but I don't know how long I can keep that up," she said. "It's a real strain trying to do several shifts at once. I'm not even trying to disguise sound, so be quiet."

"It doesn't matter," said the Leewit. "Everything stinks around here and I'll soon be as cold as the wall, anyway."

That was the hardest part. It was cold. The Leewit tried to burrow into the captain while they sat there keeping still.

And very soon, the eager Cannibals were hunting out into the swamp. All Pausert could do was hope that it was even colder and wetter and more miserable out there. It seem hard to believe that it could be.

"Well. It looks like that worked," said Pausert.

They left together, heading for the spacefield.

"Easier if we go as a bunch of gray-skins," said Goth, once they were away from the prison camp. She light-shifted them into a group of the Megair Cannibals. Because she knew the pattern, they were all ones with the collars. Other Megair Cannibals sheered away from them.

"I think we were right," said Pausert. "Most of the time with these guys, it seems to be might and numbers and rank that work their hierarchy. So as long as we look like a bunch of high lords, the ordinary Cannibals will leave us alone."

"Makes sense," said Goth.

"Yeah," said the Leewit. "Only it's not quite 'lord.' It's 'him who kills most.' One finger-bone from every fight."

Pausert blinked, thinking of the Megair Cannibal who had come to see them. That was a lot of fingers. And yet . . . he had wanted to know.

They made their way to the *Venture*. A team of Megair Cannibals was in the process of unbolting the front nova turret.

The Leewit shouted at them.

The effect was quite comical. They stopped and hastily began reassembling the unit.

"It looks like it worked," said the captain. "Give them another few minutes and we'll move the ship."

Before too long, only a single Cannibal was left in the area, one with a three-finger collar. Since he seemed disinclined to go anywhere, they walked up the gangway. The three-bone collar tried to stop them. The Leewit whistled at him, and he fell over.

"Stunner," she said. "Works well."

"You're supposed to bite off the finger. That's how you get followers," said Goth. "But I guess we'll just haul him inside and lock him in one of the staterooms."

"I am not biting off his finger!" said the Leewit.

The poor *Venture* showed some signs of looting. Much of what could be carried away easily, had been. However, it was apparent that they hadn't yet started on disassembling the ship's main components. Perhaps they were still trying to work out how it moved so fast.

Outside, night was beginning to fall on Megair 4. The rain, of course, had never stopped falling.

"I think we should go and set fire to their whole nest," said the Leewit furiously.

"Certainly the fire-control system. And maybe break the place apart while we're at it," said Goth, almost as cross.

"First we're going across to the dump," said Pausert, firmly. "I'd rather lift with a vessel that doesn't just have the Sheewash drive to rely on. We can lock the ship up. Gutting her doesn't seem to be a rush job for the gray-faces."

"Leave me here, Skipper," said Vezzarn. "I'll get the other units in and check to see if they've damaged anything else."

"Better not have," said Goth, grumpily.

A little later, Pausert and the two Karres witches—appearing to be a party twelve strong—left. Vezzarn shook the captain's hand. "If something goes wrong, I know you'll come and fetch me, Captain. I don't fancy being someone's dinner."

"You're too old and stringy to be nice eating anyway," said the Leewit, giving him a hug. "Don't worry. We got Goth and the captain."

"And we have her," said Goth, grinning.

And me, said a vatch-voice in their heads.

"Where have you been?" demanded the Leewit. "They've been messing with my stuff!"

Looking, said the vatchlet. **Big complicated dream this place. Two kinds of dream things here. Sharp hungry kind. And the soft wet ones.**

"Everything here is wet!" said Goth. "Anyway, Captain. Let's go and get on with it. You got an atomic lamp with you? 'Cause I don't think the electrics will be working in those old crates."

Pausert had, and a universal toolkit from a drawer that had miraculously been overlooked.

"You keep the *Venture* safe for us, Little-bit? Until we come back? Please?" said the Leewit.

Sure. Need someone to play with. And the dreamstuff this place is made of is happy. Not like out there. Nasty things happened there.

Sometimes making sense out of what the little vatch was saying was quite a challenge, thought Pausert. Cracked space, half-in/half-out dimensional ships. The ship's dreamstuff made of happy... about the only thing that made sense was the part about nasty stuff happening out there. And ten to one they weren't talking about the same nasty stuff.

"Well, can you keep the locals away? We want to leave, but we need to fix some things first. We need to go and get some spare parts."

Sure.

"You can have fun with them if they come," said the Leewit generously. "Not like the captain, where I told you to leave off."

Pausert made a mental note of the fact that the Leewit seemed to have gained a very high level of cooperation from this vatch. The little creature could easily stop quite a force if it wanted to. More than a mere locked airlock.

So they went.

It was almost completely dark now, and they did not encounter one Megair Cannibal in their stumbling wet progress to the junkyard of ships. Once there, it was a case of picking the best possible. The captain chose a Tullurian freighter—quite an old ship by the looks of her. She was, of course, gutted. But the Megair Cannibals hadn't ripped out her drives. It seemed they preferred their own. And her multiplier link was there. The jacks were a bit different, and the serial bus, but he could hotwire those, given a few minutes.

Down in the empty hold he found the other thing he'd been hoping for, still bolted to the little cargo-crane—a small grav-tractor, for loading. He sent Goth and the Leewit back with the multiplier link module and had the grav-tractor out by the time they got back. Walking back to the *Venture*—well, staggering

back—the captain wished there really were twelve of
them to carry it.

"What do you want it for?" asked Goth.

"I hope it'll work on the Phantoms," panted Pausert.
"They're not keen on gravity wells. I have a feeling
they won't like this either."

"If you say so, Captain. So what next? I reckon
the prisoners."

"You're right, I think," he said struggling to breathe
and talk. "If we just, huh, let me get this in, and, huh,
do a quick bit of wiring . . . tell me about the inside . . .
How best to get a safe boost out of here . . . short of
the Egger Route."

"Well, Sheewash off the ground is always tricky.
You're supposed to be a ten-year adept before you
try it." He saw a flash of teeth. "Might be safer than
your launches, though, Captain! I figured, we go fetch
the prisoners. March them over here, like they're
dinner. And put them into the *Venture*. Locked up,
after Mebeckey's last little act—I don't want them
deciding to take the *Venture* without us or something.
And then the Leewit and me go into that mound. Let
the Leewit whistle at their fire-control. Maybe at their
communications center too. You have the *Venture* all
warmed up. Then we scamper as fast as we can, try
a low launch trajectory and hit the Sheewash as soon
as we're reasonably well clear of the ground."

They'd reached the *Venture*'s ramp and the captain
had no breath to spare while he carried the heavy
grav-tractor unit into the *Venture*. But when he'd set
it down and panted for a while, safe in the dry, lit
interior of the *Venture,* he nodded. "It sounds good.
Except that I think we might as well go together. We've

all got klatha skills that complement the others. And
Vezzarn can run pre-ignition for me." He looked at the
old spacer. "Leave without us and you've got no fast
way to get past the Phantoms. So keep your nerve."

The old spacer nodded. "You came back for me,
and I learned one thing for sure, Captain. You don't
mess with Their Wisdoms. I guess the Megair Cannibals are going to learn that the hard way."

"I should have told them that you don't mess around
with the Leewit's stuff," said Pausert wryly. "She's
gone quiet and has blood her in eye. She's safer to
be around when she's just her usual noisy self."

Vezzarn nodded. "The ship itself and the engines
seem okay, Captain. But they took your Pantara detector unit. And they broke open the armory cupboard."

"Now I've got blood in my eye too," said Pausert
crossly.

"It's all right, Captain. They didn't even find my
lockup," said Vezzarn. "And the guns are in that."

"Ah! That's good news. I think we'd better take a
blaster apiece. How are you at hot-wiring this bit of
circuitry? I could try doing it myself if..."

Vezzarn looked pained. "Skipper, most of the locks
I deal with these days have hyperelectronic parts. It'd
take me less time than you. I'm not much good at
space navigation or handling take-offs and landings,
but I can do the rest."

"Good man!"

"Well, begging your pardon, Captain, I'm not. But
I'm a live man on account of you and the little Wisdoms. And to tell you the truth, the Daal promised
me a bonus to see you stayed that way, too. The Daal
is chary with money, but he pays. Hulik promised I'd

see it. And besides, there is also the matter of the little Wisdoms' parents. I'm not even thinking about going back without them!" said the former thief and agent, cheerfully, taking the looted part. "Let's get those guns."

"The part I am not looking forward to is that we've got to go out there again. I just got warm carrying that grav-tractor. You want to see if you can bolt that down and wire it up too, while we're out."

"Sure, Captain. Down in the hold?

"No, in the hold airlock."

Vezzarn blinked at him. "What?

Pausert nodded. "Going to use it in space, if we use it at all. I'll give you a hand to carry it down. It's as heavy as lead."

A few minutes later the three set out again. They held hands, as it was as black as the inside of a jungle cat out there. And, although Goth maintained their appearance as a group of Megair Cannibals, she also managed to hide their heat emissions. Unless they made too much noise, they were effectively undetectable.

"Hide our heat?" said the Leewit, shivering up against him. "I haven't got any to spare."

The prisoner compound had only one guard again. Pausert punched him on the point of his receding chin as the Leewit struggled for a whistle. "T...t... t...too cold," she stuttered out between chattering teeth. "Sorry, Captain."

It wasn't freezing, but the wind and the wet combined unpleasantly. Goth had to 'port a piece out of the gate before they could get in. And when they did, it was almost tempting to stay. There was no

wind and they were out of the rain. And the prisoners had a tiny fire.

There was also one less prisoner than they were
expecting.

The three cowered back against the wall. "Where's
the tattooed fellow from Na'kalauf?" asked Pausert,
forgetting they were light-shifted to look like Megair
Cannibals themselves.

But it was clear that the prisoners were not expecting anything but Megair Cannibals, and that those did
sometimes speak some Imperial Universum.

"You took him, masters," said Mebeckey—rather
indistinctly, because his mouth was half full of the
fleshy leaves from the trough. He swallowed and
looked nervous.

The Leewit was busy huddling in front of their
small fire. Well, thought Pausert, their day was not
over yet. And he was still angry with Mebeckey. The
fellow had proved his instincts true.

"Take off that cloak," he ordered. Mebeckey hesitated briefly. Some instinct made the captain produce
his blaster—which Goth considerately light-shifted into
one of the odd, ball-barreled weapons. The other two
had backed off. Mebeckey lifted the cloak very slowly,
to reveal a small arsenal. A heavy-duty blaster. A UW. A
butcher's knife—none of which came from the *Venture.*
He must have had them hidden in his room. Pausert
remembered the delay when they demanded entry. He
looked at the weapons grimly, furious they'd not thought
to search the room. "Drop those."

"Better do it," said one of the scrawny prisoners.
"The pain is terrible from that nerve-jangler."

So Mebeckey did. Pausert suspected that there would

be more weapons hidden on him. Captain Pausert didn't have a problem with him carrying weapons here. He just worried about the fact that Mebeckey had been trying to get into their arms supply. Wanting a weapon to defend himself against possible pirates was one thing. Disarming his rescuers, another entirely.

"Face the wall, all of you," said Pausert, roughly, still upset by the discovery. "Cover," he said to Goth, picking up and handing the allweather cloak to the Leewit. He patted them down quickly and found another small blaster on Mebeckey—a Glassite 300, a rich man's toy. The other two had no weapons. "Right. March. We are taking you to a new prison."

They walked them in the rain back to the *Venture*. The captain was amazed that they didn't get lost, actually. As arranged, Vezzarn cracked the hold loading bay and let the prisoners into it. When it was closed again, the three witches set off for the mound.

CHAPTER 26

Goth found that she really didn't like the idea of going back into the mound. The odd feeling of having brief hallucinations of small six-limbed furry creatures and their fear and misery haunted her. It was some kind of klatha manifestation, she was sure, but she was just not sure how she was supposed to deal with it. There were occasional new phenomena that the teaching patterns had never come across. Was she encountering one? She wrapped her fingers more tightly around Pausert's hand, and determinedly thought about the Nikkeldepain Academy instead.

"What's security like on that door?" asked Pausert.

"Doesn't seem to exist, Captain," said Goth. "I just whistled at it. It opened."

"The Megair Cannibals seem secure in their, well, arrogance," said Pausert. "Let's hope it works."

"Sure hope so. It's a big door to bust up." Goth had memorized the little sequence of notes—a precise, quick memory was essential for klatha manipulation. So much of it was patterns of the mind, almost burning new synapse paths, with fatal consequences if they got it wrong, that exact memorization was part of the Karres breed by now. She whistled and the low wide door slid open. Goth reflected again how odd the Megair Cannibals were. They must have to duck every time they came in. The three witches walked into the fortress as if they belonged there. No one challenged them. Actually, there were very few of the Megair Cannibals about. Goth had to wonder why. But there was a low roar of sound coming from deeper into the mound. Still, she thought, they may as well make the most of the fact that the corridors busy, earlier, were nearly empty now. All the better to bust up equipment that might stop them leaving!

There were only three operators in the Megair Cannibals' comms room. Goth was not an expert at reading expressions on the gray faces. But she would have said that they all looked sulky. The Leewit did not give her time to find out. She whistled at them. Her favorite hit-you-with-a-sledgehammer whistle. The three were no more able to fend that off than most people would be a real sledgehammer. Even the echo made Goth's head hurt.

"Okay, now we call all ships—and you whistle down the microphone."

"I've got an even better idea," said Pausert. "Give them a general call and tell them an invasion landing has been made on the North pole. All ships to make haste there—and *then* whistle down and bust the equipment, receiving and sending."

"Oh, I like it!" said the Leewit, grabbing a microphone, and starting to talk in the strange language of the Megair Cannibals. Goth had a feeling that the captain wouldn't like what she was saying, but it provoked several squawks from the system . . . and then the Leewit put her fingers in her mouth and gave the microphone the benefit of the shrillest whistle Goth had heard. In the room glass and electronic components exploded and shards whizzed past them. "That's caused a fair amount of panic. Let's go and see if we can find that poor fellow from Na'kalauf."

"Sure. Fire control is three doors down. Let's deal with that on our way past. I hope we find him in time." None of them said it, but they all knew what would happen to the man if they didn't.

They walked on down toward the noise. It sounded like a crowd, getting warmed up at some game.

And so it was. When they got closer, they could hear the cheering and yelling.

"There's an arena down here. Must be some kind of show on," said Goth.

Pausert paused. "Uh. You know what it is likely to be."

Goth hadn't thought about it, but it was rather obvious. She stopped too and touched the wall to steady herself, then wished immediately that she hadn't. Images flooded into her head. She hastily leaned against the captain.

"There was some sort of klatha surge," said the captain. "Did you feel it? We'll be calling vatches next."

"It's me," said Goth. "It started on Nikkeldepain. Something odd is going on. But we don't have time for that now. We'd better go and see if we're too late. The Leewit..."

"No way I am staying here without you," said the littlest witch. "And no way I am going outside just yet, either. I'm just about warm. And yes. I have worked out they're probably fighting and eating people. Or each other. I'm not little anymore, you know."

Goth still felt that she was, even though she was not going to try to tell the Leewit that. And she couldn't get the images that she'd got when touching the wall out of her head.

"I asked Little-bit to come help," announced the Leewit. "'Cause you don't sound too good, Goth. And there is nothing happening out there. She's getting bored. She can find anything."

He's in a cage. Off that way. The sharp-dream things are fighting and eating each other, said the vatchlet in their heads.

They followed her directions and soon found themselves in a low circular corridor. Noise of cheering and yelling came through the wall.

"Just your average happy Megair Cannibal evening out," said Pausert grimly. "I think this must lead around the arena."

It seemed to. And there was a barred entrance, with the heavy bars being crudely attached to the smooth walls and floor.

Open, said the vatchlet, and the cage door opened. Inside stood Ta'zara, the swirl-tattooed man from Na'kalauf. He didn't seem to see them. He was standing, arms akimbo, chanting something to himself.

"It's some kind of war cry," said the Leewit, by her tone much impressed.

"Na'kalaufers do it before they wrestle," said Pausert. "Hey, Ta'zara! We've got to go."

"You've killed my brothers. My companions. Now, I will fight and die like a man of Na'kalauf. I will take as many of you with me as possible!" Ta'zara charged.

Belatedly it occurred to Goth that he was seeing their light-shifted images, and probably not thinking too clearly about them knowing his name and speaking Imperial Universum. He grabbed the captain. Goth hastily dropped the light-shift. "Idiot!" hissed the Leewit. "It's us. We've come to fetch you. We said we would."

There was a second's pause. "Do you mind letting go?" said the captain, in a slightly choked voice.

The tattooed hands dropped. "I'm going mad. I'm going mad!" He began to chant again.

The Leewit stepped in front of him, stamped her foot, and grabbed him with both hands. Goth felt a surge of klatha energy. She could recognize types by now, and she'd felt this before when the Leewit had healed the nursebeast. Ta'zara wasn't injured, but not all kinds of wounds were physical.

His chanting stopped. He looked at the Leewit, incredulously.

"Now come!" she said. "Goth is going to make all of us look like Megair Cannibals. You too. But we're not. Here. Hold my hand."

He took it, very cautiously. "What you feel is real. Not what you see. Now just hold my hand and keep walking," said the Leewit, firmly, as if she was talking to very small child. "Do you understand?"

"No," he said. "But I believe. The brothers must be right. There is redemption."

"Let's go. It might be easier if you close your eyes."

He shook his head. "I am Ta'zara. A man of Na'kalauf. I know fear but it not my master," he said as if reciting. Goth realized he probably was. So she light-shifted.

"Calm down!" said the Leewit, seeing his reaction. "Feel my hand. It's just a disguise."

"A disguise."

"Yeah. A clumping good disguise. Now stop standing like you've grown roots and let's go before it's too late."

Goth could hear the Na'kalauf man pant a little, and her sister talk to him, calming him down. This was a different Leewit from the one she was used to.

They had walked a good long way towards the surface before the uproar behind them told Goth the escape had been discovered.

"I think we need to run," she said.

So they did. Behind them it sounded as if every last one of the of Megair Cannibals was after them.

The door stood before them. So did a small group of Megair Cannibals, with what Pausert now knew to be nerve-janglers at the ready. Ta'zara roared and charged. The Leewit whistled. The green passage light on the wall exploded. So did the Megair Cannibal weapons, with their holders yelping and dropping them. None of that stopped the charging Ta'zara, who was flinging Megair Cannibals about as if they were shrapnel and he their personal bomb.

Barely half a minute later Ta'zara stood, panting a little. "I know fear but it not my master," he said, looking at the fallen Megair Cannibals. Now it was not so much a recitation as a statement of faith, tinged with relief. He held out his hand. "Little lady?"

The Leewit skipped forward and took his hand. "You need to teach me how to do that," she said.

"Maybe later," said the captain, with the thought of just how interesting that might make dealing with the Leewit in a tantrum.

Goth whistled at the door, and it opened.

Outside was rain and darkness. It was more welcome than what lay behind them. They went out and the door slid closed again.

"That ought to hold them for a while. I ported a piece of door out of there. I think it was part of the opening device," said Goth. "Now all we have to do is find the ship."

"Well, let's do it together. Hold hands or I might lose you out here."

Pausert trusted to instinct to find their way to the *Venture*. He was getting quite good at that!

It was apparent that someone had figured that darkness was a shield for them. Lights suddenly came on. They still had a few hundred yards to go to the landing field and they did it at a sprint. Vezzarn started to raise the ramp as their boots clattered onto it. Glancing back, Pausert could see why. A mass of the gray-skinned Cannibals had started to pour out of their mound. The Karres witches and the man from Na'kalauf dived in through the lock, and the captain panted past Vezzarn to the control room.

"Crash stations!" he shouted. "This may be a rough take-off."

The *Venture* was warm and ready, and they boosted. It was one of the captain's trademark take-offs—erratic and touch and go, with the thrust-regulator down flat. Despite the Leewit's earlier efforts, the Megair Cannibals did get off a few shots as the *Venture* wobbled her way upwards into the cloud. But the ship did not even take a glancing hit, and the *Venture*, pushing g's, was hurtling for space.

"Phew!" exclaimed Goth as they headed toward the sun-side of Megair 4. "Are we going to go to the Sheewash drive soon, Captain? 'Cause the Phantom ships are out there waiting. There sure are plenty of them!"

So they were. The captain could see them hanging off in space, as if they were trying to englobe the entire planet.

"How is our air pressure holding out?"

Goth checked the instruments. "Down just a tiny fraction, Captain. About 99.8 points. The seal must be leaking, I'm afraid."

"Should have shoved one of those Cannibals into the hole," said Pausert crossly. "I'll need to get the Leewit into a pressure suit." He bit his lip. "I'd forgotten about the other prisoners in the hold. I want to have the Leewit use that grav-tractor I had Vezzarn bolt onto the floor in the hold airlock. But we need those people out of there—if they're in one piece."

"It has to be better than the alternative," said Goth. "If you offered me a choice between stay and be eaten and a launch without a crash-pad . . ."

"I gave 'em a mattress and some water," said Vezzarn.

"Well, Vezzarn, you and Goth and Ta'zara, go see how they are. Tell them we're in for some more maneuvers and they'd better come and get strapped in. We're in for a rough ride."

✳   ✳   ✳

The big tattooed Na'kalauf man was looking at all of them as if he'd had a couple of knocks on the head—which might possibly be true, Goth reflected. He'd stormed into the Megair Cannibals like a one-man army. "Who are you?" he asked. "Am I dreaming? Am I dead?"

"I'll pinch you if like," said the Leewit.

He nodded. "Please."

So she did. He felt the spot.

"Would it feel real in a dream?"

The Leewit stamped her foot. "I've got things to do! The captain needs me in a pressure suit and I want to get out of these clothes first. They're wet. Get up! If it is a dream, it has me in it too."

He got up and bowed respectfully. "Then at least it is a good dream. One in which I found myself and courage again. Thank you. I am yours to command, Little Lady."

"I'm the Leewit. Not 'lady'—and sure not 'little lady'! And I need you stop blocking the way and get along to the hold with me. Those other friends of yours might be hurt."

He bowed again. "Very well, Leewit. Will you accept me?"

"*The* Leewit. Like '*the* captain.'"

"But do you accept me, the Leewit?"

"If it makes you happy," she said impatiently. "Now we have work to do."

Vezzarn clapped him on the shoulder. "You'll get used to it, son. You must have realized by now that Their Wisdoms don't exactly do things the way we do." Ta'zara looked at him in some puzzlement. Obviously the term wasn't familiar to him. "I'll explain it to you sometime," said the old spacer. "Meanwhile, let's go to see to the others. I hope they're in one piece."

They went back to the hold and found the three former captives. The two thin men were doing a very proficient job of strapping Mebeckey's fore-arm to a splint they had contrived.

"Ta'zara?" one exclaimed.

The tattooed man smiled. "It's either a dream or we've been rescued."

They stared incredulously at him, then at each other. Then they dropped to their knees. "Great Patham be thanked!"

"We're not out of the woods yet," said Goth, "and the captain says he wants you strapped in. Sorry about the arm, and the bouncing around. We had to get off-world in a hurry."

"What are bruises compared to not being eaten?" said the one tall fellow.

"You've got a point. The ship's in a bit of a state. She got looted. But we should be able to find a few crash couches intact."

"You are instruments of Patham. Our gratitude—"

"Get a move on," said the Leewit.

"Contact, forty-five seconds and closing."

They'd raced into a rapid transit to Megair 4's second moon, using that for a small bit of gravitational sling-shotting for the *Venture*. But now the Phantom ships were surrounding them. And the Leewit was sitting, anchored with makeshift combat webbing, in the open hold airlock with a grav-tractor, a gravity generator intended to push and pull freight. Gravitational force obeyed the inverse square law, and for the grav-tractor to have any effect, she would have to focus the beam right on the Phantom ship.

Ta'zara was on the forward nova gun pod. He'd never operated one before, but the two Dell brothers were pacifists and missionary doctors and were no better. Vezzarn was on the aft nova guns. Mebeckey had been fed a painkiller and was strapped in. Goth was ready in the copilot's seat, with the wires for making the framework for the Sheewash at hand.

"Contact ten seconds. Five. Fire when ready!"

Pausert saw the first Phantom go from zero on the mass-detector to thousands of tons. And then there was a burst of exploding incandescence where the ship had been. Even here in space the *Venture* was buffeted by it. The Leewit shrieked with triumph. The nova guns roiled sheet-lightning across the heavens. The Leewit had plainly focused on another target because a second ship erupted. She was just as accurate with the grav-tractor as she was with her beloved nova guns. Odd marksmanship, really, for someone destined to be a healer—but the witches of Karres were a law unto themselves.

The cordon was fleeing now—still firing torpedoes but running.

"Time to go Sheewash. Can't keep it up too long here among the debris. But let's leave those torpedoes behind!" yelled Goth.

The orange incandescent fire danced and the *Venture* leapt away from the battle.

"They're still following, Captain," said Goth. With the detectors looted, she was doing a manual search of the viewscreens behind the venture while the captain dodged obstacles. They'd be out of the cluster soon and into open space. Right now, though, ship-handling took all his concentration.

"But they're keeping a healthy distance," she continued. "They're out of grav-tractor range, and we'll have time to deal with torpedoes if we spot them incoming. Can we bring the Leewit in?"

"Sure," said Pausert, not taking his eyes off the forward screens for an instant. "If she's not too tired, we can put her into the rear turret for torpedoes. She's the best shot I've ever seen. Have Vezzarn check that patch, see if we can do any more to it."

"I'm fine," said the Leewit over her suit-mike.

"Well, close that outer airlock and come in then."

"Will do. Got those clumping Phantoms!"

"Once we've got some clear space we need to go Sheewash, Captain. We're still definitely losing pressure. We won't last four days of normal ship travel," said Goth.

Pausert nodded, and yawned. "We'd better stock up on some calories then. We're further than four days out of Uldune space. I could murder a coffee and some food. Maybe we can get one of the supercargo to see to it?"

"Sounds good," said Goth. "I'll page them up."

But it soon became apparent that it wasn't going to happen. The Dell brothers were very willing, and even Mebeckey staggered up from his couch (and was sent back to it), but it appeared that the robo-butler and the food supplies had been one of the casualties of the Megair Cannibals' looting spree.

"Nothing for it but to run a bit on empty," said

Pausert grumpily. "I'd even eat those weeds that the Megair Cannibals provided for us."

The two Dell brothers looked helplessly at each other. "Your companion, Mebeckey, ate heartily of them. But we did not bring any of the fresh leaf with us. It wasn't bad. Just monotonous, and left us feeling permanently mildly hungry. It lacks, we think, some trace elements, or amino acids. We tried to get them to let us do some lab work. We think the dietary deficiency could be treated. But..."

"But they didn't want to. They think their way of life is fine," said Goth.

The Leewit came in at this point. "I'm ravenous. And they're still a long way back on us. What happened to that food?"

"The Megair Cannibals looted the robo-butler and the supplies," admitted Pausert.

"What!" The Leewit was incensed. "Those clumping useless greasy gray slabs! I think we ought to go back and teach them a lesson."

The two Dell brothers looked shocked. "But, my daughter!" said one. "We have been given the gift, our lives. We should instead be grateful. What is a little privation..."

Pausert knew that look in the Leewit's eye. Best to do some distraction before she whistled them something special. He coughed. "We're free and running, but we have problems, the Leewit."

"Like what?" Her newfound responsibility came to the fore.

"Well," said Goth. "We have a leaking ship, hundreds of Phantom ships chasing us, and no food. But otherwise nothing much."

"So can we do something about the food first?" said the Leewit. "I'm starving. I'd start on Mebeckey if he wasn't so scrawny even after eating my Winten-berry jelly."

After the klatha-energy use, they were raveningly hungry. Pausert couldn't help laughing. The two medical missionaries looked horrified. But then they had just escaped being dinner.

"I think you should go and check on the patient," said Pausert firmly. "And strap in. We're going to use our booster. Don't come back for at least fifteen minutes."

The Leewit looked darkly at the captain. "I wouldn't have really done much to them. You know why the Cannibals didn't want to eat them? Ta'zara told me. He's not the worst, you know. Anyway, the Cannibals didn't eat those two because they wouldn't fight. Wouldn't even run. No sport in them."

"And Ta'zara?"

The Leewit was silent for a bit. Then she said quietly. "They kept him for a special feast. Because he was the bravest. They hurt him really badly with those nerve janglers. Badly enough for him to be scared to face them again. He'd tried a lot of times, I think. He was...a mess inside."

Pausert knew that the Leewit was destined to be a healer. But he'd not thought of the cost of healing on herself. To fix a mind, she'd had to understand at least in part what was wrong. And she was still very young. His protective instincts surged. "But he dared again in the passage at the door."

The Leewit shrugged. "He had to. It was part of the healing, see. So I helped him not to be afraid.

But he still was. That was why he was so explosive. Winning there helped him a lot."

"You still got enough strength to help us with the Sheewash drive?" asked Goth, giving her a sisterly hug. "We need to take the *Venture* faster to Uldune, or we're going to run out of air, let alone go hungry."

The Leewit nodded. "For sure. Especially as we don't get any food until then."

"You should lay off teasing those missionaries," said Goth.

"They keep asking me to do it," said the Leewit. "So let's Sheewash."

The three of them, linked and pushing the ship, did in a bare few minutes with the klatha energies of the Sheewash drive what would have taken days otherwise. They pushed the *Venture* toward the one-time pirate port of Uldune. Afterwards, they sat, tired and hungry, in the control room. And after a few minutes the captain found the energy to start trying for navigation beacons. He got just one, faintly, and began transcribing it in.

The *Venture*'s communicators signaled a pick-up. They were back in subradio range, and being hailed. And what was more, they were being hailed on a private shielded frequency with a powerful directional beam. Someone was calling the *Venture*.

Goth fiddled with the reception. Turned up the gain. "*Venture* 7333... home in for Uldune..."

"Hulik's voice!" said the Leewit delightedly. "We are receiving you, Uldune," she transmitted.

There was no mistaking the relief in the voice. "Secure channel beam length 0.699."

Goth clicked the communicator beam length to that. "Come in, Uldune."

"Glad to hear your voice, Goth," said Hulik.

"Not half as glad as we are to hear yours," said Goth. "We're losing air slowly, and worse, out of food."

Hulik laughed. "If that is the worst worry—then I can stop worrying. Based on the directional data, we have eight cruisers and a battlewagon within half a ship day of you. Will your air hold out that long?"

"Easily. Though the Leewit's stomach may not. It's growling at us. Anyway, we're glad you happened to have some ships near to us. That was lucky."

"We got information that you were in the Megair cluster two days ago," said Hulik. "The fleet left as soon as possible."

"What!"

"You need to keep a careful lookout. There is a fairly substantial pirate fleet looking for you. Specifically for you, Goth." Hulik do Eldel paused. "You better be ready to run . . . with your special ability . . . if it's not our fleet. If they don't give the recognition call of the name of Hantis's canine friend and planet of origin."

"Will do!"

"Will keep this channel open. Call us if you encounter any ships at all. Out."

"Over and out."

Goth looked at the other two. "Someone, somehow, knew that we'd arrived on Megair 4."

Pausert frowned. "Someone who is working with the Phantom ships?"

"It's that or the Cannibals. And that doesn't seem very likely."

The intercom crackled. "Captain! Captain! There is something wrong with Mebeckey! Please come."

"There's a lot wrong with him," grunted the captain. "Besides the fact that he got something to eat on Megair 4 and tried to betray us to the Cannibals. I don't know why we saved him."

"Because we couldn't just leave him to be eaten, I suppose," said Goth, scanning the screens. "Leewit, call your Na'kalauf friend. They sounded panicky. I don't see any problems right now. I'll just get Vezzarn to the bridge to mind the shop. I have a feeling that I might need to be with you."

"I'm at the shoot first and ask questions later stage with that particular passenger," said Pausert tersely.

A few moments later Vezzarn came in hastily. "There's a lot of yelling coming from Mebeckey's stateroom, Captain."

"That's where we're off to, Vezzarn. Ah. Here is Ta'zara. We may need you to come and sit on someone. Those two didn't actually say what was wrong with him."

Ta'zara looked at the Leewit. "If you permit," he said calmly.

"What?"

"I am in your service, the Leewit. You accepted me. I am your man. Your guard-of-the-body. To honor my debt."

Goth had heard of the Na'kalauf and their honor system. But she was sure that her little sister hadn't. Well, she could probably use a bodyguard for a little while! "The Leewit's got herself her first man," she said, poking her tongue out at her sister. There was a fair amount of payback owing.

The Leewit looked utterly confused. "You saved his life. Now he owes his life to you. He is your bondsman," explained the captain, getting up and checking his blaster. "So he needs orders from you, not me."

"Oh. Well, I order you to obey the captain," said the Leewit, absorbing this. "For now, anyway. I might want to change my mind later. Anyway. I am going along to see what trouble the missionaries are in this time."

They went to the room Mebeckey had taken as his own. There was no shrieking now, so they pushed the door open.

One of the missionary doctors was taking Mebeckey's pulse. Mebeckey lay on the floor, his eyes rolled back. He was twitching convulsively.

But that was far from the most horrific aspect. Thin greenish-black tendrils were oozing out of his nose—it looked rather like jointed hair. It too was twitching. And twining and untwining around itself.

"What in Patham's second hell is it?" asked the captain.

"We don't know. But he started to have a fit earlier and next thing that plant started to come out of him. I tried to pull it out—and it tried to climb into *me*," said one of the brothers. "I pulled it off, but it has little hooks on it."

He showed them his forearm with a double row of tiny weals on it. "It's some kind of parasite, I would guess."

"Is he going to die?" asked the Leewit, pushing her way forward.

One of the missionary doctors shook his head. "His heart rate is elevated and his breathing is fast—which is natural enough, under the circumstances. All things considered, he will probably live."

With an audible ripping sound, the last of the tendrils came free of Mebeckey's nose and dropped onto the floor. Then the plant—or whatever it was—began slowly coiling and spiking its way across.

The Leewit knelt beside Mebeckey and put her hands onto his convulsing body. "No, little girl. Leave him alone," said one of the Dell brothers and reached to pick her up.

"I wouldn't do that!" said Pausert. "Leave her."

"We're doctors. He might be infectious."

The Leewit looked up. "Keep them away. And watch that thing, Captain."

"She's a healer," said Pausert.

"It might be dangerous." said the Dell brother, leaning in to pick up the Leewit—to find himself suspended.

Ta'zara held him by the collar. "What shall I do with him, mistress?"

"Just keep him away from me," said the Leewit. "I'm busy. Captain, Goth, lend me some strength?" They came forward and put their hands on her shoulders. Pausert opened himself up to the littlest witch.

Mebeckey gave a final convulsive shudder and lay still. "He's fine," said the Leewit. Then she hauled him upright and slapped his face until his eyes opened.

"Let him rest!" protested one of the brothers.

"He can rest when we're done," said the Leewit grimly. "Do you know what was wrong with you, Mebeckey?"

"Melchin." He pointed weakly at the black-green jointed hairlike mass. "The haploid stage. I thought it was dead, because it stopped controlling. . . . But I became part of the mother-plant again on Megair.

When we reached the Melchin buildings, I was told to keep you there. To keep her there, especially." He nodded toward Goth.

"The Megair Cannibals are part of your Melchin? They've also got stuff like this in them?" demanded the captain.

"No," said Mebeckey. "The buildings were built by Melchin. Cool water-worlds were their first choice for colonies. Their animals thrived best on them. The Megair Cannibals simply took over the Melchin outpost there. Made the tunnels a bit higher. The Megair Cannibals just use the ruins of what was there."

"Meanwhile, what do we do with that thing?" asked Pausert, looking warily at the slow, writhing alien life-form. "I'd say blast it to ash, but we may need to keep some of it for the scientists. How about if I put it in a small space-crate? There were a few left in the hold." .

"I reckon," said Goth. "I'll get one. You watch it, Captain."

"If it starts moving more than in little circles, I'll blast it first and let the scientists analyze the ash," said Pausert as she left.

"It is dying anyway," said Mebeckey. He stared at the filamentous plant. "The haploid needs animals to live in. Something about me poisoned it."

"Lucky you," said the captain, grimly.

"Yes," said Mebeckey.

He sounded faintly doubtful about it.

Goth came back with the space-crate. "How do we get it in?" she asked.

"Let's see if we can chivvy it in with a bit of heat," said the captain. "No one is to touch it."

It did move away from lowest setting heat from a UW, and into the crate. They snapped it closed with some relief. The crate was intended to be space-tight—so it ought, the captain theorized, to be alien-tight. But to make double sure, he bunged the little crate into the freezer, which he also locked. Mebeckey had made no objection to the fact they'd locked him into his own stateroom first. Pausert hoped he was "clean" of the alien life-form, but there was really no way of telling. And the idea of freezing the plant immediately paid some dividends as Pausert found a pack of smoked bollem steaks that had been missed by the looters.

They had something to digest along with the new information. Pausert was glad to find some food. The Leewit was still very young to be using so much klatha energy. Goth at least had a bit more experience and a bit more sense.

Pausert found he was still carefully separating Goth and Vala in his mind. That was going to take some getting used to, and he needed time to do it. The fact that Goth had not had a spare minute to change back from Vala's hair style and color made it more confusing. Pausert did not know if he wanted her to or not. On the other hand, it would make going back to accepting her as the old Goth easier. But did either of them want to? She was older now. Still the same person, but older. It was all very complicated.

Well . . . not really complicated, Pausert realized. Just very unsettling.

His feelings for Goth had been shaped by their relative ages when they met. And his feelings for Vala, the same. The problem was that those were very different feelings, indeed! He'd thought often about Vala over the years—although much less so, he now realized, after he'd met Goth. And some of those thoughts had been, well, pretty intense. You might even say, feverish. And now that he realized Goth and Vala were one and the same, and Goth was indeed getting older and coming to resemble Vala in his mind as well as in her actual appearance . . .

He forced his mind away from the matter. That was a problem for later. And Goth was talking again.

"So the information about where we were came from Mebeckey," she mused. "And the rest of this mother-plant Melchin is obviously wandering around the Empire. Presumably in the form of that ex-assistant of his, Marshi—whom you and I had a brush with back on Nikkeldepain. She seemed very strange, now that I really think of it."

"I didn't know anything about that," said Pausert. "I feel quite stupid about it now. But I wouldn't say 'wandering about.' I'd say throwing a lot of weight about, if she has the Sedmons and Hulik sending out so many ships."

"Well, you did pick up her wig," said Goth.

"That was her? The woman who kidnapped you?"

"Yep," chuckled Goth. "Boy, I had fun in no-shape looking after you!"

"You nearly got me arrested," said Pausert, smiling nostalgically back at her.

"Woo hoo! You two. Will you stop looking at each other like that?" said the Leewit. "You know, this trip is full of unwelcome visitors. You all forgot about that Megair Cannibal we locked up when we got back onto the ship."

Pausert slapped his head. "Entirely."

"He broke out," said the Leewit cheerfully. "The smell of frying steaks must have given him extra strength. He met Ta'zara and me in the passage. I think Ta'zara's mostly better now. He only bounced him around as much as he needed to, not as much as he could. He's tied the Cannibal up and locked him in again. After he gave him some water."

"You've done well with that patient," said Pausert. "He was a wreck. Now he's smiling occasionally. You should be proud."

"Yeah. It feels good," said the Leewit. "I've been thinking about Mebeckey. Little-bit says he 'tastes' better now. She must have been talking about that plant intelligence."

"Well done there too, little one," said the captain.

"If I'd treated him when he broke his arm instead of leaving it to those lame-brains, I might have caught it still alive and inside him. We could have used him to pull some very neat tricks on them, feeding them a pack of lies. On the other hand, you might not have found those steaks." She pulled a truly ferocious face. "And I guess I learned something that I am going to have to deal with. Don't like it much, though."

"And what would that be?"

"Not all your patients will be people you approve of," said the Leewit. "Or that you want to help. But you have to."

"That's a hard lesson," agreed Pausert. "We were just putting together all the pieces of story we know."

"Well, I can tell you one bit you didn't know," said the Leewit cheerfully.

"What?" asked Pausert, warily. The Leewit quite enjoyed springing unpalatable surprises on them.

This one, however, wasn't. "There are no Phantom ships behind us anymore," the Leewit said, pointing at the screen. "And if they'd left our detectors in one piece, they'd be telling you that there is a fleet of ships over there."

Goth peered at the screen. "And I think some more over there. Now which ones are friendly?"

"Well, we can go over and give them all analgesics and see if green filamenty gunk comes out of their noses," said Pausert.

"Do you think that is what made it come out?" asked the Leewit.

"Seems likely," said Goth. "Let's try hailing them, before we go to analgesics."

"It might save us quite a few, as it looks like a fair-sized fleet," said Goth, selecting the narrow-beam hailing frequency. "What ship?" she asked.

There was a pause. "This is Battlecraft *Grim*, Uldune Space Navy, Admiral Morecroft speaking," came the reply. The voice was tinged with respect. "Could you identify yourselves? You have the configuration of the ship we have been ordered to escort, *Venture 7333*."

"What is the name of Hantis's grik-dog?"

"Pul, Your Wisdom. If I might ask what planet she hailed from?"

"Nartheby. And we're glad to see you, Admiral. Any chance of a tender with some food and some extra air-cylinders? We're slowly losing pressure."

"Certainly, Your Wisdom. We have a possible hostile fleet in detector range, and so we'll make all speed back towards Uldune. Uh. If that's all right with you, that is? Or we can transfer you across to the flagship?"

"Thank you, Admiral," said the Leewit regally. "But

we have things that probably need to stay on this ship for now. Might need decontamination. Besides, we love her."

"Understood, Your Wisdom. We'll take up a defensive formation around you."

So they formed up around the *Venture*, and a few minutes later a tender dropped a spacecrate on a limpet anchor at the cargo-bay airlock.

"Perfect," said Goth. "We even have a tractor to bring that in."

Soon they had more air-pressure and enough food for even the Leewit's ravening appetite, and had reassured Hulik and the Daals of Uldune that all was well and the ship was heading for the former pirate planet under safe escort. And the other fleet had turned and scattered.

"Well," said the Leewit, pushing away her plate finally. "What's next?"

"Talking to Threbus and Toll," said Goth grumpily. "I've got some words to say to our father about business and how to leave your affairs."

"And we need to find out just who all is involved in this search for Goth, and deal with this Marshi," said Pausert. "I think we might want to hold off on telling the Sedmons that we've discovered a serious chink in the Phantom ships' armor just yet."

"We've also got to go and find the circus," said Goth, her eyes twinkling at the Leewit. "But I guess you don't want to be there for that part, eh?"

"I'll get Ta'zara to hold you down," said the Leewit, darkly. "What will happen to him and the others, now?"

"I suppose the missionaries are free to go missionarying again. I am not too sure what we do with

Mebeckey or your Megair Cannibal. As for Ta'zara," Goth scowled, "he's sworn to protect you, little sister. That's how the Na'kalauf work. But don't you even try to turn him on me. The captain will put you in a protective bubble if you do. And probably me too. But he'll let me out. And I'll make you swim home by the Egger Route."

"So when do we go to the circus?" demanded the Leewit, quite unperturbed by the threats.

CHAPTER 27

There was, of course, a limit to what could be said via subradio. There was too much potential for eavesdropping, even on an encoded and narrow beam.

"We think we may have a handle on what was happening in the Chaladoor region," said Pausert. "And a possible way of protecting against it. But there are a whole crop of extra mysteries and problems that have come up as a result."

"Isn't that always the case," said Threbus, laughing. "And how are my daughters?"

"Quite a bit older in Goth's case, and the Leewit has acquired herself a Na'kalauf bodyguard. I think, just for the meanwhile, she should keep him. Oh, and we established exactly where the Megair Cannibals have their home base. But at the moment, the Phantom ships are preventing them and anyone else passing through the Chaladoor. We only got through by taking a long route, *Venture*'s old route. An expedition that you did many years ago."

"Well, one's loss is another's gain," said Threbus. "I'd almost forgotten that expedition. It nearly bankrupted me. Paid off very poorly in terms of new discoveries or trade. So the route helped, eh?"

"You might say so," said Pausert, thinking of parts of it that he could have left out. "It was still tricky. And how goes the Imperial cultural tour?"

"Wildly," said Threbus.

Pausert had to laugh, imagining the little vatch problems. Then he handed Threbus over to his daughter—who gave him several kinds of hell about the state he had left his affairs in, back on Nik-keldepain.

Two days later they sat with Hulik and one of the Sedmons. As telepathically linked clones, the Sedmons didn't have to all be present to know exactly what was going on. And they avoided having more than one of them seen at any time. But the Leewit insisted on giving the feared Daal six hugs. Sedmon looked quite taken aback, but very touched.

"The woman called Marshi is operating under the name Tchab," explained Hulik.

"She has a criminal empire that may rival the Agandar's pirate one," said the Sedmons. "She has taken over a number of the criminal family syndicates. Moreover, it has been very difficult for us to penetrate her organization. She subverts our agents. It was more by luck than good judgment that we discovered that we were being penetrated instead, and we were able to intercept instructions about you."

The Leewit grimaced. "She's a plant."

"You mean she was put there by the Empire?" asked Hulik.

"No, I mean she's a plant. A vegetarian."

"You mean a vegetable," said Goth. "And I don't think that is quite what you mean either, Leewit. A vegetarian is a human that eats plants, this plant eats humans. She's—"

"Like I said: A plant. Like a weed. But one that grows in people." The Leewit gestured: "You know. Like really inside."

Hulik raised her perfect eyebrows. "Really?"

"Yes. And in a way she's rather like Sedmon of the six lives," said Pausert. "There is only one plant. But it has haploid plantlets growing in those it controls. They appear to be telepathically linked. Mebeckey—the first of our rescues in the Chaladoor—was a xenoarcheologist who was really the root cause of Marshi becoming infected with it. He was himself infected with the spores of the plant, and became a subordinate, but he was out of range of the telepathic plant most of the time. We think that he is clean now."

"So these things are out there, breeding and taking over humans?" said the Sedmon.

"No. Well, not if the xenoarcheologist is to be believed. This is the haploid stage. Normally the nondominant stage, with the mother-tree controlling all. To breed, they need a better host species than humans."

"That's not something I am unhappy about," said the Sedmon with his characteristic dry humor. "By the way, Hulik has something to tell you."

She blushed. "It's not public knowledge. But we are due some sextuplets."

"Sextuplets!" exclaimed Goth, looking at the still-slim Hulik do Eldel.

"It seemed the best way," said Hulik. "And Karres was very obliging in helping it happen without embryo-surgery. We owe you."

"Well! Congratulations!" Pausert shook the Sedmon firmly by the hand and kissed Hulik.

"Any nasty surprises with precog names?" asked Goth suspiciously.

"Not that we know of," said Hulik, looking puzzled. "Why?"

"Karres business," said Goth. "Best that you don't know. Anyway, I am not going to tell you. Congratulations. I am coming around to babies. But rather slowly."

Hulik looked at her. Looked at Pausert. "So tell us more about these telepathic plants. They plainly still are a problem even if they can't spread."

"I think that they *can* spread," said the captain regretfully. "I suspect that some spores were taken along by Marshi from the stasis box on the cindered world. But they have a finite supply."

"How finite?" asked the former Imperial agent and current consort to the Daal. Right then she seemed more like a deadly agent.

Pausert shrugged. "How do we know, Hulik? We know very little about these aliens. But I can imagine if that they took over one of the Sedmons, it could be serious."

"Very," said Hulik, in a tone so cold that it approached absolute zero degrees.

"I suggest that you get Mebeckey and extract as

much information from him as possible. What a trip! Have you ever heard of anyone making not one but two rescues from the Chaladoor?"

"Only the witches of Karres would even think of it," said Hulik.

"Which is one of the reasons we are very careful to stay on the right side of Karres," said the Sedmons. "We have grik-dogs to protect us against Nanites. What can we do about these plants?"

"In some ways they're less serious," explained Pausert, glad to offer some words of comfort. "It appears that a simple analgesic will make the body toxic to the plant, cause the plant to leave it. And the victim will undergo a complete recovery, it seems. Ask Mebeckey."

"I think we will," said Hulik do Eldel. "We have some very sensitive truth meters."

"And a few people guaranteed to explain to him that the truth is worth telling," said the Sedmon, making it clear that he was the Daal of dread Uldune, and the Lord of the ancient House of Thunders, where they still skinned crooks alive. Pausert hoped that Mebeckey told the whole truth and very fast. Uldune would have no problem with his criminal background. That was fine—just so long as he didn't try it on Uldune. Otherwise, he'd discover that its bloody pirate-port history was only covered by a very thin layer of varnish, a varnish that cracked quite easily.

"We've got samples of the plant frozen in a space-crate, if you want to get your scientists working on it. So long as you understand that it is exceptionally dangerous stuff. They'll have to work remotely, just in case. We really have very little idea of what we are dealing with here. We wouldn't mind knowing quite a lot more."

Sedmon nodded. "It will be done. And on issues like this, Uldune and Karres stand shoulder to shoulder." He smiled crookedly at them, and took Hulik's hand. "In other matters, of course, it is Patham's devils take the hindmost."

"We have two missionaries who can help you with that," said the Leewit, generously. "They're experts. Really."

"Although you may want the Megair Cannibal we brought along instead. He might be a better bargain," said Pausert.

Hulik laughed. "Is there anything you didn't collect on this trip?"

"Quite a few answers are still missing," admitted Captain Pausert.

That wasn't the only thing missing. Mebeckey was too.

The xenoarcheologist obviously still had some contacts with the underworld, even here on Uldune in the capital city of Zergandol. By the look on the Sedmon's face, some Daalmen were going to be working overtime until Mebeckey was rounded up again.

The *Venture* was to have a major refit, which she needed after her encounter with the Megair Cannibals. The captain, Goth, the Leewit, and her new bodyguard had to find somewhere to stay. Instinct made the captain shy away from the Daal's fortress-palace, the House of Thunders. But a guest house for visiting diplomats on the outskirts of Zergandol was a good alternative. It was a far step up from the frowsty lodgings they'd rented here the first time they'd come to Uldune, as fugitives.

It was also slightly less difficult for them to receive a secretive caller. "Olimy!" exclaimed Goth.

Olimy held his finger to his lips and set up a small device with several spidery metallic arms. "Spy-proofing," he said. "This *is* Uldune, Goth, and you can bet that the Daalmen and a half a dozen others are watching this place. My, you've grown! Looking more like your mother every time I see you."

"I think that's a compliment," said Goth.

"Oh, it is," said Olimy easily. "I had a big crush on her when I was younger. She was a few years older than me and I don't think she even knew that I was alive."

"Last time we weren't at all sure that you were alive," said Goth. He'd been disminded and in a state of suspended animation after his brush with Moander in pursuit of Manaret's synergiser crystal, when they'd transported him across the Chaladoor.

"I owe you and Captain Pausert a debt of thanks for that! Anyway, Threbus and Toll sent me. It was obvious that there was stuff you didn't want to say on the subradio."

Goth nodded. "Let me call the captain and the Leewit."

"The Leewit!" exclaimed Olimy. "Is she still the holy terror she used to be?"

"Oh no," said Goth. "She's worse. Now she has an enforcer too and not just those whistles. But actually she's grown up a lot. Nearly ready for missions of her own, I think. But I wouldn't tell her that."

"I wouldn't dream of it," agreed Olimy solemnly.

Goth went and called the captain and the Leewit using some innocent pretext. It wouldn't fool the watchers, because when they disappeared it would be obvious, but she did her best.

"So," said Olimy, once he'd been introduced to the captain and had been pummeled by the Leewit. "What weren't you saying on the subradio?"

"Well, we found out that the Phantom ships are not impervious to gravity. It seems to affect whatever mechanism they're using to move or to stay intangible. You can get at them with a simple grav-tractor. Obviously we still had to evade their torpedoes to get close enough, but once they realized we could do it, it put them off attacking us."

"Very useful. Going around the Chaladoor was making things difficult for us. But I also see why you didn't really want to inform Uldune. To have them pushing aggressively into that part of space serves no one well."

"The Daal might disagree with you," said Goth. "Anyway, that's not the only problem out there. There's Marshi, or as she now calls herself, Tchab."

"Who is directing a lot of muscle, financial and otherwise, into looking for one Vala—or, as she now calls herself, Goth," said Olimy with a grin. "She's actually proving very hard to deal with. She's taken over two of the big criminal families. Your mother was all for just going in bare-knuckle and dealing with her. But we've been trying more subtle means. Anyway, just getting to her has proved difficult. She has a very good communication network and some fanatically loyal employees."

"She doesn't have either," said Goth. "She *is* both.

She's a telepathic plant, and the communication is between her and her fellow parts of the same mother-plant. They're all just one thing, see. But I think she's the heart of it."

Goth proceeded to explain, with interjections from the other two, just where Marshi/Tchab had come from. She detailed her adventures on Nikkeldepain, with considerable interest from the Leewit, who was still very treasure minded. Filling in what they'd found out from Mebeckey, she became less so. "So it's the Illtraming that Marshi and her fellow plant-invaded are really after. Without them they'll eventually just die. Somehow this map or box came into Threbus's possession. I removed it, which led them to believe I was part of one of the criminal families."

"That's probably why she took them over," said Olimy.

"Well, then I disappeared. They simply couldn't find me because I wasn't there—vanished in time. They must have got onto the trail again about when we got to the Imperial Capital. Got DNA or retinal prints or something."

"I think we need, first, to recover that map. Probably destroy it. Humans don't need the Melchin mother-plant. Some things are better extinct. And if the Illtraming still survive out there, somewhere, they certainly don't need the Melchin back either."

Goth nodded. "They really are creepy. But the vatches, by the way, can tell who is plant-invaded."

Olimy screwed up his face as if in pain. "Not more vatch work!"

"And so how goes the dealing with the Nanite plague? Sounded as though—reading between the lines—Threbus was having fun with the vatches."

Olimy held his head in his hands and laughed. "You have no idea how much of a circus—and I mean a circus—it has turned out to be. It's effective, all right. But the little vatches are a very fickle audience. And their tastes run more to Himbo Petey than to Richard Cravan. And of course the fact that people lose their minds just after the circus has been ... well, it wouldn't take much to start plague rumors associated with them. We've had to do a lot of very careful clean-ups, post operations."

"I can imagine!"

"Yes. Fortunately the Nanites tend to estrange their victims from their families. Anyway, we think we're winning, but we'll have to keep it up for a good few more years yet."

"More touring with the lattice ships. So: we need to know: Where is the *Petey B* now? Because we'll need to pay it a visit."

"Yay!" said the Leewit, clapping her hands.

"Psaria II at the moment, Mandellin's World next," said Olimy. "We could arrange a pick up."

"Might have fun finding it!" said Goth. "And I am not saying where just in case this spy-protection is not beyond the Daalmen."

Olimy gave her a crooked grin. "You're a pretty sharp operative yourself, you know."

"I seem to be developing some new klatha skill. Not quite sure what it is, but it hit me hard on Megair. Anyway, if I was a bit sharper, and I had known what I was dealing with," said Goth ruefully, "I'd have dealt with Marshi permanently. I could have slipped her an analgesic ... Hang on. I did. I injected her in the museum, and it didn't work. Worked slowly on the fellow that was pretending to be Mebeckey, and not at all on her. She got up and ran."

"Hmm," Olimy said, considering. "It might need to be that specific kind of analgesic. Or you might have hit a button or a zipper or something, and not got enough into her."

"The problem is we just don't know. Or it might have been something else. I hope the Sedmon's scientists give us something to work on," said Pausert heavily. "The one thing about Karres work is that we spend a lot of time just not knowing enough. Feeling as if you are a rat in someone's complicated maze."

"That's for sure," said Olimy with feeling. "I'm going to take this information to someone else, who will take it on to Karres. No, I don't know where that is right now either. But there are links. And watchers."

CHAPTER 28

The repairs and refit of the *Venture* took less time and more money than Pausert had anticipated. Doing Karres's business could be an expensive pastime, the captain reflected ruefully, checking his finances. Well, Karres was good for it. And it was good to be back on the *Venture* again, the captain decided, as they boosted for Mandellin's world. They'd hidden their intentions as well as possible, but Pausert was still nervous about the missing Mebeckey. They'd saved his life, not once, but thrice, and still he'd run off. True, they'd been less than trusting after the final incident. But what did the man expect?

The Megair Cannibal, now cowed and terrified himself, was taken away by the Daalmen. When asked what they were going to do with him, the squad leader explained. "He's going to the Daals' research labs. I believe they have instructions to keep him alive and to learn as much as possible of the Megair Cannibal language. We can at least try to get that from him. Besides, they want to look at his physiology."

The Dell brothers, for all their sanctimonious piety and thanking Patham—not the *Venture*'s crew—for their rescue, were still deeply grateful to Patham for making his instruments available and happy to be back in human society. Already they were preaching up a storm on Uldune, with an impressive and not widely believed tale of great Patham's preservation of their lives among the Megair Cannibals.

Ta'zara had decided that the Leewit was the human vessel of his salvation and was planning to honor that debt, and only the Leewit could possibly persuade him otherwise. He could hardly be unaware that he was dealing with Karres witches—but that was of no importance to him, it seemed. He followed her like an adoring puppy. He had a berth on the *Venture*, because, as Goth put it, he'd just run behind otherwise, and then they'd have to feel guilty because he couldn't breathe vacuum. He was also an even better cook than the new robo-butler. And they had him teaching them the ancient Na'kalauf martial arts, which helped to pass the time on the long space journey to the agricultural Mandellin's World.

Which proved to be full of cornfields and empty of circuses. They set down and started asking questions.

The lattice ship had moved on. To the neighboring giant world of Pampez for the annual wisent round-up and fair, or so they were informed.

That was barely a two-day hop. Soon the world

of Pampez swung below them, an enormous ancient world where the internal fires had long since cooled. Light in metals and not overly endowed with water, the wind had flattened the world into an almost endless plain. The captain put the ship into orbit and got the Leewit to call port control.

A little later, as the world of greens and beiges turned below, the Leewit came to the captain's cabin. "Not getting any answer, Captain. But there are ships landing all the time. Maybe they don't have port control?"

Pausert came to the control room in time to see two vast freighters going in to land. There was no communicator chatter from them or from below. "It's possible, I suppose. It happens on Vaudevillia. But it's unlike any local government to miss a chance to collect duties. Well, let's go in. If we can deal with the Megair Cannibals, then we can deal with the local officials."

"Maybe," said Goth cheerfully. "Although Nikkeldepain taught me that some of them can make the Cannibals seem downright friendly."

"Well, those Cannibals were pretty welcoming, seeing as we were delivering fresh meat," said Vezzarn. "So where do we land, Captain? Just follow them?"

Pausert looked on the long-range scopes. "They seem to be heading for the point of those dust plumes. So I think we should too."

They did. And it soon became apparent that the reason for there being no port control was that there was no port. Just endless hard-baked flatness with huge herds of wisents being loaded. The town wasn't much of a town, either. Its only reason for being was a low

rock-ridge and an up-welling aquifer along its edge
that provided a hundred-mile-long drinking trough.
Much of the year, this town barely woke up. Right
now, however, the herdsmen were seeing that it barely
slept. And the circus was there too.

The synthasilk bunting was still bright above the
dusty town. Goth and the Leewit were both surprised
at how it called to them. Even the captain was smiling, humming his "escapists" background music. It
felt, if not like coming home, at least like arriving at
an old friend's home.

"Petey, Byrum and Keep," said the Leewit happily
to Ta'zara. "The best show in the galaxy!"

The bodyguard had rapidly become a cross between
a personal servant and a favorite uncle. He had quietly
come to ask Pausert's advice, though. "She talks to
thin air, Captain," he'd said worriedly.

"She's from Karres," Pausert explained. "They do
that." It was easier than trying to explain vatches to
him. Or klatha.

Vezzarn stayed with the ship. "I'm too old for the
circus. And I want to check that tube, Skipper. I think
they rushed the alignment."

They walked down the bustling streets of the town,
past merchants selling everything that saddle nomads
might want to part with their hard earned maels for,
and quite a lot else besides. Wind-etched and sun-
bitten men and women in leathers with extravagant
wide-brimmed hats bargained, drank and celebrated
at the town's watering holes—or just walked, taking in
the crowds, the sights, the buildings. And, of course,
headed for the synthasilk magnificence of the lattice

ship circus. The *Venture*'s crew joined the human tide flowing towards the turnstiles.

They hadn't even gotten to the turnstiles when a beaming Himbo Petey came out in person to greet them and to escort them through like visiting royalty.

"We got word that you were coming. We've been watching out for you. So here's hoping that you've come to rejoin us?" asked the showmaster. "Ethy will be here just as soon as she gets offstage."

"I wish," said Goth, as they made their way past the sideshows. "But I'm afraid that we've just come in to look for something in the second props room."

Himbo Petey twirled his mustachios. They really had improved since Karres, thought Goth. "So you won't be with us for more than six months then. I keep asking Ethy to let us tidy out that junk-pile. And she keeps telling me that I don't understand what *artistes* need." He smiled contentedly. "You have heard that we are expecting a new production!"

"Something not by Shakespeare?" asked Pausert, knowing Himbo's tastes.

"No," said Himbo, looking rather self-satisfied. "Something co-produced by the two of us. Although my input was but a small one."

The Leewit got it first. "Not more babies!" she said, in tones of disgust. "I think it's catching, Goth."

Pausert shook Himbo, now quite pink, firmly by the hand. "I'm delighted. As must be the whole of the lattice ship."

"Well, yes," said Himbo Petey. "The show must go on, and without an heir..."

"No precog names?" said Goth.

"Well, no. He'll be Himbo Junior, of course."

Goth hugged him. "Somehow the idea of a junior Himbo Junior is very cute."

"Are you selling out, Goth?" demanded the Leewit crossly. "Next thing I know you'll be all gooey about babies too."

It suddenly occurred to Goth that although the Leewit might not realize it, her little sister didn't like the idea of not being the baby of the family anymore. "You little dope! You know the terms of the agreement with the circus. You were there. It's a family business and needs a new Petey to go on."

"Oh. Well, congratulations, Himbo," said the Leewit, suddenly munificent. She looked at the ringmaster. "He'll never have as fine a moustache, though."

Himbo laughed. "Nonsense! He'll be born with one. He has a show to run."

"So how is the show going?" asked Pausert.

Himbo laughed again. "Well, you'd think that an Imperial cipher and a funding budget would help. But I conclude that the thespians think that just means more fancy stages, costumes and sets. We have a revolving stage now. And what did it do but get stuck the other day. And before that it decided to suddenly start slowly rotating midscene in the middle of that 'to be' soliloquy. I always thought that we could cut it to six words, and the stage seemed to agree with me. But our Hamlet didn't notice and disappeared . . . and the audience found they were watching King Claudius and Ophelia kissing and getting rather involved on a chair in the next set. It gave Hamlet a really plausible reason for murder, if you ask me."

Goth had to suspect vatchy interference.

"But Pampez has been good to us. Mostly locals, of course, hungry for a bit of galactic-class culture," he said proudly, "But today we also seem to have had an influx of off-world wisent buyers."

"How do you know they're wisent buyers?" asked Pausert.

"They don't wear local clothes—they're wearing suits," explained Himbo. "No one wears suits except wisent buyers here—and why else does anyone come to Pampez? Well, unless you're selling or entertaining. And then you don't have spare time to take in even the finest of shows."

They'd made slow progress, as all the show-folk were calling greetings and wanting to talk. They'd drawn level with the fanderbags. Goth had a sudden realization, as the long inquisitive mobile noses sniffed at her, that these were possibly "her" babies. She sniffed determinedly and went to stroke and pet the sensitive spots on those noses. They remembered her, too, though possibly not from their birth. But you never could tell with fanderbags.

"Mother was right," she said to Pausert. "Messing around with time is not worth the heartaches."

"I thought it was," he said quietly. "If it wasn't for someone called Vala, my own childhood would have been a lot drearier."

She sniffed again. He said just the right things sometimes. "Let's go and look in the props store and then go home," she said gruffly. "We'll come back when it's all sorted for a proper visit, Himbo. Promise."

"Missy Goth. We seem to have picked up a tail," said Ta'zara quietly.

Goth took a quick look up from the fanderbags.

There were an unusually large number of men in suits, not the local soft fringed leather outfits, in the sideshow aisle.

Himbo Petey had been running *Petey, Byrum and Keep* for a good many years and travelled across some of the rougher spots in the galaxy. He pulled his communicator out of his pocket. "Security. We have a condition amber. Get Fetz and Porro up on the gate towers and let me have what you can spare in sideshow three. Be warned. They're probably packing heat." He turned to Pausert. "Captain, something looks very odd here. Go out through the fanderbag enclosure, and up. I'll deal with this."

"Don't stick your neck out," said Pausert. "It's Karres business. We didn't expect problems, but..."

"Karres problems are my problems too, now," said Himbo Petey, looking a lot less like a dumpy, jovial, mustachioed ringmaster and more like someone you wouldn't want to argue with. "Now go."

They scrambled through the fence. And immediately trouble started to happen.

First, the suits came running up to follow. Himbo stood four-square in their way. "You can't go through there."

"Get out of the way, you fat fool," Goth heard behind them. Then she saw the flare of a blaster.

She couldn't help but turn. They couldn't shoot Himbo! Not Himbo Petey!

One of them had—or tried, rather. But he also misjudged his target speed and his target's response. Himbo Petey always carried a whip tucked into his belt, and it was not just a macho ornament. He might have had one arm singed, but he was still standing—which was more than you could say for the shooter. He'd learned a lesson about whips, for sure.

He'd also learned a lesson about being a town-bred thug and using a gun in a place like this. The wisent herders of Pampez used their weapons every day as the tools of their trade, and not just occasionally to intimidate or murder. The locals didn't use expensive blasters, but old-fashioned slug-throwers. The thug had been shot six times, at least two of those shots coming after Himbo Petey's lash had disarmed him.

Himbo looked up at the Karres witches. Goth could see other suits, whose hands had been suspiciously inside their jackets, now hastily withdrawing those hands. Himbo waved. "Go," he ordered.

They could hardly do otherwise. He was Himbo Petey, the ringmaster, and this was his circus. He gave the orders here! So they made their way along the upper walkway toward the hulk that was the second props store.

"There's more of them," said the Leewit.

Marshi's thugs had found them, and she seemed to be directing them telepathically. If they'd been "seeded" like Mebeckey, they were all a part of her.

They all had blasters. "Give them a whistle, Leewit," said Goth.

The littlest witch did, and the damage was going to cost Himbo Petey and Karres a fair amount to replace. Electronic equipment shattered. So did all the piezoelectric crystals at the heart of the modern blaster. At a guess, from this height, the Leewit must have shattered half the piezoelectric crystals in equipment across the lattice ship.

That didn't stop the orchestrated chase. They met a

group of ten "professional enforcers" running in from a side stage. They were probably quite good with guns, and maybe with things like knuckle-dusters, knives or coshes. Ta'zara, however, wasn't just *quite* good at fighting. And when you added a shrill whistle that doubled them up in pain before the Na'kalauf man and the captain had even got started, it was a fairly one-sided conflict. However, Goth realized that while it was one-sided, the enemy was committing a lot of resources to it. Marshi must have several hundred of them here, inside the lattice ship. The sounds of fighting were widespread now. And the plant-woman could coordinate her forces.

"Time for no-shape," said Goth. "Leewit, you hold onto Ta'zara. Keep him calm."

One moment they were there, the next, gone. Goth could hear her sister explaining. "It's like when we were disguised as Megair Cannibals. Only now we're disguised as nothing at all. Don't worry. You can still feel my hand."

Invisible, but holding hands, they made their way onwards. It was apparent that circus security, aided by the local wisent-herders, were engaged in battle royal with Marshi's thugs. Without functioning blasters, the thugs were finding this was not a happy place to be, since the Leewit's whistle hadn't done any harm at all to the wisent-herders' simple slug-throwers. But there were a lot of them.

Goth led them down and away from the props store a little so that the Leewit could do some whistling—and then she had to reluctantly lead them away from the sight of Dame Ethy leading a contingent of actors armed with broken bleacher-backs into the fray. Looking at her, hearing her battle-cry—straight from one of those ancient operas that Himbo had simply refused to contemplate them putting on—Goth felt sorry for the attackers if Himbo Petey had more than a flesh wound. And moreover, she relled vatches. She could imagine that they'd be less than happy about having their portable supply of fascinating dreams hurt or damaged!

The props store was locked, but she still knew the combination, and soon they were inside the old hulk, insulated from the battle that raged outside. And not knowing exactly where to start. Sorting through it all could take several touring seasons, and they didn't have that kind of time. Heaven knew what numbers Marshi had available to commit to the task, but it seemed she wasn't shy to use them all. The Agandar's pirate fleet had numbered at least ten thousand pirates strong. This, Hulik had said, was a more powerful force still. Goth simply had to find the box and get out, and then Sheewash away from Marshi's grasp.

She closed her eyes and felt for it with her mind... and then it occurred to her. The box didn't weigh more than a couple of pounds, and she knew exactly what it looked like.

She 'ported it into her hands—and then dropped it. She'd forgotten how unpleasant it felt.

"Got it. I just need a bag for it," said Goth, looking around.

Pausert bent down and picked it up. "I could just carry it." Plainly, the box did not affect him in the same way!

"I guess you could," said Goth, unsettled by her contact with the alien device. "Let's go."

They left the shelter of the hulk that was the second

props store and Manicholo and Goth's favorite hideout. Out in the lattice-tent, it was plain that between the locals, the circus-folk and the vatches, the criminals from the inner cities of the Empire that Marshi had shipped in were losing. Goth saw Himbo Petey and Ketering mounted on fanderbags, chasing several of them down.

The temptation was to join in. Common sense, however, said to get the alien box out of there and onto the *Venture*. Reluctantly Goth decided that was the better course to choose.

So, still invisible, they left the synthasilk of *Petey, Byrum and Keep* and headed toward the *Venture*— suffering, of course, from the inevitable problems of invisibility in a crowded environment.

After a few yards in the shopping thoroughfare, Goth couldn't take it anymore and led them into an emporium selling saddles for wisents. There, she changed them from no-shape into the appearance of local wisent herders. The disappointed shopkeeper watched them all troop out and continue to walk towards the *Venture*. Goth looked forward to the sanctuary of her hull.

CHAPTER 29

The open airlock and ramp were barely fifty yards ahead when the dart hit Pausert. His first and instinctive reaction, as the peculiar numbness spread through his limbs and made him fall like a puppet whose strings have suddenly been severed, was to englobe Goth and then the Leewit in a protective cocoon. He was dimly aware of a fight and being manhandled. Wanting to resist but being slack-muscled and helpless. And then...oblivion.

Goth saw Captain Pausert stagger and felt the familiar surge of klatha energy as she stepped towards him to help...and found herself in the egglike shield-cocoon of impenetrable klatha energy. The side effect of this was to have her fall like a skittle. So had Pausert—but without any transparent cocoon of force to keep him from the ground. She saw that the Leewit, too, had tumbled—also in a klatha-shield-cocoon. But her little sister was plainly not conscious, because she lay still, her eyes rolled back.

Running towards them from where they had obviously been hiding were a substantial number of men whose city pallor and clothing identified them as Marshi's men. As they arrived, Ta'zara exploded up from next to the Leewit. The first man found himself airborne, flung back into his companions. Goth began her own fight back too. Hampered yet protected inside the shield cocoon, she could still 'port objects. And sow chaos. The air itself seemed to become as thick as soup, almost impossible to see through. Objects came pelting down on the attackers as fast as she could 'port them. Ta'zara, merely one spiral-tattooed man, became four and then sixteen.

That might even have stopped them if they'd been a force of men and not just part of the mother-plant. As it was, it merely slowed them down.

Still, that was enough to call the Pampez citizenry into the act, and there were even more of them than Marshi had been able to deploy. The herders had to deal with wisent buyers. That certainly didn't mean that they liked them. Men in city-people clothes attacking people dressed like fellow herders? They had no doubt whose side they were on.

The ground shook with a close proximity launch. The *Venture* climbed skyward, and Goth realized, as the dust and smoke cleared and left them lying in the field of combat, that Marshi had gotten all she cared about. The box. The thing she called the Illtraming map. And she had something Goth cared much more about, too.

They'd taken Captain Pausert. And here Goth was, trapped in the cocoon shield Pausert had created to protect her, with no way out. Only the captain could extricate them.

The Leewit was either dead or unconscious. Ta'zara was wounded but alive and trying to stand. Goth swore furiously, angry, frustrated, desperate tears pricking at her eyelids. Had they killed the captain?

Then the hard-headed Goth, a far more dangerous person than the half-panicked Goth, reasserted herself. They'd hardly bother to take his body. She remembered now that several of the miscreants had even tried to pick her up.

Pushing his way through the fast-forming crowd of wisent-herders came Himbo Petey. He had the right tool for pushing. He was still riding a fanderbag. And up beside him was none other than Olimy. They were clearing people out of the way, and a few moments later Himbo was attending to Ta'zara.

Olimy was signing to her. "Are you all right?" at a guess. And then a floater from the lattice ship arrived, and, with difficulty, they loaded her and Leewit onto it and took them back to the big synthasilk and beam structure, to Himbo's office. Here Goth 'ported a piece of paper and pen in to herself, and then back to the Karres witch.

Marshi has taken the captain and the llltraming box-map.

How do we get you out of there? wrote Olimy.

The captain has to do it, wrote Goth. *Subradio. Tell Sedmons and Karres what happened.*

Olimy nodded. Venture *will be hunted*, he wrote.

That was a start. But Goth wanted to hunt it herself.

And when she caught up with Marshi, she was going to deliver a generous dose of weedkiller.

Can you tell me how the Leewit is? she wrote.

We can see no injuries. She's breathing. There is what appears to be a tranq dart in there with her. We assume she, and Pausert, were shot with those.

Goth could almost not breathe with relief. She felt quite faint.

We have a surgeon with Ta'zara, Olimy added.

Goth forced herself to be calm and to think. What was Olimy doing here? Either he'd been with the circus—he knew what had been going on with the vatchlets, or had been sent to watch it, when she handed information on to him. Let it be a lesson to her, she thought savagely. If they'd sneaked in disguised or even in some other ship, and then slipped into the circus, they'd not have been tracked . . .

And then it occurred to her. Marshi's operatives had been here *before* they got here. Either waiting or already searching. The information must have come from that long-eared, treacherous Mebeckey. She'd probably mentioned the circus—and it would only take the resources of a big criminal outfit a short time to track down *Petey, Byrum and Keep* as the circus that had been on Nikkeldepain when Marshi had been captured.

She needed to get out of this cocoon! It had kept her from getting hurt or captured, she appreciated. But right now she was anything but grateful to the captain for it.

Neither, when they trundled her in on a barrel, awake but definitely confused and angry, was the Leewit.

Actually, by the looks of it, when the Leewit was this angry and plainly trying out her whistles, maybe the best place for her to be was inside one of the captain's cocoon-shields.

The Leewit, once she had got over her initial fright and confusion, and the subsequent rage, which had made her head hurt something fierce with her own whistling, was very relieved to get a piece of paper and pencil 'ported in to her.

Let me out! she demanded.

Can't, wrote Goth. *They got the captain.*

The Leewit, who privately considered her older sister to be tougher than hull-metal, was surprised to see that there was a small tear in the corner of her eye.

She went quite cold with shock. Not . . . dead? Not the captain dead?

She was relieved to see, through blurry eyes, that Goth had written: *Chump. Not dead.*

Trust Goth to have guessed. Sisters did have some upsides. Now to get out of here.

What a strange thing. It was a little vatch. Even smaller than Little-bit, just a vortex of dark energy. **Some dream things are so odd.** It didn't appear to be examining her at all. **Why are you wrapped in vatch-egg-stuff?**

"To keep me safe. But I need to get out now," the Leewit informed it.

But you are long hatched. Why are you in it anyway?

Being patient and able to reason with a vatch was not something the Leewit was given to. But she had some experience with Little-bit.

"To show you what fun you can have letting me out," said the Leewit airily. "Of course, if you were really strong and clever, you could open both this one and that one. But you can't. I know I've stopped you."

Easy. You big dream things think that would stop me? I'm not a new hatchling.

As she fell a few hand spans to the floor, the Leewit reflected that being powerful didn't always make you particularly clever, and that maybe this was just as well.

Goth too was free, rubbing the bit she'd landed on and frowning faintly—a sign of intense concentration in the second of Toll and Threbus's daughters. "Clever Leewit," she said. "Now for the million mael question. Is Little-bit still around the *Venture* and can we talk her into doing stuff for us?"

He was entirely unsure where or even what he was. He stood up. Something told him this place was familiar. But that memory was buried. All that was important was to cover all, to harvest, to bring back to the mother-plant, to create more seedlings. There were other hazy memories of doing something else. Of someone important called Goth. But what was someone? There was only one. The mother-plant. He was part of the mother-plant. It would grow in him and grow in him. Eventually he would be full of the mother-plant and he would burst into a pool of motile fragments.

The idea did not worry the part of the mother-plant that had once been Captain Pausert of Nikkeldepain. He only knew that much because the mother-plant was trying to access the memories of that person that used to be. It had not known what it was to be part of the mother-plant. It had not known purpose: to cover all, to harvest, to bring back to the mother-plant, to create more seedlings.

The memories the mother-plant could access were cloudy, incomplete and disturbing. The mother-plant saw and recognized the Illtraming spacecraft. It had known for some time about the existence of the witches of Karres. But now it saw them for what they were: something that knew of the mother-plant's existence, and had somehow killed a haploid without killing the host, just as the Illtraming had deserted the purpose. Karres would try to stop the mother-plant from covering all, harvesting, bringing back to the mother-plant, and above all: stop the creation of more seedlings.

It had powers that the mother-plant feared. Powers the Illtraming had abused too, in those vile perversions of mother-plant seedships. Ships that went too fast and could not be destroyed. Ships that had forced the mother-plant to turn its last weapon onto them, a weapon that cracked the fabric of space-time itself. The mother-plant had not wished to do that. But the Illtraming would not return to the purpose: to cover all, to harvest, to bring back to the mother-plant, to create more seedlings.

Other life must exist to serve that purpose, not for any other reasons. To do so was evil. The mother-plant rooted among the motile Pausert's memories. It was difficult to access any motile from this strange species properly. This one was more difficult than most. Parts of it were blocked. Parts the mother-plant needed for this "klatha."

But at long last the mother-plant had the Illtraming device. The prime female motile was nearly full now. This had arrived just in time. The device was typical of the Illtraming motiles. They had been cunning little artificers who liked making new and clever things. Even as part of the mother-plant, that aspect of their nature had been useful and not suppressed. Like their love of decoration and patterning objects. The mother-plant knew the decoration was purposeless, did not serve to cover all, to harvest, to bring back to the mother-plant, to create more seedlings, but it had found that preventing that wasteful aspect had also smothered the creativity of useful things for the plant.

It had taken the mother-plant some days to get the new motiles to trigger the device that the Illtraming had created. Clever little motiles—to store and move the complex electronic heart to the navigation system that they had once used to guide the mother-plant seedships thus! It wasn't what the humans understood as "a map," of course. Such a thing worked poorly in the three-dimensionality of space. It was instead a vast database of stellar information. Now the mother-plant could finally see just where the Illtraming homeworld lay. Fortunately, through the archaeological looting she had obtained a powering system that could activate it. There would still be some work necessary before it could cross-reference this onto the human maps. But the mother-plant had vast resources among the new hosts. The mother-plant did not care how it spent them. But it needed its old host. And it needed it soon. The mother-plant seedlings must come to be.

Some of the motiles were allowed a fairly large degree of self-determination. Some even thought on their own, and were just absolutely dependent on the mother-plant via the hormonal feeds to their pleasure centers. This Pausert-part of the plant could be allowed no such freedom, the mother-plant knew. The Pausert-part had told her that it too would be like the Illtraming.

Still, it had brought her much valuable information. The spore planted in it had not been wasted, although there were few spores left now. The motile, it seemed, was valued as an individual—a concept the mother-plant did not fully understand—by the klatha-wielding Karres.

The mother-plant had not wasted a spore on the other captive that the Pausert part knew as "Vezzarn." It wasn't worth keeping. Too old and of too low an order in the human hierarchy. Anyway, it must have escaped. It was no longer on the ship.

The Leewit shrugged. "Maybe. Little-bit is going through a stage right now where she seems to prefer watching. Like interaction is hard work and it's a bit boring. The problem is that she goes anywhere and we don't. I have no idea how to make contact when she doesn't want to. The captain can call them. I can't."

"We need to get after the captain. After our ship."

"Yeah, but how?" asked the Leewit.

"Olimy," said Goth. "I need your ship." It was not a tone that brooked argument.

The Karres agent shook his head, nonetheless. "It's a one man scout, Goth. Besides the fact that you'd kill yourself with overuse of the Sheewash drive, just where are you going to go to?"

That was such impeccable logic that Goth could do no more than glare at him angrily.

"They've got several hours' head start, Goth. The ship could be anywhere," he said.

"Yes. Being right does not make things better for you, Olimy," said Goth darkly. "I'll still need a ship. Unless . . . I'll take the Egger Route!"

Olimy shook his head. "At the risk of being right again, assuming that Captain Pausert is still on the *Venture,* you will arrive in the post-Egger state and at best be captured and more likely be killed."

"It's a case of we need a ship and a one man scout is too small," said the Leewit. "You, me and Ta'zara . . . where is he, by the way?"

"Downstairs. They have a local surgeon with him."

"He's hurt?" The Leewit stood up hastily. "I need to go to him. What happened?"

Olimy put out a hand to stop her. "There was quite a fight after you got tranq-darted and the captain put you inside the cocoon shield. Ta'zara stopped them getting to either of you two. At last count, there were some thirty-two badly battered thugs who he personally hospitalized. He's a one-man army. But he did take some punishment. I don't think you should go there, the Leewit."

"She's a healer, Olimy," said Goth. "You see to getting us a ship. We're going to need it, and the lattice is a little bit too big and heavy."

They went down. If the Leewit was distressed by the state of her bodyguard, she did not let on. The doctor did, briefly, attempt to stop her. The Leewit was not feeling very patient, and the poor man found himself rubbing his bruised head while lying against the far wall. "I'm here," she informed the groggy Ta'zara. "Lie still. I am going to fix what I can."

The Na'kalauf man might have been having trouble getting his eyes to focus since he had a concussion, several gaping wounds, and had lost a great deal of blood, but he knew that voice and recognized the hand taking his. Goth could see him relax.

"They shed ju were orright, mistress. But better f' knowing," he slurred weakly, struggling for breath.

"And shortly you're going to be better still," said the Leewit, exercising perfect control over her voice. Goth only knew that because she knew her sister. "Gothie. Lend me some strength."

Goth had been exhausted by the fight and her klatha use in it. Time had helped a bit. But she was still bone-tired and drained. "Sure. Just . . . don't take too much, see."

The Leewit nodded, completely serious and very much more grown up. "I just need to do some things. The rest will have to heal naturally. Or later. But he's bleeding inside. In his head and body."

"Fix, little sis," she said, putting her hand on the Leewit's shoulder, feeling the surge of klatha energy.

A few minutes later they both sat down. The big tattooed man was breathing easier, and his color and pulse had improved, as the wary doctor informed them.

"Good," said the Leewit. "Now get someone to get us some food. Lots. I'm so tired I don't think I can move, and Goth is in a worse state. You can sew him up now. And give him some more blood. He needs it."

CHAPTER 30

"It seems almost a shame to wake them," Goth heard someone say. She opened her eyes. Olimy and Sedmon looked at her. She and the Leewit were lying on the floor next to the remains of the food they'd devoured before passing out. Someone had been kind enough to provide her with a blanket, Goth noticed. She stretched and shook her head, trying to clear it. One of the Sedmons? Here? How long had she and the Leewit slept?

"What are you doing here?" she asked suspiciously.

"Such a friendly greeting," said one-sixth of the Daal of Uldune. "I heard that you needed a ship. So I brought you mine."

"How long have I been asleep?" Goth rubbed her eyes, trying to get her brain to think clearly. "It's more than a week's travel from here to Uldune, Sedmon."

"You have been out for about twelve hours," said Olimy. "You need to be careful, Goth. You can kill yourself, draining that much energy."

"Had to be done," said Goth. "Olimy, you know Karres pays its debts. And we owed him. How is he, by the way?"

"Considerably better, Your Wisdom," said Ta'zara from the bed against the wall behind her. "Well enough to defend you and the Leewit if need be."

"You just stay put," said Goth firmly. "I don't want to have to do that again in a hurry."

"Is the Leewit all right?" asked Ta'zara. "I would not have had her do herself an injury for me. Your companion Olimy said you could kill yourself, draining that much energy."

"She's fine. She'd sleep through a stampede of wild bollems, that's all. My problem was just having used a lot of energy in that fight."

"And then used even more putting me back together," said Ta'zara. "We of Na'kalauf also honor our debts. My debt to her can not even be repaid with my life."

"I shall have to be more cautious than ever about offending the Leewit," said Olimy with a grin.

Goth helped herself to a slice of pie left over from their pre-sleep frantic feed. "Now, can we stop beating about the bush, Sedmon of the Six Lives," she said. "Or I will personally call a certain lady friend of mine and tell her to make your life—all of them—the equivalent of Patham's third hell."

The lord of the bloody-historied world of Uldune, Master of the House of Thunders, sat down on the floor next to her. "We caught Mebeckey. And he sang. Told us that he had passed information on to

Marshi about you needing to locate a circus. He did it for a price."

"Is he still alive?"

"At the moment, yes." The Daal tugged his chin. "It appears that the plant infestation can be gotten rid of. But it is rather like a highly addictive drug, Goth. He was desperate to get it back. That was all he asked for in exchange. He is already going through more hell than my experts could put him through. In fact, we got him to sing by giving him a palliative. He's a desperate man. You see, he got a new spore from one of her agents . . . and that rejected him too. My scientists are doing tests on him. When we got the news about the circus, we made all the speed that the *Thunderbird* is capable of. That is . . . more than we're willing to admit any ship in the Empire or Uldune can do. Not quite as fast as the Karres ships. There was a limit to subradio communications, but we did get hold of an agent on Mandellin's world. They told us you had come here. We were able to cut our journey time considerably. You see, Goth, we really do not like this situation. We're deeply concerned about this Tchab—Marshi."

"I'm sorry. She's got the Illtraming map. And the captain," said Goth quietly.

"On the other hand, it does seem that between you and Himbo Petey, and the people of Pampez, you have crippled her as a criminal power. She deployed most of her available foot-soldiers and even a large number of her capos here. And deserted them here too." Sedmon raised his eyebrows. "Can Karres never do anything unspectacularly?"

"Is the circus all right? Is Himbo all right?"

"He's been in to see you several times. So has just about everyone else in the circus," said Olimy. "And I should say the circus itself is fine too. If by fine you mean 'full-to-bursting.' They're packing them into the aisles. Even Hamlet is jam-packed and they're running a special morning show. The Pampez herders have taken them in as their own. They've almost made a planetary hero of Himbo Petey. That was why I was rather worried about you, Goth. By public demand, he rode a fanderbag around the ring and cracked that whip of his. I would have thought that the cheering would wake anyone, even halfway around the planet."

"Well, I hope it pays for some of the damages."

The Sedmon smiled sharkishly. "This is the first direct profit on my share of this investment that I have seen. You do realize, Goth, that Marshi's 'people' are by and large known and wanted criminals across the Empire. In fact, a few of them are even wanted on Uldune, and it's not something we're known for. There are some substantial rewards offered for some of them. Fortunately, dead or alive, in many cases. There have been three Imperial Security Service lighters collecting those that the locals hadn't already shot or hanged."

"Or hadn't been stood on by fanderbags, or hadn't run into the human equivalent of a threshing machine," said Olimy, jerking a thumb at Ta'zara.

"Hanged?"

Sedmon nodded approvingly. "Justice around here is swift and salutary. They were easy enough to round up—not many places to hide—and rather obvious in appearance compared to the locals. Some tried to flee out onto the plains. Others sought refuge among the wisent buyers. Except the wisent buyers—the real

ones—suddenly found that they had a good reason
to cooperate."

Olimy laughed. "Yes. I believe they suddenly decided
to increase their purchase price, too, before the hanging seemed like too much fun to stop."

"Anyway. The citizens of Pampez, the citizens of the
Empire, even some of my operatives are very pleased
with the way things have come out. And the ISS and
my operatives, and indeed, I believe, Karres, are hunting for any trace of the *Venture*, or Marshi. And yes,
the ISS are assuming that the plant-infested criminal
brethren are potentially infective," said Sedmon.

"It came out all right," said Goth. "But it's not
over yet. She could do the same, or worse again if
she finds what she needs to breed. Imagine if she'd
got those spores into your Daalmen. Or the ISS."

"Or worse, Karres," said Sedmon grimly. "She is
not a spent force yet. And we're determined to make
sure she—and this plant—are destroyed. At any cost."

Goth had a sinking feeling that cost might include
the life of Captain Pausert. She had to stop that from
happening.

It took nearly two weeks before the news came in.

"We have a positive sighting on the borderplanet
of Merega V. The *Venture* set down with four other
vessels to refuel. Marshi was seen." Sedmon paused.
"The operative is busy sending through an image.
But there is also a person that fits the description of
Captain Pausert."

Goth heaved a sigh of relief. "Let's go. You are
about to experience the Sheewash drive, Sedmon."

Olimy held up a hand. "Goth. The operative said

that he was in no way a prisoner. In fact he was seeing to the refueling."

Goth looked at Olimy. Sedmon. And then at her sister. "He's part of the plant!" she said in horror.

The Leewit ground her small fist into her palm. "I guess we're just going to have to get it out of him, Sis."

Olimy said nothing, but Sedmon bowed. "A leech was put onto the *Venture*. We can track her. If you want to make use of the *Thunderbird*?"

Goth stood up. "Farewells will just have to wait. Let's go, Leewit. Is Ta'zara fit to travel again?"

"I reckon," said the Leewit. "And we can work on him some more if need be."

"Going to go Sheewash. That takes it out of you too." She looked at the adult Karres witch. "You coming, Olimy?" she asked innocently.

He laughed. "No. You'll have to do your own Sheewash. I am coming along, but I'll be a step behind you. We've been calling people in from the Nanite cleanup. Karres herself is coming. But that's not so quickly or easily organized, as you know.

"Well," said Goth, pacing. "Let's get moving. They've got quite a start on us."

"You can't catch it all up at once," said Olimy, warningly. "There are some Empire ships, some Uldune ships, and Karres also on track. The *Venture 7333* is on a remote patch of the starways, but we're converging on them. Try to work on a delaying strategy if you get there too soon." He made no attempt to stop them. That was not the Karres way, after all.

The hexaperson was worried. The Daal of Uldune was no saint. He couldn't be, as the ruler of a planet like Uldune. Still, of late he had found that he was less unfeeling than it was good for the Daal to be. Uldune treated the witches of Karres with the respect—and the suspicion—with which a powerful and bloody ruler treats an even more powerful force. That had, in the past, proved wise. But as the Daal, he had grown up in an intrigue-filled and un-gentle environment, in which the six were, of necessity, almost entirely isolated from contact with the rest of the populace of Uldune. Emotion had largely been a stranger to the Daal... until Hulik do Eldel had woken a slumbering giant.

The hexaperson had discovered that he cared very deeply about someone. And, as if that had been a crack in his defenses, the hexaperson was discovering that he cared about other people too. Not many other people. But Goth and the Leewit had somehow wormed their way in. They were not just Karres— which was respected, but as an enemy, because all who were not the hexaperson were some kind of enemy, except Hulik. But those two small witches had become something more. He liked Captain Pausert too, for that matter. The man was just so... unbelievably undevious and well, idealistic. It had been a shock to realize that Karres too was rather like that. Yes, they were secretive. But had they been interested in ruling, he had come to realize that they could have seized power fifty times over.

The hexaperson was worried as a result. He was worried because he had come to think of Karres not merely as a powerful enemy to remain on good terms with because it could destroy or at least cripple you, but not even as an enemy. Almost... a friend. Bizarre. Not something a leader of Uldune could afford, but yet he had a feeling that he could not afford not to befriend Karres, even if it meant changing the way Uldune operated.

And he was worried for a second reason. He had seen the desperate addict that Mebeckey had become. He knew that that was the best that Goth could hope for Captain Pausert. And second, he knew Pausert's chances of survival were rather poor. His own instinct, as the Daal of Uldune, was to regard the man as collateral damage, if the opportunity arose to kill off Marshi.

Only he did not want to tell Goth that. First, it would hurt her. And second, even if he was only one-sixth physically here, and had a special cap that in theory would protect him, he thought that killing Pausert might just be very bad for his health.

There were limits even on the Sheewash drive. Both Goth and the Leewit worked at it in concert, but Goth knew that it was vital that they arrive at the *Venture* able to use klatha to its full potential. That meant not overtiring themselves. They were still pushing the *Thunderbird* along at far faster than the fastest Imperial cruiser—and her overpowered engines were thrusting her along while they rested. But it would still take at least five ship-days to intercept the *Venture*. Meanwhile, subradio information came out of the leech, letting them plot a vector.

"They're heading for the Chaladoor," said Goth, looking at the screen plot.

"So why am I not surprised?" said the Daal of Uldune sourly. He was busy with some calculations of his own, about the progress—at rather more modest speeds—of his fleet. He had ordered out all the ships he could spare. Uldune had watching enemies too.

The last probe into the Chaladoor had not been a successful one. The ships had in fact managed to send out quite a comprehensive report of the conflict with the Phantom ships.

They just hadn't been able to win or escape. The Daal had, since then, acquired some insight into what the Phantom ships couldn't withstand. But that didn't alter the fact that a ship crewed with three of the witches, using their special drive, had barely escaped. The hexaperson knew that he could not afford to lose the better part of his fleet, or Uldune—the wolf—would fall to the jackals.

There was a narrow crawlspace down along the *Venture*'s tubes. It was the sort of place, especially for a large man like Captain Pausert, that was only visited with some discomfort while doing tube calibrations. If one was really determined and crawled along a long way, one came to a slightly larger gap created by the updating of tube-liners. They'd been longer back in the long-ago day that the *Venture* was first launched as a pirate-chaser. Modern tubes were just that little bit shorter before the final choke and outer flares. That left a gap. It was a hot, noisy spot.

Vezzarn still found it the best place to be on the ship right now. He'd made himself a makeshift bed there, collected some food and water, and was prepared to wait it out until the *Venture* next set down and emptied so that he could make a quiet departure for more pleasant and safer places. It wasn't safe out there in the rest of the ship!

They'd tranq-darted him as he'd come to the air-lock, and locked him into one of the staterooms. But they hadn't even bothered to tie him up. Fortunately he'd come around and been able to use his lock-picks and leave before they'd come back. It was hard to work out quite what was going on as so many of the men now crowded into the *Venture* seemed to do things in concert, without talking. Some did talk, of course. The pilot, for one. He managed better take-offs than Captain Pausert although he was a decidedly worse ship-handler. Pausert would have done better. Except—from what Vezzarn had seen from the wiring crawlway—Pausert had somehow joined the silent majority on the ship. Vezzarn had been relieved and delighted when he'd first spied the captain. It hadn't taken the little old space-dog more than a few moments of observation to realize that this might be Captain Pausert's body, but wasn't the man he knew. Vezzarn could only be relieved that the presence of another one of the strangers had kept him from calling the captain.

He'd found that he could, with difficulty, belly-crawl and wriggle his way along to above the control room, where at least the pilot spoke and was spoken to. He'd learned a fair bit in the process. Subradio messages from frantic underlings had been coming in. It appeared that the Borozo-Shinn conglomerate had suffered cataclysmic losses. Others were moving in on their territory, and some of those left on Pampez were singing, loudly. Not all had been the silent-type part-of-the-plant.

And Marshi-Tchab, it seemed, did not care. They could all die, and it could all be lost. The criminal empire she was leaving behind was worth many millions, Vezzarn was sure. But for all the attention she paid to the squalling, it might as easily have been a piece of scrap paper that she'd dropped.

Then finally, a message came in that she did want to hear.

A set of coordinates.

They might have been what she wanted to hear, but they filled her pilot with horror. Enough horror that he was actually brave enough to protest. "We can't go there, Tchab."

"You will go where I tell you to go."

"But that is the Chaladoor," said the pilot.

"That was to be expected. Ships have dealt with the Chaladoor before."

Vezzarn was more familiar with coordinates in Chaladoor than the pilot was.

Vezzarn had managed to raid the kitchen several times.

He began wondering if he could also get to the lifeboat and get away. But as they were traveling in a formation of five ships, there was very little chance of escape that way.

But the alternative, it seemed, was to return to the Megair cluster.

And only the Wisdoms got out of there! Besides the Cannibals, the Phantoms were as thick as ants on sugar in the area.

CHAPTER 31

"Course triangulation says they're heading towards Megair!"

"We do have a gravity tractor fitted. Externally," said Sedmon almost apologetically.

Goth's stare was cold. "And how did you know about that?"

Sedmon shrugged. "Vezzarn remains in my employ. However, it would seem the technique—without considerable skill and the Sheewash drive—remains a last resort."

"If the old man is still alive, he's in big trouble," said Goth, looking up from her calculations.

"Are we going to catch them before they get there?" asked the Leewit, looking at the mess of numbers Goth had been working on.

Goth nodded. "Should do it in less than five hours." She looked thoughtful. "Have to start thinking of good delaying tactics. Unless this fancy ship of yours can take on all five of those ships."

"The *Thunderbird* has quite an armory," admitted Sedmon.

Vezzarn was watching from the crawlspace when Marshi-Tchab's small fleet encountered the Phantom ships. As usual, they appeared with astonishing rapidity. But in their previous encounters, the Phantom ships had come trickling in, in ones and twos. This time the pilot was looking at his forward view screens when some twenty or more of the spiky ships appeared at once. And they did not waste any time in launching their torpedoes at Marshi-Tchab's flotilla.

Marshi-Tchab's ships of course returned fire—futilely. Desperate evasive action followed.

Marshi-Tchab's ships had the problem that they were running straight towards the oncoming torpedoes. Even high-G turns were not effective in shaking the torpedoes. And none of the ships had the option of turning to the mysterious drive that the Wisdoms used. The Phantoms were also firing multiple salvos—something else that was new. The gunners on the various ships did manage to destroy some of the incoming space-torpedoes, but that was all.

The fight was one-sided. Vezzarn assumed that he was going to die. He just wished that he could have chosen a more comfortable place to do it, possibly one that did not have a view of ships exploding into varieties of amber or viridescent fire against the blackness of space.

✳   ✳   ✳

"Look!" yelled the Leewit. "They're under attack. The Phantom ships are attacking them!"

They were barely light-minutes away from Marshi-Tchab's flotilla. You couldn't, from here, see the torpedoes, not even on the *Thunderbird*'s souped-up detectors. But you could see the ships scatter and the riot of space guns being fired into the void—to almost no effect. Yes, there was an amber flare of someone hitting a Phantom ship torpedo. But there was also the terrible destruction of one of Marshi-Tchab's ships a few seconds later. It was plain that the flotilla would be annihilated. It was apparently plain to them also, as they were fleeing desperately.

For three of the five, that didn't help. Goth found herself digging her nails into her own palms, unable to do more than watch in horror.

"The leech is still transmitting," said Sedmon. "That means that the *Venture* is one of those two survivors."

"Thank you," said Goth, aware that her voice sounded very odd.

"They're coming back towards us," said the Leewit. "Looks like the Phantoms aren't chasing them."

As part of the mother-plant, Pausert was aware of outright panic. Illtraming ships. Many of them. The kind which had once destroyed the mother-plant.

And then the mother-plant drew comfort and confidence from knowledge held by the Pausert-plant.

There was a ship back there. It had arrived far too fast to have used the sort of drive most of these humans had available to them. It was not of Illtraming design. Therefore it must be a ship of that dangerous group of humans from Karres, the ones that used this mysterious klatha force. And the part of the plant which had once been the organism known as Captain Pausert had used it too, in times past, to evade the Illtraming ships and reach the Illtraming homeworld.

If the mother-plant could do that as well, it would be a simple matter to plant spores in some of the Illtraming. They were far better suited both to growing the mother-plant haploids and to being controlled by it. The mother-plant had much better access to their memories and thoughts than to those of humans. That was only natural: the Illtraming had been bred and shaped by the mother-plant to be a good host. As much as it was capable of understanding the concept, the mother-plant resented the sheer ingratitude of the little creatures. The mother-plant had made them what they were, raised them up from being less intelligent animals to ones that could think and reason, so that they could be better motiles to help the mother-plant with its purpose.

The mother-plant was aware that, bizarre as it might seem, the Karres humans were deeply attached to individuals. It knew that the part of the plant once called Pausert was of value to them. And they were now within hailing distance.

"The communicators are signaling a pickup," said the Leewit, pointing at the blinking LED on the control panel.

"Let's hear what they have to say." Sedmon opened the channel.

"Karres ship come in for *Venture 7333*."

Goth recognized the curiously atonal voice. "Marshi.

Also known as Tchab, I suspect. Wonder what wig she's wearing now?"

"We may as well see if she is allowing visual transmissions," said Sedmon. "I do not wish to be seen, however. It is possible that they would recognize the Daal of Uldune."

"Reckon she can see me," said Goth. "Seeing as she has been circulating pictures of me."

"I would be very afraid if I was her," said Sedmon with a slight smile.

But it appeared that Marshi was no more afraid than she was surprised, or concerned, that the crew of the ship following her should see that she was entirely hairless. "I have here a prisoner of considerable value to you. I need your cooperation if you wish me to spare his life." Pausert stepped into vision.

"What do you want?" asked Goth. "You are in no position to bargain. We have sufficient speed and firepower to blow you apart. Give us the prisoner and we'll let you go. Give you a head start of half a lightyear. You will get away alive. If we don't get him, you won't."

"We are uninterested in escape," said Marshi, uncompromisingly. "We have the purpose. If we cannot fulfill the purpose then it is best to die, along with the prisoner. And without your cooperation we cannot succeed in our purpose."

"What is it that you want from us? We need Captain Pausert's safe return assured before we are prepared to negotiate."

"We need you to come and take us through the Illtraming ships to our destination," said Marshi. "You have achieved this before by means of your klatha powers. Do this and we will release the prisoner and you."

She seemed to know quite a bit about both Karres and klatha, thought Goth. That was bad and worrying. She must have been able to access Captain Pausert's memories. But he was just as capable of using the Sheewash drive as they were.

Or was he? She remembered the story of how Mebeckey had got himself trapped in the store—unable to use his lock-picking skills to get himself out. So . . . the captain could not do the Sheewash drive for her—which implied that if the plant took over either her or the Leewit, neither of them would be able to, either.

"We know that you have the captain under some kind of control. Let him out and he can operate the drive for you."

"That will not be possible," said Marshi. "A lever of some kind would be necessary to make him cooperate. I have him as a lever to make you cooperate. You will come across to the *Venture* in a lifecraft. I will not place you under my control because you will not be able to operate your drive then."

Sedmon snapped the communicator off. "I can't let you do this," he said, keeping his voice very calm and even, pointing a stunner at her. "She has no intention of honoring her promise and anyway . . . he's hopelessly addicted now, Goth. And we cannot let her get away. We cannot have her succeed and breed."

"I know all of that, Sedmon," said Goth calmly. "I also know that I 'ported the charge out of that stunner. And what you don't know is that we have a few tools in our arsenal as Karres witches that you don't know about. For a start, if need be, unless I am unconscious, I could destroy myself, and in the process it'd take the *Venture* with me. For a second thing, we have a way of crossing space that doesn't require using a ship. Getting there...would leave us vulnerable for a few minutes. But it doesn't take very long to set things up to leave, even without a ship. If I can get into the *Venture*, I can get us out."

"By the Egger Route," said Sedmon. "I have some idea what you're talking about from Vezzarn. But, Goth...that still doesn't deal with his addiction."

"I think I can deal with that," said the Leewit. "Which is why I'm going with you, Goth. And no, you can't stop me either, Sedmon. Try and I'll let Ta'zara bounce you around. Or I could whistle at your ship's electronics and bust them up so good that you'll have to come with us, see."

"You do not go without me," said Ta'zara calmly.

"Sedmon, we will not let her get away to breed. Not even if I have to destroy the *Venture*, the captain and us to stop her," said Goth, snapping on the communicator.

"Three of us are coming across," she told Marshi. "And we can only manage to take one ship. The rest will have to stay as hostages."

Hostages? The Karres humans did not understand the mother-plant at all.

The mother-plant looked at the three in the airlock. The part of the plant that had been Captain Pausert identified them as Goth, the Leewit and Ta'zara, some form of physical defender. The mother-plant had reason to know that he was good at that. That human had been the reason the mother-plant had failed to get all of them on Pampez. That had turned out to be a good thing. It had not known it would need the klatha powers, and that being part of the plant would suppress them. They must be inferior beings, to be destroyed when the plant had completed its purpose. But for the moment, they were useful.

Could they do it with one klatha operative? One was easier to control. The Pausert-plant said no: they were not easy to control, anyway. The smaller, blonde one operated the grav-tractor with precision that must come from klatha skills—and the older could do the drive. But neither was very strong.

There was no need to keep the physical defender, though. Killing it at this stage might provoke an undesirable reaction, but she would give it a spore, and she would have it to watch over them. They seemed to believe that she, the mother-plant, could let go easily. They were welcome to their delusion.

"The bodyguard must be seeded," said Marshi, taking something in a little glass tube from a box that reminded Goth strongly of the one she'd found, so long ago, in Pausert's mother's house.

The Leewit looked at her. "Fat chance."

But Marshi was already leaning in. Ta'zara jerked convulsively as Marshi touched his hand. He pulled it away, looking at the greenish mark where she had pressed the tube to him.

"Keep calm," said Goth. "We need to see Pausert."

In her pocket were two analgesic tablets of the same type as had been given to Mebeckey.

Pausert came in from somewhere in the ship. His

eyes were empty. A few seconds later Goth had done something she'd never even tried before: she'd 'ported two tablets directly into his stomach.

They were, very shortly thereafter, searched—in a manner that Goth thought intrusive, but there was nothing personal about it. She might as well have been patted down by a tree.

It would take more than a pat-down search to find the toys that Sedmon had given them. Of course, Ta'zara could betray those. But so far the impassive-faced tattooed man showed no signs of it. He fitted right in here in some ways, Goth had to admit. He didn't show much sign of emotion, didn't say much.

"What do you need?" asked the woman. "The wires remain in the drawer at the command desk."

So she knew that much. Goth was wondering when Pausert would be affected. They'd worked out that it had taken about twenty minutes from when they'd given Mebeckey the pills to when the blackish-green plant stared oozing out of his nose. Well . . . she'd be happier out from under the *Thunderbird*'s guns. The Daal had been far from pleased about letting them go, and he might decide on expediency. That would be something he could well claim had nothing to do with him, with no surviving witnesses. Goth had no illusions about the brutal pragmatism of Uldune. She dared not lie too much—obviously Marshi had the basic information.

And to make matters more complex, she was relling vatch. *Little-bit?* she said in her mind.

Watching. This dream is very strange and complicated. The big dream thing Pausert tastes odd now. Like the other dream thing with the thing that came out of its nose.

The Leewit could probably get it to help. She took a deep breath. "I just need some space," she said to Marshi. "And the Leewit needs to get suited up and webbed into position. You could send Ta'zara to help. He would make it quicker. It would help if the captain could help me."

"No. Captain Pausert cannot."

If Goth understood the flat voice properly, it was not that Marshi would be unwilling to let Pausert help. Just that he would not be able to, because right now he was not the captain. He was a part of the plant.

The Leewit was casually walking off down the narrow passage, followed by Ta'zara. The Na'kalaufer was sneezing his head off for some reason. Well, if they lived through all of this, he could be sick properly later.

"Let the captain stay with me, then. It'll make me feel better," said Goth. "You can keep anyone else you like here, but they need to be strapped in."

She knew that there were only two chairs in the control room. There were several more crash couches yards away in the observation lounge with acceleration straps and webbing. If a plant was going to come out of the captain's nose, she didn't want it seen. But perhaps the plant would know about it anyway?

"Mistress," said Ta'zara quietly.

"Yes?" said the Leewit equally quietly.

"I have just sneezed out a small version of that thing that came out of Mebeckey's nose. I think that was one of the spores she put onto me."

He doesn't taste funny, said the vatchlet.

The Leewit took a deep breath. "Ta'zara. I don't know if this is going to work. But I want you to pretend that you are just like all these others. Be our secret agent. Watch them without them guessing."

Like the other one. The one that's hiding in the space up there.

"What?"

I think you call him Vezzarn. I've been helping him, but he can't hear or see me.

They'd arrived at the suit-bay and Ta'zara helped her into her pressure suit, and then into the strapping they'd set up at the grav-tractor inside the cargo airlock.

"You there?" said Goth in her headphones. "I'm ready when you are."

The Leewit opened the outer airlock and looked out into space. "Ready. Let's go."

The Sheewash drive blurred space. They closed on the bright suns of the Megair cluster. The Leewit kept a lookout for Phantom ships. She saw them soon enough. But they were all well out of range, and appeared to her not to be following the *Venture* at all. Instead they seemed to be holding position.

Goth confirmed that. "They're not chasing us."

She left off the Sheewash drive, and the universe stopped hurtling past. One of the reasons the scientists of the Empire were so mystified by the Sheewash drive was that it did not alter a ship's momentum. The Leewit had heard the phenomenon explained on Karres as being due to the fact that the universe moved around the ship rather than the ship moving through the universe. She didn't understand the explanation—but she suspected that the adults didn't understand it, either. Adults were given to pretending a lot.

She closed the airlock and waited. A few minutes

later, one of Marshi's impassive-faced goons came and fetched her.

"You may need us again," said Goth calmly.

The pilot who had come in with Marshi looked at her with wide, terrified eyes. Goth decided he was probably not part of the plant. "What was that?" he demanded.

"Not something you can do," said Goth, dismissively.

One of Marshi's goons—she must have them packed three deep in the *Venture*—undid the strapping. Goth got up slowly. It had been at least twenty minutes now since she'd 'ported those tablets into the captain's stomach. Yet he was just sitting there, staring into space. No plant was leaving him by his nose.

"I'd better stay close," she said. The goon stopped what he was doing, and Pausert got up and let Marshi's pilot take the controls. Pausert stood there, as if awaiting orders. Goth wondered just exactly where they were going to: the Megair cluster . . . but where?

"I need food," she said. "Both of us do, if we are going to be able do that again."

Wordlessly one of the men left and returned a little later with a plate of food from the robo-butler. Goth ate slowly. Deliberately, chewing each mouthful. It was hard after klatha use when she just wanted to wolf it down. She certainly wasn't saying anything to Marshi, but the behavior of the Phantom ships had been . . . well, very different. She wished she knew why.

The Leewit had been taken to one of the smaller rooms at the back of the vessel. Plainly, Marshi's goons had been sleeping here too, but it had been emptied to make a prison for her. They also brought her food—which was good, because she was starving.

The Leewit took advantage of the privacy to send a note to Vezzarn via the vatch. And Ta'zara came and quietly knocked and asked if she was all right. So the Leewit sent a second note to Vezzarn, telling him that Ta'zara was still part of their side. Vezzarn might wonder where the notes came from, but during all this time of mixing with Karres witches, he'd probably learned not to wonder too much, just to fit in with their plans.

A little later, Goth was pushed into the room too. The Leewit knew her sister well enough to know that she was worried and upset.

When the door was locked, Goth activated the spyshield in the chronometer on her wrist. "It didn't work. The pills didn't work."

The Leewit sighed. She wondered if she could cure the captain, if he was still infected by the plant. She wasn't sure. She wasn't even sure that she could cure the captain of the addiction, once the plant was gone. She had had no effect on Mebeckey's mind. Yet she'd healed Ta'zara—and he'd been damaged more. The difference might be that Ta'zara had been damaged and had known it, and had desperately wanted to be healed.

"Well, the good news, for what it's worth, is that Vezzarn is alive and free and hiding in the crawl spaces. And it seems that for some reason Ta'zara wasn't affected by the plant spore. He sneezed it right out again, and I think it was dying. It was going black on his handkerchief. And he still seems to be on the loose."

There was a faint rattle at the door, and it swung open, to reveal Ta'zara and a rather disheveled Vezzarn with a lock-pick. "Your Wisdoms," he said, locking the door, "I can't tell you how glad I am to see you! I didn't think you'd come and get me this time. We're heading straight back to Megair 4. I saw the coordinates."

"You mean the Megair Cannibals are Marshi's whatsit...what did Mebeckey call them? Illtraming? They clumping deserve each other!"

Goth nodded. "I'd feel sorry for any species that had been slaves. But I guess just having been a slave doesn't always make you too nice. Still, I wish I knew how we could get the captain free of this thing. Those pills had no effect."

"And yet," said Ta'zara. "I must have poisoned the plant."

Vezzarn coughed. "Your Wisdoms. Do you remember when that Mebeckey told us about these Melchin, how their slaves got some disease that killed the plant? And they ended up as the Illtraming?"

"Yep. That is why the plant that is Marshi wants to find their world. So it can have a host again. A proper one. Not us."

"Well, if Megair 4 is the Illtraming homeworld and the Megair are these hosts," said the old spacer, "maybe the disease is still there. It didn't affect the animals, the way I understood it. So maybe it's something that Mebeckey caught while he was there. Ta'zara was also there. They didn't do anything else together."

Goth bit her knuckle. Then shook her head. "But we were also there. The captain would have caught it too, surely?"

"Well," said Ta'zara. "Not if it was in the food. That Mebeckey ate quite a lot of it. And so did I, to stay alive. But I didn't see you eat anything."

"And the plant tried the Dell brother and let itself be pulled away... Okay, it might have been sick. But I think you're right! It must be the food. Must be."

"It's a gamble, Sis," said the Leewit.

"So is everything," said Goth. "*Hist!* Here comes someone. I'll hide you two in no-shape."

It was Pausert, his eyes empty. "You are needed again. There are more Illtraming ships."

"I think we can just work together for speed," said Goth.

There was an infinitesimal pause and Pausert nodded.

The Leewit calmly pulled the door shut behind her. They walked to the control room, and once again she did the Sheewash drive—just briefly—past ships that seemed to ignore them.

"It seems speed is the key," said Marshi. "Do you need more food? The navigation is difficult."

"Yes. More than last time. And some rest. It drains a lot of our energy." Goth understood, suddenly, why Marshi appeared so obtuse sometimes. Yes, Marshi had obviously gotten part of the information in the captain's head—but she got what she looked for. Not everything, obviously. And the plant was obviously not as good at joining the dots as a human would be. Marshi hadn't yet figured that the *Venture* was going straight back to where she'd come from—and the problems it had had there. Mebeckey was no astrogator, and had not provided the mother-plant with that crucial linking piece of information: *where*. The pilot had been given coordinates to fly to. He was from some inner-Empire world. He didn't know this was the Megair cluster, and that the ship's records had navigational data.

So the witches were fed again. Marshi made no objection to them taking the food back to the room designated as their cell. And Vezzarn was glad to share their meal with them.

"Now, if we can figure some way of getting some of those leaves they fed you back on Megair 4. I could really fancy some," said the Leewit, who, if she had to tell the truth, was not too good about eating leafy vegetables.

"Too far to 'port," said Goth. "And I've been thinking, don't say the name of the place. The plant hasn't worked it out yet. We'll need to get down in one piece on the planet, and I'll bet they've done some fixing since we left, more's the pity. Get some of the local food into the captain . . . and get all of us out of there alive. I'm sorry, Ta'zara. I didn't mean to bring you back to your nightmare again.

The big tattooed man just smiled. "I am starting to be like this old man," he said, prodding Vezzarn. "You got me in. You'll get me out. Besides, the Leewit," he bowed respectfully, "gave me something more valuable than anything else to a man of Na'kalauf. More valuable than merely my life."

"What?"

"She gave me back myself. My self-respect. I will never let them take that away from me again."

There was the sound of keys at the door. Goth hid the other two and the witches went out for another short Sheewash hop. Goth kept it to a few seconds, since she wanted to conserve her strength.

"We need to rest. To sleep for at least four hours," she said. "We can't do long uses of the drive and you might need us later. Stop and orbit a moon or something."

Marshi paused. "We need to get there soon. We need to find a male host for the spores."

Goth nodded coolly. "You still need to get there. And then you need to get down. The Illtraming are not going to welcome you, you know."

Plainly this had not occurred to the plant-woman. Goth decided her earlier conclusion had been right. The thing had huge advantages with being telepathically linked—but it simply wasn't very bright. Thick as two short planks of wood, actually. Not used to anything standing in its way. "We can help."

"Why?" asked Marshi.

"Because if we don't, we'll die along with you," said Goth.

Marshi nodded. "When we get down we can spore-tag the lIltraming. They respond well and fast to being part of the mother-plant."

"Glad to help," said Goth.

The mother-plant didn't twig on to sarcasm very well, either.

"It is known that you are very helpful. And very powerful. You will be rewarded by becoming part of the mother-plant."

"I can't wait," said Goth. "But we will need our klatha powers to get you down. They're not very friendly down there."

"How is it that you are aware of this?"

"We've been here before."

Then the plant-woman obviously accessed the relevant parts of Captain Pausert's memory. "Previously I had insufficient data. Light-shifts. And no-shape."

"Yes," said Goth, keeping herself as calm as possible. "Your Illtraming are very inclined to shoot first and eat anyone that's still alive to ask questions of later."

"The Megair Cannibals are not the Illtraming. They must be some form of slave. Janissaries. The Illtraming are browsers, not bred for combat."

Goth didn't think that she'd ever come across anything less slavelike than the Megair Cannibals, but she didn't say so. She wasn't sure what "janissaries" were, but she was quite ready to accept that the plant might just be wrong. The mother-plant's mind was closed on some ideas, and it certainly didn't fit Goth's game-plan to try to open it up.

The mother-plant had obviously reached some conclusions. "You will light-shift us. The other Karres human will be brought into the plant to keep you from misbehaving."

"Won't work. I need her to talk to them, and she does that with klatha," said Goth, her heart beating fast, readying herself for action. There must be all of forty or fifty of Marshi's goons on the *Venture*, she knew. And they could all act as one. Goth wished she knew what would happen when—if—Marshi died. She had a bad feeling that it might just be like cutting a branch out of a tree—hard on the branch but not fatal to the tree.

There was another pause. "Very well. There appear to be a number of Illtraming ships in orbit around the Illtraming homeworld. We will need you to take us inside that cordon."

It seemed as if the mother-plant hadn't figured out that the Phantoms were ignoring them. Goth smiled sweetly. "Sure. I'll just need some rest, and my sister."

CHAPTER 32

Hanging in the emptiness of space, Sedmon of Uldune kept his guns trained on the one remaining damaged ship from Marshi's little flotilla. Should he have tried to stop Goth, her sister and the bodyguard leaving? Should he have fired on the *Venture*? And where were the rest of the witches of Karres? His own fleet was thirty hours away. The Imperials were still farther. What should he do now? He was alone—besides the rest of the hexaperson—and vocalizing sometimes helped to focus their thoughts. He did not expect a vocal reply.

"Probably nothing," said Toll.

"Or at least that is what the best of our predictors say. The situation is highly fluid and dangerous," said Threbus.

Sedmon gaped at them. "How?...what?" was the best he could manage.

"How did we get here and what are we doing?" prompted Toll helpfully.

Sedmon swallowed. Nodded.

Threbus raised his eyebrows at the Daal. "You don't seriously expect an answer to the first question, do you? Like you, we invest heavily in research. Yes, we do know why the House of Thunders looks a little dilapidated despite the money that continues to pour into Uldune's coffers. We also have things that we do not want the galaxy to know...yet."

"And as to the second question, I would think that it is obvious," said Toll.

"Sometimes the obvious is hard to see, dear," said the big blond-bearded Threbus. "It can be right in your face and not noticed. Like the vatch manipulation of the situation on the *Venture*. Our daughters and Pausert are really quite bright, and yet they did not see it."

Sedmon was not at all sure what they were talking about, or even if he really wanted to know. Especially with Toll smiling sweetly at him like that. So he shifted tack. "What do you plan to do with that ship over there?"

Threbus shrugged. "About what you're doing, I am afraid. As it is a telepathic organism, we can't afford to make part of the mother-plant aware of our presence, because we have no desire to alarm the part that has our daughters in its toils."

"And future son-in-law," said Toll. "The miniature subradio device was a good thought, though," she said. "Well done."

"So . . . they're not in any real danger?" asked Sedmon, privately relieved. He was fond of Goth and the Leewit, he had to admit, and Hulik was more so. That wouldn't have stopped him, but still, it was good to know he'd made the right decision. "The situation is under control? This . . . vatch . . . ?"

Threbus shook his head at him. "They are in the greatest danger. And the situation could possibly erupt, according to our best precogs, into a galaxy-wide war against a telepathic foe, or something worse, that we are not sure that we could win. And while we think the vatch likes the Leewit, Goth and the captain—it might be better to say, enjoys them—it is still a vatch. An observer, mostly, as their kind are. And not a very powerful one, even if it does decide to participate."

Sedmon understood only part of that. But he understood the important part. The part about a war that even Karres was not sure it could win. They seemed very cool about it. He said as much.

Toll gave him another one of those looks of hers. "You still have a great deal to learn about parenthood."

And then they both disappeared.

Sedmon stood there, as if frozen, for a few seconds, while the hexaperson consulted with itself. Then he went to carefully check his instruments.

One recorded a gravitational anomaly less than five light-minutes away. Checking back, it had been there—where there was obviously nothing but empty space—for roughly the same length of time as he been speaking to them.

It was a large anomaly. A planetary-sized mass! Only it wasn't there now.

Sedmon recalled a long-ago conversation with Hulik

do Eldel, back when she had merely been an Imperial agent, and not a part of his hearts, and she'd informed him that the world of Karres was no longer in the Iverdahl system. She'd scoffed at the time at the idea of a super spacedrive that moved worlds, or that Karres could be made invisible and undetectable.

He went and poured himself a drink, and thought about it. The more he thought, the more sure he was that they'd only let him have the mass reading as an indication of what they were capable of. Comfort and a warning. Or were they misleading him? The witches were capable of fooling with an instrument, just as they were capable of projecting holographic images of themselves into his cabin.

It was then that he noticed that the other half of his new miniature subradio had gone missing from where it had definitely been sitting just before their visit.

He had a great deal to think about. Some uncertainty, but one thing he was clear on. He would rather have the witches of Karres regarding him as a friend than otherwise. Much rather.

He sweated a little bit, wondering how they had known that the wristwatch on Goth's arm, as well as being a miniature subradio and spyscreen, was also a potent hyperelectronic bomb.

The *Venture* had passed, undisturbed, through the last orbiting shield of Phantoms. The Leewit, well slept and fed, sat at the communicator.

Of course one had to know it was the Leewit sitting there, otherwise an observer might have thought it was a Megair Cannibal.

Listening to her, if one spoke the language of

croaks and whistles, the listener might have thought
that she was a very triumphant and successful Megair
Cannibal—having been locked into a cabin, and having escaped and captured the ship. The Cannibal
speaking to the Cannibal port control was bringing
home a shipful of fresh meat. And what was more,
a way of evading the Phantom ships that held them
prisoner here.

They were, not surprisingly, free to land.

Goth was very proud of the Leewit.

The entire exercise had had quite an impact on the
mother-plant Marshi too, Goth could tell. The plant
life-form probably had no idea how much other animals could read of the mother-plant's thoughts from
the postural cues of the host. The Leewit and Goth
would have to be very careful.

The *Venture* dropped slowly towards the clouds and
then down into them. The mother-plant was focused
on matters besides the view. The ship from which
the two witches and the bodyguard had come might
as well be taken. The craft was not damaged and
would appear to be fast in its own right, for a small
freighter. Even if something went wrong here, those
haploids still survived, along with some within the
Empire. One of them could switch sexes and become
a new prime. The mother-plant had no real concept of
anything except self. They were all just parts of her.

Closer at hand, these two witches had been shown
to be very cunning. Cunning to a level that worried the
mother-plant. It was possible that their dangerousness
and abilities outweighed their potential usefulness.

She decided it was time to use one of the tools of

the criminal gangs she had taken over: a metal collar with a highly sensitive explosive in a tube inside it. Once the collar clicked shut around the victim's neck, the circuit was complete and within four hours the explosive would detonate, severing the head, unless the properly coded signal was received. The charge could also be triggered by the same small remote used to send the deactivation signal.

The devices were useful for ensuring the cooperation of the untrustable. Trust was not a problem the mother-plant had had before. If something needed trust, it did it itself. But the collars were appropriate this time.

As soon as she had successfully enspored the Megair Cannibal motiles, of course, the two little Karres creatures would have to die. She was surprised to feel within herself some resistance to that idea. When the mind has thousands of components it was easy to lose touch with which parts were which. But none should resist her will. It took a period of self-examination to isolate the feeling to the motile that had once called itself Pausert.

That was not good. Not for one that was totally subsumed. So it too would have to be eliminated.

The *Venture* set down on the edge of the landing-field, next to a swamp—perfect for Illtraming—and, on the other side, were a number of ships that were, the mother-plant noticed, not of Illtraming design.

The Karres witch Goth asked: "Do you want us to get you in? I can escort you, light-shifted."

The mother-plant was not sensitive to the nuances of this host species, undomesticated. Perhaps for that reason, she was very suspicious.

"There is a price, of course," said Goth. "Pausert and my sister must stay here."

Aha! There was the plan. The witch planned to sacrifice herself and allow the other one to attempt to capture the ship and leave, with the part of the plant they considered valuable.

Marshi shook her head. "No. You and your sister must accompany us. She is needed to speak."

Goth slumped her shoulders. "You must promise to keep Pausert safe. You agreed to let us go."

The airlock opened. "I will leave him here, under guard," said Marshi. Pausert stood empty-eyed and chewing. Like all animals, he seemed to be constantly feeding.

She got the spore box and the collars. "Put these around your necks."

Gullibly, they did so. The collars clicked shut. She then explained what the collars would do if not disarmed within four hours.

They seemed less upset than they should be, somehow.

"Take us in to the mound," the mother-plant said.

Goth hoped she was right about the collar. Could it be 'ported off their necks? Could Vezzarn pick the lock? At least they'd gotten Marshi to leave the captain aboard the *Venture*. Goth had been hard at work 'porting chunks of the leafy stuff from the swamp into the stomachs and even the mouths of all those she could see. Ta'zara had assured her that it was just about the most common tree there. She had checked its lobular fleshy leaves with him before sending bits of it.

It was amazing how the animal instinct to chew little

tasty fragments in your mouth worked without much thought. The Leewit meanwhile kept the mother-plant distracted, talking them in to land.

They had a few hours at least to survive, to find out if it worked.

"We need close contact to enspore some of these host-creatures," said Marshi, who was walking along towards the mound as the apparent prisoner of the Leewit—who appeared to be a triumphant Megair Cannibal.

"I'll tell the Leewit," said Goth calmly, and fell back to speak to her, vanishing into no-shape at the end of the column.

"Our dear Marshi wants you to get us nice and close to the Megair Cannibals in order to infect them."

"I don't think I can do that, Goth," said the Leewit quietly. "They're clumping Cannibals... Or do you think they also eat the plants here?"

"Bound to. There is nothing else for them to eat. And they'd run out of people to eat and even other Cannibals, otherwise. Anyway, it doesn't matter."

"They'd be pretty horrible if we're wrong," said the Leewit, doubtfully. "There's a whole bunch of them coming towards us now."

"Relax. I don't like the Megair Cannibals any better than anybody else likes them, but I don't think the galaxy needs them driven by something like Marshi."

"But we need time for the captain..."

"Agreed. I thought about it before we had that last sleep. I reckon those spores are pretty fragile. Well, I hope so."

The Leewit was beginning to smile. "What have you done, Goth?"

"'Ported them out into space onto a comet. I'm pretty sure that comet is headed out-system, too, for a leisurely billion-year stroll through this system's Oort Cloud. I'd give it a push to make sure, but it's too massive for me. Yet, anyway."

Now Goth was smiling. "I gave Miss Nasty some comet-ice in that box instead. She can make the Megair Cannibals wet once it starts melting. Stop laughing, you little pest! It's hard to keep your light-shift image right when you're shaking about like that."

The people of the planet of Karres weren't laughing right now. Stealthed, and using the Sheewash drive, they should have easily penetrated the Megair cluster. But they were having limited success. It appeared that the Phantom ships could not be fooled or outrun. And although the planet had a klatha envelope around it, keeping the atmosphere in and defending it against energy weapons such as those the Nuri globes had used, the witches did not want their planet saturated in heavy radiation. It appeared that the Phantoms had been well-designed for launching attacks on planets. Very destructive attacks.

It also appeared that they had a clear perimeter past which they would not be drawn.

"The *Venture* got through easily enough," said Threbus.

The council chief Palaceles frowned. "I think we have to conclude that there was no attempt to stop the *Venture* this time. And that in her earlier flight she seems to have barely encountered these ships. We could cope with fifty, or even five hundred. But there were some ten thousand ships in that last exercise.

And in the early contacts with the *Venture*, they apparently seemed to back off from damage—now . . . well, they seem to have decided that 'stop at all costs' is the order."

He turned grimly to Threbus. "Your children are on their own, I'm afraid. This is rather what was predicted."

The Daal of Uldune, naturally, had equipped the *Thunderbird* with some exceptional weapons and detection systems. Those systems gave him ample warning of the coming attack—an attack which, using jet-packs on suits, might possibly not have been detected by some other ship with lesser equipment.

For Sedmon, the situation seemed faintly ridiculous. He began triggering his fire systems. It was rather like swatting slow-moving bugs. But, if that was what they wanted . . .

While he was at it, he destroyed their ship. And then, in case he'd missed any attackers, engaged his spacedrive and moved off a few light-seconds.

It was a lesson for this vegetable life-form that the Daal understood well. Do not be deceived by appearances, and there is always someone more powerful than you. All you can seek to do is to balance that. He just wished that he could have given the plant a message along with the lesson: don't mess with Uldune.

Still, perhaps the more generic lesson—*there are dangerous things out here you know nothing about*— would do just as well.

The Megair Cannibals surrounded them. Marshi would have had no trouble spreading her spores—if she'd had any spores left in her box. The Cannibals were poking and prodding the prisoners, in between, from what Goth could gather by tone, respectfully congratulating her sister. They were also keeping a suitable respectful distance from the Leewit. That was good too.

Marshi and her acolytes were busy pushing back, doubtless seeding "spores" as they did so.

"I 'ported Marshi's remote into the swamp where we touched down the first time," said Goth. "So we're safe until the four hour limit runs out. I think it's just about time to get out of here."

"Okay. Where to?"

"Break left and then back the way we came. Vezzarn should have the loading bay airlock unlocked. Give them your best whistle, Sis. Let's have a bit of a distraction, before you vanish into thin air."

"Okay. Just get behind me. This one causes stomach cramps. Really nasty ones."

"Doesn't make them throw up, does it? We want the stuff to stay in them."

The Leewit shook her head. "Nope. That's my number seven. Block your ears!"

Goth did. It didn't help that much, but she was really glad to be behind the whistle, not on the receiving end. She slipped the Leewit into no-shape and they ran. It was a beautiful day for Megair 4, barely drizzling. She risked a glance back to see that the progression of Marshi's plant-goons among the Megair Cannibals had turned into a merry mixture. Somewhere between mud-wrestling and an all-out mêlée.

The mother-plant had begun to be perturbed. She was aware that some plants had died trying to take control of the freighter from which the Karres witches had come. That was not particularly surprising nor distressing. It probably had a crew of the same caliber. And the death of small parts of the mother-plant happened all the time.

The gray aliens were taking an unusually long time to begin to be affected, though, to become part of the plant. The damp bare skins should have been an ideal germination ground.

Then had come the treachery.

The mother-plant itself had not felt the pain. But the host animals were quite inferior about reacting autonomously to pain. The Illtraming had had that sort of reaction largely bred out them. One could not remove it totally, of course, or fires or other sudden dangers would kill them before the mother-plant had a chance to pull them back.

This host reacted by writhing wildly, and clutching its lower abdomen. That didn't stop the mother-plant from forcing her host to reach into her pocket and press the button on the remote...

Except that it was no longer there. Instead there was just an electronic screwdriver—an object of roughly the same size and shape. Then it occurred to her. The witches of Karres possibly could teleport objects...

The gray-skinned red-eyed ones seemed to have taken what had happened as a personal attack, and one to be severely dealt with. They were busy dealing out more pain with a device that was intended to affect the host's nervous system.

It didn't affect the mother-plant. But they were outnumbered. And more gray-skins were running out of the mound.

None of them were responding to having been enspored. The plant did not, by the standards of its host, make intuitive leaps. But this conclusion was all too easy to reach. The Illtraming, vile rebellious slaves, evil beyond the comprehension of the plant, had made the skin of their foot soldiers somehow proof against the mother-plant.

Anathema! To be destroyed!

By sheer weight of numbers and physical superiority, the Megair Cannibals were overpowering the mother-plant. The mother-plant realized that it could have come so far, gotten so close, simply to have the hosts dismembered and eaten.

So be it. The plant could grow from broken fragments of tissue. And mere stomach acid would not kill it.

There was a reserve of the mother-plant back in the *Venture*. But would the gray ones not destroy that? A glance back in the midst of the fight—the mother-plant still had many eyes—said that they had already. The *Venture* was gone. But the parts of the plant inside the vessel said it was still there! The mother-plant decided she'd call some of those resources to help. The bodyguard was a powerful fighter.

Only the mother-plant couldn't find that element.

Had it died without her being aware?

The mother-plant was not accustomed to fear. Caution, sometimes. A slow burning determination for dominance, always.

Fear? No.

Even when the motherworld had been destroyed, reduced from endless forest to a slag-covered cinder, the mother-plant's spores survived. But these were new and doughty foes. And the hosts' juices were remarkably sour right now. The ones back in the Empire were still sweet. It must be the beating it was taking.

From inside the *Venture,* Ta'zara had watched as the fight raged. He'd wanted to be out there, defending the Leewit and her sister. But, he had to admit, their abilities probably made him a liability. He wasn't even sure where they were. Still, he was a Na'kalauf warrior, and the little one had given him back that pride and heritage. He would die before anyone could take it away again.

So, here on the ship, he'd taken his responsibilities seriously. He'd quietly made sure, with Vezzarn's help, that Captain Pausert wasn't going anywhere. They'd locked him into a stateroom. They had audio via the intercom and had rigged a visual input from the room, too. The two waited in the darkened hold, knowing that if the Megair Cannibals fired on the *Venture,* the ship was a sitting duck.

"Can we walk a little slower?" said Goth.

"Sure," said the Leewit. "What's up? Not like you to want to walk slower."

"Doing too many things. No-shape for us. False appearance for the *Venture.*" She waved a hand at the mound. "And porting little rocks into the spaceguns' energy chambers. If they fire, they're going to blow," said Goth. "I'm chewing energy."

She didn't want to admit that at least some of that was displacement activity. She was afraid that the local food would not have had any effect on Captain Pausert. Her range was not much above a light-second. She'd started 'porting leaves up from the world below a good two and half hours ago. Maybe it was bacteria in the local air—but he'd breathed that. Or the water . . .

The *Venture* was close now.

"Cargo bay airlock is open just a crack," said the Leewit. "Vezzarn must have got that right, at least."

"Good," said Goth tiredly. "All I want is to get out of here, right now."

"'Nother couple of yards, Sis," said the Leewit, sounding atypically considerate.

And then they were there, calling quietly to the watchers, having the lock opened slightly, and being hauled up by strong hands into the belly of the *Venture*. With a sigh of relief, Goth let go of the light-shift, as the lock closed behind them.

"Any change from the . . . plant people?" She couldn't bring herself to specifically name Pausert.

"Not yet," said Vezzarn. "But we have got the captain locked away. There are three others in that room, and two more in the entry hall. And the pilot and another one in the control room, three in the passenger lounge."

"Goth," said the Leewit. "I think it's time we took over the ship and clumping well got out of here."

"What's that on your neck, missy?" asked Vezzarn suddenly.

"It's an explosive collar that Marshi made us put on," said Goth. "She said if we cooperated she'd unlock it."

"But we knew we've got the best lock-picker in the galaxy here. So we didn't worry," said the Leewit cheerfully. "Take them off for us, will you, Vezzarn."

He suddenly looked very, very afraid. "I can't do that, Missy. That collar . . . it's got a circuit in it—if that circuit breaks, the amalite goes off. There is no way of taking it off. Amalite is so fast and explosive..."

Goth took a deep breath. "I guess I could 'port them off," she said. "Never done it with something this tight around a neck before."

But even making the attempt was delayed by the appearance of one of Marshi's goons. Ta'zara grabbed the man and threw him as he reached for a weapon. He bounced against the wall, and the Leewit whistled at him, stunning him.

"Patham! What brought him back here?" asked Goth crossly. "Well, they'll all know now. Let's move. No-shape. We need the control room."

They rushed up the passage, encountering two more en route. They were no match for the combination of the Leewit and Ta'zara.

But they'd locked the door to the control room.

The mother-plant prime haploid was still aware. The host-animal it occupied was barely so, as it was dragged along. However, it could see the tunnels of the plant nursery, so typically and carefully built and ornamented by the Illtraming. The old host animals were fond of their precious "art"—something the mother-plant had never understood, but had allowed them to create. It kept the little animals content, and it was instinctive for them to wish to decorate things.

But these tunnels had had their ceilings coarsely ripped higher so that the lanky Megair Cannibals did not dash their brains on them.

The mother-plant reached the inevitable conclusion. The Illtraming's own slaves must have rebelled. They were no more. At least not here. The ships that had so defended this place . . . It should have planned to seize one of those . . . if they had Illtraming on them? The mother-plant was having trouble accessing memory, but most of them had been drones.

The host-body the Megair Cannibals were dragging started to shake as the microscopic hyphae that had been in the host's nervous system began to withdraw. The mother-plant did not know that the Megair Cannibal had dropped the battered Marshi. It knew nothing except extreme distress. The role of prime haploid passed from it as it tried to escape.

On the Empire world of Freeman, the haploid in a human host started to grow aggressively in its human. It was the new haploid-prime. There were few of them left now, and the spores had all been lost. If the mother-plant was to survive, it would have to make some form of plan. It relied heavily on the ingenuity of the host for such plans—but this was an ingenious species.

Did any of the Illtraming still survive?

Not on Megair 4, it was sure.

It had been touch-and-go, there, Goth had to admit. The pilot had saved them, in the end. The plant-person in the room had been intent on wrecking the controls. The pilot had tried to stop him. He'd saved the *Venture* and bought them the time they needed for Vezzarn to open the lock. But he had not saved himself. And not even the Leewit could put together his burned-out chest.

Worried about the captain, they'd moved fast to deal with the rest—only to find that they didn't have to. The plants were deserting their hosts as fast as they could. The three in the lounge were lying on the floor. Vezzarn wasn't quick enough for Goth. She 'ported the lock out of the door of the room Captain Pausert was in.

And she personally burned the mother-plant parasite. The Leewit had to stop her from doing so the minute she saw it. "Let it get out completely. You don't want it to die halfway. Then it could go bad in him and cause all sorts of problems."

Goth took a deep breath. "I can wait," she said, between clenched teeth. "But I'm going to fry it."

And she did, as a startled Pausert looked on, his eyes wide, but smiling.

"You know," he said, "I'd expect my future wife to take better care of the carpets."

And then he couldn't say anything more because she was hugging him.

CHAPTER 33

"The addiction effect was on those the mother-plant kept under superficial control. Some of those goons of hers, for example."

"So you don't find you prefer it to me?" said Goth, still holding onto him.

"Great Patham, no!" Pausert shuddered. "Now, unless I am very much mistaken, we'd be very wise to get out of here. Let's get everyone strapped in and try for one of my better launches!"

He looked at the mound. At the array of protruding spaceguns. "It's going to be . . . interesting. I think we had better get airborne and go Sheewash or we might be toast."

"Got to get these collars off first," said the Leewit. "It's bothering me."

Goth grimaced. "Okay. I'm just really tired."

"Whoa," said the captain. "Is that what I think it is? Explosive collar?"

Goth nodded.

"I've got an idea. I can shield-cocoon you to fit your body, I think. And I just feel it would be a good idea."

"Clumping well just take the thing off me," said the Leewit, suddenly peevish. "I'm not too happy with that shield cocoon."

"Captain knows what he's about," said Goth. "Let him do me first, then you. We'll do it down in the hold in case it does blow."

So they did. And as the collar was 'ported . . . it exploded. But Goth was unharmed inside the cocoon.

The Leewit made no further objection. Shortly thereafter, she was free of her own collar.

"Captain," called Vezzarn over the intercom. "There's a whole bunch of Megair Cannibals coming our way. I think they're looking for the ship."

"Must have figured out something was wrong," said Goth. "It looks like theirs, but . . ."

"But we are getting out of here."

They ran back to the control room. "Strap in, and ready for Sheewash," said the captain.

"We'll do it," said the Leewit firmly to Goth. "You're dead tired. I've hardly done anything."

" 'Kay," said Goth with a sigh. "This time, Leewit. I am pretty tired. Tell you what. I'll try Sedmon's toy—that subradio communicator of his."

She strapped down in the observation lounge, as the captain pushed the thrust lever right down—and one of the laterals on full. That was clever, Goth thought.

Straight up was where gunners would predict. Now if he could stop the side blast from crashing them into the swamp...

She was looking at the Megair mound when they began firing, and saw the effects of her teleportation.

The energy—which was intended to reach out to the stratosphere—didn't leave the mound. The results were pretty spectacular.

The Leewit whooped as the *Venture* suddenly began to Sheewash toward the heavens.

"What are you yelling about?" asked her father, from the miniature subradio communicator.

"We got Captain Pausert back and we dealt with the plant, and we are out of here!"

"Wonderful!" There was no mistaking his relief. "Those Phantom ships are just about solid around Megair 4. We haven't been able to get through."

"Didn't give us any trouble coming in. They treated us like we were one of them. What are you doing on the subradio, Threbus? Are you with Sedmon?"

"We borrowed his toy. It was a bit dangerous for him to play with. Your mother wants to speak to you, too. What about the addiction part?"

"Patham's hells! We're being attacked! We're still inside the gravity well and about six of those Phantoms have tried to take us down. They've committed suicide! They're trying to ram us!"

The captain's take-offs had always been a weakness of his. But his evasive flying in the upper atmosphere was stunning. They dived towards the clouds again.

"Got away," she reassured an anxious parent. "But we're going to have to go down, I think."

✳   ✳   ✳

Pausert dived for the swamp below and then skimmed zigzagging just above treetop level. He'd seen the explosion at the Megair Cannibal base—but they still had ships and maybe they were tracking the vessel. The *Venture* wasn't built for this, but he was compensating for a lack of exterior vanes with laterals and luck. And lots of fuel! He spotted the small outcrop and set the *Venture* down. So far there was no sign of pursuit—a far cry from their first visit to this wet world.

They sat, electronics powered down, Goth using what little energy she had left to cloak the ship, the Leewit and Ta'zara ready on the nova guns. Nothing happened. Instruments picked up a high-flying craft heading in the direction they'd come from. After twenty minutes it was becoming obvious that nothing was going to happen except that Goth might need to eat all the food in the robo-butler's store.

"So," said the captain, "what now? We're safe, but stuck. And while I like the company, I can't say that this is my idea of a perfect place to spend the rest of my life."

Looking out of the viewscreen, Goth had to agree with him. Megair 4's rain came down gently. All around lay the typical Megair swamp. Miles and miles of channels, soft looking lobular trees, and more channels, trees and drifting rain, with a greenish cast to the light. They were lucky to have found a hard surface to land on. She said as much.

Pausert grinned. "Wrong. When we were diving in I hit the deep radar and got a surface scan of the local area." He pointed at the screen. "See. There are the hard spots. Not many of them. This was about the smallest, so I hoped it was least likely to be used by the Megair Cannibals. The others are in that arc over there. See—that one was their base."

"You're quick, Captain," said Goth.

"It's still like the Cannibal base one . . . a piece of rock in the middle of a swamp," said the Leewit grumpily. "It's even got a mound on the other end. So why couldn't we get out this time, and what are we going to do? Egger?" She pulled a face.

Not done here yet! said the little vatch. **Still got problems to solve.**

A suspicion blossomed in Goth's mind. "Is this anything to do with you?"

Could be. But you can't Egger out until you solve it. Stopped that! The little whirling piece of blackness abruptly vanished.

"She's getting too big for her boots," said the Leewit.

"And the worst of it is that she learned a lot of it from you," said Goth. "So she's been interfering. Big vatches like watching us solve problems, and I guess she's growing up. So what do you think she's talking about? And do you think she's really stopped the Egger Route?"

"Likely," said the Leewit. "She understands how we do it. We don't. And I suppose the easy answer is to figure out what problems she's talking about and trick her too. Not sure what she means, though."

"The Megair Cannibals, maybe? If they can't get off world to hunt, they'll eat each other, and eventually die. I suppose."

"Or the Phantom ships," said Pausert. "Where do you think they all come from? And why did they let us in?"

"Well, the first time they weren't too keen. Taken by surprise, maybe? They seem to learn, but slowly." Goth had been pacing disconsolately around the control room as she said this, taking in the changes that that Marshi and her lot had made to her beloved *Venture*. On a high rack with several manuals, webbed in, was something that had no place here.

The strange box. The thing that Marshi had sought so desperately, but had thought to be a map. Without thinking about her last experiences, merely tidying her environment, Goth took it down.

And like the last time, she dropped it. Pausert picked it up for her.

He seemed to hold it without any distress. He held it out to her. The moment her fingers touched it, she pulled them away. It wasn't right to feel that much hate and fear. "Leewit?"

"Yeah?"

"Take that box, please. Tell me if you feel anything?"

Her sister did. Held it. Looked at it. Shrugged. "Nope."

"And you didn't feel anything either, Captain. Vezzarn, let's try you."

The old spacer held the box, and examined it. "Good workmanship. It's got a tiny hole here underneath, but I can't say that I see anything else special about it, missy."

He put it down and took a tiny electronic probe from his pocket. Explored the little hole with it . . . there was a click. The box began to unfold as they watched. Very soon it was a sheet of metal and, looking carefully, they could see circuitry traced within it.

"Well, that's one little mystery solved, but it doesn't

help at all," said Goth, rather crossly. "You can't feel anything coming out of it, can you?"

The little old spacer was running one of his lock-picking tools over it. "There is some energy there," he said. "Low level. It's probably on standby."

Goth sighed again. "That's not really what I mean. It's the feelings. The images."

In her mind the Toll teaching pattern clicked in, at last recognizing the manifestations. In her mind Toll's cool voice said: "It's a rare klatha skill, Goth. Quite disturbing until you learn how to channel and control it. Powerful emotions and images leave an imprint of sorts on objects. It's the same phenomenon that gives rise to the images some people can perceive as 'ghosts'—you are just far more sensitive than most."

"Well, I wish it would go away," muttered Goth.

The Toll-pattern was cool, sympathetic, and firm. "Klatha powers don't, as you know, Goth. You can either channel them or they will destroy you. This is probably just the start of it, Daughter. You must use this pattern to put a buffer between you and it. To switch it off and allow just enough through."

She traced the thin cool intricate pattern in her mind, building the buffer. Then she undid it and did it again. Then Goth reached out and touched the Illtraming map...

It had been a navigational tool, a part of the flag-ship once. A navigational computer. And the device that identified the ship. That prevented friendly fire when the vast armada of ships—most of them robot ships, drones, had set out finally to cleanse the galaxy of the mother-plant.

Even through the buffering, Goth felt their hatred and fear of the mother-plant. It was almost overwhelming in its intensity. The mother-plant enslaved and used and killed the people. It infested them until their hair fell out and they died, consumed by the haploids' reproduction. Using the ability to surf the dimensional edges, the armada had harried the mother-plant. Many of the people had died, enslaved, fighting for the mother-plant. They hated it worse for that. But at last they'd burned the mothertrees that covered continents on world after world. Bombed and destroyed the nurseries. And then taken the battle to the homeworld. The place where the Illtraming and the mother-plant had evolved. A beautiful world of water and gentle rains.

They had set out to destroy it. The robot ships had launched wave after wave of missiles. The mother-plant's slaves had destroyed what attackers and missiles they could. But the end was certain.

And then the mother-plant had retaliated with a weapon that had shattered countless robot ships— and the flagship. It had torn pieces out of the ships in ever widening discontinuities. The flagship had crashed. The people on it had died. But the mother-plant was dead also. And the blessed-place was safe. The Illtraming's idea of the perfect world. The place where the mother-plant died.

It wasn't Goth's idea of a perfect place. But the Illtraming surely loved Megair 4. The little hairy six-legged web-foots didn't mind being wet. They were amphibians, anyway.

Goth stood up. She was unaware that she'd even sat down.

"Lots of klatha," said the Leewit quietly from the chair where she was sitting. "That was scary, Goth. But the Toll pattern said I mustn't mess with you while you were under."

"How long..."

"'Bout two days now. Scary."

"Where is the captain?"

"He and Ta'zara went to get some more of the local plant to feed the prisoners. I was all for turning them out into the swamp," said the Leewit cheerfully. "Vezzarn is keeping watch in the turret. We've camouflaged the ship as much possible. And we have found out that this place is just like the other one. The place where the Cannibals are living. That mound is full of a whole lot of tunnels too. Only they're empty." She cocked her head. "Sounds like them coming back now."

It was. The captain hugged her fiercely. "There was a sort of glow around you," he said. "The Leewit said not to touch."

"She was right. I found out how come we got in. And what we've done wrong." She pointed at the sheet of alien circuitry. "That identified us as a friend. It's an IFF beacon for the Illtraming fleet. Those are robot drones out there. They do what ordinary ships can't."

"So...why did they attack us then?"

"Because we brought back the IFF for the flagship...and landed at the base of the murderers."

Goth sighed. "I was getting it off the stones of the Megair base. It...was just too intense. And I didn't know how to make sense of it. The Megair Cannibals—wherever they came from, were invited to this place. The Illtraming thought that as they were animals, they must be allies. Friends. Good things.

Illtraming only eat plants...the only predator they ever knew was the mother-plant. You have to understand the Illtraming are basically not fighters at all. They only fought because the mother-plant had them in terror. They knew, sooner or later, it would come to their safe-haven. If it couldn't enslave them, it would destroy them. So they took preemptive steps. In the end their fleet mostly got destroyed, but so did the mother-plant. Except it seems it didn't quite."

"And so the Megair Cannibals promptly murdered and ate all of them," said Pausert heavily.

Goth nodded sadly. "It must have been like killing babies to the Megair Cannibals."

"Yeah?" said the Leewit. "They'd just been at war. They couldn't be that soft."

"They must have really hated the mother-plant to go to war with it," said Pausert. "I can understand that."

"More like they were utterly terrified of it and disgusted by it," said Goth.

The Leewit looked suspicious still. "They still fought."

"They only did so because they had to. And they used their robots to do the actual fighting," explained Goth.

"The mother-plant made the Illtraming," said Pausert. "I know that from being part of that cursed plant. The Illtraming didn't evolve to be terribly intelligent. So the mother-plant bred them for it."

"So it didn't breed them brave," said the Leewit. "That makes sense."

Goth shrugged. "They're plant-eating prey animals. Of course they weren't brave to start with. And what did the mother-plant need that for? It wanted them clever and good at making things. So the Illtraming made proxies to fight their war. When the Megair Cannibals turned up, the Illtraming thought they'd make great proxies. Only they started on the Illtraming first."

"And then, when they'd run out of these Illtraming, they went hunting in space. Only now they can't get off-world because of the Phantoms. They could deal with the Nuris, remember."

"Yeah. Maybe the Nuris enabled them to get off-world by chasing off the Phantom ships. And it's possible that the Megair Cannibals came from some other dimension through the discontinuities. Possibly exactly why Manaret and the Lyrd-Hyrier came here to the Chaladoor. Now Moander and the Nuri globes and Manaret are gone . . . the Phantom ships are back. In huge numbers."

Goth dug into the knowledge she had gotten through the eyes of the proud commander of the people's fleet. "They have robot factories on several of the planetoids here. The robots build robots that build ships . . . but they had stood down."

"Something got them going again, at a guess," said the Leewit.

"Probably us."

"What? Why?"

"The flagship went down on the mother-plant homeworld—and its IFF returned here . . . straight to the enemy base. And the Phantom ships, whose last job was simply to patrol, now believe that they need to build up for war."

"Makes sense. But they're not quick learners, those machines. Where do they get that idea from?"

"From the Illtraming, of course," said Goth.

"They're extinct, though," said Pausert.

"No," said Goth, slowly. "I don't think so. Remember, the Cannibal lord just said the prey had gone away. They're amphibians. Great artificers. Clever but not brave. The Cannibals . . . Leewit, do they have a word for 'swim'?"

"Nope," said the Leewit, after some thought. "Got some nice cuss-words for 'wet.' And I'll bet the Illtraming are still here, Sis. Right here, in fact. Well, just out there. Remember, Captain. You said those plants had been cut. You reckoned the Megair Cannibals must come here to harvest—but it didn't have to be them, did it?"

"I suppose it could have been anyone," admitted the captain.

"So how do we do we get them to talk to us? Cook the local water with the nova guns until they boil out?" asked the Leewit.

"I somehow don't think that would be too popular with them, and might just bring us to the notice of the Megair Cannibals," said Pausert.

Goth chewed her knuckle. "You say that the mound over there is full of tunnels too. I think I'd better go and have a look. See if I can get anything out of touching those walls—now that I know what I am doing. After I have had something to eat. I'm starving."

"Have some delicious Megair 4 plant leaves," said the Leewit generously. "You'll need 'em for energy. It's cold and wet in there. The mound isn't pumped out like the Cannibals' place. The water is about ankle deep. So . . . can I offer you a leaf?"

That hadn't been quite what Goth had in mind, but it would have to do. The mother-plant hadn't reprovisioned the *Venture* very adequately. It didn't care what the host-animals liked, just as long so they kept working.

Goth found that it was actually very hard to get anything from the walls of the Illtraming mound, other than the fact that it had been a happy, small provincial place. Even the little amphitheater had mere images of complex dances. Great events leaving sharp images and powerful emotions were few and far between. There were images of the people packing up and leaving...but not in a panic. And not going out? Going...somewhere. Stones...

It was not much fun exploring this place. As the Leewit had said, it was ankle deep. Water cascaded down the stairways. Dripped off the ceilings.

The odd thing was, the lowest level should have been flooded. But the water there was also just ankle deep. It must still have working pumps somewhere.

And then it came to her. She went back to the ship and called the captain and the Leewit. Ta'zara came too, because he was not very good at letting the Leewit out of his sight.

CHAPTER 34

"All right. You can come out now. We're not going to hurt you," said Goth, standing at the wall where she'd seen images of the stones.

Nothing happened.

Then there was a slight creak behind them. A click.

The Illtraming was smaller than she was. Most of it was covered in sleek black fur. The face was hairless and there was a small orange crest on the broad head, which had ears like buckets. It had six limbs—two webbed feet and two sets of arms—the first with big stubby modified paddle-fingers and the second set with three slim, delicate digits.

The soft round green eyes were wary.

"Greetings, Witch-People," it said in Imperial Universum. "We were wondering how to initiate contact."

"The way you do everything, I suppose. Nervously," said Goth.

The little Illtraming seemed to twitch all over. Goth couldn't really interpret the gesture. "We have reason to be nervous."

"It's over now."

"We are not certain that it is. There were telepathic transmissions into the Imperial region. We are not capable of telepathy but we have machinery that monitors its use."

Pausert nodded. "There are still some parts of the mother-plant that survive, yes. Back in the Empire. We'd like to take some of the plant-leaves back."

"It is not the plant-leaf. It is a virus in it, a minor pest to the plants on our world. Deadly to the mother-plant. When it has no food—no plant to feed on, it sporifies and goes dormant. The plants here have a resistance. The plants on other worlds do not."

"So are we plague carriers then? Is that why we're being kept here?"

"No. The spores have a fairly short life-span. Given a few weeks, they die. And they are quite fragile. They do not survive any desiccation."

"Oh. So why can't we go? You and that vatchlet conspired, didn't you?"

The little Illtraming looked puzzled. At least, that was how Goth analyzed its expression. "We have been monitoring your subradio and some of us were designated to learn your language. That is not a word I know."

"So why can't we go?"

"We have deduced that you are some of these 'Witches of Karres,' about which there is occasional chatter."

"So do you think that means that we're infested with the mother-plant?"

"Oh, no. You have hair. Major infestation causes most of that to fall out within a short period."

"They want us to do some dirty work for them," said the Leewit. "That's how you operate, isn't it?"

The Illtraming looked at them with those soft eyes. "Yes. After the initial devastation, it was decided to leave the Megair Cannibals in place, especially as our robot ships could not defend us. It was decided that the inconvenience of having them on the surface was compensated for by the fact that they are a terrifying force. Only you have defeated them. Twice. We watch, and they are unaware of being watched. We saw your work back at that base they took from us. We have some idea of your abilities. And we have the robot ships back. There has been considerable agitation to have the creatures removed. Our robot ships have established where the rift in space-time is that they came from. We want to send them back."

"They might be as welcome there as they are here."

It's normal back there. We're watching the dream back there too.

The little Illtraming was plainly completely unaware of the vatch. That was nice to know. "Nonetheless, it has been decided that we need them off our world."

"And you want us to do it?" asked the captain.

"Yes. We will provide you with a set of coordinates for the dimensional rift," said the Illtraming.

"And just how are we supposed to do this?" asked the captain. "I mean get them to go there?"

The Illtraming looked at them with an air of faint surprise. "They are under the leadership of the greatest eater. Challenge him to single combat and win, and they will be under your direction."

The witches looked at each other and started laughing, almost simultaneously.

Pausert wasn't laughing, though. "That's the most ridiculous idea I have ever heard of," he said. "To you we may look tough, but there is no way that I'm going to let that happen. I'd have a go but I have no chance of winning."

"I think they mean us to cheat," said Goth.

She turned to the Illtraming. "We need to confer."

The little creature backed off and sat down in the water, splashing itself.

Goth clicked the Daal's spyshield on. Then she said: "We're all pretty angry with you, Little-bit."

Why, big dream thing? They're getting very worried behind the wall, by the way. They can't hear you.

"Because you've been using us to play your game. And it's not a game."

But you've used me. And anyway, I thought you said it would be good to get rid of the eater-dream things.

There was some justice in what she said, Goth had to admit. They had used vatches. Vatches had used them too, particularly the captain, before he had turned the tables on them. Now...

"I will fight," said Ta'zara.

"No need..."

"I have a need," said Ta'zara. "I would like to get rid of the Cannibals. They killed my people. It would be good if I could free the galaxy of them." The big man flexed his muscles. "It would be worth dying for."

"It hasn't come to that," said the Leewit firmly.

There was a faraway look in the man's eyes. "No price would be too high."

"We need to extract a price from the Illtraming, though," said Goth.

"Like what?" asked the Leewit.

Pausert frowned. "Like pulling back their ships and keeping them here in the Megair cluster. They're not really conqueror material, I don't think. But we need to bargain a bit."

"They'll be longing to get back to the rain and misery most of the time," agreed Goth. "And we'll need a culture of that virus. I don't think we want it loose, but we want to have it. There are people on Karres who are really good with that sort of thing. It's like the Karres green thumb. I can't think of anything else we want."

"I have the Karres black thumb," said the Leewit cheerfully.

"Let's talk details with them, before they get too suspicious and before my feet freeze right off," said Goth, snapping the spyshield off.

The little Illtraming stood looking curiously at them. "My associates wish to know how you did that?"

"It is just one of the things Karres does," said Pausert loftily. "How can we get there?"

"We have transportation and direct access to their amphitheater. And they are in leadership challenges at the moment."

"Well, we need you to provide us with a safe, sealed culture of the virus."

"We would be glad to do that."

"And we want you to pull all your ships back from the Chaladoor, and stop making more."

There was a silence. Eventually the little Illtraming spoke. "At the moment we have pulled all our ships back here. We patrol the Chaladoor because out of the rifts in spacetime came Manaret and the things you call the Megair Cannibals."

"Doesn't seem to me that you did too well on either of those," said Pausert.

"True. But we have dealt with lesser problems. It is not a safe zone of space. So we drove all other ships out of it."

"Yeah, well, most people considered that you were part of the reason it was unsafe. Now do you agree or not?" said the Leewit. And added a word in a foreign tongue that made the little Illtraming open and close his mouth like a fish.

"We agree," said the Illtraming.

"We have ways of holding you to your word," said Pausert.

"We will honor our bargain," said the little creature. "Follow me." A door slid open in the featureless wall behind him. There was a wet passage there, lit by greenish lights. A sleek craft waited for them. Sleek, and somehow reminiscent of the Phantom ships.

"We will take you to the Cannibal arena. I assume that you will then employ the device you use to make yourselves look like the gray ones.

Goth hadn't thought that far ahead.

Ta'zara had. "I fight as myself."

"You let me do the talking," said the Leewit crossly.

"Of course. I cannot speak their language," said Ta'zara. Goth had a feeling he was deliberately misunderstanding her, but she wasn't about to point this out to the Leewit.

"But will they allow Ta'zara to fight?" asked Goth.

"We'll just have to see that they do," said Pausert. "Have you worked out what the alternative is for them? Starvation and eating each other. This place doesn't have something they need. I don't like them either, but this really will be the best solution for them."

The arena was bloody. Gwarrr the great eater stood as the body was hauled away for butchering. Yes. Many things had gone wrong. Inevitably he and his had been challenged. But no matter how many strange things had happened, he was still the greatest. The eater of foes. He was Gwarrr.

The noise in the arena was suddenly still.

All eyes looked at something, something behind him. He whipped around to face it.

It was one of the tattooed men. They were something of a legend among the eaters. They'd been the greatest of the other races to face them since the evil time when the eaters had come to this place.

"I am Ta'zara. I have come to challenge."

The tattooed man spoke the language of the eaters as if he was born to it. And at a suitable volume to make himself heard in the furthest seats, to the no-bone men in the back row.

"You are one of the lesser people. You cannot challenge," Gwarrr said dismissively. He made a gesture. "Kill him."

Several of the arena guards took the wonderful opportunity and flung themselves onto the kill. Ta'zara just stood there. The Cannibals bounced off a solidness, without quite touching him. It was as if an invisible wall kept them off.

One of the guards produced a jangler. It did not have any effect. In fact, it did not seem to have made actual contact. Another drew a blaster looted from some unfortunate spacer. It, too, had no effect at all.

"I am Ta'zara. Are you too afraid of my challenge, Gwarrr?"

Gwarrr was not sure where it started . . . but the other Cannibals began to call for it.

"Gwarrr, fight!" the chant began. Louder and louder. Tumultuous.

And the leader of the eaters knew he had little choice.

"I will fight."

He was Gwarrr. He had killed several hundred. He would eat this one's finger too.

The captain took away the cocoon shield as the huge Megair Cannibal stormed in. Pausert was a lot less confident than the Leewit was about her champion. He was ready to use the shield again at any moment. And Goth, he would bet, was ready to intervene too. He wondered just what she would teleport into the fight that would do much good, though. Even as quickly as her klatha powers had grown lately, she was still sharply limited when it came to mass. And while a small rock could do wonders inserted into delicate machinery, he was pretty sure a Megair Cannibal would barely notice it.

But the Leewit was right this time. Ta'zara used his opponent's strength against him, catching and accelerating his lashing long-nailed foot and sending it skywards. Gwarrr landed hard. Ta'zara let him get up. This time the Cannibal was more cautious. He attempted to close with the tattooed man . . . who grabbed his arms, and fell backwards . . . somehow planting both feet in Gwarrr's stomach, and tossing him into the air, to bounce across the arena. And that was just Ta'zara getting warmed up. He proceeded to use Gwarrr as a bouncing ball and throw-toy. The captain didn't want to watch after a while. The Cannibal audience did. Gwarrr was their great eater. But he had finally bitten off more than he could chew, and Ta'zara was making sure that the audience knew it.

It was a fight that could only have one end.

Pausert was glad that Ta'zara had colluded with Goth to do a light-shift of him biting off that finger.

Ta'zara walked over to the champion's chair as they dragged Gwarrr away.

"Eat," he said, as the Illtraming had explained was the tradition. "Tomorrow we return to our own place. We leave this accursed place forever. Every ship and every eater." The Leewit was proud of that speech.

There was silence.

"But . . . the enemy ships," said someone querulously.

"Do you challenge my leadership?" said the Leewit, through the finger-bone shaped speaker. The Illtraming, she had to admit, were good artificers. "I have come to lead you home."

There was another silence. Then they started cheering.

A little later they sat, spyshielded, still in no-shape, in the great-eater's chamber with Ta'zara.

"I am afraid I have to do it, mistress," he said apologetically to the Leewit. "Raider-ships are led by lesser eaters. But the whole fleet? It can only be me, unless you can somehow put an illusion of me in the command chair."

"I could if I was also on the ship," said Goth.

The big Na'kalauf bodyguard shook his head. "No. That would not be safe. I have my responsibility and this is it. They must fly into the rift. I will go. You will just have to teach me some words of their language."

Goth narrowed her eyes. "We have the coordinates for this rift. Let me get onto the subradio."

"I'm not going to let you go, Ta'zara," said the Leewit.

"Leewit. Come with me," said Goth imperiously. "Captain. Put Ta'zara in a shield cocoon. We're not having anything happen to him."

Ta'zara might have wanted to protest, but he never got the chance.

"So what do we do?" said Pausert. How easy it had become to share decisions with Goth, these days, he suddenly realized. How had he managed before this?

Goth grinned. "Exactly what he wants to do. But Karres can be close enough to help out. Cloaked, of course, but right there. We have the coordinates. We can transmit from close enough for the Leewit to do the voice and for you to shield him if need be. And then for my father to 'port him out of there. Touch-talk to the Leewit, he'll get the exact image of Ta'zara."

"But . . ." said the Leewit.

"But nothing," said Goth firmly. "He's decided he wants to be a hero. Let him. You can explain how come he isn't living with the Cannibals forever, later. It's that or send both Ta'zara and you swimming along the Egger Route. And them as well. This way he gets to feel good about it and we save a lot of energy."

Fun, said the little vatch.

And thus it was.

The eaters still in a galaxy dimensions away refer to the commands of the tattooed one who led them out of hell and back to the place of their fathers. So of course they ate their fathers and tattooed themselves.

But that too was a kind of rightness and happiness.

And the little vatch was quite correct in predicting that the explanation was fun.

EPILOGUE

Three days later, when the world of Karres swung peacefully in orbit around a hitherto planetless star some few days from Uldune, Pausert sat with his Great Uncle Threbus on the porch and discussed the things men sitting on a porch do: the destruction of worlds, star-spanning conquerors and how to stop them; and, greatest problem of all, the female of the species.

"We've more or less worked out the entire sequence of events," said Threbus. "Vatches, it appears, are quite involved in various dimensions. And have complex 'games' in them. The Chaladoor was part of her game."

"So the little vatch was manipulating things. Right under our noses."

"Well, you know how they like to watch. And set their dream things problems."

"They do indeed," said Pausert wryly. "But I hope she never planned on me being part of the mother-plant."

"No cravings to return to the plant?" asked Threbus cautiously.

Pausert shuddered. "The addiction? No, not so far as I've noticed. Look, Mebeckey had it in him for years—and I gather that being part of the plant was the first time in his life he felt he belonged to anything. That he wasn't racked with guilt about killing his first employer. It made him feel good. Look at the other victims. Many of them are criminals—and yet some are desperately trying to rehabilitate themselves now. It didn't affect everyone in the same way."

Threbus sucked on his pipe. "Well, it's true that even Mebeckey is cooperating to the absolute fullest. We've had truth-speakers listen to his testimony. He's barely strayed from the absolute truth, at least as far as he knows it."

"That's always the problem, isn't it!" said Pausert. "As far as he knows it."

"Yes," admitted Threbus. "But we've been able to cross-corroborate parts of it. I'm afraid, grand-nephew, that I was partly to blame with that expedition into the Chaladoor in '008. For a trip into dangerous territory, it was an uneventful one. I didn't realize what seed of future problems we'd brought back."

The *Venture* brought back various relics from that trip, most of which were sold to help pay for it. It hadn't been a very profitable voyage. That included the seedling drip-irrigators, thought to be goblets, that eventually found their way, along with the log of the *Derehn Oph*—one of the first ships to have stumbled